A TANTALIZING TREASURE

A Scandalous Spinsters Novel

MICHELLE HELLIWELL

ISBN: 978-1-7386487-1-9 (ebook)

9798329769524 (Amazon Edition)

Cover Design: Selena Blake and Michael Hale

Editor: Donna Alward

Also by Michelle Helliwell

The Scandalous Spinsters

A Dangerous Diversion

A Captivating Caper

Enchanted Tales

No Place for a Lady (novella)

Not Your Average Beauty

No Prince Charming

Never Trust a Rogue in Wolf's Clothing

Nothing Magical About Midnight

Praise for Michelle Helliwell

I'm a huge fan of Michelle Helliwell who writes a very special kind of love story.

— JULIANNE MACLEAN, NEW YORK TIMES BEST SELLING AUTHOR

Michelle Helliwell is a master at pulling the reader in with her stories and not letting go until the end!!

— GOODREADS REVIEW

Michelle Helliwell is truly a gifted writer. She pens page turning books with clever, memorable characters that stay with you, unique plots with heart melting endings, and gorgeous, historical settings filled with beauty, charm and warmth. Be prepared to stay up past your bedtime!"

— - CATHRYN FOX, NEW YORK TIMES BEST SELLING AUTHOR

For everyone who's had their self-worth stolen, and the people who reminded them it was right there, all along.

And as always, for Rob.

Acknowledgments

Every book comes in its own way, in its own time. Finding Maddy's story, and a hero worthy of her, took a little longer than I'd hoped. It would take even longer if it weren't for the group of people around me to help see it through the early parts of the story telling where the path isn't always clear.

Thanks to my husband Rob, often reminding me that I can actually write a book when I worry that I've lost the touch. He is often my first brainstorming partner, as well as the very best partner in life.

A very special thanks to Deborah Hale, the most amazing storyteller, for her ability to cut through the haze of overly complex plot ideas to get to the heart of the character dynamics that would form the backbone of the story you're about to read. Without her generosity, I'm certain you'd be waiting even longer to get this book in your hands.

My books are always written in the edit, and so the relationship with my editor is essential piece of the writing journey. Donna Alward, another fantastic storyteller, was so patient with me despite my pushed ahead deadlines. I always send her a manuscript I am certain is fundamentally broken, and she is there to remind me it's not, and then points me in the right direction to strength the weaker bits. Without her help, this book would not be in your hands.

Every time I entertain the idea of designing my own book cover, I spend about 30 minutes trying and realize that I cannot execute anything that doesn't look like a homemade collage (and not the pretty ones either). That task belongs to Selena Blake, my wonderful book cover designer. Finding a plus sized model in historical dress is nearly impossible, so I asked her to take a risk for me. With the help of Michael Hale (thank you!) who created the basis of a cover model I could give to Selena, she used her artist's eye and technical prowess to create the beautiful cover that is the gateway to the story you're about to read.

To my fellow writers I've met in the community over the years, both locally and virtually, I appreciate you being there. Having safe places to discuss ideas, trade 'shop talk' and negotiate the ever changing world of book publishing. Thanks for being there, both in person and on Threads.

I'd also like to take a mention of all the indie book stores who support romance authors – your support is so essential, particularly in the landscape of Canadian fiction. There are so many excellent Canadian romance authors in our midst, and readers for our books. The Dartmouth Book Exchange has been a tireless supporter of my books and so many other authors in my local community. Thanks to Sue Slade for being my book fairy, and leading this poor, socially inept author by the hand.

Thanks to the people at the Archives of Nova Scotia for their online collections, as well as the myriad of small historical societies and bloggers who pull together pictures, historical records and ephemera, preserving them digitally that make it easier for writers like me to have a window into the past, understand what currency looked like, how the trains ran (and if they did at all), and what flowers were popular to plant. Your dedication and enthusiasm about these topics are appreciated by this historical romance author, who, though isn't writing true historical fiction, wants her telling to be rooted in as much reality as is possible to tell my story.

No book in this series would be complete without a visit to The Prescott House Museum, which is the soul of Everwell Manor. Thanks to Margrete Kristiansen and the Prescott House

Interpreters for allowing me to see so many of the house's nooks and crannies, and to revisit the space when I need a bit of inspiration to move forward. Without the work of this museum and everyone who supports it, The Everwell Society would not exist.

A note for the reader

The Scandalous Spinsters series is set in Kjipuktuk/Halifax, Canada.

This is a work of historical romance, maybe even historical fantasy. For those of you who know the city, this means some of places, the streets, and aspects of the city are based in what was actually so.

But it also means that some of it is entirely my own imagination—mostly in the realm of characters, but also some places and institutions that place a central role in this story.

For my readers from the U.S., and other parts of the world, this is also a signal that I'm writing in 'Canadian English' which means you will see some spelling differences throughout the text. They are intentional—just my actual 'voice'. I trust that you'll navigate them easily enough :) .

All the best,

Michelle

Chapter One

HALIFAX, Nova Scotia, July 1876

Madeline Murray hated crowds even more than a dog-eared book or small talk with strangers while trying to buy sugar at Kenny's Dry Goods. And yet here she was, standing in MacAskill's bookshop, with two of her Everwell companions, Rimple Jones and Elouise Ashe, being jostled and squeezed amongst the horde of readers eager to buy copies of *Over the Ocean: Or, Sights and Scenes in Foreign Lands* and have them signed by the author himself.

Normally spending a day surrounded by books was not a chore, but today was not a normal day.

Well, not *entirely* normal.

When one had to switch out a counterfeit copy of a rare—and rather expensive—book with a real one, sacrifices had to be made. Particularly when that sacrifice involved the wellbeing of Mrs. Amelia Cornish, the latest client of The Everwell Society of Scandalous Spinsters and Wayward Women. A charlatan had convinced Mrs. Cornish that her prized copy of William Blake's *Poetical Sketches* was a fake and had offered to take it off her hands for a meagre sum. The very idea that a reprobate would cheat a good-hearted soul like Mrs. Cornish out of a family heirloom—and that heirloom being a book—was enough to convince Maddy to brave the bookshop on the single busiest day of the year. So here she was, enduring the endless sideways glances as a woman who, in the words of her mother, had been cursed with far too much height, hips far too broad, and hair far too red to ever to attract the good opinion of a man.

Not that Maddy ever needed one. What had Jane Austen written once upon a time? What are men to rocks and mountains? Elizabeth may have found her match in the imperious Mr. Darcy, but Maddy couldn't help but wonder if Mary Bennett didn't have the right of it in the end.

After all, there were flowers and books. Flowers came in endless variety. Some grew happily with little fuss or care at all, like dandelions, Queen Anne's lace, and Forget-Me-Nots. Others demanded particular attention. Dahlias and Delphiniums were fussy about soil and moisture. Rhododendrons needed to be sheltered from too much sun and wind. And her roses—they were the most demanding of all.

Books had far fewer requirements, but neither books or flowers expected anything from her except a little attention and her time. A rose didn't care if her skirts were not of the latest fashion. A book did not concern itself that she might have eaten one too many of Rimple Jones' delicious scones. And neither demanded that she smile.

Except today, when a book required her to put on a fashionable walking gown and venture into a crowded bookshop, her normally unruly hair pinned into an elegant chignon. Maddy hadn't had an elegant day in her life. Elouise had come to assist with today's job, using her singular good looks and natural ease to distract anyone from paying too close attention to Maddy as she made the switch. Rimple came simply because she was Rimple, curious almost to a fault, and fascinated by the world and everything in it.

"This place is an absolute crush!" Rimple whispered, her lilting Welsh accent barely audible over the din of the crowd.

"Of course it is," Elouise chimed in, turning her practiced eye across the room before flashing a dazzling smile back at Maddy and Rimple. "It's perfect."

Using the occasion of the book signing had been purposeful. The bookshop attendants would be busy with the unusual number of customers and the requirements of their author, leaving Maddy to find the volume in question and switch it out for the fake copy in her bag.

"It's not going to be on these shelves," she said, murmuring to her companions. "That book is worth a small fortune. It's going to be in that locked cabinet, behind the counter."

"If only Gemma were here," Rimple said, referring to Gemma Webber, Everwell's sleight-of-hand master.

"She's helping Jeremy host a luncheon," Elouise replied. "Right now that's probably the most important job she can do for us today."

Maddy exchanged a look with Rimple, whose seemingly perpetual smile had just dimmed. Gemma had married Jeremy Webber, a former colonel of the British army, who worked as the Private Secretary for the Lieutenant Governor. The normally shy spinster—or former spinster, Maddy reminded herself—was now wife to a man with a very public role. Since their fateful meeting, they'd encountered disturbing rumours about The Everwell Society for the Benefit of Sorrowful Spinsters and Woeful Widows — the public face of The Everwell Society. Aside from Everwell's rather scandalous mission of educating girls from all social classes and races, and providing emergency shelter for women in distress, there were whispers amongst that the upper echelons of Halifax society, sitting in their lush parlours and private clubs, of a den of lady thieves working out of old Georgian manor.

Of course the rumours, or at least some of them, were true.

"Plan A, or Plan B?" Maddy asked, eager to get on with their mission.

"Plan A is less risky," Rimple suggested. "Especially if someone decides I should leave."

Something fierce flared in Maddy's chest as she scanned the room, looking for even the slightest hint of a threat. The daughter of a Welsh Engineer and a half-English, half-Indian mathematician, Rimple's golden-brown skin subjected her to looks that ranged from curiosity to remarks of outright hostility. It didn't stop her, of course, because Rimple seemed to have a bottomless well of confidence, no doubt due to living half her life under the guardianship of two of the most self-assured and powerful women Maddy had ever the privilege to know. But it didn't make it any less taxing on Rimple, nor any more safe. And Maddy would die a thousand deaths rather than see harm of any kind come to Rimple, Elouise, or the others at Everwell.

Elouise, aware of her ability to dazzle people with a smile so bright the sun might seem dim in its presence, stayed close by. "No one is going to even suggest it," she said. Elouise was a master of the confidence game. "Rimple, let's get in line. Maddy, you get in position. Once you get the clerk to open the cabinet, wait for our signal."

"And if it's not there?" Maddy asked.

"Then we go to Plan C."

Eloise took Rimple by the arm and escorted her into the line that snaked through the store while Maddy approached the counter lined with customers and one harried clerk.

"Excuse me," she said, waving as politely as she could muster, trying to catch the clerk's eye. His gaze brushed past her as if she were invisible, moving to assist one customer on her left, before then being so ever helpful to another on her right.

"Excuse me," she repeated, a little louder, after the clerk had passed over her once more. Not that she could imagine he hadn't heard her the first time or ignored her subtle waves to draw his attention to her. "Can I—"

"The line starts back there," called out an annoyed customer from somewhere behind her. "Wait your turn."

Maddy looked over her shoulder, looking past the irate man behind her, to where Elouise and Rimple were already making their way to the front of the autograph line. This wasn't going to work if she couldn't get the man to see her. How could he miss her? She was taller than half the men in the shop by at least three inches. She blew out a low breath.

"Excuse me," she said called out a third time, suppressing the urge to reach across the counter and grab the clerk by the collar. "I would like—"

"Can I help you?"

Maddy started at the sound of a male voice, rich like Lady Em's good brandy, with much the same effect. Recovering, she looked to her left, caught off guard by the man with stunning whisky-coloured eyes who had somehow managed to appear at her side without her notice. She cast a quick glance around, looking for whomever was the object if his question, because men with eyes like that—or any, in fact—did not pay much attention to Madeline Murray. At least not the good kind.

But given he was standing close enough that the bottom of her skirts nearly brushed the tips of his shoes, and he seemed to be waiting for a reply, it dawned on Maddy that he was speaking to her.

"No," she said, angry at herself for allowing this man to distract her. Then, recalling some lesson about social niceties from Elouise, Maddy nodded at the man one more. "No thank you."

"I think you do," he replied with the confidence of a man who, with his impeccably tailored suit and objectively handsome face, probably never had to fight to command attention when he desired it. Every woman and a few men were gawking at him. And not in the way they gawked at Maddy. The attention this man attracted was nothing less than fascination. And no wonder. Lady Em, one of Everwell's two matrons, might describe him as "well put together." But Maddy had a job to do, which did not include being sidetracked by a man gifted with a face seemingly created to tempt the most pious to sin.

She turned back to the counter, where the clerk seemed to notice her at last. The wiry man with fair skin, curly brown hair, and a nose made to peer down at people, looked her way with an expression that, to her astonishment, had turned from indifference to obliging. Maddy didn't have time to contemplate the rationale for this miraculous turn, but she needed to exploit it.

"Good morning," she said, and started pointing to the locked glass fronted case. "Can you please…"

She trailed off as the clerk, who seemed a second ago to finally see her, walked past her again, turning his attention to someone standing next to her.

Maddy let go a string of silent curses.

"Good morning," came that same voice, as smooth as butter.

"How can I help you sir?" the clerk asked.

Unable to help herself, Maddy turned to watch the exchange, wondering what sort of unholy spell this man had unleashed.

"I believe this lovely lady needs your assistance," the gentleman beside her said.

Maddy paused, craning her neck to see the damsel in distress he was so eager to help.

"Of course," the clerk replied turned to Maddy, looking at her for all the world as if she'd just appeared out of nowhere. "How may I help you?"

Maddy blinked, realizing almost too late that *she* was the object of this gentleman's attention. She froze, suddenly uncertain, before the clerk politely cleared his throat. The sound cut through her confusion, allowing her to re-focus on the job at hand. She needed that book, and the only way to get it was through the man in front of her. Normally when confronted with an obstacle, Maddy's job was to swing a fist, or perhaps even level a blade at someone if the stakes were high enough.

Right now, unfortunately, she had to be pleasant.

"Thank you," she said, forcing her lips into what she hoped was a passable smile. "I believe you have a copy of *Blake's Poetical Sketches*. I would like to view it."

The clerk blinked, and Maddy knew full well why.

"I'm not..." He faltered, then regarded Maddy with more care. She'd been in MacAskill's too many times for him not to be familiar with who she was. And no librarian working at a charity school would have easy access to the funds required to purchase a rare volume that normally belonged on the shelves of academic institutions or in the private libraries of wealthy collectors.

"Is there a problem?" the man asked of the clerk, the slightest edge of impatience in his voice. By the cut of his suit, he looked as though he might very well be the type of man to have a library full of first editions and rare volumes of books sitting on shelves just because he could.

"Of course not," the clerk said brightly, clearly not eager to put himself on the wrong side of this well-dressed stranger. Turning around, he pulled out a ring of keys and opened the locked cabinet.

Maddy found herself leaning forward, scanning the shelves which held a small collection of books of all sizes, from those so small they could fit the palm of her hand, to oversized volumes. Some were bound in leather, others cloth. Most were so old the spines had no identifying marks to alert the reader to the contents. What she wouldn't give to spend time with each and every one of these.

He returned to the counter with the book and slid it in front of her. Normally it was Gemma, or even Elouise who performed the sleight of hand. *Poetics* was a rare tome—worth, according to some, more than the entire contents in the shop. Carefully, she opened the book to verify its contents.

The clerk was nearby, appropriately watchful.

And so was the stranger, who leaned on the counter as if he owned the place. She'd never met a man with such an easy charm —nor one so insistent on getting her attention. It had the perplexing effect of making her annoyed and fascinated all at once.

"What is it?" he asked.

"It's a book," she replied.

He chuckled to himself, a low, warm sound that settled on her ear and rippled through her body. Her intentionally curt reply seemed to amuse him. Perhaps most men would take that as an invitation to leave. It had been her intention. Instead, he picked up the priceless volume as easily as if he were picking up a newspaper worth a few pennies and held it out of her reach.

"I had no idea," he said, cocking an eyebrow. For a moment she thought he was toying with her, except for the crease along his brow as he examined it that suggested he was actually interested. "What makes this one so special?"

"Because this is one of the few known original copies of this work—there were only twenty-four made, and some of them even had his corrections in them. This one does. This was a gift to one of his benefactors and his wife, who supported him. You should see the inscription in the front cover," Maddy said, her heart racing at the very thought of so generous a gift. It was so romantic. "He didn't have much money at the time, so he gave the only thing he had of any value—his poetry."

She paused, realizing perhaps that she'd never spoken with a stranger in such a familiar way. Her heart pounded in her chest and she didn't know whether it was nerves or simply the heat of the crowd. But somehow, the noise faded into the background along with everyone else. It was just him and the slim volume in his hands. She reached for it, but he made no effort to return it. Instead, he seemed to hold it closer, forcing her to reach toward him. Pulling her body closer.

At any other time, she would have walked away, but there was too much at stake. She needed this book. And the fact this man so carelessly toyed with a precious work that was also the key to another woman's security flared her anger.

"Please," she said, holding out her hand. "It's very precious."

"Can I buy it for you?"

Maddy blinked. Now he was absolutely toying with her.

"It's worth more than most men make in a lifetime."

At that, he leaned into her, like a tiger she'd seen once at Downs Zoological Gardens. He lowered the book, putting it in easy reach. On reflex, she reached out for it, but he did not release his hold.

"I am not most men."

The next moment, Maddy was unable to do anything but watch as he—for she had no idea who he was—hailed the clerk and advised him of the sale. The clerk's eye's widened, apparently just as taken aback as Maddy. Old James MacAskill himself was summoned away from his authorial guest, and payment arranged. Maddy turned to Elouise and Rimple, still in the autograph line, giving them the signal to abort the diversion Elouise had planned to employ that would have allowed Maddy to make the switch with the counterfeit.

She turned back just in time to be handed the book, carefully packaged. A job they'd spent two weeks planning had been upended by one deep-pocketed stranger.

"Why are you doing this?" she asked, instantly suspicious.

He nodded, his face lighting up with an expression of bemusement that appeared genuine.

"To see you smile."

He put the book into her hands and she gripped it, desperate to hold onto something. Everything about this experience was utterly unexpected and she needed to escape. Suddenly all the heat and noise that had disappeared was back. For the first time in nearly twenty years, a man was smiling at her. And it felt real. And terrifying.

"I have to go." Maddy turned on her heel, ready to flee with Elouise and Rimple in tow before this stranger realized his mistake and demanded his book back. She took a step, coming face to face with none other than Veronica Turnbull. Diminutive in stature, the last time Maddy had seen the brew-king's wife was in the hallowed halls of Government House, where she'd inflicted the crowd of a charity event with her singing.

Though Maddy was easily a head taller than Mrs. Turnbull, the woman looked past Maddy as if she wasn't even there.

"There you are, Beau," she said, smiling at the gentleman with affection. "I wondered where you had gone off to."

"Hello, Aunt. I was just making my acquaintance with some of the more scholarly patrons," he said smoothly, nodding his head in Maddy's direction. He seemed like something out of another time, this Beau, with his smile that could melt butter in winter and a cocky sort of confidence that somehow didn't manage to be completely obnoxious.

Mrs. Turnbull's eyebrow shot up in a perfectly formed arch. Clearly, she did not care for her nephew's answer—but then, Maddy couldn't be bothered with either of them. Instead, she clutched the book tightly under her arm, ignoring the sensation that he was watching her every step. She only took a breath when she left the store, where Rimple and Elouise were waiting.

"What happened?" Rimple asked.

"I have it," Maddy said, gesturing to the package under her arm.

"It's wrapped," Elouise said, not bothering to hide her shock. "How on earth did you manage to sweet talk them into doing that for you?"

"I didn't," Maddy said. "Someone bought it for me."

Elouise and Rimple exchanged a glance, then the three walked along Spring Garden Road up to the Public Gardens while Maddy recounted the entire story.

"Beau," Elouise said, tapping a finger to her lips as she was thinking. "I think that's Beau da Silva. He's the scion of the Silver Lumber Company founder in New Brunswick. No wonder he could buy that for you—they own half the province. I had no idea he was related to the Turnbulls. Of course, money travels in small circles, and in this part of the world, those circles are even smaller."

Elouise and Rimple continued to chat, leaving Maddy lost in her own thoughts. Before long they'd reached the Public Gardens, lush from the hundreds of trees that had been planted there over the past few years. It was a place Maddy usually enjoyed visiting, but she was too preoccupied by the events at MacAskill's to show much interest.

"Elouise and I will go find Reg," Rimple said, referring to Reg Knickle, an associate of Everwell who sometimes helped out with the occasional bit of Scandalous Spinsters business. "We'll return in a moment."

The two left, and Maddy sat on a nearby bench, enjoying the shade from the soaring oak trees, when she heard Victoria Turnbull's voice from behind her. Maddy stilled, tilting her head away so as to not catch their attention.

"Your father is not going to be pleased with you squandering your money like this," Mrs. Turnbull said.

"It wasn't squandering," Mr. da Silva insisted. "I am thirty-nine years old, in charge of my own accounts and last time I checked, my last trip to New York secured da Silva Lumber new accounts worth nearly three hundred thousand dollars. And I have found a keen buyer for the old Redden homestead. I think I've earned the right to be frivolous."

"It was frivolous," Mrs. Turnbull said.

Maddy couldn't help but agree.

"Aunt," he said, and did his voice harden in a way she hadn't heard before? "If I can't make a poor old spinster's day a little brighter by buying her a trinket, then what in the hell is all this money good for?" he said.

Maddy shut her eyes and pulled in her bottom lip, biting it hard to keep herself from letting out a bitter laugh. The two continued on their walk, their voices trailing off into the distance.

Poor old spinster. It all made sense. The smiles. The teasing. She'd known in the moment there was nothing genuine or real about Beau da Silva. They were practically the same age. And while she hadn't had da Silva money, once upon a time, she'd had a dowry so large men had fought over it.

And yet somehow, she was the one who'd lost.

She tensed her body, balling up every ounce of the lingering discomfort, wishing she could take back that stupid smile she'd wasted on Beau da Silva. She counted to ten, then released the pang of bitterness before rising to go find Elouise and Rimple. And she would pretend, once again, that nothing could hurt her.

Chapter Two

BY THE TIME Beau and Aunt Vee had returned to his uncle's home, he needed a drink. Archie Turnbull imagined himself a humble brewmaster, all the while being as rich as the lord of the manor. The paradox was evident in his massive home built in the Tudor style, well-appointed with gleaming wood-paneled walls and handsome finishes. It was a counterpoint to the home Beau had grown up in, which, like the offices of Silver Lumber in downtown Saint John, exuded the might and opulent tastes of Frank da Silva.

He loved Veronica very much; she was his only connection to his mother, who had died not long after the birth of his sister Jessica. Both Veronica and Archie, unable to have children of their own, had become a surrogate family to him and his sister over the years, and a welcome reprieve from his father Frank's overbearing personality. Unlike Frank, who had never failed to find fault in Beau, his aunt and uncle were far more indulgent. But apparently even Veronica had her limits, and those involved spending a small fortune on an old book for a complete stranger.

Even if that stranger was intoxicatingly beautiful.

"I'm not sure how you are going to explain that to your

father," she said, unable to let the subject drop. "Do you even know this woman?"

Of course he didn't know her—he even failed to get her name before she bolted from the shop. But there was something utterly and unaccountably tantalizing about her. Beau was six feet tall, and that redheaded siren nearly looked him in the eye. Her face was full, her curves lush. She reminded him of a Rosetti painting he'd seen in London a few years ago. Like a creature out of time.

"It was, I admit, probably one of my least thought through decisions," he admitted. "But I have the money to spend, and we both know people who have gambled away more in a bad business deal or at poker table."

"Don't try to rationalize it," she said, carefully removing her hat pin and handing over her things to Mrs. Hayes, the Turnbull's faithful housekeeper. "I didn't think you were one for gestures, Beau. Especially with one of those women."

There was a subtle, if unmistakable shift in Aunt Vee's voice then. *Those women.* Beau had no idea what that meant, but given he needed a change of subject, he wasn't particularly in the mood to ask. Instead, he deposited his hat and gloves in Mrs. Hayes' hands, and made straight for the sideboard in the parlour to pour himself a glass of Uncle Archie's best brandy. Archie Turnbull may have made a fortune brewing ale for the common folk, but he had cultivated a taste for far more expensive luxuries.

"At least it wasn't a wedding ring," he said, plopping himself down in plush leather chair. "Then you would have something to be concerned about."

"Don't tease me," Aunt Vee said, following him into the room and taking her normal place on the settee. "I don't have the fortitude for another discussion about your marital status. Unless..." She trailed off. "Well, if you have other preferences, your secret would be safe with me. But your past behaviour would suggest you are simply unwilling to settle down. And you should. You're nearly forty, Beaumont. It's starting to be unseemly."

"What would be unseemly is foisting my ne'er-do-well ways

on a young thing that is only interested in my money. I'm more than happy to have my fortune go to Jessica's children."

Before Aunt Vee could reply, Mrs. Hayes returned, holding out a silver tray.

"Excuse me, Mr. da Silva, but this came for you." Beau rose to meet the housekeeper, picking up the envelope and frowning as he read the stamped address in the corner. It was from the telegraph office.

Beau stifled a groan. He'd left Saint John two days ago, following his triumphant return from their New York business trip. Before he left, he'd gotten into a row with his father. For the past decade, arguing seemed to be their primary method of communication. Before he'd allowed his father to get in the last word, Beau had stormed off. He was half expecting a demand to return and apologize in person.

He ripped open the envelope and unfolded the note. It took him a moment, or possibly two, to process the message, which was equal parts short and brutal.

Father dead. Your pistol at the scene. Tell me you're innocent. J.

"What's the matter?" he heard his aunt ask, the concern in her voice barely audible over the pounding of blood in his ears.

Beau sank down into his chair and handed the note to Aunt Veronica. He poured himself another glass of brandy and swallowed it in a single gulp.

"Dear heaven," she said, an unmistakable wobble in her voice. "What does that mean, do you think?" She lowered the note. "I didn't know you owned a gun."

"I picked up a revolver years ago," he said. "I didn't even think I had bullets for the thing. It's been locked away for eons. And I didn't shoot him."

Him. Frank da Silva was dead. *Dead.* It didn't make any sense.

"I didn't say you did," his aunt said calmly. "But someone clearly thinks you did."

"I have to contact Jessica," he said, fighting his way through the disorientation that was starting to cloud his thoughts. "I need to find out what happened."

"You will do no such thing," she said. "Not until I discuss this with your uncle."

His aunt's declaration struck him straight in the chest. His father was dead. Shot with Beau's gun. And the last thing Beau did was have a rip-roaring fight with his father before leaving for Halifax.

Tell me you're innocent.

Jessica's plea hurt him more than he thought possible. Beau was hardly an innocent man. He'd spent a lifetime working for Frank da Silva, an iron-fisted mogul with a sharp mind and a sharper tongue—one that seemed to grow even more cutting after his wife's death. In his youth, Beau had given himself to all the excesses that a boy with too much money at his disposal could ask for—drink, women and occasionally cards. He had a face, his father said, that could charm the devil out of his own soul, and a natural ability to put people at ease. He'd charmed teachers, women, friends, and even a few enemies. He'd used that smile and a few chosen words to get himself out of more scrapes than was probably fair. A smile and a laugh and for most, Beau da Silva could do no wrong.

Except for Frank da Silva. For him, there was little Beau did that was right. Their last meeting was so heated that Frank had sent one of his prized porcelain vases whirling at Beau's head. Even now, Beau's face burned from the anger of it.

And now Frank was dead.

"I have to talk to the investigators," he said, swallowing back the bile that tainted the back of his throat. "I'm innocent."

"Yes you do, but you need help to do it." Aunt Vee went to her side table, scratched out a note, and rang the bell for her housekeeper. Mrs. Hayes reappeared and after receiving the note and a few words of instruction, she was gone. No sooner had she exited than Uncle Archie appeared. His normally jolly expression was solemn.

The two were a study in opposites—Aunt Vee was petite, slight, but fierce in her own way. Her husband was of average height, but his bombastic personality, generous girth, and well-trimmed but rather remarkable beard made him seem larger.

"This might be a new record for you," Archie said, peering at Beau through eyebrows so thick they seemed to have a personality all their own. "You've been in town for barely eight hours and already I'm going to have the police at my door."

Beau got to his feet and raked his hand through his hair. "I swear on my life that I'm innocent."

"I've sent for that private detective I read about in the papers," Veronica said, patting the seat beside her. "I hope he'll be able to help us."

"Not that Ashe fellow?" his uncle asked, his brows forming into a deep vee as he sat on the settee next to his wife.

"What's wrong with him?" Aunt Vee replied.

"Coughlin doesn't like him," he said. "And he is married to one of those Everwell women. I'm not sure what your New Women's League would think of that association."

"You may be business associates, but any one Victor Coughlin trusts implicitly is not someone I'd leave my purse with." Aunt Vee waved her hands around, effortlessly brushing aside Archie's concerns as if they were an unwanted housefly. "I'm hiring Mr. Ashe, not his wife. Besides, he handled a small affair for Ann Kenny and she told me he was excellent. Very discreet."

Within the hour, there was a ringing of the doorbell, and a moment later a tall man in a brown suit and matching derby appeared in the door. He was Beau's height, or a little taller, with fair skin and light brown hair neatly combed back.

"Mr. Ashe," Aunt Vee said, "here you are at last. This is my husband, Mr. Archibald Turnbull, and my nephew, Mr. Beaumont da Silva."

"Dominic Ashe," he said in a clear, Boston accent. He offered his hand to Beau and the men shook hands before taking a seat.

"Before we go any further, I need to know one thing," Ashe continued, looking Beau straight in the eye. "Did you do it?"

The question took Beau back slightly, in part because of the straight forward way the American had posed it. He shook his head.

"No."

"Any idea who did?" the detective continued.

Beau pulled a folded piece of paper from his jacket and handed it to Dominic. His father had a lot of business rivals—and among those, some particularly bitter enemies. "I started making a list."

"I recognize a few of these names," Dominic continued. "Who would have access to your personal affects? Someone went through some trouble to pin this on you."

Beau sat back in the chair, trying to ignore the tightness at his throat. "No idea. It's possible any of them could have bribed someone to find my gun and use it. Frank da Silva was not an easy man to work for. If he loved you, he loved you. And if he didn't, you were out."

"And what happens to the business with him out of the picture?"

"Most of the company goes to me," he said, instantly aware of just how damning that was to say. "Jessica—my sister—is to be given a smaller stake, and a sizeable cash settlement. And Neil, my brother-in-law, is looked after as well."

"Did your brother-in-law and father get along?" Mr. Ashe continued.

"Like two peas in a pod. Neil was the son my father probably wished he had. Business driven. Loyal," Beau replied, stifling down the hint of envy that twisted. Frank loved Neil. Loved him the way Beau could have only wished of his father. "I can't imagine he would have bit the hand that feeds him."

"Someone killed your father with a gun you owned," Mr. Ashe said, looking down over the list, then back to Beau. "Was it public knowledge you had a pistol?"

Beau shook his head. "I bought it at an auction on a whim. I've never even fired the thing."

"Who knew you had it?"

"The family of course," he said, wracking his memory. "Probably half the businessmen on that list. They were at the same event."

Beau continued with the interview, giving the detective as much information as he could about his circumstances, when Mrs. Hayes returned.

"Excuse me," she said, looking from Beau to his aunt and uncle. "But the paper's just come. I think you might want to see it."

Archie rose and took the paper, pausing to read the headline. Archie was a hearty and hale man, but he visibly blanched. Aunt Vee went to his side, and her sharp gasp brought Beau to his feet. In a flash he crossed the room and took the folded broadsheet from his uncle.

Shocking Murder of New Brunswick Lumber King

Murder Weapon Found, Suspect at Large

Beau skimmed the story: Frank da Silva was found dead from a single shot to his heart in his study. The murder weapon was in the bushes on the grounds.

And the suspect? Right above the fold, was Beau's face.

It wasn't the first time Beau had been on the front page of the paper. As the only son of one of New Brunswick's most powerful families, he'd landed there for any number of reasons, and not all of them were moments his father was proud of. But even his most embarrassing moment paled compared to this.

"It wasn't me," Beau said again, handing the paper to Dominic. "Frank and I had an argument—and it was a good one. I packed my bags and took the first boat I could out of Saint John Harbour heading across the bay. I got a train from Windsor the next day and landed in Halifax. I haven't been home for two days."

"Did anyone else know where you were going?"

Beau shook his head. "I've got some property outside the city. I'd recently been offered a deal for it, and it gave me an excuse to get out of town."

"We didn't even know he was coming until he arrived at our front door," Aunt Vee said.

"Well, it seems I have my work cut out for me," Dominic said. "I have a contact at the Chronicle. I'll see what he knows about this."

"And what do I do in the meantime?" Beau asked.

"Stay out of sight," he said.

Aunt Veronica sniffed, sitting back down with a glass of something notably stronger than tea in her hand.

"We were at MacAskill's this morning. It was full of people. No doubt someone will recognize him from that image. Why don't you go to Europe, Beau?" she asked. "Just until Mr. Ashe can sort things out for you."

"Aunt Vee," he said, shaking his head. "I've got to prove my innocence and start running the company so everything Frank built doesn't run into the ground. I can't do that from across the ocean."

Silver Lumber was Frank da Silva's legacy. Beau had been groomed to run the business since his father had first discovered Beau's gift for coaxing the best deal out suppliers and getting the best price for their goods. It was a talent Beau had honed to a fine point and he'd used to great effect over the years. It had not only helped the company's ledgers, but his own personal fortune as well.

Still, it had never seemed enough. He'd spent a lifetime chasing Frank's good favour, waiting for that moment when his father would clap him on the shoulder and tell him how proud he was of him. He'd never received it. Now he never would.

At least his proclamation that he was staying was met with his aunt's approval.

"I appreciate that," she said, giving him a warm smile. "But that handsome face of yours is probably on every newspaper from here to New York and Toronto. They will have you in irons and a rope around your neck if you're not careful."

His shirt collar had suddenly become a little tighter than it had a moment ago, but Beau resisted the urge to loosen it. He'd been in tight spots before—but this was something else entirely.

"Mrs. Turnbull has a point," the detective said, pointing at the paper and handing it back to him. "The company has posted a reward for any information that leads to your whereabouts."

"What?" His uncle's voice bellowed, mixing with Beau's own protest.

"Two hundred dollars," Mr. Ashe said. "Someone is really out for your hide, Mr. da Silva."

Beau sank down in his chair, running his hand down over his face, before letting out a string of curses under this breath.

"People are going to come looking for you," his uncle said. "And they are going to start with this house."

"It would be best if we get you out of town," Mr. Ashe said. "At least while I can do some work and follow up on some leads."

"The Grove," Aunt Veronica said, then looked to her husband, and they sat silently for a moment, seeming to have an entire conversation with only their eyes. She nodded, then turned back to Beau and Mr. Ashe. "It's out of the way. You were here to sell it, Beau. Maybe you can put that off until this mess is behind you."

Mr. Ashe leaned forward, clearly interested in the idea. "How out of the way?"

"Very," she said, meeting Beau's gaze. "Emily and I couldn't wait to escape it. She hated the country. Your father was her escape."

Beau's mother had died when Jessica was barely two, and he was four. He remembered her vibrant smile and a loving nature, but little else.

"Would Beau's presence be noticed?" Mr. Ashe asked.

Aunt Vee paused, giving a thoughtful sip of her tea, before shaking her head. "We could ask the Chandlers to help out— they've been looking after that property forever and I would trust them with my life. There's a telegraph office in Windsor if anyone needed to get ahold of you."

"Someone should be with him," the detective said. "Just in case."

"Who?"

"I have someone in mind, but it may take some convincing," Mr. Ashe said, coming to his feet. "Let me see what I can do. I'll stop by the Chronicle offices and talk to Ben Miller. He might be able to tell me more than what's in the paper."

The others rose, and Archie took Mr. Ashe's hand. "You will do this, Mr. Ashe? Whatever your rates are, I'll pay it and more to find out who is determined to have my nephew swing."

"This is my problem, Uncle," Beau interjected. "I appreciate your kindness, but this is my mess. Whatever you need, Mr. Ashe, you'll have it. Name your price."

Chapter Three

PHILLIPA HARTLEY, Everwell's head mistress and unofficial head of The Everwell Society, was in the library examining the book that had been at the focus of the Scandalous Spinster's latest efforts.

"I can honestly say this might be the most unexpected ending to any job we've ever done," she said, shrugging her shoulders as the others stood gathered around her. "And given the last two ended in marriages, that is saying something."

It was mid-afternoon, and Maddy was still boondoggled by the entire thing. More to the point, she wasn't entirely sure what was the most remarkable bit of it all—that the job had wrapped up so neatly, or that Maddy's knees had managed to weaken at the thought of man with eyes like a summer sky and a smile that outshone the sun.

Weaken, that is, until a throwaway comment from his objectively beautiful mouth landed like a burr in her ear.

Poor old spinster.

Quite miraculously, her knees and every other part of her that had found itself in some state of discombobulation recovered. If she was being charitable, Beau da Silva was technically correct on all accounts. She wasn't rich. At thirty-seven she was certainly not young. And she was most definitely not married. Besides, she'd been called far worse in her youth.

You must agree the girl is quite homely, Patrick. She needs a good dowry if we're to get her married.

I got her, boys. I snagged the prized cow—

"It was more than unexpected," Elouise said, her enthusiasm interrupting Maddy's maudlin thoughts. "He was absolutely enthralled with you, Maddy. I think he would have bought you the lot of them if you'd batted your lashes at him."

The very idea of any man being enthralled with her almost made Maddy want to laugh.

"I do not bat my lashes," she said, tamping down this rather absurd feeling that had been chasing her since the moment he'd spoken to her. Besides, they hadn't heard his true feelings as she had. "He probably just wanted to goad his aunt. We all know what she and her kind think of us."

"Seems a rather expensive joke, don't you think?" Elouise crossed her arms and shook her head. "I saw the way he was looking at you. Rimple would side with me."

Maddy didn't believe in overt displays of affection, but if she did, she would have hugged Elouise. Since Maddy arrived at Everwell a decade ago, Elouise Charming—now Mrs. Ashe—seemed intent on pointing out every single one of Maddy's supposed charms. She did it so regularly, Maddy was in danger of actually believing her.

"Whatever his motives, what's important is that Mrs. Cornish gets her treasure back," Phillipa interjected in that no-nonsense way of hers. "I'll have Reg deliver it tomorrow. Maddy can have an entire evening with it before it goes back."

Phillipa was about to walk away when she stopped and gave Maddy a playful look. "And I'm afraid it will have to go back."

Maddy opened her mouth to protest but thought the better of it. After all, in amongst her small but rather impressive collection in the Everwell library were books. Some she'd borrowed on a very, *very* long-term loan while she was working on one job or another with her fellow Scandalous Spinsters and Wayward Women. Of course, none of their owners had any idea she'd borrowed them.

"Maddy!"

Rimple Jones appeared in the doorway, holding today's paper in her hands, her deep brown eyes wide.

"What's wrong?" she asked, her body immediately going on alert.

Without another word, Rimple rushed to Maddy and the others, turning the paper around so they all could read the headline. Thick black lettering proclaimed the murder of a New Brunswick captain of industry.

"And?" Maddy asked.

"Look!" Rimple pointed at the picture. There, staring back at them was none other than the man from the bookstore today. Beau da Silva. He was far more serious in this picture, obvious taken to be hung in the hallowed halls of whatever boardroom his family ruled.

And he was wanted for the murder of his father, Frank da Silva.

"Perhaps I spoke too soon," Phillipa said, taking the paper from Rimple's hands, unfolding it so she could read the entire story, which took up much of the front page.

"He's wanted, but that doesn't make him guilty," Elouise said. "Still, the good ladies of the New Women's League must be in a tizzy to be so intimately connected to an accused murderer."

Maddy tried to look over Phillipa's shoulder, but it was impossible to see the details.

"Phillipa," Rimple said again, an unmistakable discomfort in her voice, her brow dipping into a deep vee as she pulled the paper back toward her.

"What is it?" Maddy asked, alerted by the sudden change in Rimple's normally indomitable sunshine. Stepping around Phillipa and Elouise, she stood behind her friend in an effort to see what was causing Rimple's reaction.

Troubling Rumours Swirl Around Eccentric Society

Without a thought, Maddy clutched the newspaper in her hands, pulling it toward her and skimming the story. Something tightened in her gut, a thousand irrational fears coming to the surface.

Is something nefarious happening behind the otherwise pristine walls of that Georgian jewel? Rumours continue to surface from some of the most reputable corners of Halifax's parlours that the misguided aims of Miss Emma Everwell, daughter of the late Lord Everwell, have been hijacked to service an illegal ring of thieves. Not even the marriage of Miss Gemma Kurt to Colonel Jeremy Webber (retired) has ceased to quell the suspicions. Indeed, a source close to the Colonel recently revealed to this reporter—

"Maddy."

The sound of Phillipa's voice cut through Maddy's panic. Maddy looked up, not bothering to hide her displeasure at the interruption.

"Let me see," Phillipa said in that calm way of hers, all the while giving Maddy a look that suggested she would brook no opposition. Maddy let go, and Phillipa turned to the last page. Elouise, Rimple and Maddy then crowded around the head mistress, trying to read the short piece over her shoulder.

"Phillipa, this is bad," Elouise said, biting on her bottom lip.

Maddy held her breath. Normally when someone pronounced a dire judgment of a situation, Phillipa would play devil's advocate. No doubt it was because she had observed the situation before her, and viewed it in the context of the hundreds of pieces of information she had gleaned over the years and had been busy concocting not just one, but have a dozen contingencies for how to react.

This time, however, Phillipa only made a murmur of ascent before lowering the paper. As she did so, the figure of Dominic Ashe filled the library doorway.

"Ah!" he said, his gaze immediately falling to Elouise, not

bothering to disguise his delight at seeing her. "Just the ladies I need to see."

"Dominic," Elouise said, "Just the man I need to see."

She moved across the room and took his hand, his expression moving from greeting to one of concern.

"What's happened?" he asked. Elouise filled him in on the story in the social column.

"Do you have any idea who's spreading the rumours?" he asked.

"We have a good idea," Phillipa said. "A disgruntled former employee of Jeremy's. However, where she heard them is a mystery."

"Not entirely," Rimple added. "That social club—the New Women's League. She heard it at a meeting."

"Is that the group started by Emily Coughlin and her ilk?" Dominic said. "Maybe it's just another roundabout way to you get you to move."

"Possibly," Phillipa said. "But this is getting a little concerning. Thanks to Jeremy's connections, we've managed to get several of our girls hired into some of the more reputable places in the city, including Government House."

Dominic sat down on the settee and read over the piece in question. "I could take a look into it."

"I don't know if you could get anywhere near the NWL," Elouise said. "You're too close to Everwell."

"I don't think there is such a thing," he said, giving Elouise a warm smile. "I just spent the past hour with Veronica Turnbull, and she didn't seem to mind."

"You're investigating the da Silva case for her?" Phillipa said, her brow furrowed.

"I am," he said, then cocked his head. "And I think we have an opportunity here."

Phillipa crossed her arms and started pacing in that way she did when she was thinking. He hadn't said a word, yet, she already seemed to understand what Dominic was proposing.

"And before you say no," he said, raising his hands as he read her silent dissent, "consider it a chance to fix this. You know better than anyone that favours are a particularly useful sort of currency."

"The NWL do us a favour?" Maddy interrupted, rolling her eyes. "Why would they even want to?"

He picked up the paper and pointed to the picture of Beau da Silva.

"He's my newest client," Dominic said. "I don't think the ink was dry before I got a call from Veronica Turnbull herself."

"Did he do it?" Maddy asked.

Dominic shared everything he knew, including a few pieces that were not in the papers.

"Someone is clearly eager to find him," Phillipa said. "It's not every day a reward like this is offered before the case even goes to trial."

"Exactly," he said. "We have to get him out of the city. That reward is too much of a carrot for even the casual fortune hunter. I'm going to Saint John as soon as he's in a safe place."

"So what do you want from us?" Maddy asked before she could help herself.

"I need someone to keep an eye on him. Someone who knows how to handle themself."

Dominic's eyes met Maddy's and her heart jumped into her throat. Why on earth would she want to help Beau da Silva?

She opened her mouth to protest, but Phillipa spoke up first.

"Absolutely not," she said, giving her head a quick shake. "It's too much of a risk."

Maddy stifled a sigh of relief. Thank goodness Phillipa had some good sense.

"Everwell would be doing The Turnbulls a tremendous favour," he continued, clearly not yet willing to give up his case. "The man's pockets are pretty deep. You'll get a nice donation for your services, which I would add, would be one hundred percent legal. No sneaking around, no slipping keys into stranger's pockets, no cracking safes—or skulls."

"Men like Beau da Silva are not the people we are trying to help," Phillipa said. "Nor Veronica Turnbull for that matter. They can snap their fingers and get whomever they need. And they can't know about Maddy's particular training."

"They don't need to know about the martial arts or the boxing," Dominic said. "All they have to think is that Maddy is going as his housekeeper and cook."

"I hate cooking," Maddy said.

Dominic turned and flashed her a smile, which may have worked wonders on Elouise, but Maddy, thankfully, was immune.

"It's an old stone cottage in the middle of nowhere," he said, "with no one to bother you."

"He'll bother me."

Dominic sighed, folded up the paper, and placed it down on Maddy's desk.

"If it's not going to work, that's fine," he said. "I'll see if Reg Knickle can do it. Or maybe Jeremy can spare Harold Babock."

Maddy sat down at her desk, as if to signal her decision was final, when her gaze came to rest on the social column.

Troubling Rumours…

Her stomach clenched at the thought that Everwell might be in danger. Danger from an enemy she couldn't fight. She could hear Phillipa, Eloise and Dominic talking behind her, brainstorming on who could help him with this case. And while there were a million reasons to stay right where she was sitting, there was four reasons why she had to stand up.

"I will do this on one condition," Maddy said, pulling herself to her feet and looking to Phillipa. "Mrs. Turnbull agrees to find the source of those rumours and silence them."

"Maddy, are you certain?" Phillipa asked.

"No," she said. "Phillipa, you'll have to talk to her. But if you can get her to agree, then yes. I'll do it."

Maddy spent a restless night regretting her decision. There seemed no book that could distract her, and not even pouring her frustration out on her sparring bag seemed to help. She spent half the night hoping there would be some urgent message from Dominic, advising them that Mrs. Turnbull had no wish for help, but instead, Elouise had come to the door the next morning with a note for Phillipa that Dominic and Mrs. Turnbull would be by for tea to discuss the terms. Phillipa seemed pleased by this turn of events, but it had put Maddy into such a spin she'd burned the morning porridge. Phillipa graciously started another pot and ordered Maddy out of the kitchen and into her garden.

Maddy stood in the midst of her little rose labyrinth. Some of the blooms were past their prime, but the air was still beautifully perfumed by the mass of white tender blooms of her Madame Hardy roses that had been gifted to her by Tilda and Lady Em when she'd first arrived at Everwell. They'd been joined by other varieties, including the Complicatas, with their yellow centres and happy pink petals, and dramatic deep hues of the Charles de Mills. Her garden grew and flourished, but Everwell was changing, and that unsettled her more than she cared to admit. While Elouise and Gemma were still intimately involved with The Everwell Society—both the public facing society and the matters handled by the Scandalous Spinsters, they no longer lived under Everwell's roof. They still took many of their evening meals at Everwell as they always had, and those meals were more boisterous with the added numbers of husbands and extended households that had come to gather, particularly on Sundays. Indeed, Lady Em and Tilda, Everwell's matriarchs, had mused of the necessity of an addition to the dining room to house them all.

But the evenings were quieter. Elouise's regular spot on the settee was now empty. And Gemma no longer practiced as often with Maddy in their training area in the carriage house.

Something had shifted, and it unsettled Maddy in a way she couldn't quite hold on to.

And so, as she sat here on a pleasant July afternoon, about to embark on a quiet afternoon of doing something that she on any other day would have been perfectly content to do, Maddy found herself wrestling with this thing, this mood, that was hard to pin down. It had crept under her skin and stretched every last nerve of her being. Something unsettled. She felt it in her bones.

She moved through the verge, the leaves gleaming in different shades of green, some shiny, others not, her heart springing in anticipation as she approached the heart of it. There was something magical about roses. Their petals were such silky soft, delicate little things, so beautifully scented that, for just a moment, Madeline Murray could pretend that she was pretty just by being surrounded by their perfume. They didn't care if she was too tall, too fat, too grumpy, or too much of whatever it was that made the world see her the way they did. They made her feel beautiful just by being near them. And for that, she would tend to these flowers to her dying day.

There were delicate white ones, bold red ones, and a host of pinks in between. The bright pink Duc de Cambridge were a particular favourite, though it was hard to choose. But she loved them, prickles and all.

Moving toward the centre was her latest achievement—the spectacular and demanding Reine des Violettes. It was one of the few climbers in her collection, a lush, brilliant pink quartered bloom surrounded by bright green leaves. She'd managed to train it over an old section of fence, next to which she nestled a beautiful wooden bench. It provided the perfect canopy and escape to read on a warm summer day.

"There you are, my darling," she said, her heart filling up with anticipation. It was silly, and only upon pain of death would she share how much these roses meant to her. How essential they were. She approached them with the same enthusiasm and reverence she'd imagined she might approach a lover—and imagination was all she had. Which was fine. Maddy had long ago given up the idea that any man would want her for more than the dowry her father had bestowed on her, and she'd rarely seen a man that either inspired any particular excitement, nor gave her any indication that she would give them any.

Until yesterday. And then, that was someone toying with her for his own purposes.

Maddy's gaze swept over the bush, covered in lively pink blooms, framed by bright green leaves. Her heart leapt into her chest as she examined several leaves on one of the closest stems. Marring the shiny smooth surface of the leaves were a host of sickly black spots.

She swallowed back her disappointment. One couldn't garden if they weren't prepared to go toe to toe with a host of things impossible to control—weather, pests, and diseases. Every season brought forward expectation and heartbreak. The last time Maddy dealt with blackspot, it had infected one entire corner of her labyrinth, and there was still a bare spot from where the blight had completely destroyed one of her tender new varieties.

She stalked off to the small garden shed, her mood shifting from mere discontent to something between the sharp, jagged edges of panic and rage. She pushed up the latch on the shed and stepped in, grabbed her freshly sharpened pruning scissors, then spun around to leave. In her haste, she knocked over a small stack of tiny clay pots, one smashing to pieces at her feet.

Fuck.

She bent over and picked up the shards, her mother's voice in her head, chastising Maddy for her foul language. *Ladies do not use such foul language, Madeline. It's base, beastly behaviour.*

A good thing, then, that few would have considered Madeline Murray a lady. And a very good thing that her fellow teachers at the Everwell School never expected her to be. Maddy didn't believe in a god, but if she did, she would thank the relevant deity for the day Phillipa Hartley brought her to Everwell. They hadn't asked too many questions, nor judged her for her dubious past.

And for that, and so many other things, she would protect them and Everwell and everything it stood for with her life, if necessary. And that included her beloved roses.

She set the clay shards on a nearby shelf and took a moment to calm herself. Panic caused mistakes.

The other side of panic was anger—an emotion Maddy had struggled with for far too long. Harnessed, it could be useful, and on occasion, when battling a particularly difficult opponent, Maddy dipped into its dark power to help her fight through fatigue or pain. But it could inflict unintended harm. As she walked back toward her diseased rose bush, pruners in one hand, and an empty wooden bucket in the other, she worked to rid herself of the unruly swirl of emotion that would spiral. Instead, she focused on what she could manage. Yes, black spot was bad. Yes, she might lose her entire rosebush. But could she attack the problem and do her best to protect it?

Also yes.

June had been particularly damp, which no doubt contributed to the arrival of the fungus, but after weeks of wet weather, the sky overhead was a brilliant blue, with only a wisp of cloud in the sky. When she was younger, Maddy's mother used to scold her for not wearing a bonnet, letting her fair skin redden and freckle. It was one of many things her mother scolded her for.

Maddy pushed off that unwanted memory, revived as she approached her beloved garden, now lush with peonies, hollyhocks and lavender. Soon the echinacea would be blooming. The landscape was alive, the low buzz of bees searching for pollen, and butterflies dining on milkweed. Milkweed wasn't generally favoured in more fashionable gardens, where only seeds from Europe were prized. The local species, considered lesser in many eyes, were ripped out of the earth they'd been home to and protected for thousands of years.

Past the large maple tree, movement caught her eye. She paused, wondering if it was merely a bird moving through the brush when the scent of something earthy, masculine, mingled with the heady aromas of the roses, thick in the summer air and carried by the gentlest of salty breezes coming from the North-west Arm below.

Every muscle went on alert. Maddy rarely kept a weapon on her while she was at Everwell. Throwing knives and short sabres were her preferred tools when life and limb were on the line, but her small pruning scissors and a bucket would do in a pinch. She'd gone into situations with far less. Besides, she had her wits, and she had her body. It wasn't lithe, like Gemma's. But it was strong, and she would use it to protect herself and anyone—or anything—she loved.

She loved Everwell. And she loved these roses.

The unnatural rustle of leaves further sharpened her senses. She turned her head toward the noise, angling her body slightly in order to assess the threat. Through the verge, punctuated by pops of colour, she could clearly see the form of a man. Though much of his outline was obscured, her body—unreliable traitor—recognized him as the man from the bookshop.

Beau da Silva. Potential murderer of a rich industrialist, and more importantly, slinger of insults about her age and marital status.

From his gait, Maddy guessed he wasn't trying to hide his presence. Rather, he seemed preoccupied with the flowers them-selves, pausing here and there, taking in their scent, and generally admiring them. That should have taken some of her disdain away from what he was doing until he wrapped his hand around a blossom and—

He wasn't just looking at her roses. He was reaching out and… *touching them*? Indignation crept up her spine, prickling hot even in the growing heat of a summer day as he pawed at her prized Duc de Cambridge. Did he even know what he was doing? Helping himself to her passion, her sweat, and occasionally, when she worked out here without her thick leather gloves—her blood. He wasn't just inviting himself to something he had absolutely no business handling, but a diseased plant, which might easily help spread the fungus across more of the plant if he helped himself to them as easily as he did this one.

She opened her mouth, but before she could find the voice to call out and demand this interloper stop, he'd done the deed.

He'd taken one of her roses.

Her blood pounding, Maddy dropped her pruners and the bucket, rushed through the labyrinth, and came upon him just as he'd pocketed whatever blade he'd used to steal the rose. She came upon him from behind, whipping him around so she could see his face. His bright blue eyes widened in surprise and he looked about to break out into what no doubt would have been a beautiful smile. If she'd waited, he might even try and say something charming.

But Maddy didn't particularly care about his charm or his lovely eyes or his beautiful smile. He'd invited himself into this place and stolen one of her roses. Even worse, he risked the health of her entire plant. And there was a price to be exacted for that.

A second later, her body working from memory, the thief was on his back, Maddy pinning his shoulders with her hands. She looked down at him, ignoring this unwanted sensation, this heat, coming through the soft linen of his summer jacket. He squinted and let go a small cough, before looking up at her with undisguised mischief.

"Lovely to see you again."

Chapter Four

THIS WASN'T the first time Beau da Silva had been left breathless by a member of the opposite sex. But it was absolutely the first time he'd been knocked completely out of his senses by one.

He lay in the grass, perfectly still. It wasn't like he had much of a choice, considering he'd nearly had his breath knocked out of him. He sucked in a gulp of air even as his heart slammed against the walls of his chest. A halo of wild red hair above him blotted out the sun, and a pair of eyes, as hard as emeralds and just as green, stared back at him. Below that was the most remarkable bosom. It was hardly the moment to be distracted by lush breasts, but in his defence they were only inches away from his face, and Christ, if Beau was about to die here, he supposed this wasn't the absolute worst way to go.

"What in the hell are you doing here?"

He tried to put hand to his eyes to shield himself from the sun's glare and green-eyed fury kneeling over him, but her hands pressed him down into the ground. For half a second he'd considered answering her question with a charming quip, before his good sense—aided by a strong sense of self-preservation—made him reconsider. He struggled against his attacker, expecting to easily throw off the fury, only to find his efforts rewarded by being held down even harder.

Was he… aroused by this?

Quite possibly.

"I'll explain once you let me up."

"You don't get the privilege of setting the terms," she replied. "Not here, and certainly not after what you just did."

Beau blinked. What in the hell had he done? He'd dutifully arrived at the Everwell Manor as directed, even though he didn't understand the reason why a charity run by, and for, a bunch of widows and spinsters was somehow instrumental to his wellbeing. His aunt had wanted a few moments alone with the proprietors, and since Beau hadn't had the time to properly stretch his legs since yesterday, it didn't seem completely unreasonable to bide his time in this rather remarkable garden.

But now he wondered if he should have asked a few more questions.

"I have no idea where here is, and you're going to have to explain my crime." *Or at least, the one that wasn't a murder charge.*

She plucked the flower he'd just nestled in the buttonhole of his label and held it in front of him like an accusation.

"It's a flower," he said. He would have shrugged, if he could move his shoulders. "There were at least another two dozen on that one bush alone. I had no idea it was restricted."

"Do you have any idea of the damage you could do?" she said through gritted teeth.

Damage? Beau thought. Couldn't this banshee see that it was Beau who was about to be damaged?

"It's a plant," he grumbled, dispensing with any further attempts at charm, which were clearly wasted. "They grow. That's what they do."

Actually, he had no goddamn idea what plants did. His family had made a fortune cutting down trees, not growing them.

"Maddy!" Another woman's voice, calm, but commanding,

interrupted them from somewhere nearby. "For heaven's sakes, let him up."

Her call drew the banshee's attention. Even though it made no sense at all, Beau found himself oddly deprived of her attentions, which was ridiculous given she still had him pinned to the ground.

"It's quite all right," he called out, which instantly snapped her attentions back to him. He let his gaze wander for a moment from her face down to her generous bosom. Then he lowered his voice and locked his gaze right on her. "I'm enjoying the view."

Beau had always lived dangerously. But as her grip on his shoulders tightened and a look that was half befuddlement and half fury crossed her face, he had to wonder if his mouth had finally done in him. Maybe this red-haired siren would save a Saint John hangman the trouble.

Instead, he found himself hauled up to his feet. Righted, Beau was able to take in the woman who'd dropped him to the ground. This was not the same demure creature he'd met in the bookshop. Her fair skin was flushed and freckled from the sun, and her hair had come lose from its pins, a fiery crown on an impossibly lush but strong body.

Two women approached them, and for a moment Beau wasn't certain if he was in the middle of some bizarre Greek play with a female chorus about to judge him for his sins. Except these two at least didn't seem particularly eager to tear his limbs from body. Indeed, they seemed rather welcoming in comparison. One of them, the fairest of the three, he remembered being at the bookshop.

"Welcome to Everwell, Mr. Da Silva," the eldest of the ladies said warmly. "I am Mrs. Phillipa Hartley. This is Mrs. Elouise Ashe. I believe you have met her husband, Dominic."

Mrs. Hartley, a handsome woman with fair skin and keen eyes spoke with a calm but unmistakable authority. He shook hands with her, and then Mrs. Ashe, before Mrs. Hartley gestured to his attacker.

"And I believe you have already met Miss Madeline Murray," she concluded with the understatement of the year. "We should go to the house. There is much to discuss."

He brushed the grass off his sleeves, eyeing the women carefully. He shot a smile at the minotaur in the maze, who'd stalked off to retrieve a bucket and — dear Lord— a pair of pruning scissors she must have dropped before she tackled him.

"My apologies," he repeated. "I have been trapped inside since the newspapers made the rounds. I needed fresh air and to stretch my legs."

Beau's next thought was interrupted by Dominic Ashe, who approached the ladies with a friendly, unstudied air. The American didn't seem the slightest bit bothered by Miss Murray and her death stare, which made Beau pause.

"What are you all doing out here?" Dominic asked. "Mrs. Turnbull and the others are waiting."

"Yes, please get him out of my garden," Miss Murray said, turning to Dominic, arms crossed. "He took one of the Duc de Cambridge damasks."

Dominic turned to Beau with a look of simultaneous shock and amusement. "You didn't."

"My apologies," he said, then turned to Miss Murray. "I have a soft spot for beautiful things."

That line would have worked on any number of women, but Miss Murray, apparently, was not one of them. Indeed, from the taut line across her brow, it had made her more angry.

"Just because it's beautiful doesn't mean you can just help yourself to it," she said. "That bush is full of blackspot. It's a fungus. Handle it too much and you could spread it."

There was an edge to her words. Anger to be sure, but Beau knew enough about anger that often behind it, was another emotion. Generally, it was fear.

"Congratulations da Silva," Dominic said, nodding to him with undisguised amusement. "That's the most I've heard Madeline Murray voluntarily speak since the day I met her."

"I'm not sure what prize I've won," he muttered under his breath.

Dominic laughed before returning his attention to Miss Murray, his voice warm. He clearly liked the red-haired hellion.

"This will all be worth it in the end, I promise you," Dominic said.

"It better be," she challenged, giving Beau a look of disdain so sharp Frank da Silva himself would have been proud. Madeline Murray was stunning, yes, but for all the intoxicating beauty of her soft body, there was a hardness there he was in no mood to tangle with.

Beau parried her disgust with an empty smile, a defence he'd honed early in life to spare himself the worst of the pain from a thousand cutting remarks courtesy of the man for whose measure, despite Beau's near six feet, he could never quite reach.

"After you," Dominic said, gesturing to Beau, who fell into step alongside him.

Aunt Vee wished to have a private conversation with the ladies of The Everwell Society, so Dominic took him to his home, which bordered the Everwell property. Not long after their arrival, they were met by Mr. Benjamin Miller, a local journalist who, according to the detective, had good connections across the region. Miller was a squarely built man with a hawkish nose and short reddish hair. His complexion was fair, save for the ink stains on two of his fingers. Beau got the impression that this man knew more secrets about the city than anyone would comfortably admit. The three men settled in the front parlour over a pot of strong coffee as Beau relayed as many details as he could think of about his father's business, his associates, and where he was the night his father was shot. Beau had gone to his favourite club but left early to prepare for his trip to Halifax the following morning.

"And you don't have a single person who can account for your whereabouts?" Miller asked.

There was something about the question that grated, for reasons Beau didn't care to examine. If Beau were to throw a party, half the town would have been at the door. He'd once joked that he probably paid the salary of one of the columnists at the Saint John Tribune who felt the need to report on every party he attended and all the affairs Beau had been rumoured to be involved in. But at a time when he needed to be publicly seen, no one had come forward to support him. In fact, it appeared to be quite the opposite.

"If I did, I wouldn't be here now, would I?" he said with barely concealed sarcasm. "No one saw me after ten that evening."

Miller looked over his notebook, then looked over at Dominic. "I'll start making some inquiries."

"Thank you," he replied.

Miller shrugged. "If I crack this, I'll get the scoop of the year. Maybe even my career," he said. He nodded, picked up his bowler, then left.

Beau looked over at Dominic. "He's a real man of the people, isn't he?"

"He's a bit rough around the edges," Dominic said. "I suppose he has to be, given the type of work he does. But he's good, and he protects his sources."

"Let's just hope he gets his story," Beau said. "The sooner, the better. I'm already convinced Miss Murray will murder me in my sleep."

His quip brought a sharp burst of laughter from the American detective.

"There is no one else I would trust with my wife's life more than her. You don't have to be friends with her. She doesn't need to like you. But she will keep you safe. And if you were in a dark corner, you would want her in front of you."

What would Beau want to do with Madeline Murray in a dark corner? A thousand unholy, delicious things. She was so tempting in a way he really couldn't articulate. She'd gripped something carnal inside him which made absolutely no sense whatsoever. Beau da Silva liked his women bright. Warm. Open. Pliable.

Despite the fiery red of her hair, Madeline Murray was as warm as a February morning.

"It still doesn't feel right," Beau said. "I'm not one to sit on my ass while other people take care of my problems."

Mr. Ashe sat back then, raising his brows in what looked to be a flash of recognition. He put down his pen and leaned forward, elbows on the desk, his hands carefully steepled in front of him.

"Look—let me say, I've been in a position similar to yours. I know what this feels like."

"Then you know I can't be shoved off into the woods with a banshee while you and a bunch of these Everwell women go off and save my neck," he said. "They run a school, for Christ's sakes. A noble effort for sure, but they shouldn't be putting themselves in harm's way for me."

"These Everwell women have the gift of caring for people that no one else gives a sweet damn about. And that includes idiots like you and me. If they do the job—and they will—they will get more resources to keep doing what they do, and you will get that most rare of gifts."

"Life?"

"A second chance."

৩৯৫৩

Veronica Turnbull's presence in Everwell's parlour reminded Maddy of that scene in Austen's *Pride and Prejudice* when Lady Catherine de Burgh visited Longbourn. To be fair, Mrs. Turnbull wasn't as much a tyrant as Austen's overbearing aristocrat, nor even an aristocrat at all. Indeed, that title fell to Lady Em. But the strangeness of seeing this woman in their home could not be denied. After all, Veronica Turnbull had, quite unwittingly, seen The Everwell Society of Scandalous Spinsters at work. She had no idea, of course. Elouise had been in a heavy disguise, and when the job was concluded, had the plausible excuse of aiding a detective working undercover for an illustrious and very rich client back in Boston.

Lady Em and Tilda, behind the gracious hostesses that they were, had taken extra care to see to Mrs. Turnbull's comfort. Indeed, the visit had begun with all the social conventions of a normal afternoon call—pleasantries were exchanged, and cups of tea along with plates of pastries were passed. There had been discussions about the weather and the deplorable state of the spring roads, and recommendations from Tilda, a doctoress with years of experience and recently the very public endorsement of her skills by the private secretary of the Lieutenant Governor, about remedies for a cough that had been troubling Archie Turnbull.

"This has been a most refreshing afternoon," Mrs. Turnbull said, and for a moment Maddy almost wanted to believe it. She sat on the settee next to Rimple and Elouise, hands folded in her lap, watching their guest. There seemed little familial resemblance between Mr. da Silva and his diminutive aunt, except perhaps for her ability to appear genuinely convivial even when she would rather be somewhere else. "I am sorry for the circumstances that bring me here to intrude upon you."

"Sometimes the best must be made of an unfortunate situation," Lady Em said, rising to her feet and waiting for Tilda, who joined her. "We will leave the younger ladies to discuss the details. You are in good hands, and so is your nephew."

Mrs. Turnbull nodded, her smile placid but not quite meeting her eyes.

"It was a pleasure to meet you," Tilda said.

"Likewise," their guest replied, "Thank you for the advice about Archie's cough. I will speak to the apothecary about a solution."

"If they won't do it for you," Lady Em spoke up, "come see us. Miss Murray grows all the necessary herbs in the gardens. Tilda can mix it up for you if needed."

Mrs. Turnbull nodded her head to Tilda, a gesture that raised Mrs. Turnbull just a little in Maddy's estimation.

The Everwell matrons left the room. An uncomfortable silence descended, broken by the rustle of cotton and silk skirts as the women shifted in their seats. Phillipa pressed her lips together, then folded her hands, indicating to the room that the real conversation was about to begin.

"I am grateful you are able to provide some assistance," Mrs. Turnbull began. "As you can imagine, this is a rather unexpected and difficult time for my family."

"It is an unfortunate business," Phillipa replied. "I am quite surprised, however, that you were open to coming here and discussing this with us, given the obvious means at your disposal."

"I was not at all certain as to Mr. Ashe's suggestion," Mrs. Turnbull said. "But in the end, there is no one I can trust. We pay people well, but for such a sum as is being offered for Beau's return, there is more than enough incentive to alert the authorities to my nephew's whereabouts."

Phillipa stopped to take a sip of tea, her next statement pleasant, but direct.

"And what makes you trust that we wouldn't?"

A corner of Mrs. Turnbull's mouth tweaked up, betraying her amusement at Phillipa's directness.

"He was very helpful with a private matter for one of Archie's employees last month," she replied with equal directness. "I don't think he would risk his reputation by suggesting you."

Phillipa nodded, accepting her answer, when Mrs. Turnbull continued.

"Beau has offered to pay you five times the amount offered for his capture." She paused, taking her teacup in her hand, prepared to take another sip. "And any expenses related to the imposition on your operations."

Five times? With that sum, she could build a small greenhouse and fill it with exotic plants. She'd always wanted one, where she could attempt to stretch out the growing season for some of her more tender plants.

"That is quite generous," Phillipa agreed, "since you have no idea what those expenses may be."

"He is man with considerable means at his disposal, Mrs. Hartley," she replied, her gaze straying to Maddy, "as you are perfectly aware."

Maddy congratulated herself on remaining calm even as she felt heat prickle at the back of her neck. If Mrs. Turnbull only knew where that book had gone.

"Aside from the expenses incurred, we will accept no fee. We will send our most appropriate staff to stay as a housekeeper for your nephew and do our absolute best to ensure no harm comes to him," Phillipa said. "Too often we must protect Everwell and the vulnerable who come here from those with difficult and even violent intentions. This person is well trained in many of the martial arts and will come in handy. We will be very discreet."

"I have little doubt." Mrs. Turnbull's eyes narrowed slightly as she seemed to be taking the measure of Phillipa's offer. "But no fee? That hardly seems reasonable given your charitable work. He can afford to pay you."

"I have little doubt," Phillipa said with such directness it appeared to soothe Mrs. Turnbull's indignation. "But it is not his money that will seal this arrangement."

Before Mrs. Turnbull could say another word, Phillipa flipped open the copy of yesterday's issue of the *Halifax Chronicle* and presented the incriminating society column to Mrs. Turnbull. The slightest bit of pink rose from her dark blue collar.

"I want you to publicly repudiated these harmful rumours about The Everwell Society," Phillipa said, her voice calm.

Mrs. Turnbull paused, then put down the paper. To her credit, she kept her voice and manner steady.

"Mrs. Hartley," she began, in a soothing tone they'd expected.

"I would not worry yourself about such trifling gossip. Everyone knows that half the words printed in that column are utter nonsense."

"That trifling gossip is coming from an organization that has a certain degree of standing in the community," Elouise interjected, her voice calm, but firm. "And the nature of those rumours are not trifling. They are criminal in nature."

"It is nothing at all," Mrs. Turnbull protested, attempting to wave away Elouise's concerns with a flick of her wrist. "Do you think I would be here if I believed for a moment this was a den of thieves?"

"You arrived in a hired cab," Rimple said, her normally bright demeanour a little more pointed. "And just a moment ago you stated that you don't really trust anyone. It matters to us what the people reading these papers think of us."

Phillipa cast a glance at Elouise and Rimple, before turning her attention back to Mrs. Turnbull.

"It makes it difficult, if not impossible, to place our students with families in respectable homes when an organization with the clout of the New Women's League, which you helped found and currently oversee, is publicly saying such things about us. It is damaging in the extreme," she said. "Find the source of the rumours and publicly discredit them. We can trade on reputations—your nephew's innocence for our own."

Quiet descended again, as Mrs. Turnbull assessed the measure of Phillipa's challenge. For a moment, Maddy wondered if the woman would waver. She was clearly a proud woman. Hopefully, she was not a petty one. These rumours needed to be quashed and only Mrs. Turnbull had the power to do it.

"Just because I say something doesn't mean they will go away."

"Just because we are sending one of our best people to guard your nephew doesn't mean we will be successful," Phillipa countered." But we will do our very best and stake our reputation on ensuring it doesn't happen. We will try to help, at least."

Mrs. Turnbull took a sip of tea, her eyes glancing down at the paper once more. Though the room was full, it was quiet save for the gentle clink of the porcelain cup as she set it down on her saucer.

"We have an agreement."

Chapter Five

BEAU HAD BEEN GIVEN four hours to pack whatever belongings he required and return directly to Everwell Manor. Unlike his father's house, which was heavy with dark wood and a sense of self-importance that imposed itself on those who crossed its threshold, Everwell Manor was bright and welcoming. He breathed in the scent of lemon oil from freshly polished wood, mixed with smells from the kitchen and the fresh summer breeze carried up from the Northwest Arm.

In the morning he would head out of town and go into hiding with Miss Murray as some kind of…nanny.

Miss. Murray.

Christ.

His sleeping quarters were humble—a room normally was saved for unannounced women who needed an urgent refuge from a violent partner. It was small but comfortable, and even though the evening was warm, a gentle breeze from the window refreshed the room. A small bouquet of flowers—none except lily of the valley that he could name—sat in a pretty little vase next to the washstand. Everything at Everwell seemed somehow at home, even if none of it quite made sense to Beau. Then again, he'd never really felt at home after his mother passed. Funny how that just occurred to him.

Beau pulled the coverlet up to his chin, trying to get comfortable. The eccentricity of the place spoke for itself. The relationship between Miss Everwell, a white woman whose manners and accent marked her as a member of the British Upper Class, and Mrs. Gilman, whose brown skin and hair tied neatly and wrapped in an elaborate scarf, would have been the source of no end of gossip. He had not been there ten minutes before he comprehended that the nature of their relationship was not, as one might be tempted to guess, based on the general treatment of black people as an underclass, a pairing of employer and servant. A very quick study of their body language and manner suggested to Beau something even more remarkable. They weren't just equals. They were partners in life.

And then there was Miss Murray herself, who'd returned to the house after his arrival, her face ruddy, strands of hair glued to her skin with a slick of sweat at her hair line. She had a pair of canes in her hand because, according to Rimple Jones, she'd just returned from her training ring, where she had been practicing some type of martial art. Given their meeting in the garden, Beau couldn't help but wonder what would happen if he found himself on the wrong side of those canes.

And he always seemed to be on the wrong side. What had happened to that woman he'd met in the bookstore? The wide-eyed beauty who spoke with such passion about poetry and handled that volume with such reverence that might have made him yearn to trade places with a book?

There was no time to linger on that now. As Beau's head hit the pillow that night—a pillow that was, like the rest of him, at Everwell Manor rather than his uncle's mansion two miles east—he realized he'd spent far too long in the plodding world of business. Generally, "planning" took several days of meetings with a small army of managers, their secretaries, and if done right, at least three bottles of good Scotch.

He tossed and turned, conscious of every squeak of the bed frame underneath him. Rest was pointless when his thoughts ran in a thousand different directions. It didn't help that he'd spent far too much of the day reading and re-reading the nearly cover-to-cover stories in the *Halifax Chronicle*, filled with the accounts of Beau's so-called friends and colleagues who were only too happy to proclaim that Beau's fractured relationship with his father must have induced him at last to murder. Aunt Vee promised to send a note to Jessica, in the hopes of getting a better picture of what was happening. He could only hope his sister had faith in him.

After what felt like hours, Beau tossed off his covers, lit a candle, then fumbled for his pocket watch. It was barely three in the morning. He'd been given a nightshirt and robe—slightly out of fashion but, Beau couldn't help but notice, impeccably tailored. They'd belonged to the former owner of this room who, once upon a time, had been the butler to the matriarchs of this strange place.

He opened the door, conscious of every step. No doubt Miss Murray was a few feet away in her own bed, lounging like a lioness—confident, strong, and yet somehow capable of terrifying anyone she felt was a risk. He should be happy, he supposed, that he was to be the object of her protection. Beau half expected to wake her and found himself curiously disappointed when he'd made it to the bottom of the stairs without her notice.

Beau went to the library. Surely there was a volume on the shelves that would either induce sleep or indulge his imagination enough he would forget his troubles until morning. Either was preferable to staring into the darkness waiting for the morning and the flight to the mysterious refuge that, until yesterday, was merely a bit of land he'd hoped to dispose of as quickly as possible and pocket the reward.

Once he arrived at The Grove, the old Redden homestead, perhaps he could form a true value of the property so he could demand a better price. He'd always had a gift for assessing the true value of something—a business deal, a piece of machinery, or real estate. He might be there for a fortnight at the very least, and with nothing to distract him from his troubles, he would turn his mind to what he was good at: making money.

A faint shimmer of light danced on the floor under the half-closed door of the library. He paused, wondering if one of his hostesses were up. No doubt it was Miss Murray, waiting to glower at him from a corner of the room.

"Hello."

Beau started, caught off guard by an unfamiliar voice that belonged to someone far younger than any of the women he'd met thus far. Obscured by shadow, Beau could make out the figure of a young child, no more than ten. She had dark brown hair and golden-brown skin.

"You're up late, aren't you?" Beau asked.

"Very late," she agreed, not particularly bothered by the observation. "So are you."

"That I am," he said. "Do you need help?"

She shook her head. "Miss Murray said I could come here anytime I couldn't sleep."

"You're not afraid of the dark?" he asked, genuinely curious. When he was that age, he'd been terrified of the dark. An overactive imagination, his father had said. If he was to be a man, he had to learn to conquer those fears. The dark he had managed. Failing his father was another matter.

"Not particularly," she said. "My name is Lucy."

"Hello Lucy. My name is Beau," he said, unsure about whether he should leave the child in peace. "I couldn't sleep either." He held his candle up to the shelves. "Are there any books you recommend?"

"I'm reading this book of fairy tales right now," she said.

"Do you like it?"

The girl shrugged. "Some I like. Most I don't."

"Why is that?" he asked, genuinely curious.

"Most of them are little white girls with yellow hair. They are all poor, and very meek, and very beautiful," she said. "And many of the princes are very, very stupid."

Something in Beau's heart twisted as he considered this girl with her big brown eyes, curly brown hair, and warm dark skin.

"You could write your own fairy tale," Beau said. "And make smarter princes. Or none at all, if it suits you."

Her eyes narrowed, and it seemed to Beau that she was appraising him with a guile beyond her tender years. "I've tried, but the words in my head go faster than my hands."

Beau held up his hands, wiggling his fingers.

"Luckily for you, I can write quickly." He pointed at the desk. "I bet there is some ink and paper. We could start right now. You tell it to me, and I'll write it down."

Maddy sat on the stairs, her heart slamming against her chest. She'd been lying in bed, awake since Lucy had crept down the stairs into the library. The child had always been a restless sleeper, and since an accident that had nearly claimed her life the year before, it had only gotten worse. Maddy had allowed her to use the library, teaching her how to light the lamp so she could read. Some mornings, she'd wake early to find Lucy asleep on the settee, a book still in her hands.

She never slept when Lucy went downstairs. Not soundly, anyway. While it was unlikely that any harm would come to the child safe within the bounds of Everwell, the chance was not zero. So she remained awake.

Besides, Beau da Silva was here. She was hyperaware of his presence, which she attributed to the same compulsion she had with Lucy. It was Maddy's job to keep everyone safe, and she made sure she did it. So, when the telltale click of the door latch from Foster's room broke the silence, Maddy was on her feet. She wasn't light footed like Gemma, but she knew every squeak on those steps and how to avoid them, even though she was at least eighty pounds heavier.

She paused on the steps, allowing the darkness to envelope her, and listened. While she was not expecting anything untoward, she knew that some of the children who'd come into their care could not be alone in a room with a man without reliving a past trauma. Lucy, however, was not one of them.

Indeed, there seemed to be a natural affinity between the two as they discussed their favourite books. She was at once transfixed by their easy camaraderie, and yet strangely envious of it. Maddy had never found being with others easy. She always appreciated Gemma's quiet, and Rimple's capacity to carry on a conversation without her, while making Maddy seem effortlessly a part of it.

She couldn't catch all the conversation from her perch on the stairs, and the moment she saw Beau's form move toward her desk, she gripped the railing, prepared to run down the stairs and pull him away. The light from his taper shed just enough light for her to make out what he was doing… which was taking dictation from Lucy.

She found herself relaxing as she watched them, her head resting on the banister, staring off into the distance while snippets of quiet conversation wafted up the stairs. Before long, she found herself nodding off.

The sensation of a hand on her shoulder caught her off guard. She opened her eyes, an old instinct flaring inside her and she grabbed at her shoulder before springing to her feet.

"Good morning."

Maddy's eyes blinked as she focused on Phillipa Hartley, standing two steps above in her dressing gown. Maddy rubbed her hands over her eyes and stretched the kink out of her neck.

"What time is it?" she asked, stifling a yawn.

"About half past five," came the reply. "Still early."

In the summer, six o'clock was the hour when the house started to wake and get ready for the day, but the morning light had already cast a warm glow over the house. A quick check of the bedroom doors confirmed that aside from Phillipa's and Maddy's, the occupants were still asleep.

"How long have you been up?" Phillipa asked in hushed tones.

"Lucy had another restless night," Maddy said.

"I see," Phillipa said. "I assume she didn't go back to bed?"

Dread dropped like a stone in Maddy's stomach. There was a second staircase, originally build to be used by servants, near the kitchen that led upstairs, and continued right on to the third floor, where the children slept. Lucy and Beau could have returned to their respective rooms for the evening, without passing Maddy on the stairs.

Maddy rose, then padded down the stairs, stopping at the entrance to the library. On the settee was Lucy, curled up in her usual position, a coverlet pulled up over her, looking contented. Relief flooded through Maddy, relaxing the tension in her shoulders, when the sound of a gentle snore came from a corner to her right. There, sprawled in a chair, long legs stretched out, was Beau da Silva.

His mouth was half open, the sole hint of normalcy on an otherwise perfect form. A single lock of his chestnut brown hair fell across his forehead, and there was the distinct shadow of a beard on his chin, which somehow managed to make him look more appealing. Underneath his robe—which Maddie recognized as Foster's—he was wearing one of Foster's old nightshirts and thankfully, he'd had the presence of mind to throw on his trousers. But his feet were bare, and there was a generous amount of exposed skin at his neck where the nightshirt gaped open.

He was, even with his mouth hanging open and snoring to wake the dead, beautiful.

How Lucy even managed to sleep with that racket was something of a miracle.

"Well now," Phillipa said behind her in a low voice, so warm Maddy could practically here the smile in it. "I'd say our new client has made himself quite at home."

Maddy managed to drag her attention away from Mr. da Silva to her desk, where he'd been writing. Sitting in her chair. Using her pens. She sighed, trying to excise some of the nervous energy from her bones. She would need an hour in the carriage house with her fighting canes just to siphon this storm out of her.

She spun on her heel and stalked off to the kitchen. It was early, she was tired, and needed coffee to think straight. Or even to be civil. Phillipa followed, and in the way she had of knowing what Maddy needed, got the fire going in the stove while Maddy filled the kettle.

"Won't he wonder why I'm going to guard him, Phillipa? Won't he ask uncomfortable questions?"

"Maddy, my fierce warrior," Phillipa said, reaching up to Maddy and gently cradling her face in her hands. "I know you just want to lock everything up tight and let nothing in. I wouldn't be suggesting any of this if I didn't think you could do it. Besides, Dominic's been talking to Ben Miller at the Chronicle. He might uncover some valuable leads that will help bring this to an end sooner than later."

At the mention of Benjamin Miller, Maddy started. The man had his nose in much of the city's underground comings and goings over the years, and seemed unafraid to report on even the most sordid news that might tarnish the otherwise sterling reputations of the city's elite. He'd even come to Everwell a few years ago, to do a piece for the paper.

Maddy crossed her arms. "With respect, Phillipa, the more people we involve, the greater the threat. Miller doesn't know about us."

"Dominic's consulting business is fronting the case. He can very publicly consult anyone without even a hint of involvement of Everwell, aside from the tangential issue of being married to Elouise," Phillipa continued. "Our primary job here is to keep Mr. da Silva safe until the real killer can be found, or at least until it can be proven unequivocally that he can't be guilty."

"And if we can't?"

"Then we will have done what we can," Phillipa said. "We

work hard, but we are not magicians. Sometimes the jobs don't work out."

There was Phillipa's never-failing pragmatism. The women of Everwell had managed to conjure the impossible more times than Maddy could count. It was a mix of preparation, hard work, and sometimes, dumb luck. And while they'd never been caught, and their secret seemed to remain secure, there were times when they hadn't managed to get the ending for the client that they'd hoped. But they had to try. Those rumours had to be quelled. They were too close to the truth. A truth that could harm Everwell so deeply, it may never recover.

She had a debt to Everwell she would gladly spend her entire life repaying. This job was just another instalment.

After few fortifying sips of coffee, Maddy was in a far better mood. She was still upset that Mr. da Silva had left her ink bottle open, but at least now she didn't want to dump the remainder of it over his head.

"Good morning Miss Murray, Mrs. Hartley."

Lucy's salutation grabbed both adults by surprise. She stood in the doorway, clutching a small sheaf of papers.

"Good morning Lucy," Phillipa said, greeting the child with her customary warmth. "What do you have there?"

"I wrote a story!" she said, bounding into the kitchen, her small body vibrating with excitement.

"You did?" Phillipa asked, casting an eye to Maddy. "When?"

"Last night. It's not quite done. I might like to change a few pieces yet," Lucy replied. "If it's good enough, I might ask Mrs. Ashe if we can use it for this year's play."

Lucy held up the pages to Phillipa, who examined the pages. "Did you write this?"

"I talked, and Mr. da Silva wrote it down. That way I could just think about my story," she said.

"This is quite good, Lucy," Phillipa said. Maddy looked over the pages Lucy laid in front of her. It was a fantastical story about a girl and a fox. She suspected Mr. da Silva may have, in some places, employed some editorial license to smooth the prose, but it was clear he took the job seriously.

Phillipa handed the pages back to Lucy. "Why don't you take it to your room, and over tea we'll look at it together with Mrs. Ashe?"

"I will," the girl said, then bounded out of the room and up the stairs.

She turned away and disappeared up the back stairs.

"Well," Phillipa said. "It seems our Mr. da Silva is not only a buyer of expensive books, but a scribe as well."

Our Mr. da Silva. Maddy wanted to brush off the moniker. He'd arrived a little more than twelve hours ago. He was nothing more than a beautiful interloper. A ruiner of pens.

And a willing scribe to a budding storyteller.

Maddy fought her own urge to soften at that last descriptor.

"I'll go and rouse him," Phillipa said, interrupting Maddy's thoughts. "He might like a cup of coffee after a night in that chair."

"I'll do it," Maddy said, almost before she knew what she was saying. Phillipa, famous for her unflinching demeanour under the most trying of circumstances, arched a brow.

"He's in my library unattended," Maddy grumbled, satisfied with the perfectly rational explanation for her rather irrational response. "He's no doubt already ruined one of my pens. I don't want him doing any more damage."

She picked up the small tray Phillipa had assembled with the coffee, a small sugar bowl, and some cream from the icebox and let out a low breath before marching across the hall.

The snoring had stopped and Mr. da Silva was out of his chair and at her desk. Again.

"What are you doing?" she asked, gripping the handles of the small tray.

"Good morning." He looked up and flashed her a smile that was probably meant to disarm her. Instead, it flared something deep inside. A phantom pain, from a time when a man had used just such a smile to win her heart, only to sacrifice it to sate his desire for a piece of her family's wealth. Of course, Mr. da Silva didn't know that. No one did.

She stood still, the way she did with the students when they were getting rowdy. Sometimes silence was more effective than words. It was a trick she'd learned from her mother, of all people. Her mother had wielded silence with the same sharp precision she'd used her words.

"Do you always use that smile of yours to beg for forgiveness instead of permission?" she asked at last.

He shrugged. "I can't help it if it works much of the time. What's a few pieces of paper?"

"To a man who runs the largest lumber company in the northeast, I suppose nothing," she said. "Our circumstances are a little more dear."

He set down the pen, genuinely chastened. "My apologies, Miss Murray. I'm a little out of sorts. I'm not used to being so dependent on other people."

"I brought you some coffee," she replied. "You must have slept horribly in that chair."

He rose and accepted it from her, but stood nearby, looking eye to eye. "Beats the gallows."

"Before you send off any notes, check with Dominic," she said. "If your whereabouts are traced here, you put Everwell at risk—and I can't let that happen."

"Of course not," he said. "I have a contact in Boston, and I've asked him to send something to the company on my behalf. Throw them off my scent as it were. He owes me a favour."

Maddy couldn't disguise the surprise that must have come over her, because Mr. da Silva flashed that telltale smile.

"You didn't think I'd be that smart," he said.

Damn him for reading her mind. "You don't know what I think."

"I have a long history of people underestimating me, Miss Murray," he said, and Maddy couldn't help but wonder at the hint of bitterness that marred that otherwise cocky grin. "Though I might be a tad bit disappointed you have."

Maddy swallowed the unexpected sting of his retort. The warmth of his body and the brushing of Foster's silk robe against the wood of her desk as he rose captured her attention. He gave her a cursory glance, then walked to the door.

"I didn't see the book," he said, pausing just before he left. "Did you not like it after all?"

The book? Heat rose into Maddy's cheeks even as she pushed away the sensation that he cared if she'd displayed the expensive poetry book.

It was already gone, delivered by Reg Knickle to Mrs. Cornish. According to Reg, Mrs. Cornish had been moved to tears upon its return.

It had been so hard to give it up. Maddy had loved it. Loved it the way she loved so many of the other books in her collection—they were filled with beautiful plates of flowers or pages of verse. Words she could lose herself in, if only for a little while. But there had been something even more particular about that one book, and Maddy would die a thousand deaths than admit to anyone, including herself, why it had been so hard to part with. He'd bought that book for her because he'd decided she'd deserved such a beautiful gift. Even if it was just to aggravate his aunt.

"It's where it belongs," she said at last, as much to herself as to him.

"By your bed, I hope," he said, raising his eyebrows, a sly grin on his face as he walked out the door.

Chapter Six

MADDY RAN her fingers over the spines of the books stacked on her bedside table. Normally, choosing a book to read was a pleasurable sort of agony. In the most private parts of her imagination, she imagined them as suitors, eager that she might bestow her favour upon them. Even alone, her cheeks warmed with embarrassment at the idea. She devoured fairy tales, yellow-backs, and romantic poetry because they allowed her the fantasy that, at least within the pages of the books, she might be worthy of a man's desire. It was a secret she would take to her grave rather than reveal.

She pulled out a slim volume of John Donne's poems and a copy of *Sense and Sensibility* from the pile, sliding them in her case alongside a few other titles. If she was going to be miserable for an undetermined length of time watching Beau da Silva, torn from her roses and the safe familiar space of Everwell, she reasoned, she could allow herself some modicum of comfort.

She'd just closed the trunk when a knock at her door snagged her attention. Recognizing the quick taps as Rimple's, she called out for her to come in.

"How is the packing?" her friend asked, poking her head around the threshold.

Maddy looked down at the modest chest sitting on her bed. Once upon a time her mother would have insisted on her packing an entire wardrobe for a trip like this. This time she'd packed far more books and equipment than changes of clothes.

"Done."

"The train departs in an hour," she said. "Phillipa's got her watch out."

Maddy wanted to roll her eyes. "Is *he* ready?"

Rimple nodded, walked into the room, sat on the bed, and took Maddy's hand.

"Thank you for doing this," Rimple said, her lips into a tight smile, a shadow of concern crossing her normally sunny disposition. "I know you don't want to."

It was a reminder to Maddy that whatever dislike she had for Beau da Silva or Veronica Turnbull, it did not matter. She knew the power of rumour to tear apart a life.

She swallowed an unwanted lump of emotion that threatened to shake her voice. "I'm doing this to keep those NWL busybodies off our backs."

"I'm sure Mr. da Silva will be so happy, he'll do more than cover the expenses for the job," Rimple said, her normal levity returning. "You will have the best little greenhouse in the city, I promise. Maybe good enough to grow a lemon tree in. I'll work on the designs while you're gone."

Before Maddy had the time to consider what kind of miracle of physics Rimple would pull off to create such a thing, there was a second knock at the door, and it opened to reveal Gemma Webber.

"Nearly ready?" she asked.

Maddy swore under her breath. Clearly Phillipa was marshalling the troops.

She paused long enough to check that her short blade was in her boot, and the second was strapped to her back, under her jacket. Her throwing knives were already packed amongst her books.

"I have never been late for an assignment and I'm not about to start," Maddy grumbled, hoisting the chest off the bed. "Let's go."

Rimple and Gemma exchanged a look.

"Next time I'm just going to make Phillipa come up here herself," Gemma said. "Are you trying to make me not miss you? Because that is impossible."

"I miss you already," Maddy said, not bothering to protest when Gemma put her hands on the other side of the trunk to bear the weight. She bent down and planted a kiss on Gemma's head.

They were not halfway down the stairs when Jeremy Webber, Gemma's husband and a wall of a man by nearly any measure, took Maddy's trunk and carried it the rest of the way where his daughter Ivy was waiting, along with Phillipa and Lady Em. The door was open, and just beyond it, Maddy saw a carriage waiting to take her away.

"I'll get this on the carriage." The deep, crisp tones of Jeremy Webber's voice broke through low murmur of activity coming from just outside the front doors of Everwell. Maddy caught the flush of anticipation in Gemma's cheeks as she gave her husband a warm smile. "The train leaves within the hour. Phillipa is waiting."

"I'm starting to wonder if Phillipa is worried I'll change my mind."

"I'm sure she worries about you," he said, giving her a knowing smile. "But not about that."

Maddy almost smiled in spite of herself. She liked the retired British Colonel, despite the fact that he'd married one of her dear friends. He seemed to understand her role as protector, and perhaps of anyone here, might empathize with the war going on inside her. To protect Everwell, she had to leave it.

She pulled on her gloves and fastened her wide-brimmed straw hat to her hair with a pearl-tipped hat pin, taking a quick glance in the mirror to ensure it was on straight, then headed outside. A small crowd waited for them, and she felt the weight of

Beau da Silva's whisky-eyed stare. He stood by the carriage, deep in conversation with Dominic, Jeremy, and Reg.

Phillipa stood with the other Everwell women, Lady Em and Tilda among them, along with a few of the students. As if sensing her unease, Lady Em took Maddy's hands, her eyes sparkling with what could only be mischief.

"I'm excited for you, my dear," she said. "You deserve a pleasant sort of adventure."

"Lady Em," Maddy said, her eyes straying toward Mr. da Silva, "I'm not sure how pleasant it will be to mind a peacock."

"I suspect you will manage quite well," she said in that no-nonsense way of hers. "I've heard rumours about the old Redden property. You might find yourself far more at home there than you might think."

"I can't ever imagine any place being more at home than this," Maddy replied, trying to keep the wistfulness out of her voice as she took one more look back at the home that had been her salvation in more ways than one.

"Everwell will always be here for you, my dear," Lady Em said. "But do not deprive yourself of a chance to see something new."

Lady Em's expression softened to something like sympathy, and Maddy found herself swallowing back unwanted emotion. What was happening? She'd been on more jobs than she had fingers and toes for, and she had gone to several on her own, watching in the shadows to ensure the others were safe.

"Maddy," Phillipa said, inspecting her in that sisterly way of hers. "As always, the most important thing is that you return home safely. While I don't expect too much trouble—"

"—which I will deal with if it comes," Maddy responded.

"The Redden property is adjacent to a small farm, and the owners—the Chandlers, are known to Mrs. Turnbull. They have acted as caretakers to the property for many years," Phillipa said. "Mrs. Turnbull has already seen to it that they are aware of your arrival."

"And you trust them?" Maddy asked. "What if they are interested in the reward?"

"Maddy, if I hadn't learned to trust people, I wouldn't be at Everwell," Phillipa said. "Sometimes you have to risk it."

Maddy didn't know if she could risk it. Trust had come with a perilous price that she'd paid for with her self-respect and nearly her life. What could she make of a man like Beau da Silva? His smooth charm threatened to lower her defences even though the very first thing he'd done was misrepresent his intent with her. He'd batted his eyes at her one moment, and then when her back was turned, told his aunt the only reason for his attention was pity. Trusting him was the very last thing she would do.

She walked toward the carriage, a small crowd of Scandalous Spinsters and Wayward Women in her wake. Squaring her shoulders, she strode past Beau da Silva, who stood at the carriage door clad in a brown traveling suit that was no doubt tailored to emphasize his best features, which, Maddy had to concede, were all of them. Only a faint shadow of unease darkened what seemed to be a carefully constructed display of nonchalance about the very real threat he was under.

He held out his hand to assist her into the carriage, which she ignored. Instead, she had her foot firmly planted on the running panel when Ivy Webber, Jeremy and Gemma's daughter, marched up to her with the same aristocratic bearing as her father. She stood alongside Mr. da Silva, giving him an appraising once over that made him chuckle. The low, warm sound slid down Maddy's back and settled in her belly like a generous swallow of brandy.

"Miss Murray, do not fret about your gardens," Ivy said with such earnestness Maddy couldn't help but smile. "Sylvie has volunteered to help Miss Jones with the blackspot. And I have decided to do a watercolour study of your plants so that you will not miss any of their beautiful blooms."

Ivy was a talented artist, like her father. Between Jeremy and Phillipa, who was an artist in her own right, Ivy's natural talents were sharpening a little more each day.

"That is very kind of you," Maddy said, nodding in appreciation. "I look forward to seeing them."

"And we will save your birthday party for when you return," Ivy called.

Maddy stifled a groan and schooled her features, which was no easy feat given the undisguised amusement that lit up Mr. da Silva's face as he watched this exchange with far too much interest.

"How did you discover that?" she asked the girl.

"Lady Em told me," Ivy said. "She knows everyone's birthdays."

Maddy didn't like celebrating her birthday. It had never been a particular cause for celebration, according to her mother. But Lady Em made a particular point out of fussing over everyone's birthday.

"She does," Gemma said, approaching them and taking her stepdaughter by the shoulders. "And everyone's favourite cake. Though Maddy doesn't have a favourite. At least none she's ever told us."

"We shall have to guess," Ivy said, then turned to Mr. da Silva. "Or perhaps you can solve the mystery while you are gone."

"I will do my very best," he replied with a conviction that felt entirely too real, even though it was no doubt that same look he gave everyone he wanted to ingratiate himself to before insulting them the moment they were out of earshot.

"Right then," Phillipa called out, glancing down at her watch with that look that told Maddy the time for dawdling was over. "There is a train to catch."

At Phillipa's signal, Maddy scrambled into the carriage before Mr. da Silva could resume his offer of assistance. The carriage ride would be the most uncomfortable part of this awkward situation, she reasoned. As he took his seat opposite her, the carriage, which would comfortably hold four and a little less comfortably, six, felt suddenly claustrophobic.

Maddy waved to the small band of spinsters as they pulled

away. All the while, she felt the weight of Beau da Silva's attention resting on her. Something in her hardened, and she pulled back her shoulders, lifted her chin, and clasped her hands in front of her.

"You have a someone who misses you," he said as the carriage rumbled toward the road. "A bunch of someones. It must be nice to be so well thought of. After all, you were the one nearly making us late by having a throng of people seeing you off, promising to look after your gardens and books and whatever else. And promise to make you cake."

"Well, we miserable old spinsters have to take our pleasures where we can."

His eyes widened ever so slightly, betraying his surprise, before he schooled his features and flashed her a smile.

"I apologize for that," he said, with an earnestness that took her off guard. "I didn't wish to draw my aunt's attention to you. She is lovely but can be quite the overbearing sort when she thinks a woman is trying to take advantage of me. It was rude in the extreme to speak of you in such a way."

Maddy swallowed her surprise at what seemed to be a heartfelt apology.

"You don't strike me as the type of man who is particularly lonely," she said. "I've read about you."

One of his eyebrows shot up in a look of utter amusement. "You have?"

Maddy bristled at the sly smile on his perfect face. He seemed amused by the idea that she'd been interested in him. It was, in some ways, a window into a glamorous world she once might have known in some measure, but was now lost to her. Which was fine, since it wasn't one she'd ever really wanted. Not at the price it would have demanded of her.

"I wanted to be prepared," she replied, shrugging off his smile. "I need to know who amongst your friends and associates seemed most willing to want to see you hang, or at least sell you out for a rather modest reward."

If her answer meant to sting, Mr. da Silva seemed impervious.

"I don't have friends," he said so casually that it might have struck Maddy as sad if she wasn't so prepared to dislike him. "And as for my associates, I would say at this juncture, it might be all of them."

The idyllic aura of Everwell faded into the distance, swallowed up the lush canopy of maple, oak and elm trees, as the carriage made its way to the train station, located near the harbour. Halifax reminded Beau very much of Saint John in essentials, clinging to its British connections, a busy port city that came with all the trappings, both good and ill: shining waters, working wharves, and a veritable forest of masts edging the shore from small schooners that would transport goods and people along the shore to areas that were still in winter largely impassible by road or rail. Alongside those vessels were the newcomers, their signature smokestacks belching out black effluent from the coal-fired furnaces deep within their iron hulls. The difference came in the scale and the source. Halifax, hanging between London and New York, with its deep harbour, ice free even on the bitterest winter day, made it the natural stopping place. It started its life as a military town and remained one, the British still occupying it even after Nova Scotia became part of the fledgling nation of Canada.

But Saint John had a mighty river and behind it, the dense New Brunswick forests that supplied lumber to not one, but two powers—the British empire and the emergent American markets. Frank da Silva had built his fortune cutting into the great swaths of those forests, sending lumber to London, New York, and beyond. And even though those iron-hulled steamships now took that lumber across the Atlantic much faster than the wooden ships, his father had still viewed them as a threat.

Then again, Frank had viewed nearly everyone and everything as a threat. The only people he seemed to have a modicum of time for was his sister, Jessica and her husband, Neil. Neil was in some ways the son Beau could not be—compliant, eager to please, and an excellent head for numbers. Had he instigated the manhunt for Beau? Neil had a healthy respect for Frank, and maybe even loved the man. If Neil believed there was a rivalry between them, he was mistaken. In the race to win Frank's respect and maybe even affection, his brother-in-law had been the clear victor. Beau had spent a lifetime trying to secure his father's approval. It was the only pursuit he'd failed at.

Getting from the train station to their compartment was blessedly unproblematic—at least until the compartment door was shut and they'd taken their seats. His body was acutely aware of hers. He seemed to feel her every movement, even though there was more room between them here than in the relative snug quarters of the carriage.

Almost immediately, she pulled a pair of reading spectacles out of her reticule and fastened them behind her ears. Her head tilted down, and her attention was apparently fixated on the same volume she'd used to ignore him all the way to the train station. The effect, which should have made her appear even more matronly and impervious, managed to intrigue him—an effect which no doubt would have mortified his surly chaperone. Miss Murray, on the other hand, seemed completely unaware of this unexplained witchcraft with which she was effortlessly affecting him. Everything about her was a challenge, and that stirred his blood.

"What are you reading?" he asked, desperate to try to engage her in something approaching pleasant conversation.

"A book," she said, not bothering to look up.

"I would never have guessed," he said, not bothering to hide his acrimony. He turned his head toward the window, watching the harbour disappear as they headed north. "Can I ask what exactly I have done to deserve your ire?"

She glanced up at him over the brim of her glasses.

"You have taken me away from my garden. I have a new species of hollyhock that was about to bloom, and now I'm going to miss it," she said, glaring up at him. "And Rimple Jones makes the best chocolate cake you will ever eat in your life, which she normally bakes on the first of August, and knowing my luck, I will be with you instead."

"If it makes you feel any better," he said, trying to stifle a grumble. "I would much rather you were doing those things instead of being here with me."

Her lashes fluttered; Beau saw a flush of pink creep up from under the collar of her stiff, green linen jacket. She stilled, and it occurred to Beau his words might have been misconstrued.

"It will take as long as it takes," she replied, before turning her attention back to her book. "And there is nothing either of us can do about it."

They sat in silence which could have been minutes, but felt like hours. More than enough time for every bit of self doubt, and every angry word exchanged with his father to replay in his head.

He rose, driven to his feet by a torrent of unwanted memory. He needed coffee. Or a whisky. Or anything to escape the oppressive silence.

"Where do you think you are going?"

He paused, oddly excited by her question. It was still unpleasant, but there was an urgency to it. Like she actually cared about what he was about to do next.

"To stretch my legs."

"Are you certain there isn't someone waiting out there to break them for you? Haul you back to New Brunswick and collect their finder's fee?"

He paused. He wasn't entirely certain of anything anymore. Except that he'd spent a lifetime being berated and managed by his father, and he was damned certain he wasn't going to be managed by Miss Murray, no matter how beautiful she was. It was his neck on the line, not hers.

"Maybe it's a chance I'm willing to take."

With military-like efficiency, she closed her book and grabbed her valise from the rack above her. He expected her to reach in and grab a set of knitting needles or some other type of needle work that women of a certain age occupied themselves with. Instead, she snapped the clasp shut, grabbed the bag and… left.

Beau stood at the door to their tiny compartment and watched Miss Murray walk away. Part of him was impressed. Knowing when to walk away was an excellent negotiation tactic he'd employed successfully on more than one occasion.

It didn't explain the strange, unsettled pressure in his gut, though. A sensation that was growing as the time stretched and she had not reappeared. He stood there for a nearly half a minute before it finally dawned on him she wasn't coming back.

He called after her, but she either didn't hear him over the din of passengers and steam, or chose not to.

Beau groaned. Should he let her have her fucking tantrum or whatever this was? Didn't she realize he was the client?

A client she was walking away from. But more importantly, she was walking away from him.

He strode after her, smiling apologetically at the stream of people eager to take their seats before the train left. Ahead, he caught the flash of green from her skirt as she disembarked.

Panic grew. Was she abandoning him? Because it absolutely fucking felt like it.

Urgency fuelled his steps as he jostled through the crowd, "excuse me" falling out of his lips in an endless string of apologies. At last, he reached the platform where Miss Murray was speaking to one of the porters.

"What are you doing?" he asked in a harsh whisper so loud anyone with a set of ears probably heard him.

She turned away from the porter, actually smiling—the first genuine smile she'd given another human being since they boarded. Something broke apart inside him, making him inexplicably envious. Especially when it disappeared the moment she turned to face him.

"What does it look like?" she asked, narrowing her eyes, and even though he didn't hear her say it, he felt her follow up with *you idiot.*

"I have no idea." He actually did have an idea; he just didn't want to say it out loud.

"You made it clear just a moment ago that you see no problem risking your own skin rather than sit with me in silence for a few hours. To put off your own comfort for even the smallest amount of time for the larger goal of potentially saving your neck. If you aren't willing to put in the time or energy, why should I give up the things I love, the people I actually care about, to do it for you?"

There was no look of triumph in her eye. No sense of victory. She simply turned away from him, went about her business, and left him to sit in his own discomfort.

And it was damn uncomfortable.

"Don't you want my aunt's help with those rumours?" he challenged.

"Of course," she replied, seemingly unbothered. "But we've gone this long without their help. We can manage if we have to."

Beau knew the art of negotiation meant having the nerve to walk away and leave it all on the table. In order to risk great reward, you had to be prepared to lose.

Too late, he realized, she could walk away—or better—turn him in and get the reward. And she clearly had the nerve to do it.

Why did it have to be this woman, of all people, who was reminding him that the one neck he was risking was his own?

"I'm sorry," he blurted out, quite possibly before he knew what he was doing. "I am grateful for your help. I really am."

In what was probably only a few seconds, but felt like an eternity, she turned to him, looking him over. For a second he wanted to crack a joke or say something that would deflect from the unsettled feeling he had in his gut. Instead, he just stood there.

Whether she was aware or not of his internal struggle, he wasn't certain. But the relief that flooded him when she turned toward him and nodded was palpable. He blew out a long exhale.

She turned back to the porter, her smile a little more apologetic this time, as she spoke a few more words to him. A smile he wanted for himself. Why, he had no clue. It was clear she held him in absolute contempt. And he'd given up looking for approval from those closest to him. It had never been worth it in the end.

A whistle blew a second time, announcing the train's imminent departure. A few last-minute passengers made hurried dashes toward the train. Miss Murray took a few steps and to Beau's surprise, paused. It occurred to him she was waiting for him. Whether it was out of politeness or simply to ensure he was, in fact, coming, he wasn't sure. But she was there all the same, with a look of anticipation that wasn't unpleasant.

It wasn't everything. But it was a start.

Chapter Seven

BEAU AND MISS MURRAY settled back into their seats, the hem of her skirts tantalizingly close to his legs. She seemed blissfully unaware of the closeness, far more preoccupied with her valise. She pulled a book out for herself and was about to close her case when she paused.

"Would you like something to read?"

Beau couldn't decide if Miss Murray was attempting to be pleasant, or trying to entertain him, like a child needing distraction. Either way, it was an invitation to conversation, and he took it.

"Depends on my mood I suppose," he said. "I can't say that curling up with treatises by dead Romans intrigues me. But I'm not above a good detective novel by that Collins fellow. And I do enjoy poetry."

She rooted through her bag a moment, then produced two volumes. "Romantics or Elizabethan?"

Beau bit back a smile. It seemed so at odds that a woman of Madeline Murray's severe countenance would be traveling with not one, but two books of poetry. But then he recalled the utter joy she'd displayed at the bookshop when they'd first met. This woman who seemed to ensure, like her beloved roses, that her thorns were on display. He suspected they were there to protect the soft and vibrant beauty she tried to hide.

What would he give to touch that softness?

"I'll take the Elizabethan, thank you," he said, accepting the smaller of the two volumes from her. It was beautifully bound, with an exquisite leather cover. Beau carefully thumbed through the pages, which were edged in a beautiful gilt. There was a printer's mark on the inside page.

"Is... this a first edition?" he asked, studying the binding which looked ancient, though he was no expert.

"No idea," she said, not bothering to look up from whatever book she'd suddenly found so engrossing.

Beau returned his attention to the inside cover, squinting at the flourished signature produced by a pen centuries ago. Was that... *Christopher Marlowe?*

"Is this—"

"Yes," she said, answering his question with all the nonchalance of a person who might have been agreeing with him that the day was fine, or that carrots were in fact the worst of all vegetables, instead of confirming the book was signed by one of the premier poets of the English language.

"Did this come from MacAskill's, too?" he asked, genuinely interested.

She shrugged. "I can't recall. I found it somewhere."

"You found a seventeenth century copy of Sir Phillip Sidney's poems once in the possession of Christopher Marlowe?" he asked, genuinely incredulous. "Let me guess—you plucked it out of a bookshop you happen to be strolling by, where it had sat dusty and unappreciated, lost amongst a load of lesser works?"

She actually looked up at him and considered his question, then shrugged her shoulders.

"Sort of," she said. "It's amazing what people have right under their noses that they don't appreciate."

"But you do."

"I do."

Beau had no words for the utter conviction in her answer, but something slammed in his chest. Was that his heart, maybe? Did he even have one anymore? He knew, he wanted to tell her, what was right under his nose. And he wanted her to know that he was worthy.

"I appreciate you trusting me with it," he said instead.

"I don't trust anyone with my books," she said, snapping her satchel shut.

If Beau had dared believe that he'd managed to have made some sliver of progress finding his way into Miss Murray's good graces, she'd closed that door with her comment. And while he hadn't expected her to suddenly be civil, he hadn't expected her insinuation of his character to sting. Beau gathered his senses and reminded himself that it wasn't worth trying to prove himself to a person who didn't care.

"Did you want me to stow your satchel for you?" he asked.

"No need," she replied. "I might need something from it."

"Another book?" Beau said, taking his seat. "You seem to have an entire library in there."

"Weapons," she said, as if she were talking about books, or flowers, or anything else.

Beau blinked. "Weapons?" He knew she was being hired as protection, but it still seemed ridiculous that he would have a woman as a bodyguard. "Don't tell me you have a set of pistols in there."

"I don't use firearms," she said, brushing off his comment. "Too much noise."

Beau stifled a nervous laugh.

"And how often do you feel the need to be stealthy with a weapon?"

"I work in a place that shelters women from their violent husbands," she said. "I feel the need far more often than I should."

The matter-of-factness of her reply set his jaw on edge. Was that part of the reason she was loathe to accompany him?

"Besides, if someone recognizes you, they may have little compunction about subduing you by whatever means possible to collect their reward," she continued. "What do expect me to do? Throw a book at them?"

Beau supposed she had a point.

"I don't actively make a point of hurting anyone," she said. "My role is defensive." She turned her gaze back to the book, inexplicably making Beau feel envious of the volume to which she freely gave her attention. And he found himself wanting some of that attention for himself.

"Can I ask how a woman becomes a bodyguard?"

"The same way a woman does anything," she replied, idly flipping a page. "In spite of all expectations and obstacles put in her way."

"You don't look the like type of person who's going to use a knife in a fight," he said, more to himself than to her, given she'd seemed more enraptured by the sonnets of a dead poet than Beau.

"What do I look like?"

The challenge in her question—and the subtle narrowing of her stare—was unmistakable, but Beau could have sworn he detected the hint of a nervous swallow as she waited for his reply.

What did Madeline Murray look like? Like no other woman he'd ever encountered. She was his height, or possibly an inch taller, with shoulders that upon reflection seemed able to carry the weight of a thousand worries. She was hard, and yet she was soft. She had a full mouth, and a generous bosom and hips. Madeline Murray wasn't dainty. She wasn't overtly charming or classically beautiful.

She looked like a goddess—a Ceres, a Demeter, a Faerie Queen.

"Not a miserable old spinster," he said instead.

The faintest hint of a smile quirked at the edge of her lips and she looked away again, down toward the safety and silence of her book. Beau contented himself with the subtle flush of pink rushing into her cheeks, before turning back to his own.

. . .

The journey passed uneventfully. By the time Maddy and Mr. da Silva disembarked at the station in Windsor, they had settled into companionable silence. Having collected their baggage, they waited for Mr. Chandler, a trusted associate of Mrs. Turnbull, to take them the rest of the way.

According to Mr. da Silva, the Chandlers had been neighbours of the Reddens for two generations, trusted with keeping the property maintained long after it had been regularly unoccupied. Mrs. Turnbull had alerted the Chandlers about Beau da Silva's arrival, using the pretence that he was coming to personally survey the property ahead of the sale. There was no allusion to Frank da Silva's murder, or the bounty on Mr. da Silva's head.

The Scandalous Spinsters were highly experienced at coordinating people to accomplish a feat of the extra-legal variety for a client, but this arrangement was between The Everwell Society and Mrs. Turnbull. That subtle but critical distinction meant that the contact with the Chandlers had been handled by Mrs. Turnbull. This left Maddy with a crater of doubt about the trustworthiness of their new neighbours.

By now, Dominic would be on his way to Saint John to find the real culprit, or at least cast enough doubt on the existing theories to allow Mr. da Silva to return home with his innocence established. She could only hope the detective employed his usual cunning and solved the case quickly. Behind Mr. da Silva's effortless charm there was a sharp intellect and a quick wit she would have to guard herself against. Not because she might be under his spell, though. Never again would she fall prey to a handsome face or the pretty words of a well-dressed man promising her the moon.

Maddy shook off her woolgathering and looked past the platform to the road, which was busy with the comings and goings of a small town. Thankfully, she had not seen any posters advertising the bounty for Mr. da Silva's whereabouts. Instead, she tamped down a curious wave of envy growing inside her at the barely disguised looks of interest thrown in his general direction by women passing by.

They did not have to wait long before a cart pulled up alongside them. The driver was a man her age or a little younger, wearing a straw hat, trousers, and a jacket Maddy suspected was used for weddings, funerals, church suppers, and picking up strangers from the train station. He had fair skin and dark blond hair.

"Good morning," he said, looking over Beau, then taking off his hat and nodding to Maddy. There was something about him— his smile perhaps—that was not dissimilar to Mr. da Silva.

"I'm Dan Chandler, and this is my son, Teddy." He nodded to the boy sitting next to him. Teddy looked to be in his early teens, with short black hair, fair skin tanned by the sun, and bright inquisitive eyes. "I believe you are the people I'm to take to The Grove."

"You have found us," Mr. da Silva replied. "I'm Beau da Silva, and this is Miss Murray, who is my—"

"Housekeeper," she interjected primly, sniffling her discomfort. At her age, she hardly needed a chaperone—those days were long past her. Still, she was not good at play acting. That was Elouise's job.

"I can help you with your things," Mr. Chandler said, hopping down. He and Mr. da Silva shook hands, before picking up Maddy's trunk and hauling it to the back of the cart.

Maddy watched the crowd as the men hauled the luggage onto the farm cart. Clearly the Chandlers had taken advantage of the trip to load up on a few supplies, and there was some rearranging required to ensure everything fit snugly and provided room for seating.

Even though the task took only minutes, impatience ate away at Maddy's attention. Every moment they lingered was another moment someone could recognize Mr. da Silva. She turned her attention from the crowd to the wagon, trying not to be distracted by the way his fine wool coat pulled across his shoulders.

"There is no need to take up an entire side of the road."

Maddy turned to the source of the grumbling. It emanated from a well-dressed man with a remarkable set of sideburns, hawkish nose, and an unmistakable air of pomposity. While there was, in fact, plenty of road for him to move around, he stood there waiting for Maddy to move. Unwilling to subject herself to his ill will, or Mr. da Silva to his attention, she moved out of the way.

"My apologies," she said, then stepped aside for him to pass. He returned her apology with a caustic stare.

"Next time, watch where you are going." He brushed by her, muttering to himself. "Oversized cow."

The insult caught her ear. She turned away, giving herself a moment to let the hurt roll off her shoulders. She looked over to the wagon to see if it was finally loaded properly so they could leave. She was greeted by the sight of Beau da Silva, jumping off the back of the wagon, directly in front of the man, a thunderous look on his face.

The man blinked, clearly taken aback by his path being blocked a second time.

"I didn't realize it was acceptable to insult a woman for simply standing on the road," Mr. da Silva said, the lightness of his tone at odds with the edge in his stance. "You will apologize immediately."

Blood flooded the man's cheeks, regarding Mr. da Silva with the dangerous countenance of someone whose overinflated ego had just been shattered. Maddy, warring between mortification at the attention and Mr. da Silva's defence of her, watched the two intently.

"Come," he continued when the man merely sputtered, not moving as quickly as Mr. da Silva had liked. "I'm sure you have somewhere of dubious importance to be. Apologize."

"And what is she to you?" the gentleman sneered, casting a side long glance at Maddy.

Mr. da Silva put himself between Maddy and the cad.

"Do not mistake this congenial conversation for a lack of anger on my part," Mr. da Silva said, his voice low and laced with ire, his jaw tightening his smile into something that struck Maddy as pure threat. "The lady definitely has better things to do than be insulted by an undersized steer. I insist you apologize so we can both get on with the busy nothings of our day."

The man stepped back, swallowing, his face a touch paler than it had been a moment ago. Mr. da Silva may have said he wasn't a man prone to violence, but he certainly sounded threatening in that moment. He stepped back and looked up at Maddy.

She recognized those eyes. Like a shade from her past, here to haunt her. Icy blue eyes that belonged to Malcolm's friend Nelson Taylor, one of a handful of young men Maddy's parents had tried to induce into marrying their contrary, oversized daughter.

A lump formed in her throat and she struggled to remain calm. Perhaps it was just the strain of the trip. After all, the Maritime provinces were small, and family ties cut across the region. It was entirely possible that this man was only distantly connected to the Taylors from southern New Brunswick. The young Nelson had been handsome, with curly brown hair and square shoulders. The man before her walked with a stoop, and seemed far too old to be the same man who'd been invited by her parents to the dinner parties they'd held as she'd been trotted out as marriage material with a healthy dowry as the prize.

"My apologies," he said, his lips twisting as he attempted a halfhearted smile, mostly to satisfy Mr. da Silva. Maddy did not dare watch him too closely, but there seemed to be no flicker of recognition. Only disdain.

That she could manage. Recognition would shatter her completely.

Maddy fixed her feet to the ground, her fingers reaching for the knife she had tucked in a sheath on her left forearm. She wanted to take Mr. da Silva by the arm and drag him to the carriage. They were drawing a crowd. She nodded in acknowledgment, unable to speak. She just wanted this to be over.

The man scurried away like an angry badger, and Maddy swallowed the jagged panic she'd been holding.

"Are you all right?" Mr. da Silva asked, concern clear in the lines around his eyes. It was clear he wanted to press the issue, but she couldn't let him—for both their sakes.

"It's time to go," she said, clearing her throat. "Before you draw any more attention than you already have."

According to Mrs. Turnbull's notes, the journey would take a couple hours depending on the state of the roads. Eager to get out of sight, the two climbed into the cart.

Maddy sat in the back and watched the world go by, the unpleasantness of her encounter to shrink into the distance as they made their way out of town. Mr. da Silva sat on the driver's bench with the two Chandlers. It didn't take long for the men to fall into an easy rapport.

The roads were a little dusty but not overly rutted, and the horses went at a steady pace. The countryside was pleasant, alternating between wood and meadow, the landscape dotted with little hills, and the air was heavy with the sweet, earthy scent of grass. Sometimes the road took them by tidal rivers, the muddy red-brown waters highlighted by borders of lush green tidal grass. The countryside was sparsely populated by the odd farm, and in the distance, what appeared to be a Mi'kmaq summer encampment.

The afternoon was warm, and Maddy was glad for her straw hat. Unlike Gemma, whose skin bronzed in the summer, and Rimple, whose naturally darker skin warmed even further during the season, Maddy's skin turned an unholy shade of red if she was not careful, her freckles blossoming like asters in September.

At last, the cart slowed. Mr. Chandler signalled to the horses to make a left turn, leading them down a much smaller lane—so narrow in fact, Maddy wondered what they would do if they came upon a team of horses coming from the other direction. It soon became apparent the risk was almost negligible.

They continued on until they came to a ragged fence that bordered a small field, where a couple of cows lazed under a tree. Further up the hill was a few outbuildings, and a farmhouse that looked to have recently had a fresh coat of paint.

"Is this it?" Mr. da Silva asked.

Mr. Chandler shook his head. "That's our farm. That and all the woods we just passed. Where we're going is just up ahead."

The farm disappeared from view, back into the trees. They seemed to be going to the absolute edge of nowhere. Without the Chandlers, they would invariably gotten lost.

The cart turned onto a gently curving road that snaked through the woods, the trees providing a welcome shade from the canopy overhead. A small sign, cut on board made grey by time and weather, was nailed into the side of a large maple tree. It announced The Grove was close by. Maddy started to wonder if Mr. da Silva's property was indeed little more than a shack in the woods.

That was, until she saw it.

Outside of her books, Maddy had never allowed herself to be romantic. Romance was wasted on the beauties of the world, who had so many kind looks and words sent in their direction by those eager to woo them. She was thirty-seven years old. She was taller than many men, and somehow hard and soft in all the wrong places. The very idea of romance simply hurt too much. The pursuit of it had nearly ruined her.

But there was an undeniable lump that tightened her throat as the stately oaks drew her gaze to rest on the prettiest stone cottage she had ever seen.

Not that she'd seen many stone cottages, of course. There were only a few, generally created by more well-to-do immigrants from the British Isles who yearned for the feeling of home. In the Maritimes, even the most stately houses were made of wood, which was plentiful. But there was something about it that held

Maddy's attention, drawing her to the edge of the wooden seat. Something solid. Something timeless. Something magical.

The buggy came to a gentle halt near the entrance, allowing Maddy to see the building in greater detail. What looked to be a small, storey-and-a-half structure was in fact larger, as the building had been set into the side of a hill that sloped down and away. On the south-facing side was a mass of tangled green that looked to be overgrown grapevines. The paint on the sturdy wooden door and the window frames had long since faded, with only the slightest hint of the oxblood pigment that covered them. She couldn't help but wonder how pretty they might look with some window boxes beneath them.

The sliding of trunks from the back of the wagon broke Maddy out of her reverie. Chiding herself for allowing her attention to be stolen, she cast a glance around for Mr. da Silva, who had disembarked and stood on the ground, looking up at her with an unreadable expression. He held out his hand, which she viewed with suspicion.

"I don't bite," Mr. da Silva said with that effortless charm of his. He smiled a moment, then took a pause. "Come now. It's been a long day."

An unnamable shame pinched at her heart, warring with her to do something so very normal, like take his hand. Maddy wasn't graceful. She lumbered, her mother had often told her. She wasn't interested in having Mr. da Silva bear the weight of her as she stepped down.

But he stood there, so bloody expectant. Like he wanted to help her. To her great surprise, she relented. She told herself it was out of some misplaced desire to play nice with him. To allow him to pretend to be useful. If that was what he needed to feel better, so be it.

She placed her hand in his, determined only to rest her fingers in his as lightly as possible while she gripped the edge of the cart with her other hand, allowing the sturdy wooden vehicle to bear her weight. But as his fingers wrapped around her hand, a shock of warmth rushed through her body, and before she was able to recover her senses, he'd held out his other hand, robbing her of the chance to use the cart to steady herself as she stepped down.

"There you go," he said, giving her a reassuring smile. "I have you."

Robbed of her ability to answer him with anything but a nod, she had no choice but to allow him to help her down. His touch was traitorously soothing, alleviating some of the discomfort from the long day of travel.

"Thank you," she said. He nodded in return, and she expected him to reply with some witty allusion to his gallantry. She found herself studying him for any sign of polite disinterest, or worse, disgust. Instead, he seemed equally as transfixed as she.

The rumble of her trunk being pushed across the back the cart broke the spell, and she pulled her hands away, eager to rid herself of this unwanted softening at his touch.

Of course, there should be nothing about Beau da Silva that Maddy might want. Even if he was the reason she found herself in the middle of a woodland with a fairytale stone cottage, she'd had to leave Everwell and all her friends behind because of him. Once upon a time, she'd been forced to run away, and had spent too much time scared and alone. Then she'd learned to protect herself, then others, because she'd learned in the most horrible of ways that if she did not, no one else would. And today Nelson Taylor had appeared—a shade from her past who only reinforced her need to protect herself.

Except for the most inconvenient thought that just as she'd wanted to protect herself by making herself invisible to him, Mr. da Silva had done the opposite.

For an unfathomable moment, Beau da Silva did have her.

Chapter Eight

THE UNNAMABLE AWARENESS that had been humming in Beau's veins since he'd first sat in the carriage with Miss Murray had finally subsided by the time he'd hopped out of the Chandlers' wagon. But the moment she'd begrudgingly accepted his hand, it had flared anew, running through his blood like a fine brandy. The touch had been brief, and she'd briefly locked eyes with him out of what he suspected was politeness. As she walked away, an echo of longing prickled under his skin.

Shoving his hands in his pockets, Beau turned his attention to the property that only a few days ago he'd been so eager to sell. His mother had grown up here, and, according to his aunt, eager to flee as soon as she'd been able. Beau could see why. This modest but sturdy building, built by the grandfather he never knew, stood watch over a flock of sheep and little else. His memories of his mother were few, but she seemed to thrive on company, on dazzling everyone in the room. Here, she'd only had her family and some farm animals to keep her company.

Still, the country was pretty enough. The gentle rolling hills and mature trees were certainly inviting, if one liked that sort of thing. Liked the quiet. And it was *so* quiet. Not that Saint John was a metropolis on the scale of New York or even Toronto, but there was always something to catch his attention. Perhaps he was more like his mother than his father had given him credit for… and credit was something Frank had given Beau precious little of.

He hauled the luggage from the back of the buggy, distracted by the notion that his knees might buckle under the weight of the trunk he'd watched Miss Murray handle at Everwell with little strain. He'd never been one for ridiculous notions of manliness, but if pressed, he would have noted a small blow to his ego.

"What on earth did you pack?" he asked Miss Murray, gripping the leather handles. "Cannon balls?"

"Books," she said.

"All of them?"

Miss Murray rolled her eyes then approached, clearly ready to give her assistance.

"I am being babysat by a woman, Miss Murray" he said, pulling the trunk out of her reach just as she went to grab the sturdy leather strap. "Allow me to salvage some of my masculine pride."

Whatever the strain to his knees or his back, the hint of a smile that seemed to pull at her mouth lessened the pain.

He heaved the trunk to the faded red door, when it magically opened. He was greeted by a woman of modest height, her Mi'kmaq heritage evident in her dark brown eyes, black hair, and straight nose. She greeted Daniel Chandler with a warmth he returned, welcomed Miss Murray with a gracious smile, then regarded Beau with undisguised curiosity.

"You're Emily Redden's son," she said simply.

Her greeting took Beau off guard. The only two people who ever spoke of his mother were his father and his aunt. To hear it from a stranger left Beau with a curious sense of loss—as if there was an entire part of him he hadn't realized he'd been missing.

She beckoned them inside and led him to a small parlour. He lowered the trunk to the floor, then turned to face her. They stood in silence, and Beau had the sense she was taking the measure of him. He brushed it off as mere curiosity at having her days upended by this unusual request of his aunt's.

He outstretched his hand, eager to end the examination. "Beau da Silva."

"Annie Chandler," she replied, accepting his greeting. "Here to take a first and last look at the farm before you sell it?"

Beau kept his smile in place, but there was no mistaking her disapproval at Beau's plans.

"It might not be his last," Daniel Chandler said, appearing from behind his wife, his eyebrow raised in that way a man does when he's too polite to outright say what's on his mind. "Nelson Taylor might be afraid to offer it now. Mr. da Silva here nearly took his head clean off his shoulders."

Beau blinked, taken off guard by the name. Nelson Taylor was the estate agent for George's College, an expensive private school in Windsor that had styled itself on the elite private schools like Eton, or Deerfield Academy in the U.S. Only a week ago, Beau had traded correspondence with Taylor about the details of a possible sale of The Grove.

For her part, Miss Murray, who'd been quiet, even by her standards, went unexpectedly ashen at the mention of the man's name. The moment their eyes met, she looked away. Clearly the encounter had left her more hurt than she'd initially let on. Despite her brusqueness, she'd clearly been injured by Taylor's callousness.

"Mr. Taylor is a miserable man on a good day," Annie said, giving Beau a second look. "I'm sorry he was the first one you met when you got off the train."

"You're not the only one," Beau replied. Not that he had time to think about the sale now, but there was no chance in hell he would do business through Nelson Taylor. He'd speak to the Board of Governors himself about the sale if he had to.

"I'll show you the rooms, then leave you to get settled," Annie said. "There still is some work to do, but we made up the beds, so you'll have someplace comfortable to sleep."

Miss Murray asked about fetching water, the condition of the hearth, and half a dozen more practical questions. Annie answered them all, leading them downstairs to the lower floor which had a dining room, kitchen, dairy room, and another room that might have been a study.

"I figured you'd be hungry so there's some hodge podge," Mrs. Chandler said as she brought them into the dining room. It was a bright room that, while modest in size, had a sort of faded elegance and an excellent view he found appealing. On the small table there was a pitcher of raspberry shrub, bread, bowls, and a large terrine.

All the while, he felt Annie Chandler's appraisal. He was long accustomed to having the eye of everyone in the room, something he normally appreciated. But this was different. Did she know about the charges against him and was too polite or afraid to mention them? Was she merely curious about the long-lost connection to this house reappearing after so long? Or, most likely, was she not pleased with the thought of having her life up ended by the sale of the property?

"Thank you," Miss Murray said, her manner one of detached politeness. "That's very kind."

"There's a pump in the kitchen, and the water is potable," Daniel said. "We'll be just next door. Teddy will be by tomorrow to see if you need anything."

The Chandlers left, and Beau, famished, walked to the small feast prepared for them. He pulled off the lid of the green-and-white porcelain terrine and stirred the contents, bringing colourful chunks of young carrots, peas, green beans, and new potatoes to the surface as the rich smells of butter and cream reached his nose. It reminded him that he hadn't eaten in hours.

"Neither business nor adventure can happen on an empty stomach," he said, ladling the hodge podge to his bowl. "Come, Miss Murray, so we do not leave Mrs. Chandler's efforts wasted. Unless you think she is trying to poison us."

He said that last bit as a bit of a throwaway remark, but when he looked over to Miss Murray, he wondered if she was, in fact, entertaining that very notion.

"I don't know," she answered, her gaze still fixed on some point out the window. "She was looking at you just a little too closely for my liking."

"No need for jealousy," he tsked, before helping himself to a long drink of tangy shrub. "It's entirely unnecessary, I assure you."

She turned her head, her eyes narrowed, clearly irritated with him.

"She was staring at you."

He shrugged. "Look at this face. I can't help it."

"That face is in half a dozen newspapers between Saint John, Moncton, and Halifax," she said, clearly unimpressed with his attempt at humour. "You gave everyone within fifty feet of us a reason to gawk in town."

Beau blinked. "He insulted you."

"Yes, he did. But they were just words, and no one else heard them."

The lack of emotion with which she answered took him aback. Why was she so indignant?

"I did."

"You are not my protector, Mr. da Silva," she said. "Quite the opposite. And if you're not careful, which you apparently have no interest in being, that face will be attached to a man hanging from the gallows."

Silence fell like a stone between them, leaving a heaviness in the room. Sarcasm and humour had been weapons he'd used in equal measure as a shield—and occasionally as a rapier— to his father's unending disapproval. After one of Frank's usual tirades, Beau would cut him off with a jibe or a bad joke, and then leave the elder da Silva and his cloud of insults for drinks with his friends in his club, or a rendezvous with one of the local society widows.

But here, with Madeline Murray standing silent and goddess-like, laying out the stark reality Beau now found himself in, his deflection fell flat. Whether she was aware or not of his internal struggle, he wasn't certain.

"If you don't think for a moment I do not appreciate how serious this is, I can assure you, I do," he said. "But I am not prepared to unload my anger on Mrs. Chandler. No doubt they are simply curious—and perhaps a little suspicious—about a person encroaching on property they've probably used as their own for some time. We are the interlopers here, Miss Murray, not them."

Miss Murray crossed her arms. "Too many people will sell their soul, or someone else's, if given the opportunity and the right inducement."

There was something about the way she'd said it that struck Beau as more than simple paranoia. And of course, he knew that to be absolutely true in the business world. Still, he found it difficult to automatically think the worst of people unless, like Nelson Taylor, they'd proved themselves to be.

He ladled some of the hodge podge into a second bowl and beckoned for her to sit. "Have you always gone through the world thinking everyone is a threat?"

"No. And that was my mistake," she said.

Something in Beau's chest twisted at the idea of a Madeline Murray who, once upon a time, went through the world with an open, trusting heart. A heart that had been clearly damaged so badly that she would look upon a genuine offer of hospitality with suspicion. It inexplicably saddened and angered him. Perhaps his misplaced concern was merely a way to keep his own worries at bay. Miss Murray was right. He'd noticed Annie Chandler's attention, and it had made him uneasy. She seemed to be studying his face, of all things. And it wasn't because she found him attractive, measuring his character. He'd brushed off the sensation as merely an overactive imagination, but apparently he wasn't the only one.

Chapter Nine

A MARATHON of chores dominated the days immediately after Beau and Miss Murray's arrival at The Grove. While the Chandlers had done them the blessing of airing out the mattresses which, by some miracle, had not become home to several generations of mice, Beau and Miss Murray's hasty arrival at a house mostly unoccupied for the past twenty years did not give the caretakers time to get the place entirely in order. The chimneys needed a thorough cleaning, and the rest of the place was in dire need of a good wipe down. While Beau prided himself on his physical fitness, he'd gone about it in the way of his upper class peers—rowing, boxing and other sports condoned as appropriate for a man of his stature. It was a life, he realized, his grandparents, who were by all accounts simple, hardworking people, might have found suspect in the extreme.

Still, Beau could not help but marvel at the overall state of the cottage. When he'd first been told about The Grove, he wondered if he'd inherited a well thought of, but not well taken care of, shack in the woods. But every part of it was built to last. The walls might need washing and perhaps a new coat of paint, but the roof was intact and the windows watertight.

The work inside was enough to keep both he and Miss Murray

so busy neither of them had time to breathe, and provided Beau temporary relief from his worries with the law. Occasionally Daniel and Teddy would come by to check on their progress and offer a hand, which they both accepted. Despite Miss Murray's wariness about the Chandlers, the task at hand was so monumental that she relented in her protest about their presence. Daniel seemed a good, honest man, and Beau found himself looking forward to chatting with both him and his son, Teddy. They wanted nothing from him. There were no angles they were trying to exploit. After years in boardrooms and clubs shaking hands with people who looked at him only as an opportunity to profit—an activity Beau himself participated in and excelled at—it was shocking how novel it was to be with people who expected nothing from him.

Beau was scrubbing down the walls in a room that once upon a time might have been the room his mother shared with Aunt Veronica. It had a beautiful view to the back of the property, where the Chandlers' sheep were happily grazing amongst the lush pastures. It was odd to think of her and Aunt Veronica living here. Both women had a penchant for finer things and they certainly both rose to social heights that made a place like The Grove seem like an entirely different world.

"Good morning."

Beau looked up from his labours to see Annie Chandler standing in the doorway, a basket in her hands.

"I thought you might need more eggs," she continued, looking over at Miss Murray. Miss Murray was in the bedroom across the hall, scrubbing down walls, all the while watching their neighbour with barely veiled suspicion.

"She seems somewhat protective of you," Annie said, her face bright with amusement.

"I suppose she is," he said. Only because she was paid to be so. Which was fine. Beau certainly didn't need mothering. He was a grown man. But the idea that someone might in fact be invested in him for reasons that had nothing to do with his wealth, or his name, or what connections he might be able to leverage was a tantalizing one. "Miss Murray is an excellent housekeeper. Very dedicated to ensuring the walls are clean."

Annie looked between the two, then turned to Beau. "Are you here because of the murder?"

Beau swallowed, the heat prickling up the back of his neck, before turning his attention back to Annie. "You know about that?"

Annie laughed. "We go to town once a week this time of year. Your face is on the post office wall."

"Is that why you've been watching him?"

Miss Murray's voice pulled his attention away. The rag she'd been using was in her hands, which were red from the water. She stood just outside the door, looking absolutely thunderous.

"Don't you worry, Miss Murray," Anne said. "Your man is safe here."

Miss Murray's eyes widened at the statement, and then she let out a laugh.

"He's not my man. I'm here to keep him out of trouble," she replied, giving Annie Chandler an appraising glance. "Is he in trouble, staying here?"

Annie Chandler was not bothered by the edge in Miss Murray's voice. Instead, Annie turned to her and smiled.

"Once upon a time, The Everwell Society helped out a friend of mine who was in a bad way," Annie said. "I couldn't imagine they would risk what they do to protect a rich white man who supposedly killed another one unless they had a good reason."

Miss Murray just nodded, her gaze straying to Beau. It was a strange experience, having two women discuss his character as if he wasn't even in the room. But he learned something else. The Everwell Society did have a reputation, beyond the one his aunt wanted to dismiss. It was not the Turnbull name, the da Silva wealth, or even the Redden connection that allowed Annie Chandler to help Beau.

It was because of Everwell.

"I didn't kill my father," Beau said.

A smile quirked at the side of Annie's mouth. "No, I don't think you did."

Beau had little time to dwell on the curious expression, or the confidence in which she'd offered her opinion about his innocence. Daniel and Teddy bounded up the stairs, the entire Chandler family apparently determined to help get the place in order. With Annie's help, Miss Murray had boiled water for laundry while Beau and Daniel, with Teddy's help, created a makeshift line to hang clothes.

As the five ate supper together in the early evening, a potent mix of contentment and yearning settled on Beau as he looked out the window at a small line of shirts and linens catching on the breeze. That night, when he lay in bed with freshly laundered sheets under him, it occurred to Beau that he'd never given clean bed linen a second thought in the entirety of his life. They'd always just been there. Growing up in Saint John's most exclusive neighbourhood had inoculated him against many of the petty hardships of his fellow men. Hardships that Miss Murray and the ladies at Everwell knew well and did their best to lessen for those who'd sought their aid. He drifted off, wondering if any of the students at George's college would appreciate the effort it took to allow them to fall asleep under sheets that smelled like a summer afternoon.

Birdsong roused Beau from a restless sleep. Gentle morning light bloomed under the curtains, framing the windows. Once upon a time, he'd have been coming home at this hour after an evening of merry making with friends or a pretty widow looking for his company. Both activities had provided distraction from the hollowness of a life built on one business conquest after another. But he was closer to forty than thirty, and now those vapid pleasures only served to remind him of the absences in his life. Last night at supper, he'd witnessed the deep connection between

Daniel and Annie, who seemed to have entire conversations with one other without exchanging a word. Or the way they took joy, and occasionally exasperation, in Teddy's exuberance. It opened up something inside him that, alone in the dark with only his thoughts for company, he'd found himself wrestling with. It was an undeniable yearning for something he couldn't name and definitely should not have wanted. Christ, he had a business empire at his fingers—one he'd helped build. He'd given the better part of his adult life to it in the vague hope to earn his father's respect, if not love.

And now Frank was dead, and Beau didn't know what he wanted anymore.

Movement from the other side of the door pushed aside the ball of uncomfortable thoughts. Miss Murray must be awake. The image of her rising from bed, her wild red hair falling in a tangle of unruly curls down her back and over her shoulders, managed to drive away any thoughts about his father, the business or the Chandlers. Throwing off the covers, he shook off the morning chill, then refreshed himself with a splash of lukewarm water he'd poured into the washbasin from a nearby jug. He pulled on a pair of trousers and a clean shirt, not bothering with a collar. As he fumbled around for a clean pair of socks and boots, he made a mental a list of today's chores and tried not to linger on the fact there was a gorgeous redheaded banshee in the room across the hall.

He pulled open the door to find Miss Murray standing on the other side of it, only slightly disappointed that her hair was already pulled up, though it did provide the distinct advantage of displaying the lovely curve of her neck and the exact place he imagined putting his lips to taste that beautiful skin.

"You're up early," she said without ceremony, and Beau couldn't tell if she was disappointed or surprised by his appearance.

"And you, I am sorry to say, are completely dressed," he said, unable to help himself. "What time do you have to rise in the morning to get all that hair into place? Or are you some faerie queen, and you coax some supernatural force to do it for you?"

Her lips twisted into some nameless expression, and Beau wondered if he had utterly befuddled her, which was entirely more satisfying than appropriate. But considering she was somehow befuddling *him*, it was only fair.

"Of course, you wouldn't have to coax them, would you? They'd just want to."

She blinked then, and Beau realized he'd said that last thought out loud.

A flush of pink rose in her cheeks, and she turned away and marched down the stairs, breaking the spell she'd somehow put over him.

Beau stood at the top of the stairs, watching her disappear out of the corner of his eye, and feeling suddenly poorer for the fact she was gone from his sight. Ridiculous. He didn't want her approval, did he? He'd spent a lifetime trying to earn the approval of his father and failed. Years of trying to prove to Frank he was smart enough, sharp enough, charming enough to be the man his father had wanted him to be.

Beau had somehow never been enough.

A crash from below interrupted his thoughts. He bounded down the stairs and into the kitchen, where Madeline Murray was crouched down and gathering up a heap of broken crockery.

Chapter Ten

"DAMN, DAMN, DAMN." Maddy cursed under her breath as she took stock of the broken crockery at her feet. She bent down and started picking up the larger pieces, gathering them in her apron.

So much for a quiet morning. Now that the house was mostly to rights, she'd hoped she could focus on the tasks she was actually looking forward to: unpacking her books and tidying up the overgrown kitchen garden. Perhaps there would be a cutting or two she could take back to her own garden at Everwell before it was plowed under for a school for boys with an overabundance of privilege.

What could I do with a garden like this?

If only she'd had the money her parents had set aside for her dowry. Her father, Patrick Murray was a very wealthy man—not as rich as the da Silvas, but still respectable. Malcolm would have married her, taken her money and she would have been left in a loveless marriage with a man who'd thought her abhorrent.

She swallowed the ugly memory as she gathered the shards at her feet. She had a garden at Everwell, and Mr. da Silva was in the business of making money. Her dowry, while substantial, would not have been enough to compete with an exclusive school like George's College. He wouldn't just give this all away.

To her surprise, he'd worked hard and without too much complaint since their arrival at The Grove. And—though she would rather die than confess it aloud—it was no hardship to watch him. His long, lean muscles had glistened in the sun as he and Daniel put up the poles for the clothesline. And when he'd taken a moment to splash a bit of clean water on his face after several hours of helping Teddy chop wood and clean out the chimney, Maddy had stopped to watch. It was unfair that he resembled a slightly soiled Adonis after all that work while she'd been on her knees with water-soaked hands, hair that had all the appeal of a rusted steel brush, and cheeks as red as an overripe tomato.

The exercise at least helped to distract her from the fact that Nelson Taylor had crossed her path. Any faint hope she'd had that he'd been a distant relation of that hateful man had evaporated. The name had landed on Maddy's ears like an exploding keg of black powder. Nelson Taylor had been a rival suitor of Malcom Ferguson—Maddy's fiancée.

Former fiancée.

Malcolm was dead, and Maddy had run as far as she could from the rumours that she'd killed him. Dread descended on her like a fast moving storm. If Nelson had recognized her, there would be more than just Beau da Silva's neck on the line. That awful story in the *Chronicle* would be nothing compared to the devastation Everwell would face if it came to light that they'd had a woman accused of murder living under their roof. Maddy had no defense against the power of story told by man like Nelson Taylor. Even her parents had believed it. If it weren't for Phillipa Hartley, she would never have found a second chance at life. Everwell had protected her when no one else would. She owed Phillipa and the society everything.

"Should I be happy this found the floor before you threw it at my head?"

Mr. da Silva's casual sarcasm interrupted Maddy's worries. He stood in the door, his hands in his pockets smiling at her with a look that seemed to be equal parts humour and concern.

Maddy tried to ignore him as she resumed collecting the broken pieces of pottery. Her entire body was dangerously aware of him, making the task far more difficult than it should have been. The sting from a sharp piece of smashed crockery slicing through one of her fingers was the price of her inattention. Instinctively she dropped the shard, which landed with an unceremonious clink in her apron, and put her finger to her mouth.

Mr. da Silva approached, undisguised concern crinkling his brow as he crouched down opposite her. It stirred Maddy in a way that, if she'd cared to think about it, she'd never quite experienced. And she did not care to think about it.

"Let me see," he said.

"I'm fine," she replied, pulling her finger away, betrayed by the blood flowing freely over it. It was only a small gash, but the cut was ragged, and deeper than she'd realized. Still, between her time in the garden and the occasional job for the Scandalous Spinsters that had been a little too close for comfort, Maddy was hardly bothered by a cut.

"I have no doubt," he replied, even as he took her hand, unbidden, and wrapped it in a clean handkerchief he produced from his pocket. He applied gentle pressure to the wound. "But let's make sure."

A pause settled over them, dulling every other sensation. The sounds of the birds fell away, as did the smell of the coffee beans and every other thing except the heady presence of Beau da Silva, crouched next to her, his hand wrapped around hers. Even the gentle throb from the cut faded, unable to compete with the thrumming of her heart.

What was this feeling? Maddy had no words for it. Whatever it was, she was certain it was dangerous. It softened her, when she needed to be hard and on alert.

Eager to break this curious spell, she straightened, pulling her wounded hand away while using her other to hold onto her apron, full of pieces of pottery.

"I said I was fine," she grumbled.

"I never said you weren't," he replied, his tone warm and strangely comforting, like the crackle of the hearth on a November day. He pulled out a chair from the heavy wood table, and with only a nod, bade her to sit. To Maddy's surprise, she did.

He found a broom and cleaned up the mess. Beau da Silva's normally suave demeanour and reputation as a shrewd man of business seemed at odds with the man in his shirtsleeves sweeping a kitchen floor. His natural elegance while doing the most mundane tasks commanded her attention.

"You're surprised I can hold a broom," he said, giving her a sly smile.

"I might be," she conceded.

"When I was younger, I ran a fishing camp for American industrialists," he said. "I did a little bit of everything, especially in the beginning."

"Do you still have it?" she asked. She'd heard of businesses like these, particularly along the Miramichi River, where there were fishing lodges that mixed rustic simplicity with a certain genteel luxury that provided a retreat for wealthy men looking for an escape and some of the best salmon fishing in the region.

He shook his head. "I sold it years ago."

"Why?"

"Silver Lumber," he said, a rare tightness appearing along his jaw. "The lodge was taking my focus away from the family business."

His answer left her wanting to know more, which, given her aversion to small talk in general and Beau da Silva in particular, surprised her. But there was something in the way his movements had become more rigid, as if he were sweeping away a ghost along with the broken crockery that had piqued her curiousity. Instead of giving into it, she rose, prepared to get on with the business of grinding coffee beans. He cocked an eyebrow and gave her a look that made her insides flip.

"I didn't say you could get up," he said, his playful tone and arched brow a counterpoint to his commanding words.

"I don't recall any reason why I have to listen to you," she replied, even though she sat down again. "On the contrary, you are to follow my orders."

"As enthralling as that sounds," he said, filling the kettle with water from the pump, "I am not particularly good at following orders."

He flashed her a smile, then turned away and carefully placed the vessel over the fire, then stoked the coals. The act provided Maddy an opportune moment to appreciate his backside, which, she could not help but notice for the eighth or ninth time since they arrived, was exceptionally well formed. All of him was well formed, and picking the most alluring part of him seemed an impossible task. Still, if anyone asked her opinion—which she would not give under any circumstances—she would have said that his forearms commanded her particular attention. Roped with lean muscle, they hinted at a physicality that was more about flexibility and speed rather than brute strength.

"Let's see that hand," he said, returning to her, his movements more efficient and businesslike now, though still edged with a bit of the softness he'd displayed earlier.

"You don't have to bother with me," she said.

"I know," he replied. "But you should know I am a selfish man, Miss Murray, and I like to get my money's worth out of my investments. After all, if someone does come to the door trying to haul me back to Saint John for their two hundred dollars, you can't defend me if your hand is festering. I'll be out my payment to Everwell."

Before she had the chance to answer, he gently pulled the cloth away from her cut, the white cloth now marred by blots of dark red. She held her breath as the air found the tear in her skin.

He frowned as he examined the cut. "Did we pack any sort of medical supplies?"

"Tilda wouldn't have sent me fifty miles from home without any," she replied.

"Right. Stay put."

He disappeared into the dairy room behind the kitchen, then reappeared moments later, looking triumphant. He set the box down on the table near her, picking through the contents and eyeing labels, before pulling out a roll of clean bandages. He set it down, then noticed the book sitting on one corner of the table. She'd put it aside for this morning, hoping to finish the last few pages while the water was warming for the coffee.

"A little early morning reading?" He opened the front cover. "The Scarlet Pimpernel. I've not read this one."

A well of embarrassment rose inside her, and on impulse, she pulled the book away, wincing slightly as the fabric cover pulled at the cut in her finger, bringing a fresh well of blood.

"Let me take that before you bleed all over it," he said, gently taking the book from her hands and setting it beside her. "I'm not going to hurt your book."

He gave her a wink, then examined a few of the bottles, some of which were common elements like iodine and alcohol, along with a few of Tilda's special tinctures she'd mastered over a lifetime of learning and practicing her art as a doctoress. Beau found the alcohol and a few bandages, dabbed a clean bit of linen with the clear liquid and without ceremony, held it to Maddy's finger. The sharp cold sting was expected, and while she was able to swallow an intake of breath, he caught her flexing to pull her hand away.

"Now now," he said, tsking at her in mock admonishment. "Just keep still like a good girl."

Almost against her will, Maddy laughed out loud, surprising them both.

"I haven't been a girl in a very long time," she said. "And I don't know if I've ever been good."

"Well," he said, pulling away the swab gently, examining the wound once more before wrapping it up, "that's something a man likes to hear."

"Are you deliberately trying to vex me?"

"Perhaps," he said. "But people who are good all the time are boring, don't you think?"

"And people who are bad are a lot of work," she said. "There's nothing wrong with good. It just depends on whose definition of good. I've just never been particularly adept at being whatever type of good women are supposed to be good at."

"This seems like far too in-depth a conversation before breakfast, don't you think?" he asked.

"But— "

"Do not try and distract me with those pretty eyes of yours." He playfully waved a finger at her, then pressed her book into her uninjured hand. "For heaven's sake, Miss Murray, take your novel and go sit somewhere you won't be overcome by a need to clean something."

Unwilling to betray herself, Maddy practically ran upstairs to the parlour, stopping at the bookcase in front of her, desperate to grab a single thread of her control. Her finger throbbed from the gash, but the rest of her hummed with warmth from the echo of Beau da Silva's touch. There was something about his manner— playful and soft and yet demanding—that was traitorously compelling.

Those pretty eyes of yours. He'd said it as casually as if he'd noted that the grass was green, or that hens laid eggs. The phrase sent a cascade of emotion rushing through her veins—confusion, then a fleeting sense of delight, chased away by panic. His smiles, his warmth, his pretty words—those were the tactics of a man who was trying to make the best of his situation by treating her with common civility, or at worst, condescension.

That wasn't the worst. The worst had been learning she'd been at the centre of a devastating game that had men fighting over her with romantic gestures and pretty words in order to win her father's fortune. Even now, she could recall Malcolm's face when he coolly told her the deal had been done, and they would in fact be wed. The moment he'd tried to ensure she couldn't go back on the agreement. He'd forced himself, and she, in a moment, forced back. And now Nelson Taylor—who'd eagerly participated in those games—had reappeared.

For that much money, I would kiss a hog in a skirt.

Tears burned at the back of her eyes. She blinked quickly as she cursed the memories and the power they still had over her, nearly two decades later. She put the heels of her hands to her eyes, willing the emotion to stop.

"I thought you might want some breakfast."

Maddy pulled her hands away, then whipped around, chiding herself for allowing the unwanted memory to distract her to the point she'd been taken off guard.

He paused, his casual smile broken a second time by a look she was coming to learn was concern.

"I'm not disturbing you, am I?" he asked.

"Of course you are," she grumbled, turning back to the shelf to shield herself from his gaze. "I should be in Halifax, looking after my blighted roses."

Her abruptness had done its usual work. He set down the tray on a nearby table, and turned to leave without any further attempt at conversation. She'd wounded him for no good reason but to protect herself. Shadows of a darker moment, long ago, edged into her thoughts. The night she'd learned the truth about her engagement. The night that led to Maddy being wanted for the same crime Beau was about to be tried for.

Murder.

Inexplicable panic rose in her chest, then settled, weighed down by regret. She held her hands to her belly in a pale attempt at calming her fear he might go. What was this sudden and inexplicable desire for his presence? She should just tell him to go and spare her the rejection she was certain was coming.

"I'm sorry," she blurted out, overcome by another emotion she didn't want to name. "I'm in a foul mood this morning and it's not your fault. Please stay."

Beau paused, struck by the tremor in her voice. Despite the lushness of her body, Madeline Murray presented hard angles and bristles, like a porcupine ready to strike if anyone got too close. He'd known from the moment he'd walked in the room that she was nursing a wound much deeper than the one on her finger. That he'd been stung by her response was another matter he'd bury under a mound of other, supposedly more important concerns. Right now, he found himself absolutely bewitched by the pink rising in her cheeks, and the subtle, but unmistakable plea in her dark green eyes. Madeline Murray had no idea what effect those eyes of hers had on him.

He pulled out a faded, red chair and she wordlessly accepted the invitation to sit. Beau picked up one of two plates of simple breakfast he'd prepared and handed it to her.

"Thank you," she said. "I didn't think you could cook."

"Fishing camp," he reminded her. "Breakfast was my specialty."

He smiled as he caught the flash of surprise in her expression.

"Handsome and handy," she said. "We could use you at Everwell."

In spite of himself, Beau found himself momentarily taken with the idea. "It's the least I can do," he said. "Besides, you're wounded."

She rolled her eyes at him. "It's a cut."

"I've seen men die from cuts." Beau said, knowing full well he was deliberately stretching the truth. That cut was to one of the foremen at a lumber yard, and the 'cut' was so large and of such a grisly nature the poor fellow had bled to death.

"This is twice I am hearing about a man dying in your proximity," she said. "Maybe I should turn you in and get the reward myself."

"And then you would deprive yourself of my company," he said. To his utter and inexplicable delight, he managed to coax a smile from her that she tried to hide behind her coffee cup.

Beau gestured to the chest full of books she'd brought for a trip they'd both hoped would be as short as possible. She was going to run out of shelf space long before the trunk was emptied.

"You must be an incredibly fast reader."

"Actually no." She paused, as if carefully considering her answer. "I like to take my time with a book. To savour it."

Beau swallowed a groan. Did she have even the slightest idea what she was doing to him?

"Why Miss Murray, you really are a romantic," he said.

"I am not," she protested, a familiar edge creeping back into her voice. Her armour was coming back into place, and Beau was overcome with the absolute necessity of figuring out how to pry it loose.

"There is nothing wrong with that, you know," he said. "Not everything has to be logic and hard angles all the time. The world is better with some softness."

He set down his cup, rose and walked over to the small trunk she'd carted from Everwell. Inside was a tidy line of books that had been packed with great care. He scanned the spines, some of which appeared absolutely ancient. The mix of titles were eclectic. Poetry, two novels, a book of philosophy, and—

He paused, and looked again, partially because the title was in a complex blackletter script, and partially because it was in German.

Vollstandiges Ring-Buch.

"Your tastes are quite eclectic," he said, carefully pulling the book out of its place, and opening the cover. He flipped through the pages, which were full of illustrations demonstrating different stances and techniques for disarming an opponent. How many times had she had to employ these stances to keep herself and the people of Everwell safe?

"Didn't your parents teach you to ask before you help yourself to someone else's things?" she asked, setting her plate aside.

"Come now," he said, lowering his voice in that way he did when he wanted to draw in a potential client to close the deal. "You can't deny me a book, can you?"

"I hardly think a man in your position has been denied anything."

Beau couldn't argue the point. Though he'd been denied the one thing he'd worked his entire life to earn—his father's respect—he'd long given up on that dream. With Frank dead, it was gone forever.

Unable to shrug off the discomfort, he thumbed through the pages, looking over the top of the book at Miss Murray. He was goading her—a deliberate move to distract himself from the old wound.

"How about your good opinion?"

She rose to her feet, crossed the room, and reached for the book, but he pulled it away. He looked at her out of the corner of his eye, knowing full well he was playing a dangerous game. And just as he was about to congratulate himself on his tactics at playing it, Beau felt himself temporarily discombobulated owing to the fact he'd been spun around, his arms pinned to his side and temporarily unable to see thanks to his shirt being yanked over his head and pulled tight across his mid-chest. By the time he'd righted himself, the book was back in Miss Murray's hands, and the only salve to his ego was the unmistakable hint of smug victory on her face.

"Miss Murray, if you wished to undress me, simply ask," he said, brushing off his wounded male pride with his most reliable weapon—sarcasm. He tucked in his shirt and raked his fingers through his hair, trying to put it back to some semblance of style. "You may find that I am most agreeable to the question."

"You seemed determined to make this arrangement of ours as unpleasant as possible," she said.

"And you seemed determined to hate me," he said. "I cannot help but rise to that challenge."

"Does a man of your fortune and circumstance require the good opinion of an old maid whose entire worth can be found in a few trunks at her feet?" she asked.

"Those closest to me that I believed knew my character now deem me capable of murdering my father, Miss Murray," he said. "So perhaps I am more invested in your opinion that you might think."

The room stilled as a note of tension wound between them, like the calm before a gathering storm. Why did her estimation suddenly mean so much to him? Was it simply that she was here? He hadn't experienced this level of urgency with Dominic Ashe—the man he'd actually hired to help him—or even his aunt and uncle. Why did Madeline Murray matter at all? She was here because she was being paid, not out of some urgent need to help him.

"I wouldn't be here if I thought you were guilty," she said at last. "The Everwell Society wouldn't be jeopardizing our reputation otherwise."

"And that is important to you."

"It is everything."

Her words hit Beau like a blow to the chest, robbing him of his ability to speak for a moment. How must it be to have such a sense of belonging? Envy, ridiculous as it was, crept inside him, twisting at his insides. How could he be jealous of a charity? But there it was. That conviction in her voice, that quiet fury driven by an absolute love and devotion to a people and place that she loved. For all his wealth and status, no one seemed as interested in protecting Beau as much as Madeline Murray was determined to protect Everwell and everyone in it.

To her, Beau was a job. To Frank, he'd been a tool for making money.

Beau couldn't help but wonder if his gravestone would have the words "A means to an end" engraved under his name.

Beau nodded, then flashed a smile, the same smile he used to cover over a thousand hurts. And Christ, he didn't even know why it pained him so. Of course she was here to help the people she knew, trusted, and quite probably loved. He didn't know why, but for just a moment, he didn't want Madeline Murray to be here for her duty to Everwell. He wanted a scrap of that devotion. It was ridiculous, given they were barely acquaintances, and certainly not friends. He didn't deserve it.

But how he longed to have it.

Chapter Eleven

BOTH MISS MURRAY'S plans to dig in the garden and his own to survey the property were scuppered by a thick band of ominous grey clouds that settled overhead almost immediately after breakfast. The light but steady rain continued for the rest of the day, and the entire day following.

Beau had been eager see the land for himself, which according to Aunt Veronica, was a good fifty acres of rolling hills, bordered by forest and a small tidal river. It must have had some potential, otherwise an exclusive college would not be offering him a small fortune for it. Frank da Silva might be dead, but Beau was still his son, and he'd become rich doing what the da Silvas did better than nearly anyone—taking the land and harvesting it for whatever it was worth and then selling it.

What worth did this place have?

It was a question he'd often asked of himself, and came up wanting.

To occupy himself, Beau spent much of his time reviewing old ledgers and notes made by his grandparents. It was a fascinating window into a part of his story he'd been blithely unaware of. When he'd first set eyes on The Grove, his curiosity had been tempered with disappointment. The place was solidly built but the interior would have benefited from a fresh coat of paint or some paper on the walls. The kitchen needed updating, including the addition of a modern stove instead of relying on an open hearth for cooking. And the privy… well, that just needed to be rebuilt. When he'd run a highly successful business bringing in wealthy Americans looking for excellent fishing in the Miramichi River, he prided himself on having the right mix of simple, rustic surroundings mixed with some basic refinements—good food, a comfortable bed, and modern plumbing.

Still, the investment of a little elbow grease had already done wonders. With every bucketful of dirty water he'd tossed away after wiping the place, Beau felt himself connecting with the faded beauty of the place. When he and Teddy Chandler had finished cleaning the chimney and had the fire burning properly, Beau felt a rush of accomplishment he hadn't recalled in ages. Even Miss Murray had gifted him with a genuine smile which gave him far more pleasure than was rational.

The idea that she considered herself an old maid bothered Beau. What injuries of the heart had she faced that had left her without the promise of love? Not that love and sex had anything to do with each other—he'd lived a lifetime with a scarcity of the first and a respectable harvest of the second to know the truth. But Madeline Murray was a romantic soul. He knew it as surely as the sky was blue, despite her attempts to keep that sky hidden under a thick carpet of dark cloud and rumbling thunder. Because every time he'd seen a break in those clouds, it was dazzling.

After a day and a half of rain, and with no end to the cloud cover in sight, Beau climbed the narrow stairs to the attic to check the water tightness of the roof. Satisfied to find it dry, he'd turned his attention to a handful of his grandparent's belongings, including a battered straw hat that once upon a time made a comfortable shelter for a small family of rodents, a box of odd buttons, and a weathered, hand-stitched volume full of the most bizarre recipes that should have been as dry as dust, but were in fact, fascinating. There were multiple notes in the margins, apparently made by his grandparents, and their own recipes added on scraps of paper stuffed between the covers. Thoroughly engrossed, he lost all sense of time, looking up only when he heard the creaking of the attic steps. He was gifted a view of Miss Murray, and was inexplicably pleased she'd gone in search of him.

"There you are," she said, a line of concern on her brow. "Would you like some tea?"

"Miss me?" he replied, unable to help himself. Because he'd missed her.

She rolled her eyes, but Beau saw the hint of a smile on the edge of that delectable mouth of hers. Her expression turned from feigned irritation to undisguised curiosity.

"What is that?"

"I'm not exactly certain," he answered, carefully closing the cover. "I think it's part *Mrs. Beeton*, part *Domestic Medicine*, and part witchcraft."

She stepped forward, looking from him to the book and back again. The movement was surprisingly tentative, as if she was fighting her own enthusiasm. Beau stifled a laugh. He'd wooed women with smiles, teasing innuendos, and any number of expensive trinkets. None of them had worked on Madeline Murray. Not that he was trying to woo her. But here he was, sitting in an attic in wrinkled trousers on an old dairy stool poring over an old book and suddenly he couldn't drive Miss Murray away if he tried. And he didn't want to try.

"May I?" she asked.

"Of course," he said. "Perhaps, you can help me decipher it."

They went down to the kitchen and perched side by side on the wooden bench at the kitchen worktable. A teapot sat on the table, its precious contents wrapped in a linen tea towel to keep the pot warm. The smell of the woodsmoke mixed with the subtle scents of Miss Murray's rose-infused soap, along with the scent of the old book in front of them. He pushed it toward her. In her eagerness to take it, her fingers brushed against his, sending a small shock of intense awareness through his veins. She pulled her fingers away, even as that familiar blush crept up over the collar of her cotton blouse.

It could not be his imagination. She'd felt it too. Beau stifled a smile of satisfaction, even as the echo of that brief touch lingered.

"It's like two books were taken apart and restitched into one," she said, as if the touch had not happened, even though she kept her eyes glued to the book, carefully examining the binding. "It seems like the last third of the book is completely handwritten."

"What do you make of it?" he asked.

"I can't speak for the witchcraft," she said, "but your first assessment doesn't seem too far off the mark. There are recipes in here for feeding the sick, tonics for any number of ailments, and a few for making soap. And—" She paused, her brow crinkling into a frown as she squinted slightly, clearly trying to interpret a passage that, if he had read her expression correctly, suggested either morbid fascination or disgust.

"What is it?" he asked, unable to help himself. Without thinking, Beau slid closer, holding out his hand. She opened and slid it back toward him, her finger pointing to the top the page.

"There's a recipe for forcing mustard seeds into greens in the space of a morning," she said. "With hot horse manure."

"You don't want to try it?" he said, genuinely curious. "Just to see what happens?"

"Would you eat salad that was pulled from a fresh pile of horse manure?" she asked in such a manner that Beau knew in a heartbeat Miss Murray's answer to that question.

He shrugged. "I've been accused of worse things," he said. "I'm curious enough."

Miss Murray gave him a questioning look, and then shook her head. "You and Rimple could set up an experiment. Cow, Horse, Sheep. Which one grows it faster. Your grandparents would be proud."

The casual way she talked about his grandparents sent a curious ache through him. What would they think of his discovery of this book? All through the volume, there were little snippets of writing in the margins. An echo of their lives in his hands. He flipped back to the front pages, where there was an inscription by Verner Redden, his grandfather, and a second by his grandmother, Maisie, whose hand was equally present in the margins of some pages where some of the ingredients had been scratched out and substitutions made.

"They must have had an interesting garden," she said, gazing out the kitchen window to a spot that even to Beau's untrained eye had been treated differently than the meadow surrounding it. "You can see where it was, though it's frightfully overgrown. When the weather clears, I'll take a look out there and see what's salvageable."

"There's a bunch of tools in the barn," Beau said, tamping down the urge to remind her that there was little point in salvaging a garden for a place where neither of them had any intent to stay. "I have no idea what state they are in, though if the Chandlers have been keeping up the outbuildings, the spade might even be sharp."

Miss Murray poured them each a steaming cup of tea and added a bit of milk in each of their cups while Beau fetched a couple of biscuits and jam. It was, he had to admit, sort of pleasant, sitting here with her in this humble little kitchen with its large hearth that must be outrageously warm in the heat, despite the large windows. Meanwhile, Madeline Murray was too busy looking down at the book, studying every page, soaking it up as if she was deciphering an ancient manuscript, looking for some hidden secret. Her mouth moved silently, reading to herself, and then she looked over at him, pointing to the book. Her eyes widened with something that could only be excitement. Joy. And damn it all if it didn't make him feel a little joy, too.

"This is very interesting," she said, looking up at him, gifting him with an expression that lit up her entire face. "There are plants in here I didn't know could be grown in our climate. Brugmansias, for example. You have to be careful with those. And—"

She paused, her eyelashes fluttering in surprise before she schooled her features. She closed the book.

"Something wrong?" he asked. He'd been staring, he realized. Caught up in what he suspected was the rare occasion of Madeline Murray being happy. And something about that both elated and saddened him at the same time.

She shook her head. "I'm sorry—this is your family treasure, not mine."

She pushed the volume toward him and he responded by resting his hand on hers. He'd intended the impulsive act only to let her know he was in no hurry to end her enjoyment. But the moment his body made connection with hers, desire, excitement rushed through him, followed by a nameless wanting that welled from deep inside and made him go still. The only sound in the kitchen came the steady thrum of the rain and the pounding of his heart in his chest.

Her gaze brushed over his face, resting on his mouth. Was that his imagination, or did she part her lips slightly? They were soft and full, like the rest of her, and Christ, Beau wanted to taste them. If he'd been honest with himself, it was nearly his first thought when he saw her in the bookshop, and he'd dreamt of it more than a few times since. Those lips seemed to be the answer to a thousand questions he didn't even know he had.

Should he kiss her? He sure as hell wanted to. Did she want to be kissed?

A soft, intoxicating heat rushed through Maddy's body. Was she imagining the invitation in his gaze? Because her body seemed to be answering it. She was certain she'd been frozen to in her seat, but somehow their bodies had moved closer, her entire being prickling with delicious awareness of him.

Yes, she was a thirty-seven year old virgin. Yes, she read romance novels and romantic poetry until her heart and body ached. Still, Maddy knew how to satisfy herself. She learned more from books than just how to sow seeds or deflect the blow from a dagger.

But this... this was different. She suddenly didn't need to imagine the tenderness of a man's touch. She didn't need to read about the way someone's heart might drum in their chest so loud that even the heavens might hear it.

Did Beau hear it? Maybe he was trying, because he came closer—or maybe it was her—and somehow, his lips brushed up against her cheek close to her ear, and her body responded with a single word.

"Beau."

The word flitted through the air, landing somewhere between them. As she realized what she'd done, panic barrelled toward her, like the scream of an oncoming train. Malcolm had heard her heart beating in her chest, too. Right before he announced to his friends that he'd won her hand. Did her heart break, or simply freeze that night? She couldn't remember anymore. It had just seemed to stop working.

The memory intruded on the present like the guardian it had become. Deep in her heart, Maddy knew no one would look at a woman like her and a man as beautiful as Beau da Silva and think that there could be any physical attraction between them.

Well—on his side. Because Maddy did have eyes that worked and she knew how absolutely devastatingly handsome he was. Even the subtle marks around his eyes and along his brow that marked his age only highlighted his beauty. Whoever had named him, named him well.

She pulled her hand away and pushed herself to her feet. The act was clumsy, jostling the table so much her mug of tea shook, dropping neat little circles of liquid on the sturdy wooden table-top. Maddy ignored what might have been a flicker of hurt cross his face.

"I've got a headache," she said, clearing her throat, trying to keep her voice steady. "It's probably the weather."

Maddy forced herself to remember why she was here. The

greenhouse of her dreams would nearly be funded with the proceeds of this job, which was to keep Beau da Silva safe from harm. But right now there was a greater danger, and it came from her own body. She darted out of the kitchen and upstairs to the relative safety of her room.

As expected, he did not follow.

If she'd been at Everwell, she would have retreated to the corner of the carriage house she shared with Gemma for training. There, while Gemma practiced on ropes above her, Maddy had a straw bag to punch and kick. Mats to flip over opponents. She even occasionally boxed with Jeremy Webber, Gemma's husband, an accomplished pugilist in his own right. Once the rain stopped, she promised herself, she would find some private space to practice with her knives and the retractable cane, a gift from Lady Em. There was a barn and acres of land primarily occupied by trees, birds, and the Chandlers' livestock. She would use it to put some space between them. She'd only been on the job for a week, and already she felt herself softening around Beau.

Beau.

She rolled her eyes as her stomach clenched at the way she'd uttered his name, breathy and wanton. And what was worse was the sharp intake of breath she heard when she'd put her lips to his ear. It had sent a bolt of heat straight to her core—and scared her to death. She'd nearly kissed him.

She'd never been kissed like that.

Never been kissed at all.

Chapter Twelve

AFTER RETIRING EARLY, Maddy spent most of the night re-reading her favourite passages in *Sense and Sensibility* and trying to put Beau da Silva out of her head. Then, deciding reading Jane Austen might not have been the best antidote for her current state of mind, she set down her book and rearranged her clothes hanging in the small wardrobe. While she was refolding her stockings, she found a small bit of paper shoved at the back of the lower drawer. It was a fragment of a note—a poem actually, and one she recognized: *The Passionate Shepherd to His Love*, by Christopher Marlowe. The initials H.C. were scrawled at the bottom. Setting the paper aside, she returned to her task, until boredom finally induced her to rest.

The following morning, Maddy woke to a bright blue sky, birdsong, and a rolling green landscape that had grown even more lush, if such a thing was even possible. She rose early and went to the kitchen, hoping to avoid Mr. da Silva without appearing as if she was trying to, and soon discovered that she had failed.

"Good morning," he said, walking into the kitchen, reaching for the pot of coffee she had just brewed. "How's your headache?"

There was no innuendo, no awkwardness on his part. Was he

taking pity on her, or genuinely unaware of the embarrassment she had found herself in yesterday? Both were awful, but if she had to choose, she'd rather the latter.

"Better," she replied, determined to go about her day as if she hadn't spent the entirety of last evening in her room nursing the mortification in her chest.

"Did you take a sleeping powder?" he asked. "I knocked on your door, but you didn't answer."

"I did," she lied. She'd heard him knock on her door late last night. "I fell asleep not long after I crawled in bed. I must have really needed the sleep." What she'd really needed was for Rimple Jones to build some sort of contraption that would enable her to go back in time and keep herself from trying to kiss Beau da Silva. The fact he'd gone and checked on her may have made it worse. Or was it better? She couldn't be certain and why was she suddenly concerned about it?

He poured a generous dollop of cream into his coffee cup. He took a tentative sip, then went to the window looked out over back garden.

"That pergola along the side of the house needs to be repaired," he said. "There must be a mill around somewhere, don't you think?"

Maddy blinked. "You don't mean to do it yourself?"

"Believe it or not, I actually like doing things for myself," he said, a hint of discontent in his otherwise cheerful demeanour. "This is my property. Maybe I want to invest in it."

"I thought you wanted to sell it," she said. *Sell it to Nelson Taylor,* she added silently.

"I'm entitled to change my mind." he said, as if the opportunity to make a small fortune, or spend one, was nothing to him. "Besides, if I can show its potential, I could make far more out of it."

Something deep inside Maddy bristled at his offhand comment. Of course that was it. The money. People with money were always about that. Just like her parents. Every new dress, new pair of shoes, every new diet tonic, every new contraption to pull in her belly, all for the express goal of fixing Maddy to ensure that Patrick Murray got the best family connections for his investment in his daughter.

"You can't go to the mill," she replied. "The entire point of this is that you stay hidden."

"I'll ask Daniel Chandler to take me—I'll pay him for his trouble." He rubbed his hand across his jaw, emphasizing the stubble he hadn't yet shaved. "Besides, people are not going to be expecting to see me here, and not without a starched collar."

Even more casually attired, without the pomade that had kept his golden-brown hair styled in the way of fashionable gentlemen, he somehow looked as dashing as ever.

"Ask Daniel to get the wood for you." she said. "You are not going to get carted off in a sack back to Saint John."

Unwilling to listen to him argue the point, she took her coffee cup and walked to the back door and opened it, where it seemed like the kitchen garden, tangled and overgrown as it was, was waiting for her. Expectant. Dill and thyme were still evident, along with great swaths of mint. She breathed in sweet smells of grass, sweet peas and clover, which soothed her in a way few other things did. Being here was not entirely bad.

Before she knew what she was doing, she was bent over, pulling at this plant and that. Just exploring, she told herself.

Was it just exploring when she'd gone to the little garden shed and pulled out the hoe so she could cut through some of the weeds? Of course it was, she decided. After all, it was in her best interest—and certainly Mr. da Silva's—to know where there was potential for danger, and if she discovered a host of little clay pots and gardening implements, it was a happy coincidence indeed. On her return, she saw Mr. da Silva, standing in the garden, surveying her progress. He wore a straw hat he must have found in the cottage somewhere. It suited him.

"I thought you were going to bother the Chandlers," she called out, "and leave me in peace."

"He's already done that," came the reply, but not with Beau da Silva's voice.

Maddy gave a start. Perhaps she needed new glasses after all, because it was Daniel Chandler, not Beau da Silva, giving her a broad smile. A familiar one. It was the second time she'd been struck by this odd sense of familiarity about a man she'd just met.

"Apologies," she said, approaching him. "For both my manners and for Mr. da Silva."

As the distance closed, it was not difficult to note the similarities. Daniel Chandler was perhaps an inch or two shorter, his build a bit broader, and hair far more wheat coloured, but there was something in his eyes and his smile that was remarkable in his similarity. Even the way he rested his hands on his hips.

"Not at all," he said. "I'm sure Annie is happy for the solitude, and I need some new fence posts."

"Is the mill far?" she asked.

"Just outside of town. We'll be a few hours. Plenty of time for you to make some progress," he said. "My father and I were keeping this up, but we've been busy this year helping our daughter set up house near the shore."

"Did Mrs. Turnbull ask you?" Maddy asked. "It seems like a lot of work, especially if it isn't getting used."

Mr. Chandler shook his head. "My father used to help out the elder Reddens quite a bit. They had no sons, and they treated him quite well. We've always kept it going, and used what we could out of it."

"We found one of their books in the attic. They grew some remarkable plants."

"The soil here is very good," he said. "My father learned a lot from them."

"And your father is still living?" she said. They hadn't seen any indication of the elder Mr. Chandler.

"He is," Daniel answered. "He's getting on but still a very active man. He was visiting my daughter up in Avonford. She was married last year, and he misses her. He should be back in a few days. He'd be very happy, I think, to know someone like you was here to tend to it."

Maddy inexplicably brightened at the thought of meeting the elder Mr. Chandler. Anyone who shared an interest in gardens or books was generally good company, and someone who might have particular knowledge of plants was especially welcome. If he was anywhere near as affable as his son, he should be quite pleasant company. And maybe there was something she could learn she could take back to Everwell.

A pang of something—something so unfamiliar and potentially troublesome that she found herself putting a hand to her chest—distracted her. It wasn't strong enough to be regret, but rather a sense of missing…but what? Was it Everwell? Of course she missed home, but this was something more. New. It was missing…*this.*

Maddy straightened, as if the idea was so utterly impossible it threatened to toss her off balance. The Everwell Society saved her. She owed Phillipa, Lady Em, and Tilda her life. She'd always been safe there and kept them safe in return. Whatever this sensation was, she had to rid herself of it.

Before she could contemplate it further, Mr. da Silva approached with Teddy at his side, jumping around with the twitchy energy of a fourteen year old. With his straw hat and simple trousers, white shirt, and vest, Mr. da Silva looked very much like he belonged at The Grove. Like he'd always been a part of it.

"Careful Daniel," Mr. da Silva called out. "If you touch the plants, she might toss you over her shoulder."

Maddy smiled in spite of herself, even as a look of curiosity crinkled the skin at the corners of Daniel's eyes.

"He once plucked a rose from my garden without my permission," she said to Daniel by way of explanation.

"Which apparently was against the rules. I didn't know there were rules about gardens," Mr. da Silva said. He cocked an eyebrow, that familiar sly grin coming back that Maddy was coming to adore. Well, not adore. Adore would suggest she liked him. But she did like that smile. She liked it a lot.

"There are rules about touching people's things without permission," Maddy said, quietly ignoring the fact that she had in fact broken that rule herself more times than she cared to admit. But only books. Books that were unloved and unappreciated. "And there are many, many rules about gardens."

Mr. da Silva was looking at her again in that way of his, like he was smiling at her, and yet there was something deeper under his shiny smile. A wanting. It couldn't be possible, or course.

"We should get moving," Mr. Chandler said, "if you want to get a head start on your pergola. We'll be the rest of the morning to get to the mill and back. We can probably get started on it this afternoon."

"You're not going," Maddy said, crossing her arms. "We discussed this. Daniel was going to fetch the wood."

"My dear Miss Murray, you will find I am a stubborn man as well as a selfish one," he replied. "I'm going with him."

"Fine," Maddy said, shaking her head. "I'm coming."

Despite Madeline Murray's fears, the trip to the nearby mill in St. Croix proved uneventful. Even with the danger of rutted roads from the wet weather, the Chandler's sturdy cart and sure-footed horses made good time. And if anyone recognized Beau from a public notice, there was no evidence of suspicion. Indeed, one of the men assumed he was a relation of Daniel's, and Beau decided to allow that impression to remain. Better to be known as a distant cousin of a local farmer than an absent landowner who also happened to be wanted for the murder of his father. For her part, Miss Murray watched from her perch in the carriage, studying every face with the same appraising look he'd imagined a lioness might give to any intruders threatening her brood.

"We should take the opportunity to check the telegraph office," Beau said, after the wood was loaded. "We already have the horses out, and it would spare us the extra trip. The messages are all going to be addressed to the Chandlers, so no one would be the wiser. Would it be worth the risk, do you think? After all, we might get good news, and you can be back to Everwell sooner."

Miss Murray blinked, staring at Beau as if he had sprouted an extra head, neither of which contained a lick of sense.

"It's too risky," she said, looking between Daniel and Beau. "If you get spotted in his wagon, they may not come for you in the middle of town, but they'll know exactly where to find you. And if they're motivated enough to come looking for you, they might not give a care who gets in their way."

Damn this woman and her good sense. Beau glanced over at Daniel. The very last thing he wanted to do is bring the Chandlers into his mess any more than was necessary.

"What if I ask about a canvas tarp?" Daniel offered. "I saw a few lying around the mill. They might be willing to part with one, and you could settle underneath it. Between that and the lumber, no one should think twice about it."

"Are you certain?" Beau asked.

Daniel pursed his lips slightly and shrugged. "I think it would work."

Both men looked to Miss Murray, who crossed her arms and surveyed the wagon.

"Let's give it a try."

Daniel went to the mill foreman and returned with large piece of canvas, and tossed it on the back of the wagon. Beau climbed up the back, scrambling over the lumber, taking the tarp with him. Even with the wide brim of her straw hat shading her face, there was a tension cutting across her brow that Beau felt determined to dislodge. He wanted to believe she was truly concerned for his wellbeing beyond the mere transactional nature of their relationship.

They made their way into town. Since the rail lines had been laid down, the coaches from Halifax had almost entirely disappeared, passengers choosing the faster, more comfortable journey to Windsor by train. As they approached, Beau sat down on the bed of the wagon between the stacks of lumber and prepared to pull the tarp over himself, when to his surprise, Miss Murray settled beside him, then helped him pull the canvas over them. The warm-sweet smell of the linseed-treated canvas filled his nose and with the sun overhead, cast a dark orangey glow over them. Crowded under the tarp, they were forced to sit next to each other, Miss Murray's arm and hip pressed into his, the fullness of her skirts spilling over onto his trousers. The weight of them felt strangely comforting.

The rumble of the cartwheels and the steady clopping of horses came to a stop.

"We're here," Daniel said. "I won't be long."

Neither of them dared speak, even to whisper. While there was little chance they would be heard over the general noise of the busy town streets, it was not zero. Miss Murray sat next to him, her posture as stiff as a coiled spring.

Time stretched as they waited. Between the two of them, and the heat of the afternoon sun, it was growing uncomfortably warm under the tarp. Beau started bouncing his knee as he began to grow impatient. It was an old habit that he'd mostly rid himself of—an unfortunate tell, Frank used to say, that could let competitors know he was nervous.

Before a memory of Frank berating him for that habit had fully formed, a firm hand landed on his knee. Madeline Murray fixed him with a stare, her lips forming the most perfect 'no', without breathing a word.

"Master Chandler," came a voice nearby. Very nearby. "Is your father about?"

Beau stilled and Miss Murray, who'd turned to silently admonish him, was still looking in his direction, not daring to move.

"He's just gone to the telegraph office," Teddy answered, with the detached politeness of a young boy answering an adult.

"I have a letter for him and seeing you here saves me the

penny to mail it," the voice said. Beau strained to recognize it, because he had heard it before. "See that he gets it, will you?"

"Yes sir," Teddy answered.

"Mr. Taylor." Daniel's voice entered the conversation. Like his son, Daniel was polite, but the warmth Beau had become accustomed to was notably absent. "Can I help you?"

Mr. Taylor. Nelson Taylor. Beau recognized the voice.

"Just saving myself the postage to send you a letter," Mr. Taylor said, his voice laced with that brightness that Beau himself had employed when he was trying to disarm someone he wished to make a deal with. "I haven't heard from you since we spoke a few weeks ago. I wanted to ensure it was in writing, to let you know it is a serious offer."

"I appreciate that," Daniel said. The cart lurched slightly. Daniel must have hopped into the driver's seat.

"Doing some work around the property I see," Mr. Taylor continued.

Mr. Taylor was only a few feet from where Beau and Miss Murray were hiding. So close, Beau was certain that if he breathed, it would be noticed. It was hot under the canvas now, and beads of sweat ran down the side of his face. It was all he could do not to scratch his nose. For her part, Miss Murray's hand was still on his leg, but her grip had tightened, digging into him as if she was holding on for dear life. Save for her stillness, she gave no sign of fear, or panic. But there was something about that stillness that prompted an unexpected flare of emotion—that same anger that had caused him to lash out at this same Mr. Taylor, who'd insulted Miss Murray when they first arrived.

Without thinking, he laid his hands on hers. She did not pull away.

"There's always work to be done," Daniel said, with the same polite tone as his son. "I should be getting on now."

"Of course," Mr. Taylor said. "I hope we'll be in touch."

To Beau's relief, the horses started moving, and the cart heaved forward again. He and Miss Murray stayed still, under the thick protection of the tarp. They stayed as they were until Daniel called out.

"It should be safe now," he said. "You can pull that off your heads."

Beau didn't need another invitation. With his free hand he pulled the tarp off, squinting from the sudden brightness. Miss Murray pulled her hand away, wiping the errant strands of hair that stuck to her face from the heat. Her expression was equal points relief and indignation.

"Never again. Do you hear me?" she said under her breath. "You do not move from The Grove until I get a letter from Dominic or Everwell telling me they have arrested someone else. You may get to run that empire of yours when this is over, but you will never get to do that if you can't listen to me."

The fierceness of her tone that left Beau fighting his instincts reply with a joke or some rapier sharp comment to deflect her criticism. But her panic, laced through those harsh words, deterred him.

"Was that who I think it was?" Beau ask, awkwardly turning himself toward Daniel.

Daniel gave a quick nod. "The very same."

Beau sucked in a quick breath. Nelson Taylor, the man he'd been corresponding with since his decision to sell The Grove. The man who'd insulted Madeline Murray.

"What does he want with you?" he asked, even though it wasn't his business. He shouldn't feel obligated to the Chandlers —a week ago he hadn't even known they existed. But given everything they'd done for him of late, never mind the years spent keeping an eye on the otherwise abandoned property for his aunt, he felt a sense of responsibility for bringing a man like Nelson Taylor into their sphere. And while he really didn't know the man, Beau had learned everything he needed to about his character the day he so casually stomped on Madeline Murray's dignity.

Beau's answer was silence, and he wondered if Daniel had

heard. He was about to ask the question a second time when Teddy reached down and put two envelopes in his hand.

"You're a popular man," Daniel called out, "and not in a way I think you want to be. Your face was all over that office. If I hear one more off-hand comment about me being a long-lost relation of a murderer, they might see my face on a poster."

Miss Murray had commented early upon their arrival that the two men bore a resemblance, but neither of them saw it. Beau looked up at Teddy.

"Do you think we look alike?"

Teddy shrugged in that way young people did when they didn't want to get involved in adult conversations. "You don't look that different."

Beau was about to turn his attention to the telegrams, which had been addressed to Daniel to aid in their subterfuge, but Miss Murray had already snatched them from his hand. Without ceremony she'd ripped open the one from Dominic Ashe. Even before he had the chance to ask, he heard the sigh of disappointment rush from her lips. Without looking at him, she handed it over.

The message was short and written in an agreed upon code that, to the uninformed, read more like a farm report than a murder investigation. It took a moment for Beau to decode it, but the meaning was clear: he was still a wanted man. There was a request for information on a few members of the board, as well as his sister and brother-in-law.

While the news was frustrating, it was unexpectedly tempered by his need to remain at The Grove. While he'd been utterly entranced with Miss Murray from the moment he'd laid eyes on her, the attraction had been physical. Over the past days, an undeniable tension wound between them. And while Beau wasn't entirely certain the attraction was mutual, he'd caught the way she'd looked at him when she believed his attention was elsewhere.

But beyond his body's desire for hers, something else had started to become evident. He liked spending time with her. She had a quick mind, a fierce sense of the world, and a romantic soul that intrigued him. And he found himself not yet ready to let that go.

It was selfish, he realized, but selfishness came as naturally to Beau as negotiating a troublesome business deal. For her part, Madeline Murray looked straight ahead, watching the trees rush by, her thoughts gone to a place Beau knew he could not reach. No doubt she was back in Everwell, with her friends and her garden. A place she loved.

And Christ, how he envied that. He could buy Everwell a hundred times over, but he couldn't have what she had. No wonder she wanted to go. No wonder he didn't. And wherever he eventually landed, he would be without her.

Because he would have to go. There was nothing about his life —not the money, the glittering parties, or even the travel to even bigger places with more money and more parties—she would find irresistible. There was only him, and he was certain he wasn't enough. He had never been enough.

He tucked Dominic's note away along with tangle of emotion it had brought, and turned his attention to the second. It was from Archie. A second offer had come from the board of George's College, with a plea for urgency in the decision.

The fact the offer had gone to Halifax gave Beau some assurance. If the Board of Governors knew about the charges against Beau, which they must have by now, they were not particularly bothered by them, and they had no idea he was close by. Clearly, they were eager to buy, sweetening the pot by increasing the asking price by five percent. If that offer had come even the morning he'd arrived in Halifax, he would have signed it without hesitation. But everything had changed.

Had Daniel Chandler received a similar offer, Beau wondered? Was that the root of the conversation Mr. Taylor had with Daniel? The Chandler property bordered the same river, and while it was perhaps more visible from the road, was still graced by beautiful rolling hills and beautiful forests. Unease pricked on the edges of his thoughts.

Beau shoved the note back in the envelope, tucking in into his jacket pocket. Until Dominic uncovered the real killer—or at least proved beyond a shadow of a doubt Beau's innocence—there was no hurry to sell the property or deal with Nelson Taylor.

It was nearly suppertime when they returned to the farm, and Beau's shoulders sagged with relief as the cart turned up the secret road, snaking its way through the old forest. His chest rose with anticipation as the trees gave way to the view of the little stone house at the top of the hill. The cart slowed, the horses pulling a much heavier load, the clacking of the cartwheels drawing the attention of Annie. A second figure Beau didn't recognize appeared in the door.

"Grampa!" Teddy yelled, waving at the man who took off his hat and waved it at the cart. "He's back early."

The cart came to a stop at last. Beau's back and legs were cramped from the way he'd been sitting for the better part of the afternoon. Madeline Murray, however, was already on her feet, towering over him, her hand outstretched.

"If you're going to toss me out of the wagon, I know I deserve it," he said.

She looked down at him, one brow carefully arched. "If I break your neck, I won't get my greenhouse."

"Good to know my worth." He took her hand and she helped pull him to his feet. He held onto her hand before she could try to let go of his grip.

"I'm sorry. I've done plenty of stupid things in my life," he said, "but rarely thoughtless ones. It came from a misplaced desire to save some effort, and perhaps a delusion that this is one situation I cannot talk myself out of."

She looked him up and down, taking the measure of him. When she nodded her acceptance, he blew out the breath he'd been holding.

She turned away and allowed Daniel to help her out of the

wagon before Beau jumped down himself. Daniel was waving him over to the house.

"Come meet my father," Daniel said, then turned to the man standing beside Annie.

Beau approached, catching the elder Chandler's attention. He gave Beau the same appraising look that Annie had.

"You must be Emily's young fella," he said. "Hollis Chandler."

Hollis Chandler was similar in build to Daniel, and at least twenty years his senior. His hair was grey, trimmed short, and his chin was covered with a tidy beard.

Beau took his hand and gave it a hearty shake, all the while trying to dispel this curious feeling of connection he had with a man he'd only just met. He wanted to brush it off as a long-standing familiarity with his mother, but it felt even deeper than that.

"It's been a while since anyone called me young," Beau said at last. "Beau da Silva."

After what felt like a prolonged moment, the two men released their handshake.

"I was sorry to hear about your mother's passing," Hollis said, and there was a heaviness of real grief that crossed the elder Chandler's brow as he spoke. "I knew her, when she was younger. Lovely girl."

"Daniel said that you helped out here when you were younger," Beau said. "I'd love to know more about that. About my grandparents, too."

Hollis nodded, and it seemed to Beau he was taking a long time to speak. In his enthusiasm, Beau wondered if he'd asked too much of him.

"Happy to," he said at last, his voice almost rough.

"We didn't expect to see you back until Friday," Daniel said. "How's Jeannie?"

Hollis cleared his throat.

"Your girl's doing just fine," he said. "I was getting a bit homesick. Especially for this young fella here," he continued, beaming as Teddy ran to him with a great bear hug that was lovingly returned. A pang of envy at the easy way of father, son, and grandson skittered across Beau's insides. Frank da Silva had never been a particularly affectionate man, and Beau could hardly remember a time when his father had held his hand, never mind enveloping him in a hug. He'd viewed such affection as a sign of weakness. By the time he was Teddy's age, a smile from Frank da Silva was the most he could hope for.

Soon the timbers were out of the cart in a tidy pile beside the fallen pergola and the Chandlers, including Hollis, had departed, disappearing out of sight down the winding wooded path. As they left, Beau found himself watching the Chandlers leave, as if there was something there, right in front of him, that he couldn't see.

Chapter Thirteen

MADDY LAID out a simple supper while Mr. da Silva washed up. She was still rattled by the events of the afternoon. Hearing Nelson's voice had nearly paralyzed her with a terror she'd thought she'd outrun. It wasn't until the cart had pulled away that she'd even noticed Mr. da Silva's hand on hers. But it had managed to comfort her in a way she hadn't expected. She'd still been furious at him, a byproduct of her own fears that she dare not share. His apology was surprising yet heartfelt. Still, the biggest surprise of the day had come when she'd been introduced to Daniel's father, Hollis.

If she'd brushed off the idea that Daniel Chandler and Beau da Silva seemed to have the same smile, she could not so easily dismiss the fact that Mr. da Silva and Hollis Chandler not only had the same smile, but the same eyes. No wonder Annie Chandler had been taking the measure of Mr. da Silva the moment she'd laid eyes on him.

She had a thousand questions... and most she was afraid to ask. Beau da Silva was none of her business—except for their official business, of course. There seemed little time to waste in answering Dominic's questions about his brother-in-law and other senior members of the Silver Lumber Company, but after meeting the elder Mr. Chandler, that urgency had been swept aside, replaced by more pressing questions.

"You've created a feast," Mr. da Silva said, standing at the door and wearing a fresh shirt and vest. His hair was swept haphazardly back, as if he'd just run his fingers through it. "I'm starving. Thank you."

"We can thank Annie," she said as they sat down to a feast of cold chicken, fresh potatoes, and tender new peas.

He loaded up a plate for her and a second one for himself while Maddy poured two glasses of raspberry shrub. Quiet descended, as if both of them understood that starting a conversation might lead down several rather uncomfortable paths.

"I guess you are stuck with me for a little while longer," he began. Maddy couldn't help but notice that Mr. da Silva's normal humour had left him. Indeed, he sounded almost apologetic.

"I guess I am," she said, then took a drink of the bright red shrub, sneaking a look at him from over the rim of her cup. His brightness had dimmed, and she felt strangely compelled to try to bring some of it back. She would miss her birthday, which was in three days. But that meant she had to stay here, in this magical stone cottage with a kitchen garden ready to be brought back to life. That alone would be a consolation. And then there was Mr. da Silva. "But Mr. Chandler—Hollis that is—mentioned to me there is a berry patch, down past the barn. That might be something to occupy me."

His lips finally edged up into a bit of a smile, which, given how angry she'd been in the wagon this afternoon, shouldn't have made her as happy as it did.

"I'm glad you're not disappointed," he said, and the way he looked at her, he seemed to mean it. Beau da Silva seemed to mean everything he said—at least when it came to her.

"Are you?" she asked.

"I'll be happy not to have my character questioned," he said, digging his fork into the heaping pile of boiled new potatoes. "And the threat of hanging gone. But there are far worse ways to spend my time." He smiled but there was a cloud behind his eyes. "Dominic wants to know about Jessica and Neil."

"Perhaps that can wait until tomorrow," she replied, surprising herself. "I think we can both agree today has been full of twists and turns."

"More than a few," he said, giving his head a shake. He sat back in his chair and settled his fork on his plate. "On the other hand, one decision was made for me today."

"What is that?" Maddy asked.

"The offer from George's College," he replied. "I'm not going to sell. At least not through Taylor."

"You're not?" she blurted out, inwardly wincing the eagerness. Whether or not he sold The Grove had nothing to do with her. But she was inexplicably happy at his decision.

He shook his head, then picked up his fork again. "I wonder if he—Taylor that is—is pressuring the Chandlers to sell their farm," he said. "I'm worried that if I sell, it would put extra pressure on the Chandlers. Another reason not to have that Taylor fellow profit from this place."

Maddy's stomach clenched at the mention of Nelson Taylor. It drove away her appetite, and she found herself picking at her food.

"Why would you be worried about the Chandlers?" she asked. "You've told me more than once you're a selfish man."

"I have," he said, scooping another forkful of supper into his mouth. If Maddy didn't know better, she'd have guessed he was trying to avoid the conversation.

"Except you're not."

He looked at her as if she'd suddenly declared it to be winter and that pigs were flying by. He paused, grabbing his glass and taking a sip of his drink.

"Don't look at me like that," she continued. "You are many things, Beau da Silva, but you are not selfish."

He set down the glass and sat back in his chair, his brow carefully arched. "And what things am I?"

"You're rich," she said, holding up a finger as she prepared to count his attributes one by one.

"Undeniably," he shrugged, his lips turning up in a smug grin.

Maddy lifted another finger. "And cocksure."

"Of course."

"But you're also hardworking," she said, "And you are concerned about others."

"I thought you were going to tell me I'm handsome," he said, gesturing toward her hand. "That would make a perfect five."

"Did you recall my comment about being cocksure?" she said, hiding her smile behind a long sip of her shrub.

"I don't want the Chandlers to lose their property," he said.

"They aren't your concern," she said. "Or they weren't until now. What's changed?"

"They are good people," he said, suddenly fixated on pushing the peas around on his plate. "And I don't need this property. They need their farm."

They continued eating in a comfortable silence. She'd pushed enough.

"Hollis Chandler seems like a nice man," he said, just when Maddy thought the conversation had come to an end.

"He does," she said. "He probably knows this property better than anyone."

"He knew my mother," Mr. da Silva said, almost abruptly, as if his thoughts were forming as he spoke. "He had the same dreamy look about him when he spoke about her that Frank used to. Frank called her his Helen of Troy. A face that would launch a thousand ships." He gave his head a little shake, as he found a bit of humour in a memory. "If anyone could turn Frank da Silva into a romantic fool, it was my mother, apparently. Maybe Hollis Chandler was the same."

Beau da Silva could turn her into a romantic fool, Maddy thought. Was he a Willoughby, or a Colonel Brandon? At one time she would have written him off as the first. But she was no longer a romantic fool.

Romantic fool.

The memory of that scrap of a poem she'd found in her room rushed back.

Then live with me and be my love.

H. C.

Almost on impulse, Maddy rose. "I have something to show you. And before you say anything, I know I shouldn't be doing this because it's none of my business."

She rose and ran upstairs, returning with a piece of paper.

"I found this the other day, and I set it aside. I didn't know what it was at the time. But I think—I think Hollis wrote this to your mother."

Gently, she unfolded the paper, brittle with age, and placed it in front of Beau.

The Shepherds' Swains shall dance and sing
For thy delight each May-morning:
If these delights thy mind may move,
Then live with me, and be my love.
- H. C.

Beau as he seemed to retreat into himself as he stared at the page. It was so unlike him that it she wondered if showing him that note was the right thing to do. She was here to protect him, after all.

She fought the urge to wrap him in a comforting embrace and absorb some of the confusion he was feeling. To protect him. But protecting him from the truth seemed like cruelty.

Instead, she took her seat and returned the simple gesture he'd offered her this afternoon.

"Beau?" she said at last, lightly placing her hand on his. She didn't know if he would rebuff the gesture, but he did not stiffen at her touch.

At last he looked up at her, and she caught the now-familiar look of self-deprecation. She expected some kind of joke, a deflection from whatever storm he was trying to calm. Instead, he grabbed onto her hand, holding it as if he were holding onto the gunwale of a boat to keep himself from falling overboard. She should have been self-conscious about her hands, which were rough from days of cleaning and gardening. But he didn't seem to mind. And she didn't mind the way a river of warmth ran down her spine to her core.

"You called me by name," he said. "You must really be feeling sorry for me."

She shrugged, resisting the urge to reach up and smooth the lines of worry from his brow.

"It's short and I'm not a woman of many words. Why use four syllables when one will do?"

Beau stared as he held the delicate piece of paper with his fingers. Hollis Chandler hadn't just known Emily Redden.

He'd loved her.

A thousand uncomfortable thoughts prickled under his skin. The odd way Annie had greeted him when they'd first arrived. The foreman who had mistaken Beau for Daniel's relation. The haunting sense of knowing Beau had experienced when he'd shaken Hollis's hand. The curious answer Annie had given him when he protested his innocence in killing Frank da Silva.

I didn't kill my father.

No, I don't think you did.

In a moment, that knowing rushed at him like a train, slamming into chest, forcing him to lower the paper to the table. Annie was right. Even if he had pulled the trigger at Frank da Silva, Beau couldn't have killed his father.

His father was alive, and living next door.

A gentle breeze wafted in the room, picking up the delicate lace curtains they'd found packed away in the attic a few days ago. It brought with it the sweet smell of the meadow and wild-flowers and carried away the haggard breath he'd let go.

"Why don't I wash up," she said softly, "and then we'll go for a nice walk. It might help."

They sat there, Beau holding onto her, idly running his thumb over her knuckles.

"How about we both wash up," he said, letting go of her hand, which brought a pang of something like absence, which was ridiculous because she was still right there beside him. "And then maybe we can go find this berry patch."

After the dishes were done, the two stepped out into a beautiful summer evening. The sun was still bright, but shadows started to stretch across the landscape. They walked in amicable silence for a while, the sound of crickets filling the air, Miss Murray's presence the only balm for the torrent of Beau's unsettled emotion.

"Are you going to talk to him?" she asked at last.

Him. There was no need for more. There was only one person on his mind.

"I don't even know what I'd say," he said, letting out a bitter laugh. "I've rarely been at a loss for words."

"I saw the way he looked at you," she replied. "I think he knows. Or perhaps he wonders, at the very least."

Beau shook his head. "I don't know much about how my parents met, but I do know my mother had gone to Halifax to visit Aunt Veronica, met Frank, and they were married shortly after."

"Do you think your—" Miss Murray paused, clearly looking for the right word.

"Frank?" Beau answered, sparing her the trouble. "I think so. I think he always knew. I mean, it all sort of makes sense."

"What do you mean?"

"I never seemed to be enough for him," he said. "Don't get me wrong, he never laid a hand on me. Not in anger. But not in love, either. Especially not after my mother passed. I gave up trying get any real affection from the man..."

"Is that why you call him by his given name?" she asked.

Beau shrugged. "I called him Father when I was younger, but as I grew up it just didn't seem to fit our relationship. He didn't seem to mind. Maybe we both knew somehow that it was the right thing."

"Do you miss him?"

He shrugged, then dragged his hands through his hair. "You know the crazy thing is, I sort of do. He was a bastard, but he taught me a lot about the business. He expected me to take it over. Even if he did know, he never begrudged me that. And I know the man well enough to know he didn't give a hot damn about appearances. He would have cut me out of the will entirely if he didn't think I'd earned it."

"If he gave you his entire company, I have to say you earned it," she said, giving him a smile that was somehow kind without being condescending. "And maybe he loved you in his own way."

"For a woman of few words, you seem to pick all the right ones," he said. "Thank you."

"I read a lot of words," she said. "I am the school's librarian after all."

Her lips turned up in a smile that Beau couldn't help but return. Every time she graced him with a bit of humour, he felt like he'd discovered something precious about her.

Serenaded by the chirping of crickets and the trilling of sparrows, they paused at a small bench just outside a small, fenced area that housed the berry patch, surrounded by the stillness that Beau had spent his adult life running from. It had been part of the reason he'd decided to sell The Grove. Sitting with the quiet only served to remind him how alone he'd been. He wasn't miraculously cured of that, but still, it was much more tolerable with Madeline Murray beside him. And through the cow path was a man who was quite possibly his father. A man who had tended a berry patch his grandparents created for years, perhaps out of some kind of devotion to them, or the woman he'd once loved.

Beau wanted to laugh at the irony. Here he was, the scion of a family who'd built a fortune cutting down forests, standing amongst the labour of a man who seemed to take genuine joy from teasing more berries from the soil.

"I have no idea how to feel," he said at last.

"Your world has just been turned upside down," she said. "You get to feel however you want."

There was a certainty in her words he found both comforting and intriguing. Of course, Madeline Murray wasn't a young child. She was a woman who'd no doubt had her fair share of experience with the world, both good and bad.

"I feel like I want to get drunk," he said.

"You never know with Tilda. She might have packed a bottle of whisky in case of emergencies," she said, then brightened. "Of course, Daniel and Hollis will be here first thing, so you might want to treat it like a minor emergency."

Daniel. Beau had spent the entire day with his brother. And his nephew. Christ, he was going to swoon and it had nothing to do with the way a lock of Madeline's hair kissed the curve of her neck. He wanted to reach out and take her hand, pull her close, and feel the lush curves of her body against his. The last time he'd come close to kissing her, she'd pulled away.

"I really need that drink," he said.

"Do you know what might be better than whisky?"

Was this some trick question? Beau knew perfectly well what was better than whisky for pushing aside a host of inconvenient feelings, and it largely involved him worshipping Madeline Murray's body and losing himself in what he was certain were the most perfect of breasts.

Of course, he knew better than to suggest it. And clearly whatever she had on her mind wasn't sex.

"I have not spent enough time with women to learn the trick of reading their minds," he said. "You'll have to help me."

"I suspect you've spent plenty of time with many women," she said with a stiffness that he hoped might be a carefully contrived mask for something close to envy. "Come with me."

She led him to the barn, taking a moment to strike a match and light one of the lanterns hanging up inside. Until he'd arrived here, he hadn't spent much time in barns, but this had clearly been well taken care of, smelling like old timbers and fresh hay. It was big enough to shelter a few large animals, and no doubt the Chandlers had used it over the years to store extra equipment.

She hung the lantern on a nail overhead, and Beau noticed a large canvas sack stuffed full of straw, hanging from a chain in the ceiling.

"Is this what I think it is?" he asked, poking at the makeshift punching bag. He'd seen plenty of these—some in posh gentleman's gyms, and others in dark corners where bare-knuckled men beat themselves silly for the betting spoils of the audience, rich and poor.

"It's not quite the real thing," she said, running her hands over the rough fabric, the surface jagged from the edges of straw trying to poke through. "But it will do in a pinch."

He was tempted to walk away and return to the house in search of the whisky that he hoped to hell would somehow be hiding in a corner. But there was a glint in her eye—an invitation—that made him want to appease her.

He curled his fingers into a fist and threw a halfhearted punch at the makeshift punching bag. It barely moved.

"It's a good thing I'm here," she said. "If anyone was determined to grab you, you wouldn't stand a chance."

"I don't want to hit it so hard I'll throw you off your feet," he challenged. It had been years, but he used to box. He knew his way around a ring. And then he remembered Madeline Murray had come with him because she was supposed to handle any threats of physical violence coming Beau's way. He remembered the knives. The books on martial arts. And her off-hand remark about having to ensure the safety of the women at Everwell from anyone who presented a threat.

Her lips turned up into a daring smile. "You won't."

He obliged her, this time with a right upper cut and a left hook. The bag moved haphazardly, like his form.

"Again," she repeated. "And don't worry about your form so much. This isn't a boxing ring. The opponent is inside you. Just let it out."

Beau focused on punching the bag. With each strike, he imagined the life he'd known. The man who'd raised him, now dead. The family next door who might very well be his. How everything he understood about himself might no longer be true. After endless strikes at the bag, he paused, his breath heavy, his heart pounding.

"Frank loved Neil—my brother-in-law," Beau said between ragged breaths. If there was little Beau could do right in Frank's eyes, there seemed to be nothing Neil could do wrong.

"But he didn't raise Neil," she said, throwing him a linen towel to wipe the sweat from his brow. "And he didn't will him control of the company, did he?"

Beau mused on that. It was always assumed that Beau would take ownership of the company but Neil's keen business sense and his gift for numbers, as well as his devotion to Beau's sister, all but secured him a key position at Silver Lumber. Beau had always assumed that Frank gave the company to Beau because he was his son.

But he might have assumed wrong.

"Did Neil suspect, do you think?"

"Do you mean about me not being Frank's son?" Beau shook his head. "I don't think so."

"But you're not sure," she prodded. "Could there have been rumours? You said he and Frank were close. Would he have ever betrayed that in confidence?"

Beau blinked, stunned by the implication she was making. He couldn't imagine Frank betraying that fact to anyone. But that didn't mean Neil couldn't have had his suspicions.

"If they were as close as you say, maybe he discovered the truth," she said. "Just because people are your relations doesn't make them naturally better or more inclined to love you," she said. "Sometimes they can be the ones who will hurt you most."

There was something—a subtle little catch in her voice. And maybe he misheard it, his own tattered emotion billowing like a ripped sail in a stiff wind. But it caught his attention. He turned to her, her red hair being gently tugged this way and that by the sweet evening breeze, the sun, starting it's slow descent, lighting up her face and heightening the fiery glow of her hair. She seemed at once strong, yet brittle. Like she was speaking from behind the dull ache of an old wound. The idea that anyone might have hurt Madeline Murray tightened something primal in his chest. His mind went immediately to Nelson Taylor who'd insulted her that day on the platform. The people he'd been so eager to sell this place to. The people who just offered him even more money than he'd originally asked.

And the people who would no doubt make an unequally ungenerous offer to the Chandlers.

And how did he know that?

Because he might have done the same thing. It made good business sense. Making money was what a da Silva did.

But he wasn't sure he was a da Silva anymore.

Beau raked a hand through his hair. Neil had the ear of the upper levels of Silver Lumber. He could have very easily convinced them to put the price on Beau's head if it was the company he wanted. Through Jessica, he'd have it if Beau was out of the way. And Neil knew about Beau's pistol. They'd been together when he bought it.

"I want to be wrong about this," he said. "For my sister's sake, if nothing else."

"Maybe you are, but we need to get this information to Dominic," she said. "It will give him something to go on."

"It will kill Jess if he's guilty," he said.

"Your sister is probably stronger than you think," she said, looking in him the eye with a flash of defiance. "She's lost her father. She doesn't need to lose her brother, too."

Chapter Fourteen

THE NEXT MORNING, Beau was cutting through the thick tangle of grape vines that had claimed the old pergola. Pulling the old one down and rebuilding it promised to be a full day's work, and Madeline had already been up early, making coffee, baking, and creating a small feast to fuel the work.

He should have been exhausted after a sleepless night, but as the first light of dawn caught the treetops, he was dressed and out the door. There was too much on his mind, and the only way to push through it was to move. By the time the low rumble of cartwheels and the gentle clinking of harnesses caught his attention, he already had most of the grapevines pulled away.

"Good morning!" Daniel called out as he and the rest of the family came into view, the now-familiar cart trundling up the road.

The Chandlers. His father, mostly likely. And his brother.

Beau waved back, aware that the simple act of being relaxed, that had come to him so naturally yesterday, took far more effort today.

"You're going to be fine." Madeline's calm voice broke through his nerves. She'd just stepped out the back door, smoothing her apron as she approached. "This is supposed to feel awkward."

"I feel like you're a nurse, preparing me for something painful."

"As Tilda would say, I think you'll feel a little something. It won't necessarily be comfortable, but it's not really painful. And you'll be much better afterwards."

Her reassurance buoyed him, but not even the warmth in her smile could do much to alleviate the twists in his gut. Only yesterday, he'd known who he was. A da Silva. The wealthy son of a proud, thunderous, mighty titan of industry. He made money, and he was good at it.

As the wagon drew near, and he saw Daniel's face with Hollis beside him, that certainty slipped away.

A moment later, the Chandlers disembarked and began unloading the tools. Beau couldn't help but feel every glance in his direction. It would drive him crazy if he couldn't get this out into the open. But he would do it privately first, with Hollis.

"Why don't you take the horses to the barn?" Madeline asked him. "There're sitting empty. Perhaps Mr. Chandler can help."

Beau wanted to roll his eyes. She really wasn't one for subtlety, was she?

"Perfect," Daniel said, displaying no hint of awkwardness or even awareness of the tension running through Beau. "Dad, do you mind? Teddy and I can set up the sawhorses and we can get to work."

Hollis shook his head and gave Beau a warm, if tentative glance. It occurred to Beau that it was entirely possible the note he found between Emily Redden and Hollis Chandler was nothing more than a youthful romance, and that every time Hollis looked at Beau, he saw her. But Beau had eyes, and every time he looked at Hollis, he saw a little bit of himself.

Or was he imagining that, too?

"I suppose you know the barn better than I do," Beau said, as he hopped back into the cart while Hollis took the reins. He'd never been a man who found conversation hard to come by, even in the most tense of business negotiations. But this was something else, and he felt woefully unprepared.

Hollis gave the reins a gentle flick, and the horses started a leisurely walk to the barn.

"I spent a lot of time here, helping sweep out that barn," he said, then pointed to a patch in the roof that looked darker than the shingles around it. "Damn near killed myself slipping off that roof trying to patch it. If it wasn't for your mother, I probably wouldn't be here now."

The sudden and casual mention of his mother made Beau's stomach lurch, even as the horses came to a stop. They hopped down and started unhitching the two Canadian horses from the cart.

"You knew my mother really well," Beau asked.

Hollis' eyes lit up with a gentle fire.

"Yes," he said. "But I think you know that, don't you?"

"I didn't really know it until yesterday," Beau replied, then pulled the letter from the old recipe book out of his pocket and held it up. "Though I think Annie knew from almost the moment she saw me."

The older man's eyes softened as he laid eyes on the note, and Beau held it out to him. Hollis's hands, which were still strong, shook just a little as he reached for the folded paper.

"We found this in the cottage," he said. "I assume you are H.C."

A strained smile tightened Hollis's jaw as he read over the yellowed page. He blew out a low breath, as if trying to steady his emotions, before folding it up and giving it back to him.

"I didn't know she'd even kept that," he said. "Of course, I suppose she didn't, if you found it here."

A fresh hurt seemed to cut across his face, and it occurred to Beau that whatever memories this man had of Beau's mother, they were wrapped up in a fresh wave of emotion that wasn't necessarily pleasant.

"Emily was a real firecracker," Hollis said. "Smart. Hot

headed. But I loved that about her. I thought she could run the world if she had the chance. You must have missed her, when she passed."

"I was eight," Beau replied, his mind going back to the horrible night the pneumonia took her. "I missed her very much. I remember her being a very vibrant woman."

"That she was. This place was far too quiet for a girl like her. She wanted to outshine the sun if she could."

"When did you last see her?"

"Not too long after I sent that note," he said. "We were in love —or at least in that way young people sometimes think they are. I offered to marry her, you know, after—" He blushed. "But she never wanted to. I don't know if she knew at the time you were inside her."

"Did you?"

"Not right away, no," he replied. "Her parents took the family to the city, Emily and her sister. She met your father there."

"But not my father."

Hollis shook his head. "I suppose not. According to your grandparents, he swept her off her feet and offered to marry her on the spot. And she said yes."

"That must have hurt."

"It did," he said. "For a while, at least. Your mother and I probably wouldn't have suited each other. And living here would have killed her—or killed what made her special."

"She was very special," Beau agreed. "If you ever get to meet my sister Jessica, you'll see a lot of my mother in her. Fiery. Smart as hell."

"I'd like that, I think." He smiled, then looked Beau up and down. "But you turned out mighty fine. I hope Mr. da Silva raised you well?"

The question caught Beau off guard, and he wasn't sure how to answer it. Beau had wanted for nothing—food, clothes, shelter, schooling—he had the finest of all of it. But looking back now, he wondered if Frank knew—if not about Hollis, then at least about the his mother's pregnancy. After all, if they married not long after meeting, Beau would have been born two months early weighing a strapping eight pounds.

"He did," Beau said at last. Frank had never been loving. He'd been demanding as hell. But he'd never laid a hand on him. "Frank da Silva wasn't the easiest man to be around. But he let me try to prove myself to him, and he must have trusted me enough to leave the business to me."

"Well, I am sorry to hear about what happened to him," Hollis said. "But I am happy to see you and know you're well. I had always wondered about you. I read in the papers about you from time to time. But I was never sure you were mine until I saw your picture in the paper not that long ago."

"That must have been a shock," Beau said.

"It was on both accounts," he said. "But I knew you couldn't have done it."

"Thank you," Beau answered, struck by that conviction, that faith which could have easily been misguided. "I don't know why, but that means a lot to me."

"You're my son," he said, his voice wavering a little. "I've always had faith in you."

Hollis's statement rippled through Beau, nearly forcing him backward. In all the years he'd been with Frank, all the effort, the endless search for his approval, had he ever felt as if he'd truly earned it. And yet here was Hollis—a man Beau never knew— who believed in him simply because he wanted to.

Beau smiled, swallowing the lump of emotion in his throat.

"Did my grandparents know?"

Hollis shook his head. "I never betrayed your mother's confidence. It's hard for a woman, of course. I would have married her, and at the time I would have believed me the right person to be her husband, but I would have been mistaken. In the end, we found the people we needed. A few years later I met a nice girl— Shirley Oickle, Daniel's mother. She's passed, God rest her soul, but we had a good life together."

Beau considered that. He never recalled his parents being unhappy. Frank had doted on his mother. She was the only person whose will he bent to, and he did it willingly. Beau didn't remember any unhappiness. Any fights. The darkness came for Frank, and possibly for Beau, after she was gone.

"What about Daniel?" he asked, after he had time to compose himself. Beau recalled the jokes at the mill, and the curious look on his face when he went to the post office. Daniel may not have noticed the likeness, but it had not escaped others. After seeing them all together, he might have put it all together.

"I think he suspects something," Hollis confirmed. "I'll talk with him tonight, but I wanted to speak with you first."

With the horses stabled, the men walked back toward the house, the conversation turning to much more mundane matters, such as how long ago the grapevines had been planted, and the excellent homemade wine Hollis's wife had made. As they approached the house, the others were already busy, preparing for the work ahead. All the while, he sensed Madeline watching him. Watching out for him.

While the men cut the timbers, Madeline and Annie collected the grapes that couldn't be left to ripen.

None of this should have mattered. He'd intended to sell the property, and what George's College did with the grapes, the vines, or even the old pergola wouldn't have mattered. But every day he was here, Beau saw something: possibility. It was something that seemed to come naturally to Madeline, who spent every minute she could bringing the kitchen garden back to life.

One might argue she was having the same effect on him.

After the work on the pergola had begun in earnest, Maddy and Annie took their reclaimed grapes into the kitchen. Maddy had never worked with grapes before, and she was eager to explore what was possible with them. She showed Annie the Reddens'

book, and they laughed in mutual fascination at the suggestion that rooting mustard seeds in hot horse manure could produce leaves in hours. As they flipped through the pages, exchanging stories of past gardening successes and failures, Maddy noted the differences in technique from the lessons she'd gathered from her own experience with those of Annie's, informed by generations and generations of local knowledge from her Mi'kma'ki elders. Overall, the morning passed quickly with contentment—something Maddy never dreamed she'd feel outside the walls of Everwell.

The school had been Maddy's home for seven years. More than a home—a haven. After years on the run from a murder charge, Maddy had found her way to Boston. She'd worked in a factory there for a time, always looking over her shoulder, waiting for the day the Ferguson family would find her and take her back to Cape Enrage to pay for the crime of killing their beloved son. She'd met Phillipa Hartley there, saving her from a man who'd cornered Phillipa in an alley. On the spot, Phillipa had offered Maddy a lifeline—a place at Everwell. It took some time, but at last, it felt like home. So much so, she could hardly imagine another.

Until now.

In amongst the pages about mustard greens and poultices, was a recipe for verjus, which used sour grapes to make an acidic liquid to be used like a wine vinegar in cooking. While the men worked on the pergola, Annie and Maddie pressed the grapes using a cider press they had Teddy fetch.

Once the last of the juice had been pressed and decanted into bottles that created more than enough verjus for both households, they rinsed down the mill and let it dry in the sun. They took a short break, finding a bit of shade on the eastern side of the house. Maddy wiped the sweat from her brow with the edge of her apron.

"This heat is something else," Maddy said. "I should have worn my hat. I must look like an overripe tomato."

"Why don't you go put your feet in the water?" Annie said, then pointed to a line of trees past the meadow. "If you head down past the berry patch, you'll see the path that will take you through the trees to the river. Nice place to stick your feet in, or even wash your hair, especially on a hot day like this. Go and breathe in the cool air by the river. That's good medicine."

Maddy looked over her shoulder, where Beau and the others were still at work. His skin was bright from the exertion, and the way he wiped his brow with the back of his hand shouldn't have been as tempting as it was. And from the way her stomach fluttered when he caught her watching him and gave her a wink, he was far too alluring. She'd never been so aware of a man in her entire life. He seemed to be aware of her in a way that was so completely new she didn't know what to make of it.

She'd been led astray once—wooed very publicly by several men who, as it turned out, wanted only one thing from her. While it was still quite common for women to be prized for their dowry, the cruelty and notoriety of the game they'd played at her expense had marked her. Once upon a time, she remembered Elouise Ashe telling her that men could never be trusted. Of course, that was before Elouise had met Dominic, who, it turned out, was an incredibly trustworthy man. So was Jeremy Webber, Gemma's husband. Logically, Maddy knew good men existed, just like Félicité Parmentier roses, but her chances of seeing one in the flesh was practically non-existent. Following Malcolm's betrayal —and the horror that came after it—she was quite unwilling to trust herself.

After catching herself straining to listen for the sounds of Beau's voice, she got to her feet. At the very least, the cold water would help drive any thoughts about Beau da Silva and his taut muscles out of her mind.

"Excellent idea," she said. "I won't be long."

Even as she walked away, she found herself fighting the urge to look over her shoulder, her attention drawn to Beau like a hummingbird enraptured by sweet pea blossoms. She even thought she'd caught him watching her, but before she had the chance to indulge in the idea, she reached the edge of the pasture. Ahead lay that most irresistible of temptations — a winding little path. Stands of maples, oaks, and beech trees stretched high overhead, the floor carpeted by ferns and to her delight, little clumps of spotted coralroot—a plant she had only seen in a pamphlet put out by the Nova Scotia Horticultural Society.

The sound of gently moving water joined the birdsong and hum of insects. The air turned cool and fresh as she walked amongst the trees, and bright ribbons of light danced off the moving water just ahead of her. Lured by the prospect of running her hands and feet in the cool water, she continued on the path, which sloped gently downward until she came to a small clearing. Just beyond was small waterfall.

A little bubble of joy caught in her chest.

The gentle mist cooled the air even further. No doubt the past two days of rain had made the waterfall more lively than it might normally have been. Drawn to edge of the little river, she carefully bent down and dipped her hands. It was cool but given her exertions today, refreshing. She hunched over the water, quiet in her own thoughts. It had been a long time, she realized, since she'd been so alone like this. And yet, she didn't feel lonely. And not really afraid. She'd been afraid for so long. Afraid that the law would catch up with her. Afraid that she would die alone in a square for a crime she didn't commit, her body hanging for ridicule in death just as it had been in life.

Taking one more moment to ensure she was alone, she unlaced one boot, and then another, and untied her garters. She rolled down her stockings, then folded them and set them neatly on a little pile of rocks along with her boots. Carefully navigating the pebbles and rocks, she winced here and there at the odd sharp rock that found the balls of her feet before reaching the water's edge at last. The cool water skimmed her toes, and she hitched up her skirts even further, taking a few tentative steps in the water up to her mid-calf. How gorgeous would it be to submerge herself, and lose herself in the sensation? Could she risk it?

She straightened, looking back over her shoulders one last time, then, before she could change her mind, walked quickly back to the shore, where she untied her skirts and petticoat, and slipped off her blouse, draping them over a nearby branch. Unable to stifle a grin, she went back into the water in her underthings, shuddering a little bit as she walked deeper to the pool near the waterfall. When the water came just above her waist, she paused, then plugged her nose and plunged herself beneath the surface.

Chapter Fifteen

AFTER SEVERAL HOURS OF WORK, which included a few splinters
and the occasional cuss word, the pergola came back to life. The
grapevines had been given an unfortunate haircut to accommo-
date the new section, but according to Hollis, the trim would not
hurt them, and would in time return them to their former glory.
Beau wiped his brow with a handkerchief he'd bought at a shop
in London, never imagining the fine silk would be stuffed haphazardly in his trouser pockets while he performed manual labour.
Not that he'd been afraid of hard work. In the early days of
getting his fishing camp running, when he was still searching out
the right people to work with, he'd had little choice but to pick up
a hammer, a saw, or even a broom, and he'd never minded it. In
fact, there was a certain satisfaction and insight that came with
understanding how much work was needed to make something
successful. It was that same insight that served him well at the
negotiating table. It wasn't just a firm handshake and the right
joke that broke through the sometimes tense conversation
inherent in a deal where hundreds of thousands of dollars might
be at stake. A little understanding went a long way to disarm the
shield of the man on the other side of a business deal.

Eager to push on through the day until the job was done,

lunch came late. The dining room table had been informally set, filled with sandwiches, shrub, ale, and a pile of oatmeal cookies. They'd each helped themselves, then taken their plates outside to sit on the benches outside under the large maple at the front of the house to take advantage of shade. Beau had looked for Madeline, but she was nowhere to be found. He swallowed the sting of disappointment with a large gulp of beer. She seemed to love the property more than he did, and had appeared excited this morning at the prospect of having the pergola repaired.

"Your grandparents would be pleased to see this," Annie said, looking approvingly at the work. "Daniel's mother used to make a lovely wine from these grapes. Maddy and I helped ourselves to a look at your grandparent's big green book and found a recipe that we tried."

At the mention of Madeline's name, Beau's heart leapt a bit in anticipation. Christ, he was going mad for a woman who seemed as interested in him as she was the prospect of a den of snakes. He'd spent a lifetime with a man who'd done his duty to Beau, and no more. He wasn't going to lose his heart to a woman who, despite what he could offer her, would do the same.

"You could spend a lifetime going through them all," he replied.

"That sounds like a lovely challenge," she said. "And a wonderful way to honour them."

"I don't know if it's possible," he said. "According to Miss Murray, there are recipes that call for plants that aren't known to grow here."

"Maybe you just haven't found them," she said. "She told me you were going to do a survey of the property, but you haven't done it yet. Maybe it's time to see what you have before you find yourself giving it away."

"Annie, leave the poor man alone," Daniel said, looking up at his wife with a mischievous smile. "It's tiring being on the run from the law."

"Like you would know," Annie said, her brown eyes lighting

up at her husband's gentle teasing. "Daniel's idea of playing fast and loose with the law is when he decides to plant his beans three days after a full moon."

Beau smiled, ignoring the pang of envy at the easy way between them, and indeed the entire Chandler clan. Sitting on the other side of Daniel was Hollis, idly tousling his grandson's thick black hair over a shared joke. Over the course of the morning, Hollis had shared anecdotes and memories about The Grove. He told Beau about the berry patch, which had started long before he could remember and flourished under Beau's grandmother's watchful eye; the swimming hole, under a little waterfall where the Redden and Chandler children used to go for a reprieve from the heat and the watchful eye of the adults. And most tantalizing of all, something he'd referred to as the keyhole garden. Hollis had mentioned it almost by accident, but when Beau pressed him on it, he waved it off. Perhaps it had been the rare source of unhappy memories or those with Beau's mother that he didn't wish to share.

After the sandwiches were devoured and the last of the cookies were washed down with the dregs of ale and shrub, the Daniel and Hollis brought the horses up from the barn. They'd given much of their time, but the Chandlers had their own farm to tend to and it was time to leave. Beau also knew that Hollis wanted to talk privately with his family about this part of his own past that joined Beau to them.

Beau also wanted to ask about the offer on the Chandler farm, but because he was in the midst of a family he didn't know until yesterday was his own, he'd decided there was a better time and place for that conversation. Besides, he'd firmly set aside the idea of selling the property. He was not yet ready to acknowledge what was behind that unwelcome hesitation, particularly when some of it had to do with his feelings for a striking, redheaded siren who wanted nothing to do with him.

And yet, as he looked over at the repaired pergola, catching sight of bunches of green grapes waiting to get fat and sweet under the sun, something else bubbled up inside him. The same feeling he'd had once when he'd come across that perfect little spot on the Miramichi River where the salmon were jumping and there was no one but him and an abandoned shack to see them: possibility.

"Maybe you should take a look for the swimming hole," Daniel said as he climbed up into the wagon, joining the rest of the family. "It's not far. If you follow that path and then go through the trees, you'll find it soon enough."

Beau nodded. "I'll do that. Thank you for your help today. I owe you a supper, at least."

"Ah, but Miss Murray would probably be cooking it," Annie said with a mischievous grin, "and I think she deserves a bit of a rest, don't you?"

Beau smiled at that. What did Miss Murray deserve? If he could, he would give her an entire library and a garden as large as she wanted. He could still recall the excitement when she was looking through the recipe book.

Something twigged in his memory.

"She does," he said. "I think it's her birthday soon."

"Is it?" Annie said. "Well, I think that deserves a celebration, too."

"I think it does."

"Well, I will make a cake then. You can't have a birthday without a cake," she said. "We'll keep it a surprise."

"But only if she likes them," Teddy pipped up. "Jeanine doesn't like them."

"You're right," Hollis said, then turned to Beau. "She's my granddaughter. Lives up near the shore. Hates surprises."

A curious feeling came over Beau. He had a niece too. It was a good thing he didn't mind surprises—the good ones anyway. Did Miss Murray even like surprises? He remembered the way her eyes lit up when he'd bought her that book in Halifax. Maybe she could have one more good surprise.

As the Chandlers made ready to leave, Beau pressed the

telegram for Dominic in Daniel's hand, along with a couple of bank notes to compensate him for his time and effort. Daniel and Teddy would take the note back to the telegram office in the morning.

After they left, Beau stood, hands on his hips, staring up at the stone house. The windows glistened in the sun. Madeline Murray had begun to work her magic on the back garden, where plants like marjoram, thyme, and sage, long forgotten, had been freed from a choking mass of weeds and overgrowth. And the pergola was already more inviting. In a year, maybe two, it would be back to its old self, encouraging a visitor to take a magical little journey to the back garden under a canopy of lush grape vines.

A year, or two. Would he be here in a year or two? Even if Beau managed to have his innocence proven, he did have a company to go back to. A legacy to continue. Despite their differences, Frank had put that faith in him, and Beau wasn't particularly interested in letting him down once more.

The joy he'd felt a moment ago was sucked out of him with such a force it left him hollow inside. Once upon a time he would have filled that hole with drink, or a game of cards, or some other distraction. Now, even if they were available to him, he was certain they would not have the power to fill that well of yearning. On impulse, he looked around for Madeline, ignoring the twinge of disappointment at her absence. Annie had told Beau she'd gone for a walk, possibly to the small meandering river that edged one side of the property. Perhaps he would find her there.

He skirted one of the pastures that the sheep had clearly not yet inhabited. The foliage grew tall, with a mix of green grass, tall yellow flowers that resembled dandelions, delicate white flowers that looked like lace, and clover. No doubt Miss Murray would know every species, and how they might be used. Ahead, the path diverged, one segment of it partially blocked by the massive roots of an upended tree.

A hare bounded out from the bottom of the felled tree, startling him from his thoughts. He uttered a small curse, then watched the animal, equally startled, disappear into some nearby undergrowth. At the base of the bright green leaves, something unusual caught his eye: a small edging of dark stones, three high, gently curving off and out of sight.

Intrigued, Beau moved to examine them. They continued, curving away into the undergrowth, under the boughs of an overgrown apple tree. He followed the brickwork, which, despite some missing stones, was remarkably intact. In some places it disappeared under the haphazard plantings different from anything else on the property. A modest orchard of apple, pear, and plum trees, overgrown but bearing fruit, stood on his right. The brick edging continued, bordered by daisies and wild roses, leading him on, until it came to a halt where a small bridge had been built over a brook bubbling underneath. The boards were largely intact, but it was clear that he was the first person to walk over this threshold in a very long time.

On the other side of the bridge was a little wooden gate with a strange pattern—like a keyhole —cut into the centre of it. A rush of excitement caught in his chest as he recalled Hollis's mention of the keyhole garden.

Beau was nineteen the last time he'd been struck by such a thrill. He'd walked into a small fishing cabin in the woods in northern New Brunswick. Nearby, was the mighty Miramichi River. It was spawning season, and the salmon were rushing. He'd seen that old cabin and that river, and he'd known in his heart what he could do with it. For five years, he'd had a successful little business, built out of nothing but his own belief and a lot of sweat. But he'd done it.

His father had demanded he sell it, to concentrate on the family business, hinting that any deflection of his efforts was viewed as some kind of betrayal. He'd always mourned the loss of it and the sense of satisfaction it had given him. But swayed by a more urgent desire—to claim, for even a moment, the respect, and possibly even love, of his father—he'd left it behind. Left it for a tantalizing promise that had died with Frank da Silva.

He wasn't sure how long he spent walking the small paths, some of them so overgrown with ivy or some leafy monstrosity that they were practically impassible, lost in his own thoughts. It would be an impossible task to bring them back to life. For him, anyway.

But not for Madeline Murray.

He retraced his steps, going back across the little brook, under the apple tree, and back down into the woods toward the brook. Eager anticipation drove his steps. He imagined her sitting on a rock, her feet dangling in the water, reading a book. If he was very lucky, he thought, maybe she'd left down her hair.

He was about to chide himself for his schoolboy fantasies that his very grown up body was finding pleasurable, thank you very much, when he realized that the object of said fantasies was nowhere to be seen. A pang of disappointment—one that was becoming far too common when he was devoid of her company—rushed through him. Had he missed her? It was possible that in his meandering discovery of the overgrown garden, she'd already packed up and gone back to the house.

Except he caught a glimpse clothing, draped carefully over a large tree branch, and a pair of ankle boots sitting on guard underneath them. Beau turned toward the water again, then wondered if he should, given that the evidence suggested Miss Murray was here, but in a spectacular state of undress. His body went hard at the mere suggestion, as if the promise of a week's worth of fitful dreams and meanderings of his mind would be presented to him.

He paused, afraid to look further. After all, it was one thing if a woman undressed for you, but it was another thing entirely to be sneaking up on a person in a private moment. He'd heard stories about one of his father's secretaries who was let go for having a penchant for helping himself to the personal moments of the female staff in the household after a small hole was found in the wall between his room and that of a couple of the female servants. His father, upon some reflection, may have been an asshole to many, Beau included, but he had some level of basic decency. A twinge of something—regret maybe—twisted. Frank da Silva had not been good person. But he hadn't been an entirely bad one either.

Beau was about to turn away from the small river when something caught his eye. He turned, his gaze immediately drawn to the rush of water tumbling over the rocks, splashing loudly into the dark pool below. At the base of that pool was a lone, solitary figure.

It took a moment for him to realize it was Miss Murray. She was lying utterly still, eyes closed, her face one of utter peace and contentment. For a moment, he wondered if she was sleeping, which would have been ridiculous. She looked like something out of one of those Rosetti paintings he'd seen once when he was in New York. Like an Isolde, lying in a boat, her red curly hair in a halo around her, dying as she mourned her lost Tristan. Beau could never imagine love hurting so much that one's heart would actually break. But there was something about Miss Murray that made his heart fill with something so utterly light and full that it squeezed the air out of his lungs.

Of course Isolde, if she ever existed, was long dead, but Miss Murray was…

He paused. She was so…still. And she wasn't completely undressed. She had a corset and drawers, and weren't corsets heavy? Maybe she'd somehow hit her head on a rock, or had a sudden fit of whatever brings normal, healthy people to their knees. When he had his fishing business, he'd pulled a man out of the Miramichi after he'd slipped and hit his head on the rocks. If Beau hadn't been there, Hugh Evans, one of his first and wealthiest clients, would have drowned.

Beau's stomach dropped and he went flying into the water.

Chapter Sixteen

Bliss.

The rush of the waterfall and the gently churning water mixed with the sound of her own heartbeat. Maddy floated for what seemed like forever and yet no time at all, her body freed from layers of clothing. While Maddy rarely wore any of the more stylish trappings her fellow spinsters did, she did use a corset to support her chest and back. She'd briefly considered leaving that on the bank along with her skirts, but changed her mind. After all, she had no idea if Teddy Chandler might come by to rescue an errant sheep, never mind the challenge of putting herself back into it with a sopping wet shift underneath.

It was so easy to imagine herself as a character from one of those Arthurian Legends—Isolde, maybe—pining for her lost Tristan. Or maybe Maid Marian, off in the woods, hiding from the sheriff, waiting for Robin Hood. It was silly, really, to want those things. For years she'd been looking over her shoulder, alone, waiting for the day she'd be discovered and taken back to face her punishment. Having someone else rescue her felt like a fantasy. It didn't hurt to indulge in it, even for a brief moment... did it?

Maybe The Grove's beauty was playing with her imagination. The place awakened something inside her that not even Everwell had. She wanted to think it was the pretty rolling hills and the possibility in the overgrown kitchen garden, or even the beautiful berry patch. But there was something else, too—something she absolutely needed to guard herself against. It was the expression on Beau's face when he looked at her. Because it wasn't like Dominic or Jeremy. They certainly respected her, even liked her. But Beau was different. She'd caught his lingering stare in the small mirror that hung by the front door. The vulnerability he betrayed. It made this golden man a little less shiny. But far more attractive.

Madeline.

The muffled sound of her name caught her attention, pulling her away from her disjointed feelings. Her attention sharpened, and through the woosh of rushing water, she sensed a change. Her body went on alert, but before she could react, something gripped her shoulders. Alarmed, she opened her eyes only to see another set of panicked eyes staring back at her and her upper body being pulled from the water.

"Madeline!"

Propelled by fear, she came into her strength, pushing whoever this was away from her. She stepped back, her feet skittering over the rocks, trying to find her footing. She wiped the water from her eyes with the back of her forearm and raised her fists ready to fight, instantly regretting the fact she'd left her knife in her boot on shore.

"Thank Jesus you're alive."

The sound of Beau's voice, along with that damnable beautiful face of his, cut through the haze of confusion. Wet hair plastered to her face like a web, obscuring her vision. He stood an arm's length away in his trousers and shirtsleeves, hands up, a line of worry on his normally placid face.

She, on the other hand, was utterly mortified. Once the excitement subsided, she pulled her arms across her chest, then dunked down into the water in some vain attempt at preserving her modesty.

"Of course I'm alive," she said, trying and failing to keep her voice steady, even though she was only a few feet away from Beau with nothing between them but some very clear water and her underthings, which, save for her corset, were utterly transparent. "Why were you sneaking up on me?"

"I called out but you didn't answer," he said. "You were just very… still. I thought you might be drowning."

There was something in his looks—something urgent. He'd been afraid. Afraid for her.

"I'm not some fairy tale princess," she grumbled, ignoring the fact that before he arrived, she'd allowed herself to imagine it. "You don't need to save me."

"You don't know how many times I saw people who loved to fish but couldn't swim. They got in over their head. Some of them didn't make it." He locked eyes with her, and Maddy was struck by the earnestness she saw there. It occurred to her, with something approaching genuine shock, that Beau da Silva never told her anything but the truth.

"Well, you can plainly see I'm fine," she said, trying to brush off the warring sense of delight and mortification at being in front of him so completely vulnerable. "I have to get to shore."

He nodded in recognition that this meeting of theirs, unintended as it was, was now incredibly awkward. He put his back to her, then called over his shoulder.

"Do you need help?"

"No."

She lifted herself out of the water. She hadn't taken more than a few lumbering steps toward the shore when she landed on a sharp rock. Wincing, she pulled her foot away and stumbled. Choosing between her modesty and having rocks embedded in her face from a fall, she decided the later would be more painful, and flung her arms out in front of her.

Her actions were unnecessary. Beau was there, one arm around her back, his hands on her arms, steadying her before she fell forward.

"I've got you."

It should have been awkward. It should have been mortifying. Here she was, practically naked and soaking wet, her drawers clinging to her body. For a moment she was struck by the very real urge to sink into him, let him bear the weight of her. Rely on him to get her safely to shore. To let him do for her what he had no doubt done for countless other women—be gallant and charming.

To rescue her.

She was afraid to look him in the eye, fearful she would be lost in the hypnotic spell he weaved without even trying. Her gaze trailed down his body. His shirt was wet from his midsection down, clinging to his body. Before they'd taken more than a few steps however, an old fear rose inside. She shrugged, a half-hearted attempt to push him away, but it appeared that Beau da Silva was not having it.

"Can you allow me to be a gentleman just once?" he asked, half exasperated, half playful. "If I'm going to ruin these perfectly good trousers, I should have a good excuse."

"Fine," she said. "Just keep your eyes forward."

He looked at her, cocking an eyebrow and giving her a perfectly devilish smile that made Maddy wonder if her knees would actually buckle.

"As long as you do the same."

Maddy reddened, then turned away, her eyes fixed on the shore.

"You don't have to keep shifting your weight," he said, as if sensing what she was doing. "I've got you."

"I'm bigger than you," she protested, as if that was the only explanation required.

He turned to face her, and a line of irritation spread across his brow.

"Did it ever occur to you that I might like helping you? That I respect you enough to let you know if I might need you to shift your weight or to stop for a moment?"

The exasperation in his voice, and the implication—that he wasn't bothered by her size—was a far more bewildering thing than it should have been.

He guided her to a large rock a few feet from the shoreline. Away from the canopy of trees, it was warmed by the afternoon sun, and despite its hard surface, offered some comfort.

"Thank you," she said, as she tried to wring out the edges of her drawers.

"You weren't even drowning," he said. "My attempts at playing the gallant hero were misspent."

Were they? She'd never been rescued by a man before. Maddy stilled even as the thought formed, remembering the moment when they'd gotten off the train, and Nelson Taylor had insulted her. Beau had nearly started a fight on her behalf. Even before then, he'd bought that near-priceless tome for her, saving her the worry of having to nick it. Of course, he had no idea that he'd helped her in that way. But he'd seen, somehow, that her heart needed something, and he'd given it to her. Beau da Silva seemed to make it his mission to make her feel safe. It was so strange.

So tempting.

She studied his face—really looked at it. There were little lines at the corners of his eyes. He had a small scar, just peeking out underneath his hairline. She realized he had a small fleck of blue in one of his eyes. He seemed, at that moment, incredibly shy. She fought the traitorous urge to run her fingers through his disheveled hair.

"It's the thought that counts," she said, unable to keep herself from smiling. "And I appreciate it. I really do."

"You really do have very pretty eyes," he said, then, as if sensing her imminent retreat at the compliment, he plucked a small ribbon of her hair in his fingers, held it up, and pulled a face before unceremoniously dropping it. "But your hair... I have seen old mops less tangled than this."

This time she did laugh—it was loud, and she was pretty sure she snorted just a little bit as she struggled to find breath. She wiped a tear from the corner of her eye, then caught a look of utter joy in Beau's face.

"What?" she asked, as she tried to pull her hair out of her face and into some sort of order.

"It's good to hear you laugh," he said, with a grin so infectious Maddy returned it. They both grew quiet, a creeping yet tantalizing tension between them. There was no sound, save the gentle rush of the waterfall, and the insistent call from a blue jay from above them.

He stood and gestured to her hair.

"Let me help you with that."

"I think you've helped enough," she said.

He arched an eyebrow, which Maddy knew was deliberately done to disarm her and quite handily did the trick. "My gallantry knows no bounds."

He stood behind her, and though the sun was warm, a shiver of pleasure went through her as he carefully raked his fingers through her hair in an effort to detangle it.

"You don't like compliments," he said, oddly matter of fact.

"I—" She paused, uncertain how to proceed. "I find them difficult."

"Because you are too modest for your own good?" he asked.

"I'm not too modest," she protested. "Is it possible to have too much modesty?"

"Take it from someone with far too little," he said in that self-deprecating way of his. "It is entirely possible to have too much."

Whether it was his hands on her hair, or the warmth in his voice, or the very careful way he worked the strands of her hair so not to pull at her scalp, Maddy felt herself giving way to his question.

"I was supposed to marry a man who was very generous with his compliments in public," she said, thinking back on Malcolm Ferguson. Malcolm had a full crop of dark hair, a million-dollar smile, and an eye for making money.

"I know the type," he said. "They came after my sister in droves. Smooth talkers, looking for her money."

"Malcolm used to tell me how pretty I was," she said. "How my hair was like liquid fire, or some nonsense. He couldn't wait to be married to me. He was going to be the luckiest man in town."

"And he would have been," he said with a confidence Maddy found she couldn't share.

She remembered the horrible sinking feeling that had come over her the moment she'd called on him unexpectedly. He was with his friends, and they'd been drinking. And he'd told them he'd how he'd managed to snag the Murray fortune. He'd managed to convince old man Murray that his oversized daughter with the face that could stop a train in its tracks was the only woman for him.

"Only because of my dowry," she said, her voice dropping to a whisper as she recalled the words that had wormed their way into her heart. "He told his friends he'd won the prized sow."

She'd spoken so softly, it took a moment to understand what she'd said. But there was something in the air, and it was fragile. When his brain put finally this impossible thought together, his stomach dropped. Finally, it all made horrible sense. Every time he'd flattered her. Every time he'd tried to tell her how dazzling she was.

She cleared her throat, and it occurred to Beau that she might be crying. Something inside him shifted and he was tempted to turn her around, but he stopped himself. Madeline Murray was an intensely private person. Instead, he continued to untangle her hair, partially because it felt so damn good to touch her, and partially to keep himself rooted to this space, instead of finding whomever it was that broke Madeline Murray's heart and handing his arse to him. His fingers worked her curls, and before he knew what he was doing, he'd braided her hair back in a simple plait and tied it firm at the end with the damp handker-chief he'd stuffed in his pocket. It was hardly expert work, but it would keep it from tangling as it dried.

"There," he said, putting his hands on his hips, trying to lighten the mood. "I don't think I'm in danger of replacing any one as a ladies' maid."

She reached back and felt the braid. "Thank you."

"Please tell me you didn't marry this idiot who clearly wasn't worthy of the dirt under your boots," he said at last. The idea that she may have found herself tied to this absolute asshole set Beau's jaw on edge. He swallowed his anger and sat down beside her, reaching out to hold her hand. He half expected her to push him away, but instead, she gave him the most heartbreaking smile.

"Not for his lack of trying," she said. "I went to my father and demanded he call off the wedding. My mother wouldn't hear of it. She said I was lucky to have anyone want me."

Beau was renowned for his poker face while in the middle of intense negotiations, but his ability to keep his emotions hidden were failing him now. This woman brought out every ounce of passion he had. The idea that her mother would be so heartless to her own daughter must have been all over his face.

"She was a beauty," she continued, answering Beau's unasked question. "She gotten far on her looks, and I had always been a disappointment, I guess. But my father must have been consid-ering it, because Malcolm came to see me."

"To beg forgiveness?"

"To force me," she said.

If the police had found him before this moment, he would have said he wasn't a man given to violence. After that moment, that would have been a lie. He turned her gently, facing her, and her hand. It may have been a decade too late, but he needed her to know she wasn't alone.

"I didn't let him," she said.

He gave her hand a gentle squeeze. "I am so sorry they were so horrible to you. You didn't deserve it."

"Maybe I did in the end," she said.

"How can you say that?"

"Because he died," she said, then looked straight at him. "And I think I may have killed him."

Beau paused, giving himself a moment to measure his response to her shocking admission. "You weren't sure?"

"He forced himself on me," she continued. "He'd been drinking heavily. He said so many horrible things to me, but he seemed determined to make me the cause of all his ills. His failed job prospects. His inability to find a prettier wife."

"You don't have to tell me this," he said.

"I have to tell someone," she said, her eyes bright with unshed tears. "It's been so long. I can't live with this anymore."

Beau smiled and brushed a few strands of hair from her face.

"I suppose I'm the best person to tell," he said, happy to play along. "I mean, if I go to the police and turn you in, I'm not doing myself any favours, am I?"

His joke brought a smile to her face as she squeezed his fingers.

"I fought him off," she said. "He was smaller than me, and the drink had made him unsteady. He'd been forcing himself on me, when I kicked him off and ran. I didn't dare look back. I thought I'd heard him yelling after me, but it was so confusing."

Maddy stopped for a moment, those last moments a horrible blur she could no longer recall with clarity.

"The next day the local constable was at our door," she continued. He'd been found dead from a wound to the side of his temple. I must have pushed him harder than I thought."

"That wasn't your fault," he said, putting his hand to her face. "You did what any man would have done. Defend yourself."

"I wasn't going to let anyone hurt me anymore."

Something in Beau swelled then, fierce and protective. It was as if he'd never made a vow before—and maybe he hadn't. But he was never going to let anyone hurt Madeline Murray. Never again. If it cost him every last cent, every scrap of his self-worth.

"Is that why you look after those girls at Everwell?" he asked.

"Partially," she said. "They need someone to look after them."

"And who looks after you?" *Because I want to.* He would look after her until his last breath.

"My fellow spinsters," she said. "We all look after each other, in our own way."

He wanted so badly to put his lips to her exposed shoulder and taste her skin, which was starting to turn pink under the sun. Instead, he got to his feet, looked around for her clothes and boots, and presented them to her.

"Well, I'm going to look after you," he said, ignoring the curious glance. "At least for the rest of the afternoon. As much as I would personally love to see you in nothing but your drawers, I don't feel prepared to answer to any of the Chandlers if one of them came back this way looking for a stray ewe." He gave her his best cocky smile, and to his great delight, a blush crept up the side of her face.

Even though they'd just been side by side, she insisted he turn around until she was dressed.

"There," she said, button up the last button on her blouse. "I'm ready. I'm eager to see the pergola."

There was something about her not-quite-put-together appearance that threatened to drive him wild, but this was not the time for him to be thinking with what was in his pants.

"Much as I would be thrilled to dazzle you with my carpentry skills," he said, "I've got something else to show you. Are you ready for a little adventure, my lady?"

Chapter Seventeen

ANTICIPATION HUNG in the air as Maddy looked at his outstretched fingers. Taking his hand felt dangerous in a way she couldn't quite articulate. But she had just confessed all to him, hadn't she? Somehow, Beau had become a safe place to share some of the most horrible pieces of herself. Her worst memories. And that brought a lightness she hadn't expected.

Taking a breath, she put her hand in his. As he wrapped his fingers around hers, the feeling of his warm, masculine hands, so foreign and yet so unbelievably right, reached deep inside her. Just like how the sun's strength would touch her flowers, encouraging them to unfurl their petals.

He led her up the foot path, through the wood, until they reached the clearing. But instead of guiding her back toward the house, he turned in the opposite direction, where the elaborate root system at the base of a fallen tree formed a natural wall. He guided her around it, taking care that she not catch her foot on a root.

"Where are you taking me?" she asked, as her curiosity started to get the best of her. The scent of clover filled the air as the wildflowers and grasses danced lazily in the summer breeze. The path underneath their feet was thick with grasses, but alongside she noticed the suggestion of a stone formation, almost like a little ha-ha wall. She was about to point it out to him when he stopped. For a moment, she feared he would let her go, and Maddy could not help the relief that he apparently had no intention of doing so.

"Almost there," he said, smiling at her with a giddiness she could only recall seeing in the eyes of the Everwell students on Christmas Eve. "In fact, I want you to cover your eyes."

"Beau da Silva," Maddy said, not bothering to disguise her incredulity at his request. "Perhaps I have just read too many novels or penny dreadfuls. But going with a strange man into the woods, blindfolded, generally doesn't work out well for most women."

"I am hardly a stranger," he said, putting a hand to his heart with that characteristic flair she was, despite herself, coming to adore. "And what are you reading? Clearly not *A Midsummer Night's Dream*. Or *Snow White*."

Maddy blinked. "I've read *Snow White*—the huntsman is there to cut out her heart."

"Ah!" he said. "But he doesn't, does he? You just need to go off into the woods with the right man."

"And you are the right man?" she asked, unable to stop herself from smiling.

"I hope so," he said, with an earnestness that at one time she would have felt was out of character, but now understood to be genuine. "Or at least, I hope I'm not the wrong one."

"No, Beau da Silva," she said. "You are not the wrong one."

There was never a moment when Maddy didn't think that Beau da Silva was handsome. The gods had blessed him with more good looks than seemed fair. She was confident he could have any woman he wanted. But the way his eyes lit up in that moment did something to Maddy she thought impossible. It was as if her good opinion of him mattered more than anything in the world. If he kept looking at her like that, she might be in real danger.

How was it possible that a man's smile could make her feel this way? So utterly important?

"How about I promise not to try anything dastardly, which, given the fact that I saw you store two throwing knives in your boot this morning, would be a remarkably foolhardy idea," he said, a twinkle in his eye. "Now, cover your eyes. I'll guide you the next fifteen feet or so, and I promise it will be worth your while."

"Fine," she said, ignoring the thrill in her chest she felt at the way he was looking at her—as if her joy was the only thing that mattered to him. She closed her eyes, and then, because that was clearly not enough, she put her hands over them as an extra measure.

"I'm going to lead you up slowly, so you don't trip," he said. In a moment, she felt him behind her, one hand at her back, one hand at her elbow. It was peculiar, this sensation. Unfamiliar. She should, frankly, be hating this. She should have felt vulnerable, but the heat of his hand through her clothes, and the subtle warmth of his breath from behind her had the opposite effect.

Of course, she could open her eyes at any moment. He had not bound her in any way. Except, perhaps, that she was spellbound by his playfulness. This desire, almost palpable, to delight her.

Their paced slowed, but with every step, she reached out with her other senses—the smells carried on the breeze, a subtle drop in temperature from where they may be walking in the shadow of trees, and underfoot, the sense that the ground beneath had changed from the uneven but soft ground of the meadow to something harder. Stone, perhaps. Interesting.

Everything about what she was doing seemed wrong. She was here because her job was to have her eyes wide open, looking for the danger lurking in the shadows. But Beau's intoxicating smile and playful expression had convinced her that this was absolutely safe.

"Nearly there," he said, whispering in her ear. It was impossible, but she felt like she could almost see his smile.

Maddy felt his hands on her shoulders, and a gentle pressing as he tried to control her steps.

"Can I open my eyes now?" she asked. She wasn't sure whether to be impatient or excited.

"Almost," he said. His hands were gone from her body, depriving her of his touch. But she sensed him standing close, and then, almost whispering in her ear, she heard. "Now."

Maddy dropped her hands and opened her eyes. And blinked.

She'd had no idea what to expect. Perhaps a small clump of columbine, or some other plant in the nearby wood.

Instead, he'd found… heaven.

Beau stood beside her, his chest tight, watching her with the same urgency he'd felt when presenting a new investment opportunity to his father. But there wasn't thousands of dollars at stake, nor the company's reputation. Why was he so damned nervous?

"Oooooh!"

It wasn't a string of words. But the wonder from that single syllable was worth an entire soliloquy.

Madeline Murray didn't communicate with words. She obviously loved them, given how much she read. But right now, it was the rush of pink flooding her cheeks, and her hands, trembling as she'd covered her mouth, that told him everything he needed to know.

"How did you find this?" she asked as she recovered her voice, even as she studied the riot of tangled vines and overgrown jumbles of flowers.

Quietly, he let out the breath he'd been holding and shrugged his shoulders, as if her good opinion didn't mean everything to him. "Purely by chance."

She turned to him, giving him a curious look, before having her attention dragged away by some delicate pink blossom that grew on feather-green branches.

"Did you see this?"

Her voice had a giddy lightness to it that he didn't recognize. She was gently handling the trumpet shaped blossom, looking at it with the same excitement he'd seen in his father when he'd reviewed a particularly profitable quarter.

He walked over to her.

"It's a milk and wine lily," she said as join her. "I've never seen it before, except in a book. There are half a dozen species just in this section I've never seen anywhere. This is the most incredible thing I've ever seen in my life."

She looked at him with such happiness, such gratitude. With joy.

Something tightened in Beau's throat. When was the last time that anyone had ever gazed at him the way Madeline just did?

"By the looks of things, I don't think anyone has tended to this for years. Even Hollis hasn't been here since the days he was with my mother. A storm must have knocked over the tree back there and obscured it from view."

"Maybe this place held too much meaning for him," she said. "And it hurt to come back."

Beau considered that. Hollis had mentioned the garden in an offhand way, and when Beau had questioned him about it, he'd seemed distinctly uninterested in discussing it further.

She paused, putting her nose into another flower, then carefully inspected its leaves. She treated these plants with such tenderness and reverence, Beau was practically jealous.

"This garden was very carefully designed," she said, walking slowly to negotiate the path, which was obscured in many places by a carpet of vines and overgrown bushes that forced her to duck or push them aside. Rather than be taken aback by the wildness, Miss Murray seemed to revel in it. "It's overgrown, but you can see there are no straight lines. It allows you to always be discovering what is along the next curve."

Beau followed, his mind wandering to forbidden places, like the curves of Madeline Murray's body.

"This must be the garden from your grandparents' journals," she said. "How exciting for you."

It was an unexpectedly difficult question for Beau to answer. His grandparents obviously wanted this to be part of Beau's life— they'd willed this to him, after all. But he had commitments to the da Silva lumber empire, and even if Frank wasn't his father, he'd raised Beau and trusted him to run it. After a lifetime of chasing the excitement of the next dollar, the next contract, the next distraction from a life that was wanting something that he couldn't quite see, couldn't quite reach, Beau wasn't sure if he knew what to do if he stopped. Or how empty he would feel if he did.

And then he watched Madeline bending over a clump of plants, her long, red braid draped around the back of her neck, and realized he wasn't feeling empty at all.

"Your grandparents must have had curious, open minds," she said after a moment, interrupting his woolgathering.

Beau frowned. "What makes you say that?"

"It's all around us," she said, gesturing to the landscape, somehow able to decode the message in the unruly mass of green that surrounded them. "Look at these plants."

Unlike the family business, which seemed to delight in going into the wild places and leaving destruction in its wake, this little garden was nature run riot. Butterflies and moths flew from one plant to another, unperturbed by the presence of what may have been the first newcomers to their domain in years. Sunshine glinted off the ethereal threads of spider webs. The hum of bees, busy gathering pollen, made the air come alive. It looked like chaos. Beautiful chaos. A garden fit for the faerie queen that stood in its midst.

"I'm looking," he said. "But I'm not sure what I'm looking at."

"Here," she said, holding up a spindly branch between them, beckoning him closer. Beau ducked under the brush, standing next to her. It was the first time since they'd arrived that Madeline Murray seemed at ease. Maybe even happy. And since he'd arrived here—after years of being unable to live up to scratch in the eyes of the men in his family, years of toiling in pursuit of another man's dream—it was the first time he'd been, too.

"See these?" she said, pushing back an overgrown brush. "These are milkweed. Many people tear them out, because they think they're weeds, but the butterflies love them. And next to them are Tickseed. They don't do well in my garden, but being up against this stone probably helped. And these—" She moved past them to a mass of plants with green heart shaped leaves and larger green husks. "I've only seen these once before, in a book. They are called winter cherries. You have to be careful with plants. Some can come in and take over, smothering out everything else. That's what this is, unfortunately. But we could dig it out, I think."

"We?" Beau asked. "The last time I came near a plant of yours, you nearly took my head off."

She turned and gave him a sheepish look.

"But these are yours," she said, holding out her arms, encompassing the magic around her. "This is your magical kingdom, Prince Charming, not mine."

This was his kingdom. A kingdom that he'd been offered a respectable amount of money to sell.

"I have one more thing to show you," he said, pushing past the discomfort of an idea that a mere fortnight ago had seemed like the best way to get rid of a property he had no interest in.

"Do I have to close my eyes this time?" she asked.

He shook his head. "Follow me."

On impulse, he held out his hand again, and she took it without hesitation. He suppressed the thrill and led her past an obelisk, its iron form covered by a crawling ivy. Along the way, she paused to fawn over some blossom or another, or tsk at a planting she may have felt was a mistake. He stood dutifully, trying to pay attention even as he was fixated on the fact that she'd not let go of his hand. Heat wound through Beau's body, making him hard in all the usual places, while somehow leaving a soft, breezy feeling inside of him. Did she feel the same?

At last, they approached a stone wall, thoroughly covered by a thick verge of creeping roses save for an opening directly ahead. He heard her gasp and smiled as he turned to see her own mouth in a tidy little O.

"I think this section was the rose garden," he said as they ducked under the canopy of green leaves. "Some of them are more thorns that flowers but—"

Whatever explanation he had planned to offer—which as far as information was concerned, was very little—stopped as the most unexpected thing happened.

Madeline Murray kissed him.

And it wasn't just a peck on the cheek, or even a short kiss on the lips owing to some overwrought excitement at seeing a mass of roses in more shades of pink, white, and yellow than he thought possible.

Her lips were on his mouth, pressing hard, her hands on his shoulders, holding herself steady. The sensation of it nearly weakened his knees. She broke the kiss suddenly as she'd initiated it.

"I shouldn't have done that," she blurted out, her eyes as wide as saucers. "I'm sorry. I don't know what came over me."

"Why not?" he asked.

"I don't—I don't—" she sputtered, before doing the most uncharacteristic thing he'd seen her do: bury her face in her hands and turn away. "I don't know how."

It took a moment to process what she'd said. As a kiss it had been clumsy, but a clumsy kiss from Madeline Murray still lit a fire inside him that went straight down to his nethers. He'd had just a hint of the fire he knew was inside her, and like a man coming in from the cold, he was desperate for more.

And then he had another thought—a thought that twisted inside him. Madeline Murray had never been kissed. Or at least, not by someone who deserved her.

He turned her around, gently pulling her hands from her face.

"Madeline Murray," he said, tracing her hairline with a touch. "I'm going to kiss you properly, if that is all right with you. You are an extremely intelligent woman, and I'm certain you will be a quick study."

She nodded, suddenly shy. It was endearing and yet there was something about it that tore at his insides. This beautiful woman, who did not know she was beautiful—cast aside by those who by rights should have cared for her.

He would. He would care for her until his dying day. He didn't know how to entice her to love him. But he would try.

And he would start with a kiss.

He put his lips to her cheeks first, pressing gently into the soft flesh, tasting the sweetness of her. She sucked in a breath, which encouraged him to plant those kisses lower, along the edge her jaw, down to the tender flesh just below her left ear. Every touch brought a new delight—a little sigh here, a deep breath there. The space between them closed to nothing, and the sensation of her lush bosom against his chest threatened to end him. He hadn't even found her lips yet, but even through her skirts, she must have felt his arousal.

He pushed away a few stray tendrils of her hair, then placed his lips on hers. He pressed gently at first, waiting for her response. Her lips, sweet as any berry he'd tasted, were soft, and in response to his touch, her mouth opened slightly. He took the invitation. He cupped the back of her head with one hand, his other hand grazing one of her ears, and kissed her lips, trying to be gentle, wanting this to be everything she needed it to be while trying to control his own need to pour every ounce of his longing into her.

Instead, she kissed him back with such a fire that Beau feared on the one hand he would be consumed by her, and on the other, knew he would happily sacrifice himself on that pyre. Just as he'd thought he'd lose himself completely, she broke the kiss.

"I..." she stuttered, breathless, as she stepped away. "I should go."

Chapter Eighteen

Maddy stepped back, mortification driving away the sensual pleasure of the kiss like a heavy April rain could drive away the warmth of a spring sun. She turned away, unable to bear his reaction. His disgust. What he must be thinking of her.

Maddy had fought bodyguards and drunken husbands hell bent on dragging their wives and children back home. She'd faced them all, even when she was scared, channeling that same fury she'd conjured that night Malcolm Ferguson had come for her.

But there was no fury now. This was something else—and it scared her to death.

Who knew what a proper kiss was? Apparently, Maddy didn't. Beyond the chaste brushing of lips on her hands from Malcolm, Nelson, and a handful of other suitors her parents had lined up for her, she'd never been kissed before. And once upon a time she'd been so grateful for those kisses, for that small bit of attention, because she'd thought it genuine, instead of a cruel game to win her hand and her dowry.

But this... this was something outside all experience. And like a child given her first taste of toffee, she'd wanted more. She wanted to devour him. That desire, that need—so fiery and hot— scared her like nothing had for a very long time. Putting the full force of her shame into her feet, she turned on her heel, eager to put this entire thing behind them. She'd taken only a step when his hand caught her arm.

"Madeline."

His voice was warm and disarming.

Why was she so scared? Maddy had lived with fear of one sort or another for so long, she'd thought she could manage it all. But this—this magical feeling that had swept over her and pushed aside, for even a single moment, that old wound? This was beyond her experience. The taste of him was still on her lips. The subtle feeling of his whiskers stung her skin. It had all been so new. So strange. So wonderful. And so terrifying.

"I should go," she said, carefully erecting the walls that she'd foolishly allowed to fall. Her brain groped through the haze of pleasure his kiss evoked, searching for some flimsy excuse for why she had to leave this magical garden and the soothing warmth of his touch as fast as her legs could carry her.

After she'd fled from home, Maddy had sneered at the women who swooned over a bouquet of flowers. Like the syrupy bits of flattery and chaste kisses, the only flowers she'd received were those given to her by men who'd been desperate to win not her favour, but her father's. The first time she'd been gifted flowers in any genuine way was when Jeremy Webber, Gemma's husband, had given her African violets from a local hot house as a thank you for giving his daughter Ivy boxing lessons. But that wasn't romantic—that was a gesture between friends. Beau da Silva, a man she was contractually obligated to watch and who she'd told herself more than once that she didn't particularly like, had just offered her an entire garden. He wasn't even giving it to her—he was simply showing it to her. And in response, she'd thrown herself at him like some kind of doe-eyed maiden being swept off her feet by an errant knight.

Emphasis on errant.

"Don't go," he said. His grip was firm, but not hurtful. "I enjoyed it."

She turned slightly, casting her glance past him to a mass of calendula that had managed to self-seed, no doubt encouraged by the warmth of the half wall they had been growing next to. It took her a moment, but at last, she steeled herself to look him in the eye.

"You're just being kind."

"I'm not that kind, Madeline," he said, his gaze darkening. "I'm rather selfish. I've made myself rich—and Frank da Silva even richer—by seeing the value others overlook."

Maddy frowned, fighting her body's desire. Though his fingertips barely touched her, they brushed up against the light cotton fabric of her blouse, the sensation tethering her as surely as if he'd held her tightly. She shouldn't let him touch her. Shouldn't allow him to soften her like this.

"You were prepared to sell The Grove sight unseen," she challenged, needing to recover.

"George's College was offering a substantial amount of money for this land," he said, then leaned in close, as if he was sharing a secret meant only for her ears. "I just said I was selfish. I want what I want, Madeline Murray."

Her heart pounded so loudly in her chest she was certain he could hear it. Did he want her? It seemed impossible—just like this garden. Yet, he'd made his pleasure plain. He wanted her. And she wanted him.

"What do you want from me?"

"I want to worship you, Madeline Murray," he said, with such deliberation and confidence it shocked any protest she was about to voice. "Worship every inch of you."

With slow, deliberate movements, he traced circles in the palm of her hand with his fingers, then brought her hand to his mouth and between breaths, kissed the tips of her fingers.

"I want to see that lush skin in the sun and kiss every freckle. I want to taste the skin behind your right knee, and where the curve of your hip meets your legs. I want to run my tongue along your belly. I want to lose myself between what I have imagined to be the most perfect set of breasts to ever exist."

"When have you been imagining my breasts?" she whispered, in a vain attempt to keep her breath steady. This man was disarming her with every word out of his beautiful mouth.

"Since the day in the bookstore," he said, running his lips over the back of her knuckles, the warmth of his breath rushing over her skin. "Since the first moment I saw you, standing in that store, like Tatiana. I have never wanted anything more, Madeline Murray, than to make love to you."

He lowered her hand, and her entire body shuddered from the deprivation of his tender kisses. Until today, she'd never been kissed. Until today, she'd never known what it was to be really and truly wanted by a man in such a pure, carnal way.

Maddy had read countless books—some tragic, some serious and meditative. But her favourites—the ones she read over and over, in the quiet moments when she was alone, were her romantic stories. Gallant knights who pledged their love and their bodies to beautiful women of the court. She'd wished a thousand times for someone to look at her like she was worthy of such devotion. Such attention.

It was possible he was lying. But he had nothing to gain. The dowry was gone. Madeline Murray had nothing but herself to offer.

I want what I want.

"I have no idea how a person is worshipped," she said in little more than a whisper.

"I have had weeks to consider it," he said, with a conviction she found difficult to comprehend. But before she could think it more deeply, he claimed her mouth, and she was lost to a world of sensation.

Even though he'd seen her nearly naked by the river, this was different in every possible way. Any lingering modesty was gone. He trailed soft kisses along her neck as he unfastened the buttons on her blouse and pulled it from her shoulders, unwrapping her with all the care of an elaborate Christmas package. The hooks on her skirts were no match for his nimble fingers, and soon they were in a puddle under her feet, leaving her in nothing but her drawers and corset. When he pulled the delicate ribbon on her corset cover, he kissed the top of her breasts, sending an aching need through them. In response she'd wrapped her arms around his waist, pulling him against her, savouring the hardness of him.

When he'd unhooked the last of her corset fastenings, exposing her breasts to the sun, he'd stepped back. Panic edged through the haze of pleasure that had enveloped her, and she found herself fighting the urge to put her arms over herself.

"Is there something wrong?"

Beau saw the hesitation in her eyes—that flicker of self-doubt that he was determined to dispel. His mouth went dry as she stood before him like Venus in her garden. She only had her drawers on, and he'd rid her of those soon enough.

"Only with my imagination," he said, his voice a low growl, pulling off his shirt. "I wanted to give my eyes something to feast on before my hands and my mouth take over."

He pressed gently up against her, so she would not be mistaken about how his body wanted hers.

"Do you feel that, Madeline?" He'd been stiff as a board since they'd been on the shore, but he wanted her to know how much he desired her. "You are a feast for a man's eyes."

His ran his hands over her body, cupping her breasts, lifting them to his mouth, teasing her nipples which were already at a delicious, tender point. Every inch of her was so sensitive to his touch. He realized, with both a tinge of sadness and excitement, that he was the first to grab her hips, cup the generous cheeks of her bottom, and revel in the fullness of her breasts. Every moan, every breath urged him on, and it was difficult to keep his own lust in check. But he promised he would worship her, and he would take his time.

With more strength than he thought possible, he broke his kiss. He took her skirt and spread it on a soft piece of ground, then undid the lace of her drawers. Biting back a moan, his hands itched to graze the strawberry blond mound that stood as a crown at the top of her legs. But that would wait.

Carefully he helped her to lie down, then, kneeling in front of her, pulled off her boots, the hilt of a small throwing knife flashing in the sun as it peeked out of a specially made pocket. Facing her once more, he ran his hands long the length of her calves, and, brushing his fingers up along the softness of her thighs, he slowly removed her stockings. It occurred to him them that he would buy her some silk ones, embroidered with her favourite flowers. Her gaze was soft and heavily lidded, signalling to him that she was lost to a world of her own sensation.

He lazily stroked tiny circles behind her knee, first with his fingers, then his mouth. She tasted like sunshine and waterfalls and—to his utter delight—roses. The fact she'd anointed herself with rose perfume brought a smile to his face. This private little part of herself was just another treasure he'd discovered. Naturally, and for comparison, he had to kiss her behind her left knee, just to be sure. She let out the smallest of giggles, and there was a shyness in it he found endearing. It was at odds with her fulsome beauty, on display for him alone.

"Are you ticklish, Madeline Murray?" he asked.

"I don't know," she said, genuine curiosity in her voice. "I suppose I am."

He loved her sounds. Every sigh, or a sharp intake of breath, sent a new rush of desire through him. He'd known from the moment he saw her that he wanted her. But he'd never understood, even in that moment of want, how deep his desire ran.

He brushed up against her sex, taking in the undeniable elixir of her readiness. He felt her hips move as he did so, as her body searched for the pleasure she had been too long denied.

"Not yet," he said, as he peppered her belly with soft kisses. "I promised I would kiss every inch of you. And I'm a man of my word."

Her fingers tangled in his hair, stroking the back of his neck. He loved the subtly possessive way she'd reached out, as if she was bestowing her grace on him. He kissed his way back down to the mound of strawberry blond hair between her legs. As if she'd sensed his intention, she parted her legs. The moment he put his lips to the side of her thighs, grazing just the outside of her sex, she gave a pretty little sigh.

Soon his tongue explored her soft folds, wet with anticipation of him. Gently, he inserted a finger inside her sex. She stiffened slightly, then relaxed again. With small, steady strokes, he moved his finger, then inserted another, all the while administering his attentions to clitoris. He'd barely touched it when she came, crying out, lifting her hips toward him as the full force of her orgasm moved through her.

He lifted himself up, resting on his knees, stroking her legs as she opened her eyes. Her face was flushed from her climax, but she looked up at him, her brow furrowing.

"What about you?" she asked.

"I wanted you to have your pleasure" he said, eager to assuage whatever cloud threatened to overcome her. It took every ounce of control he had not to spill his seed in his own trousers. "I didn't expect you to risk yourself for mine."

"I am used to risk, Beau da Silva," she said, "I trust you to be careful."

I trust you.

It was all the invitation he required. He positioned himself over her, finding her opening. Her body yielded to him, and he buried himself in her tight, lush folds. Soon they were moving in a gentle but urgent rhythm, the edge of his own climax coming. He slowed, wanting to make this last. But as he looked down at her, her hair spread out like a fiery halo, her lips full and parted from their kisses, his body could no longer wait for the rest of him to come to terms with what they were doing.

And more dangerously, what it felt like. It was pleasure, yes. But it was so much more than that.

And that was new.

She cried out a second time, and Beau, sensing his own climax threatening to overtake him completely, pulled out, spilling his seed on the ground.

They laid together quietly for a few moments before rising. For a second time today, he helped her dress. They didn't speak for a while, both contented with the silence.

"I hope that wasn't too uncomfortable for you," he said at last. While he'd suspected she was a virgin, the exquisite tightness of her, and the momentary hesitation on her face as he entered her, seemed to confirm it. "This wasn't the softest surface to lie upon."

"It was much more enjoyable than I had imagined actually," she said.

He couldn't help but start at that assessment of his lovemaking. True enough, the setting was not quite what he imagined, and he'd imagined their coupling more times than he'd dared count. But all of them involved a bed, or at the very least, a roof.

"Dare I ask what you'd imagined?"

"No, you may not," she said, blushing again. "And I was reasonably well read on the subject."

"Now I must know what scandalous books you keep by your bedside," he said, equal parts aroused and intrigued by the notion of Madeline reading books of that nature. The very thought threatened to make him hard all over again. "You really don't need to do any more to make me dream about you, but you just keep on doing it, don't you?"

"There is nothing wrong with being informed about the sex act," she said. "Though there is so very little about how you feel."

"This is when the poets are useful," he said.

"Most poets are male," she said. "I don't know that any of them had ever explained that."

"Maybe you could write a book then," he said. "For educational purposes, if nothing else."

She stopped to examine an overgrown hedge, carefully examining it before moving on.

"I would rather spend my time in a place like this," she said with a sense of conviction Beau found himself envious of. "I'd rather be outside, with sun on my face, working with these glorious plants."

"Why do you love them so much?" he asked.

"I don't know," she said. "I suppose it's because I can come to them as I am, and that seems to be enough."

She was enough for him, he wanted to tell her.

How many times had he wished he'd been enough? How many times had Frank berated him for his early failures? A breeze rushed through the garden, dancing through the scraggly blooms, whipping up a torrent of memory that he'd normally kept buried under a heavy layer of business meetings, parties, and other diversions that he'd used to drown out the loneliness.

"Perhaps I should take up gardening," he said, more to himself than to her.

She looked at him with a peculiar expression—as if she didn't understand or didn't believe his insinuation. And, if she had read the social columns in the papers, it would be more than natural she wouldn't believe him.

"My father—Frank that is—was a demanding man. He loved my mother, his company, and his children in that order. I'd struck out on my own—with my fishing business, but after a few years, he wanted me to come back to Silver Lumber. I wasn't happy about it, but it turns out this face and mouth were far better at making money than either of us realized." He paused, his hands itching to reach out and take her hand. Instead, he clasped them behind him as he walked.

"Why did you go back? Was the outfitting business not working?"

"It was doing great," he said. "But Frank rarely asked me for anything, and I thought— "

"You thought it would be nice to be needed," she said. "Needed by someone you loved."

Something in Beau's chest tightened, as if she'd unknowingly hit on something so tender he hadn't had the opportunity to prepare himself.

"I spent fifteen years at the company chasing that man's respect," he replied, taking a moment to clear his throat to rid himself of the sadness that had trapped itself there. "And now I know, I suppose, that I probably would never have earned his love."

"Well," she said, her manner circumspect, "if he was going to will you the company, and he loved it so much, he must have trusted you with it. Maybe that was his way of expressing it."

Beau turned that over in his head. Frank was many things, but sentimental wasn't one of them. And he couldn't care less about appearances. If Beau had failed him, the company would have gone elsewhere—maybe even to his brother-in-law.

Beau dragged his hand down his face. He hoped to hell that Neil had nothing to do with Frank's death. Frank liked Neil. Hell, he probably loved him.

But he respected Beau.

"Maybe," he said, something loosening in him. Years of resistance, of numbing himself to the emptiness of working for a man who would never love him, started to yield. He let go a long, low breath as he tried to channel the whirl of pain, of loss, of grief for the complicated man who'd raised him and given him his name. "Christ, I think I might even miss the old man. I just realized I didn't even get to pay my respects at his funeral."

"When Dominic solves your case, you can go back to Saint John and do that," she said.

While the idea of not swinging from a noose appealed, the very last thing he wanted to do was the thing he'd always thought he'd been born to do—take over the company.

But Frank da Silva wasn't his father. Beau's father lived a half mile away.

And his heart, he realized, was sitting in the hands of the woman walking next to him.

Chapter Nineteen

BEAU WALKED along side Madeline as they made their way out of the garden. She, at least, seemed able to delight in her surroundings, pointing out one plant or another as walked back to the entrance. Perhaps it was her way of shielding herself from any awkwardness that had arisen from their coupling. Beau remained silent, still grappling with a torrent of emotion that left him completely out of his depths. Normally his carnal activities were like much of his life; satisfying in the moment for both parties, but largely transactional.

Crossing the little bridge, they soon came upon a large oak tree that had been felled by some mighty storm.

"Did you see this?" Madeline said, pulling Beau out of his thoughts. She'd jumped over a bit of brush and pointed to a series of markings in the tree. They were weathered, but there was no mistaking the initials:

H.C. + E. R.

Beau was silent as a wave of melancholy washed over him. An echo of a past love, and heartache, scratched into a tree by two people whose brief affair had created him. He'd never experienced a broken heart—at least, not from a lover. That his parents

—or at least Hollis—had, brought him a measure of sadness he hadn't anticipated.

"I wonder if they would have been happy here," he said.

"Perhaps for a while," she said. "But perhaps what your mother did was best for both of them, in the end. She was quite brave, I think."

"Risky," Beau answered, unable to keep the sharpness at bay. Why did this hurt him so much?

"Men do risky things all the time, and are celebrated for it, even when the stakes are much lower for them," she countered. "Your mother clearly knew she would not be happy here. To have that knowledge at such a young age is a gift. They would have had to marry, and how sad would it have been for the both of them, and you, if that one event had left them in a loveless union?"

Beau sat with that for a moment. For all Frank's faults, he worshipped Beau's mother. There was nothing he wouldn't do for her. The one solace he now possessed was that Frank and his mother may have been reunited. He'd showed Beau what it meant to be head over heels for a woman who was, as far as he could recall, equally in love with him.

"You're a wise woman," he said, fighting the urge to pull her into his arms and kiss her again. It was a selfish act, he knew, because he wanted it to soothe his own hurts.

"I have the gift of distance from all this," she said. "It's easy to seem wise when the pain isn't your own."

The back of his hand grazed hers, sending a tendril of longing throughout his body, begging him to reach out and take her hand. But she had already turned away.

They continued on toward the house. "What will you do, when this is over?"

If she had asked him this question two days ago—heck, maybe even this morning—he would have known the answer. But basking in an afterglow of lovemaking had left him paradoxically satisfied and greedy for more. He was surrounded by the equally tempting threads of possibility in this tangled garden, with its riot of colour, scent, and untapped potential. Everything he thought he wanted had tilted.

"I have to run that company," he said, as if to reinforce to himself what was expected of him, even if the thought of the day-to-day running of a lumber empire made Beau want to crawl out of his skin "People depend on Silver Lumber for their livelihoods. Frank worked too hard for it."

"What will you do with this land, then?"

She might as well asked him how he would walk to China.

"I don't know," he said, and smiled to himself at the pleasure he took in being able to be honest with her. He had no idea. But he'd seen the way she'd looked at it—with such longing. "What do you think I should do with it?"

"Gift it to someone who will love it," she said, her expression bright with enthusiasm. It was so contagious, it seemed to swell in Beau's chest. "Someone who will tend its gardens. I could see it being a lovely haven for people who need nature's embrace."

"Gift it?" Beau said, and in that moment, he realized that perhaps he was Frank's son after all. "The proceeds from this would make a tidy legal fund."

"I am sure the contents of your closet could be sold to make a tidy legal fund," she said, a darkness edging her tone.

"Do you want it?" he asked.

If he had offered her the moon, she would not have looked more surprised than she did at this moment.

"I have Everwell," she said, as if that was the answer to everything.

"Do you?" he asked. "Do you plan to stay there forever?"

She nodded with what he might assume to be complete confidence, save for the hint of doubt in her eyes.

"What happens to the place when Miss Everwell dies?"

"Tilda will run it," she answered.

"Mrs. Gilman is of an age," he said. "I assume—and certainly hope—that you will outlive her. She is at least twenty years your senior."

"Thirty, actually," Maddy said.

"More to the point," he said. "Does it go in trust?"

"Technically, Rimple Jones is their heir," Maddy offered. "She has been Lady Em's ward since she was a child. The property will be hers when the time comes. But Rimple would never throw us out. Everwell will endure."

"But do you want to stay there forever?"

Why was he pursuing this? He'd bedded Miss Murray. More to the point, he'd deflowered her. Still, he'd expected that the encounter would satisfy whatever hold she had on his senses. Instead, it magnified them.

"I suppose I do," she said. "After all, it has all my books and my gardens. And I have work there. My life is there. Everyone I care about is there. And everyone who cares about me."

Not everyone, Beau wanted to shout.

"Nothing about this appeals to you?" he asked.

"But you are not really offering it to me," she said. "And beautiful as it is, I couldn't do this on my own. I wouldn't want to."

Maddy and Beau returned to the house in companionable silence, each lost in their own thoughts. Beau had promised to worship her, and he'd made good on that promise. And if it was only once, to sate his own curiosity, Maddy had selfishly taken the experience and pleasure for herself. She would not let Malcolm Ferguson be the last man to have touched her; a touch that had begun in deceit and ended in anger. If there was nothing else between her and Beau, he had given her something more. Beau had given her pleasure, and more importantly, the sense that she was, in that moment, the one thing he desired.

His provocative question about Everwell played in her mind. The place was not immune to change. Students came and went. As the city's circumstances changed, and not for the better, as the number of people knocking on their doors looking for help grew. Foster, Lady Em's beloved butler, had passed away several years ago. And in the past year, both Elouise and Gemma had found husbands and no longer resided under Everwell's roof. She would love Everwell and be devoted to it until her dying day. But there was something magical about The Grove. Just like there was something about Beau.

The sky, which had been brilliant blue with a few blousy clouds, darkened as they approached the house. As if amplifying Maddy's internal turmoil, the wind picked up, moving through the grass, and tossing the leaves in nearby trees, showing the silvery backs of the maples.

"I think it's going to rain," she said, peering up into the sky. "I think we got back just in time."

"Making love under a summer rain seems like a wonderful idea," he said, coming back to that playful part of himself. "Don't you think?"

"Perhaps," she said, trying hard to suppress a smile. She was completely out of her depths. The idea of Beau making love to her in a summer rain sounded as equally appealing as him making love to her by the fire on a cool fall evening—like a dream. A dream she was terrified to have.

"You are hard on a man's ego," he said. "But lucky for me, mine is strong enough to bear it."

A few drops of rain started to fall, and they quickened their pace. As they got to the house, Beau let out a curse.

"Shit," he said, gesturing to a handful of tools that had been left aside. "I was supposed to take these to the tool shed. I guess I was too distracted by the thought that I might find a beautiful woman bathing herself in the river like a forest nymph."

Maddy blinked. He kept saying these things, these words that should have been lovely and wonderful but, even after everything, felt like an illusion—some sleight-of-hand trick.

"I'm going to get these out of the rain before they rust," he continued, seemingly unaware of her unease. He picked up the tools and ran down the path toward the tool shed.

Maddy watched him go, partially because that's what she was here to do, and partially because she seemed unable to help herself. But after all that had happened this afternoon—as wonderful and thrilling as it was, she felt a compulsion to turn away… as if she needed to detach herself from him.

She continued toward the house, the raindrops falling here and there, as if the clouds themselves were uncertain of their intent. Maddy paused at the pergola, taking a moment to appreciate the work Beau and the Chandlers had done. Soon, however, the rain started to fall in earnest. She ran inside the back door, surprised by the contentment that settled on her like a warm embrace as she entered the house. She brushed it off as nothing more than the relief one might feel from getting to shelter in the middle of a rain. After all, the only place she could truly be at home was Everwell. Everwell was where she belonged. This was only a job. A job she'd only taken to keep Veronica Turnbull and her NWL cronies from exposing the truth about The Everwell Society.

Who here was the selfish one?

After returning from her room to refresh herself and change her clothes, Maddy was about to start supper when the sound of carriage wheels caught her attention. At first, she assumed that the Chandlers had returned, perhaps to take back a large piece of lumber, but as she peeked out her window, which looked onto the back of the house, there were no horses. Frowning, she walked to the front parlour window, where a small but well-equipped gig sat in the same path where she and Beau had upon their arrival. Her body tensed, and she immediately felt for the small knife she'd tucked in her sleeve when she realized she hadn't strapped it on. It was too late to retrieve it when a knock at front door stopped her in her tracks.

On impulse, she grabbed her apron, hanging on a peg near the front door, and tied it around her waist. Smoothing her skirts and schooling her expression, she fell into the mode she had time after time at Everwell.

She pulled the door open and her stomach dropped.

Nelson Taylor stood on the front step. He looked up at her, regarding her with an expression that moved from disinterest to discontent.

It took every ounce of Maddy's strength to keep herself fixed where she stood.

"Good afternoon," she said, keeping her voice polite and firm, and not giving a tinker's damn he was standing in the weather. "Can I help you?"

"Is Mr. da Silva about?" he asked. "And do not tell me he isn't at home. I know he is in the area."

Maddy stifled a groan. Nelson Taylor was many things, but stupid was not one of them.

"He is not," she said, which was a lie and yet somehow perfectly true. Convenient, that. "Is there a message I can give him?"

"He can't be far," he said, rather insistent. "I can wait and speak with him, or I can bring the authorities. Your choice."

Maddy pressed her lips together, carefully trying to decide her next move. She was here to play Beau's housekeeper as well as his bodyguard, and she didn't want to overreact—yet. It would have been so easy to send Nelson to the ground and make him regret ever coming to this door. But that would send him straight to the authorities, and further prejudice them against Beau. Elouise Charming, Everwell's talented actress whose ability to use disguise was second to none, often reminded her fellow Scandalous Spinsters that people generally see what they expect to see. Nelson Taylor shouldn't expect to see Madeline Murray, the naive girl that had been at the centre of that cruel game he, Malcolm, and a few others had concocted. He expected to see an aged, humourless spinster who was housekeeper to Beau da Silva, the man from whom he wanted to buy this property.

She led him into the parlour and silently congratulated herself that she remembered to offer him refreshments. She was tempted to lace it with something from the big recipe book, but had not yet come to the remedies on laxatives. She decided, however, that if she was ever to try forcing mustard seeds in fresh horse dung, she knew exactly who she'd feed those greens to.

Beau returned as she prepared the tea. Despite the fact his clothes were rumpled and wet from the rain, he was still as handsome as ever.

"I saw some horses," he said, coming into the kitchen and wiping his face with a linen towel, his expression far more guarded.

"Nelson Taylor is here," she said. At the mention of him, Beau stilled, took her hand, and gave it a gentle squeeze. "I was going to send him away, but he knows you are here."

"You don't have to go back there."

"He didn't recognize me," she said, gently pulling her hand away. She had to be sharp now. "At least, I don't think so."

"You don't need to say anything else, Madeline," he said. "I can deal with him."

"But I'm here to protect you," she protested. "That's what you are paying me for."

His eyes went hard then. "I am not paying you to put yourself in that kind of danger."

"I'm not afraid of him," she said, swallowing the lie. Nelson had found Malcolm's body—had seen her run and reported her crime to the local authorities. She'd lived in fear of him ever since. "Do not use my name around him—he could use that against you. It might put you in greater jeopardy."

"He's here to see me," he said. "He's been talking to the Chandlers. A brute with a shovel might be beyond my skill, but a greedy man looking to make a bargain? That is my specialty. Give me five minutes."

He gave her a reassuring smile, then bounded up the stairs. Maddy followed, carrying a tray with tea and a few of the biscuits Annie had brought over that morning. Her arrival barely drew

Nelson's attention, as he'd already concluded that she was beneath her notice. She had to keep it that way. He was standing in front of her bookshelves, pawing her precious books. It took all her self-control not to tear him away from them and throw him out the front door.

"He will be here shortly," she said as she set the tea down and poured out a cup for him.

As if on command, Beau appeared in the doorway. Somehow, the man who'd ravished her in the garden in his shirtsleeves had disappeared, replaced by this polished gentleman in a fresh suit, looking every bit the relaxed country gentleman.

"Can I help you?" he said, putting on a polite, disarming smile. He turned to Maddy. "You may go."

His dismissal was one of an employer to a servant, and it jarred Maddy more than she'd imagined. Still, it was part of the charade she'd agreed to, and a moment like this, it truly mattered. Maddy nodded silently and left.

She would not go far.

Chapter Twenty

BEAU RESISTED the urge to watch Madeline leave, focusing all his attention on his uninvited guest. Despite the fact Nelson Taylor was of average height and had the build of a gentleman, he bore the manners of a man who needed to prove his importance. Beau had been so blinded by his anger at Mr. Taylor's slight toward Madeline near the rail platform, he had not noticed the man's reddish-brown hair or his rather remarkable beard.

But there was something more today in the way he pulled back his shoulders, puffing up his chest like a pigeon prancing around a park bench. It was a sort of confidence that came from knowing you had the upper hand.

There was no doubt why. At the moment, he had Beau's life in his hands. Taylor was coming to make a deal, and with terms so utterly in his favour, he could walk out of here a very rich man. Clearly Taylor knew who he was. But Beau had always found it useful to acknowledge any advantage that his opponents thought they had. If they thought they could use your shortcomings against you, they would. It was far better to own one's harmless indiscretions rather than have them weaponized. Patricide was far more than harmless, but the principle still held, especially since Beau was innocent.

He decided the best defense was to deflect that pomposity with his own. Confidence was king when your neck was on the line—in business anyway. Frank had taught him that, and it had been a good lesson.

His uninvited guest had been pawing at Madeline's books, helping himself to one of the volumes. Taylor slid the book back on a nearby shelf as Beau held out his hand.

"Beau da Silva." Beau introduced himself with the same ease he used in all his business dealings, a signal to Mr. Taylor that his being here did not rattle him in the slightest. "And you are Mr. Nelson Taylor."

His opponent nodded curtly. "I represent George's College."

They shook hands, then Beau gestured for them to sit.

"This is quite an eclectic little library you have here," Taylor said, gesturing to the shelves that housed Madeline's books. "I didn't know you were a rosarian."

"I spent some time in Boston with the Gardners," Beau replied. "They have a remarkable garden built right into the courtyard of the house. I was hooked."

The story was partially true. He had been to dinner parties in Boston several times at the Gardners. He'd made the connection through Hugh Evans, whom he'd saved from drowning.

Taylor appraised Beau carefully. There were far too many unspoken questions in the air.

"I take it you are here to discuss the offer for the property?" Beau asked, eager to get this man out of his house as soon as he could with as little damage as possible.

"Yes indeed," he said. "I just paid a visit to the Chandler farm, and decided to take the opportunity to call on you personally."

"Let's get to it then," Beau said. "My housekeeper has provided tea, but if we are going to get into the business of negotiations, then perhaps something more bracing is required."

Mr. Taylor waved off Beau's offer. "My client has been anxious about the sale. They are eager to acquire the property, so they can proceed with their plans."

"And what would those plans be?" Beau asked.

His question seemed to take the man off guard. What the buyer of a property wanted to do with it was not really his business. When Beau had originally decided to sell, he hadn't given much thought to it. Of course, that was then. Before he'd found he enjoyed reading in the chair near the window in this parlour, or taking his breakfast with Maddie in the dining room, which had lovely sun in the morning. Before he'd found his grandparent's recipe book and fixed up the pergola with his half-brother.

Before he met his father.

And most definitely before he'd discovered the garden and made love to the most beautiful woman he'd ever met.

"To build a new school of course," Taylor replied. "The plans are quite remarkable. There will be enough room for two hundred students, all from the most desirable families across the northeastern United States as well as the local area. An oasis where young minds can be encouraged."

Soon Taylor was rambling on about a chapel, a gymnasium, school rooms, a library. Stables for horses. Lodging for students, faculty, and the small army of staff required to run it.

"They, of course, will be lodged on an adjacent property," Berwick continued.

"Adjacent?" Beau replied. "Do you mean the Chandler property?"

Mr. Taylor nodded. "We have made them an offer as well. Contingent of course on the sale of this one. It would have no value to us without this one as well. They have been resistant to the idea. But I'm certain once you and I come to an arrangement, they can be made to see reason."

Beau's gut tightened. This was the matter Taylor had pressed Daniel about. Despite Daniel's non-committal tone, perhaps the Chandlers were interested, if the money was good enough. Daniel had a daughter living in Avonford, a small town on the Bay of Fundy a few hours away. Hollis had just come from visiting her.

But he'd heard Daniel talk about the plans they had for the

farm. How he hoped to give it to Teddy one day. If Beau sold the property, the Chandlers would have to move.

He'd just lost the man he'd thought was his father.

He could lose the man who was.

Beau took a moment to gather his thoughts. Used well, silence was a powerful tool. Instead of filling the air with mindless conversation, Beau took his time, spooning a bit of sugar into the tea Madeline had poured out for him. He stirred the liquid, watching the sugar disappear, then picked up the delicate porcelain cup he and Madeline had found packed away in a crate. All the while, he felt Nelson's stare boring into him.

"I've been rethinking the offer," Beau said. "Now that I've arrived, I've become quite taken with the property."

"I didn't think a man of your reputation would be interested in an old house and a barn," Taylor replied, his voice edged with forced nonchalance. "Unless, I suppose, he needed a place to hide from the law."

Beau laughed. He couldn't help it. The moment Taylor had shown up at his door, Beau had known. It was out now, and Taylor had shown his cards.

"An innocent man doesn't need to hide from the law," Beau said, taking a sip of tea. "You're a lawyer, aren't you? You should know that. Unless, of course, you are more interested in keeping the guilty out of prison."

Taylor narrowed his eyes and idly stroked his beard. "If you're not hiding, why are you here? No one's lived in this house for at least twenty years. And you hardly look like the sentimental sort."

Once upon a time, Beau would have agreed with him. He hadn't been particularly sentimental. Frank had only been interested in what he could earn.

"I was already making plans to visit and conduct an informal survey of the property when this business happened," he said. "If I were guilty, do you think I would come here, of all places, when I could find a lovely little apartment in Rome and live out my days unbothered by the cold or a court in New Brunswick?"

Beau watched Taylor study him, trying to pick apart the truth. Beau had to believe this statement to the core of his soul to be convincing. And he could only hope that the heavily coded message he'd sent back to the detective might help the case get solved.

"In fact," he continued, putting on his best smile, "we recently were informed of a very promising break in the case. I expect to be back in the boardroom at Silver Lumber in a fortnight. At the head of that boardroom table, I might add."

He put down the cup and leaned in, as if inviting Taylor in on a secret.

"Please tell me that a man of your intellect would not be so eager to collect a mere two hundred dollars," he said deliberately, choosing each word carefully, "only to lose out on the potential of future business with Silver Lumber or any of our customers across New England. Contacts who might be eager to send their sons to George's College."

Nelson stilled, the implications of Beau's threats landing on his shoulders. It was a hollow threat, though Taylor couldn't know that. Without any word from Dominic, Beau's future was still very much in jeopardy. But the last person Beau would ever do business with was a man who'd treated someone he thought beneath him so abominably. Especially if that person was Madeline Murray.

"What kind of business?" Taylor asked, once he'd recovered himself. As Beau suspected, the man was driven by a familiar principle: greed.

"Once the charges have been cleared, we can discuss it," Beau replied. "Do we have an agreement?"

Beau could tell the man was wavering. Besides whatever fee he was charging the school trustees, Taylor would no doubt earn an extra fee if he sealed the deal. He had to be as invested in Beau's innocence as Beau himself.

"I will consider it," Taylor said at last, getting to his feet and leaving his business card. "In case you need someone to keep you out of prison and in the board room of your company."

From the room across the hall, Maddy peeked from behind a lace curtain, watching Nelson hop into his gig and drive away. The rain had already start to let up, but her insides were roiling. She stood motionless, watching the horses, not daring to look away until they were out of sight.

"He's gone," Beau said, leaning against the sturdy wooden door frame, projecting an effortless sort of calm that Maddy wished she could bottle for herself.

"How can you be so calm?" she asked. "He could turn you in in a heartbeat if you don't give him what he wants. You're still a wanted man."

"Only by you I hope," he said, his lips turning up in a sly smile. "You've quite ruined me for anyone else."

"This isn't funny," she said, pushing aside his compliment, knowing full well it was an attempt to soothe her. Instead, she found herself only becoming more agitated.

"I'm not trying to be." He pushed himself off the door, walking into the room, the nonchalance gone, replaced with an unbreakable sense of confidence. "He's not a threat to me."

"How can you be so certain?" Maddy crossed her arms and turned toward the window, watching the gig until it disappeared. "He just tried to blackmail you."

"And I turned the tables," he said. "Nelson Taylor is many things, and greedy is one of them. Silver Lumber is a big company. We control a lot of the markets and have access to many of the same people that George's College wants to use to populate that school. If he turns me in, I will simply reach out to my contacts and tell them to stay away."

"They don't have to listen to you if you're swinging from a rope," she said.

"Why do you always expect the worst to happen?"

"Because the worst happened to me," she snapped. "And that man was right in the middle of it."

Beau crossed the room in three strides, standing in front of her, brushing away a stray lock of her hair. She fought the urge to sink into him and allow his strength to support her.

"It happened to you," he said, his mouth crinkling into a soft smile that made her feel safe. "You've been through some truly horrible things, and you are still here. You've shown me over and over just how strong you are."

"What if I don't want to be strong anymore?" she said, cursing herself for the unwanted hitch in her voice. Tears pricked the back of her eyes, and she blinked, desperate to keep them at bay. "What if I want to just want to sink in a chair with a book and not worry who might be coming to the door, or what they say about us in the papers? What if I just want to work in the garden, and go for long walks, and just live without having to worry about everyone else?"

Maddy turned away, fighting to keep her emotions from spilling over.

"Madeline," he began, his voice low and soothing. "You don't have to be strong for me. I don't deserve it."

Maddy warred with herself, wanting his touch and yet hating herself for desiring it. If only her fellow spinsters could see her now—completely undone by a man.

"That is why I am here," she said, unable to look at him, even as she found comfort in his presence. Comfort she didn't deserve. "Or have you forgotten?" Because only an hour ago, she certainly had.

A second knock at the door interrupted them. Maddy jumped, then realized it was coming from downstairs.

"It's the kitchen door," she said, pushing past Beau, just in case Nelson had returned. This time, she had her knife safely in place.

Maddy took a deep breath then flung open the door. Teddy Chandler stood on the step, wearing a toothy grin.

"Good afternoon Master Chandler," Beau said, standing beside Maddy. He spoke with that effortless charm of his, as if he and Maddy hadn't just been bickering about blackmail and his safety. "How can I help you?"

"Mom and Dad wanted to invite you to supper tomorrow," he said. "You too, Miss Murray."

Maddy noticed that Teddy was looking up at Beau with undisguised curiosity. She wondered if Hollis had spoken with the family about this prodigal son.

"We'd love to," Beau replied. His voice was even, but there was something there—trepidation perhaps—in his very short answer. More so, amazingly enough, than when Nelson Taylor had been sitting in their parlour only a few moments earlier.

Beau's parlour, Maddy silently corrected herself.

They invited Teddy in for a few cookies, but the boy politely declined. He kept looking at Beau, and Maddy was confident his parents had made Teddy aware of this long-lost connection. He spilled out the essential details, such as the time they were expected, most importantly that his mother was making a cake, before running off back toward home.

"Well," Beau said, raking his fingers through his hair. "We've just been invited to a family dinner."

Maddy rose early. Birdsong peppered the early morning stillness, a welcome reprieve from the cacophony of thoughts running through her head. She'd spent half the night staring at her bedroom door, lit by a generous moon, wondering if Beau was awake. Her body, traitorous thing that it was, craved his touch. Even worse, her heart craved his boundless confidence that Nelson posed no threat.

After a simple breakfast of boiled eggs, toasted bread, and strawberry jam, she spent time in the kitchen garden. She'd wanted to harvest some raspberries, but would not allow Beau or the house out of her sight. For his part, Beau continued to work on the pergola, brushing the first of several coats of linseed oil on the wood to help preserve it. While Beau was confident Nelson would not return, she was not so certain. Occasionally she paused from her gardening to walk around the house, carefully surveying the meandering path that would bring any visitors to the property.

Still, the day passed fruitfully enough, and by mid-afternoon, Maddy and Beau stopped their labours to prepare for dinner. After she put her tools away, Maddy refreshed herself with a cool hand bath and dressed for dinner. She hadn't packed anything remotely appropriate for the occasion. Her fellow spinsters, however, most definitely had. There, at the bottom of her trunk, was a lovely pink skirt she'd worn once before, as part of an ensemble Rimple had made for her for a job she and Elouise had done at Government House last year. Maddy smiled in spite of herself. No doubt Elouise and Rimple were responsible for putting it there. While the evening bodice she'd originally worn it with was far too fancy for their surroundings, pairing the corded silk skirt with a fresh white blouse would be just the thing. She took time to brush the dirt from her boots and make them some-what presentable, especially when the dinner was meant, no doubt, to welcome Beau to the family.

A small clock in the dining room chimed the hour, signalling the time to depart. Maddy stopped in the hall and gave her hair a cursory glance. She'd sat in front of one looking glass or another while her mother stood over her shoulder, dishing out her endless criticisms while a hapless maid tried to contain Maddy's wild hair or fade her freckles with some homemade concoction. Mirrors had become a reminder of her shortcomings, and she'd come to dislike them. There was always an improvement to be made. Fixed, as if she were broken. Even at Everwell, she had to endure Elouise's well-meaning sessions in front of a mirror. And while Lou loved Maddy's wild hair to the point of envy and delighted in her freck-les, it was exhausting.

So when Beau stopped beside her while she was attempting to shove a hairpin back into place, his question took her aback.

"Am I allowed to tell you you're beautiful?" Beau asked.

Maddy grimaced. While they had both enjoyed the love-making in the garden, Maddy could not just rid herself of the lingering distrust that came with the compliment. Beau seemed to genuinely admire her. Why was it so hard to accept? She knew he was not Malcolm Ferguson. Malcolm had had the veneer of charm, but it had been stretched over a littleness of character that could not stand even the smallest test.

A fresh wave of guilt—that same guilt she'd carried with her for nearly two decades—landed on her shoulders like a lead cloak. Yes, she hadn't intended to hurt Malcolm, even though he had every intention of hurting her. But it did not change the fact that a man was dead, and even if she had fought to protect herself, she was partially responsible.

The story in the society pages of the Halifax Chronicle haunted her. Last fall, during the Red Coat Job, Gemma had heard rumours through a member of the New Women's League that Everwell not only housed women of questionable character and possibly thieves, but something even more dark... a murderess. Gemma had told the story over tea laced with a generous helping of whisky after it had all concluded. While most of her fellow spinsters had laughed off the accusation as something so ridiculous it belonged in the bin, Maddy—who was not given to drink of any kind—swallowed her tea in a single gulp. Only Phillipa Hartley knew her entire story, which meant Lady Em and Tilda did, too. How the whisper of that dark chapter in her life had followed her here, she did not know.

And yet Beau wanted to know if he could tell her she was beautiful.

"I don't know," she replied at last.

"Would you deny that the sun rises in the morning?" he asked.

"Of course not," she replied. "That's a fact."

"So is your beauty," he replied.

She rolled her eyes. "You are beautiful," she said, turning to face him. "And that is a fact."

"Why is it I am beautiful—thank you—and you are not?"

"Because look at you!" she said. "Your face could be put in a dictionary beside the very term. It's what Rimple would call an 'objective truth.'"

He cocked an eyebrow, not bothering to disguise his disbelief. "So what you are telling me is that your opinions matter, and mine do not."

"That's not what I am saying," she said. "You have not had a lifetime of people trying to improve you."

"That's a rather remarkable conclusion to have." An unmistakable edge dampened his usual lightness. "How well do you know me?"

She blinked, taken aback by his question. "I—"

"I spent a lifetime with a man who tried to turn me into a version of himself," he said. "And I suppose he partially succeeded."

"I hadn't thought of it like that," she conceded. "Because you seem like a perfectly fine man. A very good one, in fact."

He'd called himself selfish on more than one occasion, but the longer she spent with him, the harder it was to believe. He treated the Chandlers with respect. He treated her with respect. And after she was able to move past the fear of encountering Nelson Taylor on the street, the fact that Beau was willing to defend her honour so easily was something she would not forget.

Beau da Silva was a good man in a world where it seemed hard to be a good man and be celebrated for it.

"I believe you are humbling me," he said, his cheeks flushing from her compliment. "Mark that down in one of your books, Madeline. I can't recall the last time that happened."

"How about I let you tell me how beautiful I am," she said. "Because perhaps I need to be a little less humble."

He cocked an eyebrow, looking at her with the same eagerness she'd seen in tigers at feeding time at Down's Zoological Gardens.

"Where do you want me to begin?" he asked, his voice low and dangerous. "At the top of your head, or the bottom of your feet?"

Chapter Twenty-One

AFTER A RATHER BREATHLESS—AND entirely too short—round of lovemaking, Beau and Maddy managed to put themselves together in time for supper, arriving at the Chandler's door at the appointed time.

The Chandler homestead was built in the common fashion of many farmhouses in the area, with whitewashed boards and window sashes accented in green. Unlike The Grove, this was very obviously a working farm; the nearby barn was full of animals, and below, fields full of potatoes and grain glistened in the gentle summer evening light. Under the windows, there were boxes full of violets, pansies, and a host of other plants that Beau could not name but gave the house a welcoming glow. Nearby, the twinkling of a homemade set of chimes adding their gentle music to the birdsong and leaves that made up Mother Nature's symphony. Through the nearby window, which was open, notes of savoury herbs and roasting chicken wafted through the air, rousing his appetite.

Beau put his hand to the door and after a moment's hesitation, gave it a gentle tap. It had been ages since he'd been this nervous. An old fear clawed at him, and despite Madeline's assurances that they would not have invited him here if he was not wanted, it lurked under the surface. The endless demand to prove his worth had not stopped with Frank's death. Indeed, it had crystallized it to a fine point. Now he was standing at the door of a family he didn't know until two days ago, and part of him wondered if he would pass their test.

They stood expectantly for what seemed like a long time. He missed the sensation of Madeline's arm resting on his. She'd taken it as they walked over, listening to him as he wrestled with his nerves about meeting a family and navigating a relationship that was new to all of them. But as they approached, she'd released him, a cruel reminder of this unusual dance of identity they found themselves in and for the sake of propriety.

No one is going to make you marry me.

He'd had to content himself with the hint of her scent and the weight of her skirts brushing against his leg. But my, how hungry he was becoming for her. One taste was normally all he required of a woman before the fascination waned. As he tortured himself with the implications of his insatiable need for her, the door opened.

Daniel Chandler stood in the threshold. His brother. Beau had no idea what Hollis had said to them, but all the confidence he'd found in his dealings with Nelson Taylor deserted him.

"Good evening," Beau said, then held his breath, waiting for the awkwardness. Instead, Daniel's face broke into a wide smile as he held out his arms, welcoming Beau with an embrace.

It was the strangest sensation, this warm welcome. Beau had rarely been so warmly embraced after his mother passed away, particularly by a man. Frank was never one for outward signs of affection, at least where Beau was concerned. He wondered if it was his imagination, this distinct sense of a bond between them. But it felt real.

They released their embrace. Annie stood alongside her husband, waving them inside.

"*Pjila'si,*" she said in the tongue of her foremothers. "Come in," she repeated in English. "Make yourself at home."

She winked at Beau, and he realized that in some way, he was home. He was excited and nervous all at once as he crossed the threshold. He wanted to reach out to Madeline. Her presence wasn't just intoxicating. It was comforting.

"These are for you," Madeline said, offering a bouquet of flowers and greens she'd picked earlier. Like Madeline herself, the arrangement was bold, full of unexpected pairings of colour and shapes. "I'm a horrible baker, but I do know something about plants."

"More than a few things I'd say," Annie said, then gestured toward the front parlour. "Beau, why don't you sit with Hollis and Teddy, and get to know your family. Maddy, perhaps you can come with me and pick out a vase for these."

Madeline looked to Beau, asking him the silent question—*will you be fine without me?* Even now, it seemed, she was on guard for him. He nodded in return. She followed Annie, disappearing toward the kitchen. It was ridiculous that he felt her absence when she was only a few dozen feet away.

He followed Daniel into the cozy parlour where Teddy and Hollis stood. Anticipation crackled in the air, and Beau found an expected hitch in his breath as he was hit with an overwhelming sense of longing. He wasn't sure what to do with his hands, until Hollis held his out.

"I know that you weren't expecting any of this," Hollis said, "and you don't owe me anything. But if you are welcome to it, perhaps we can shake hands?"

Beau held out his hand, and this time, knowing this man was his father, found it wasn't enough. He moved in closer, motioning for an embrace. A hug from his father.

What started as a tentative embrace turned into something more. Comfort and longing mixed with each other—sensations he'd sought in the bottom of a whisky glass, or in late night negotiations chasing a business deal, or the satisfaction watching the bottom line of the company grow to earn even the most passing acknowledgment from Frank. But those memories were hollow.

Right now, it felt as if Beau had spent a life time in a windowless room with only an oil lamp for light, and had just stepped out into the daylight for the first time.

And, like looking at the sun, it brought tears to his eyes.

He squeezed them shut, trying not to make an ass of himself when his heart was suddenly so full he thought he might burst.

"It's all right, my boy," he heard Hollis whisper in his ear. "God didn't go through the trouble of giving men tears if they weren't meant to fall from time to time."

Something inside him broke apart at that gentleness. And for a moment or two, he held on and let those tears fall.

At last they broke the embrace with a gentle pat on the back, and soon the tears turned to laughter. Save for Teddy, who was treated to a bottle of root beer, whisky was poured and toasts were made.

"I guess you got a little more than just a stone house and a berry patch," Daniel said as he took a seat on a chair. "Of course, I got a little more than just a headache from some rich stranger who was planning to sell my best sheep pasture without taking a look at the place."

Beau took a sip of his whisky.

"You must have been thrilled to hear I was coming," he said. "Trust me, I wasn't thrilled to be here." Until someone shot Frank da Silva and framed Beau for the crime.

A sliver of grief ran through Beau, and he shifted in his seat at the memory of the man who raised him as his own.

"Teddy," Daniel said, "Why don't you go see if your mum needs any help in the kitchen?"

Teddy, who had the sense of being dismissed, gave his father a pleading look to stay.

"I know," his father said, answering his unvoiced question, "but we have some private things to talk about."

"Is it about the letter?" the boy asked. "I know about that."

Daniel and Hollis exchanged a look before returning his attention to Teddy.

"Why don't you finish putting up the paper streamers in the dining room?" he said, clearly unwilling to discuss what was a sensitive topic in front of company. "That would be a big help. Just don't let Miss Murray see."

The second suggestion, which piqued Beau's interest, seemed to sit better with Teddy, who stopped in front of Beau on his way out of the room.

"Can I call you uncle, then?"

The boy's directness and the request took Beau a little aback. Not because of his question, but because of the word "uncle". Jessica and Neil did not have children, and the title was a novel one to Beau.

"I suppose you can," he said, sounding out the phrase several times to himself, trying it on like a new suit. And like one tailored for him, it fit perfectly. "Uncle Beau has a nice ring to it, don't you think?"

Teddy nodded, gave him a wide, toothy grin, then proceeded on his mission in the dining room.

"Are the streamers for Madeline's birthday?" Beau asked.

"They are," Hollis said. "Annie made her a cake. But it's meant to be a surprise."

Beau smiled to himself. First, at the Chandlers' thoughtfulness, especially Annie's. He'd been thinking of Madeline's birthday from almost the moment she'd mentioned it to him. What present would be good enough for a woman like Madeline Murray? She didn't seem to care for jewels. He'd bought far more expensive trinkets for women he didn't care for, mostly because it was so easy to go to a jeweller and ask for something flashy. It was easy, it was expensive, but in the end, it was meaningless.

Of course, the book he'd boughten her was not an everyday gift, but he would buy her an entire library of precious volumes if he could. Maybe when this was over—when Dominic Ashe finally solved this case and he could go back to Saint John and get things to rights there—he would take Madeline to Boston or New York or even London, to the best book shops, and let her have her pick.

Something twisted. When this was over, Madeline Murray was going back to Everwell. Unless he could induce her to go to London, or Boston, or anywhere beyond her beloved rose gardens.

And the only way to do that was to marry her.

Beau smiled, thinking back to their encounter in her rose garden back in Everwell. He'd landed on his back, nearly breathless. Of course, he'd been rendered breathless from almost the moment he'd met her.

"Can we talk about Taylor's letter?" Beau asked, idly swirling the amber liquid in his glass. "Was it about an offer from George's College?"

Daniel exchanged a look with Hollis, then nodded.

"What you do with your property is your business. We didn't want you influenced by us."

"He came 'round to see me yesterday," Beau said. "I told him I wasn't selling."

"Won't that fella turn you in?" Hollis said, his brow furrowed with concern.

"We came to an agreement," he said. Men like Taylor could be bought, and Beau could afford it. If Dominic solved the case, he could walk away and never worry about this ever again. "I'm not worried about him."

"You seem confident," Daniel said.

"Too confident," Hollis repeated. "You must get that from your mother. There wasn't much that scared her."

A shadow passed over Hollis' face, and Beau wanted to ask more about it, but this was not the time.

"I've handled men like him before more times than I can count," he said. "I know what they want, and I've always managed to give it to them while still getting what I want."

"How did he take it?" Daniel asked. "Word has it the college was offering him a bonus if he could secure both properties."

"He wasn't thrilled, but it's my decision. I'm not inclined to be kind to the man, after what I saw of him when we first met."

"Well," Hollis said, "I suppose that's a relief. I helped build this house with my father and his father, and I'm happy for Teddy to have it if he wants it. And I think your grandparents would be pleased to know you're not going to give up The Grove."

"What were they like?" Beau asked, genuinely curious. "Knowing Aunt Vee's inclinations, as well as my mother's, I have to say I can't imagine them growing up here."

"They were good people. Fair. And probably a little eccentric," Hollis said with a far-away look in his eyes, as if he were catching memories and holding on. "I helped out around the property, seeing as they had daughters. Not that they weren't put to work, because of course they were. But they were very private people. I always suspected they came from money, though. Your grand-mother spoke with an accent. Not sure what kind—but it sounded like one of those Slavic tongues."

Beau thought back to the book, and to some of the recipes he saw there. They were unusual to him, but he would return to it with fresh eyes.

"Were my mother and my aunt happy?"

"I think so," he said. "Your mother, she was restless. It was probably hard for her. Emily sparkled. Once she found a fancy necklace of her mother's and she snuck it out of the house and showed it to me. She was so excited. She imagined her mother was a princess—a runaway princess, living in the woods. And you know, I have to wonder about it. It was like nothing I'd ever seen."

The idea of his mother wearing jewels didn't surprise Beau in the least. Some of his clearest memories of her was her wearing her jewels. He got Hollis to describe it, but nothing caught in his memory. He would have to ask Aunt Vee about it when this was all over.

Beau asked Hollis more questions, but this time about Daniel's mother, and about his family. The niece who lived in Avonford, that he hadn't yet met.

Teddy bounded into the living room followed by Annie and Madeline.

"Supper is ready," Annie announced, giving Beau a little wink.

Something was amiss. Maddy could feel it in her bones. It wasn't a bad something, but a something nonetheless. She could tell by the twitchiness in Teddy's body language. The way Annie, who was normally as calm as a soft summer morning, nearly lunged at her when she offered to take a basket of freshly sliced bread out to the dining room. And now, she saw a spark of something in Beau's eyes that bordered on mischief.

The ease of the three men with each other brought a smile to Maddy's face. She'd gone with Annie to give Beau the time and privacy to have conversations with Hollis and Daniel without her hovering about. Normally she should have been happy to have the break from him, having been her near constant companion for over a fortnight. But as she helped Annie in the kitchen, tossing salad greens and generally making conversation, she found herself distracted by Beau's absence. It was utterly ridiculous, given he was under the same roof. But she found herself missing his presence. He somehow steadied her, filled her up while turning her world upside down at the same time.

"I'm starving," Daniel said, rubbing his hands, signalling his hunger and eagerness for the feast Annie had been cooking. And it was a feast, as far as Maddy could tell. This was a family reunion of sorts. The Chandlers, reunited. A missing piece of the puzzle, now back into place.

Where did that leave her?

She wasn't lonely—not entirely. Part of her had been lonely for so long the sensation had become familiar. She had her Everwell Spinsters, of course, and she did miss them. Her birthday was tomorrow, and if she were home, they would have had a little party for her. Rimple would have made a cake, and she would have been presented with a new book. And another year of her life would have come and gone. But tonight, and indeed, this entire adventure, was not about Maddy. It was about Beau, and it was about helping Everwell. Phillipa had promised her funds from this job to help build a new greenhouse. That was a present, that for years, Maddy could only dream about.

"Shall we?" Beau said, walking to Maddy and offering his arm, which felt so good. So right.

And she took it.

They walked down the short hallway to the dining room. Maddy's breath caught in her throat as her heart filled with an emotion she was coming to recognize as joy.

The room was beautifully lit, sparkling in the warmth of a fading sun glinting from a single stained-glass window to the west. Garlands made from paper flowers in the shapes of peonies and cabbage roses were strung from the ceiling. It created a lush sort of fairy garden hanging above her.

She turned to Beau, about to gush about how wonderful it was for them to go through all this to make it special for him, when she spied a beautifully decorated chocolate cake sitting on a side board, and above it, on a sign that it looked like Teddy had made himself, read the words: HAPPY BIRTHDAY MISS MURRaY.

She blinked, and kept blinking, trying to keep the tears at bay. Maddy didn't cry. She certainly never cried publicly.

"Beau told us about your birthday, and the cake your friends make for you," Annie said. "I'm sorry you are missing your friends."

"Thank you," she said, turning to Annie and smiling through blurry eyes. "You didn't have to go through all this trouble just for me."

"Don't you worry, Maddy," she said, looking at Beau and smiling conspiratorially before turning back to her. "I get to decide what trouble I want to get into."

"I think my sign is pretty good too," Teddy pipped up. "Though I almost forgot the 'a'. I hope you don't mind."

"It's perfect," she said. "Honestly, I have never seen anything so perfect in my life."

"Well, that is somewhat disappointing," Beau said, cocking an eyebrow and looking so devilishly handsome she wanted to kiss him right there. "I assumed the moment you first met me you'd already crossed that threshold."

"Hey," Daniel pipped up, "I think I got the looks in this family. Eh, Annie?"

"Well you got them both from me," Hollis said, looking for all the world like a man at peace with himself.

"I think that is enough Chandler bravado for one evening," Annie said. "Come and sit, before it gets cold."

They all took their seats. The table was lavishly set, and Maddy was certain every bowl and plate in the house had been put on display just for her benefit. At her place setting, there was a small posy of wild rugosa roses in a small glass cup.

It was, compared even to the faded elegance of Everwell Manor, humble in size. But there was no less joy around that table. Beau sat beside her and all felt incredibly right. Plates were passed, toasts were made, and the cake was served. And though she would rather die than admit it to Rimple, Annie's chocolate cake may have been the best she'd ever had.

Throughout the evening, she felt Beau staring at her, and a warm tingly sensation spread through her body. She yearned to reach under the table and brush her hand up against the hard muscle in his legs. They had only made love a few hours ago, but her body wanted more of his. She wanted the comfort of his warmth, the elixir of his touch, and the way his smile lit up her insides like nothing she'd ever experienced.

As the tea was poured, and the last of Annie's dandelion wine was drunk, Maddy was content to listen to the stories around the table. Stories about how Daniel and Annie met, stories about Daniel's mother, that Hollis told with the bittersweet melody of a man still missing the love of his life. And every once in a while, she looked up to see Beau smiling at her as if she was a brilliant shining light in the darkness. Part of her realized that maybe, just maybe, there was nothing she enjoyed more in the world than the way he looked at her. Nothing more wonderful than the way he made her feel.

Beautiful.

And as the laughter rose from the table at one of Daniel's stories, somewhere in the corners of Maddy's heart, a different sort of yearning took root.

The thought, impossible as it seemed, that there was a life to be found outside of Everwell.

Chapter Twenty-Two

A FULL MOON made the lamp Beau held as they walked back from the Chandler farm almost unnecessary. It had been a magical evening. They had welcomed him and Madeline unconditionally. They had traded stories about the past, and Beau discovered that he and Daniel had the same sense of humour and the same self-effacing ego. And most importantly for Beau, they had made Madeline feel as if she were the most special person in the world.

And she was.

That realization hit him square in the chest. Yes, he had wanted to bed her from the first moment. He'd been struck by her presence, quiet and yet magnetic. He'd been tantalized by her fiery red hair, her lush curves, and eyes that told everyone who dared hold her stare that she was not a woman to be trifled with. For Beau, that had been an absolute dare.

But he'd chased women before, like he'd chased money—for the challenge. The thrill of not letting something he wanted get away.

In the past few days—and probably more than that, since it was coming on so slowly he'd assumed his cock had still been in control—he realized that whatever his feelings were for Madeline, they were far deeper and urgent than just bedding her. And that had been magnificent. It continued to be. But there was something more. She was becoming necessary. And her happiness had, most unexpectedly, become more important to him than anything in the world.

The fact that the Chandlers seem to understand that, made them important too—even if Hollis Chandler had only been the neighbour next door. For that reason alone, Beau would have thrown out the entire deal with George's College to save their farm.

Sometimes he wondered the rather useless question…*what if?* What if Hollis and Beau's mother had managed to stay together? What if he had been raised next door?

It was a pointless exercise, of course. His life, and that of both his parents, would have been completely different. His mother had been very happy with Frank. If she harboured any regrets, she never expressed any to Beau. And while Hollis still carried some fondness for Beau's mother, Shirley had clearly been the love of his life.

Beau knew from the moment Daniel embraced him that selling The Grove to anyone was out of the question. Yes, he would lose the substantial offer George's College was making. The ease with which he was now letting that go would have, not so long ago, seemed impossible. Beau da Silva didn't lose money. He made it. Even when he'd sold his beloved fishing lodge, he'd made a good profit on it. Chasing the next dollar seemed like the only way to get Frank's attention, if not his admiration. And that had filled the emptiness inside him.

Now, The Grove, and everything about it, filled him with joy.

"If you weren't at Everwell," he asked, his heart pushing forward the question before his brain had the chance to consider the better of it, "and you didn't have to worry about anything, what would you do?"

Moonlight mixed with the lamplight, casting her pale skin in an unearthly glow. She paused, and it was obvious she was thinking.

"If money was no object, do you mean?"

"I suppose so," he said, realizing yet again that for him, money largely hadn't been an object, except to chase. But it had rarely been a barrier.

"I would have a wonderful garden," she said, "and a library."

"But you have that at Everwell," he replied.

"I do. But I am always on guard there. Always on lookout," she said. "If I could, I would put all that energy in to growing things. Using those plants to create beautiful things."

"Like what?"

Even in the pale light, he could see she was blushing. "You'll think it's silly."

"Madeline Murray, there is nothing you could say that I would consider silly."

"I would like to make things that let people feel pretty—nice soap, for example," she said. "Gemma brought me home some lovely French milled soap from Montreal when she was there. I've made rose oil before. And then maybe I'd put it in a shop and try to sell it. Or give it away, to women—or men for that matter— who need a little something. When women come to Everwell, sometimes they come with only the clothes on their back. They've been beaten down by life. They are scared. And maybe they've never felt as if they deserved something nice."

Beau's heart twisted a little when he considered her words. How many times had Madeline felt like she hadn't deserved something beautiful?

"It seems like such a simple thing—a bath, fresh clothes, a safe place to sleep," she continued. "I always make sure there are fresh flowers in the room, and we sometimes make soap and scent it with the rose petals from my garden. Or other things."

"That's not silly at all," he said. "Providing someone a little dignity, a little bit of joy is never silly."

The moonlight hinted at the smile on her face as they continued on in companionable silence. Soon they were through the path, where the house stood waiting for them, its slate roof glistening in the silvery glow from the heavens.

"What if you had the ability to pursue that," he said, an idea gripping hold of him so tightly he stopped in his tracks. "To have your garden and your books and make your soap. Would you want it?"

"I can't," she protested, stepping away from him as if he were offering her something dangerous. "I'm so busy at Everwell, it would be hard to— "

"But what if you weren't at Everwell?"

The question seemed to hang in mid-air, the only sound the odd hoot from an owl in the nearby woods. Her brow crinkled in confusion, as if the question didn't make sense.

"Just pretend," he pressed, as gently as he could, trying to stem his own excitement. "You like to read. If you were to read— or perhaps write a story, and your main character wanted to have their gardens and their books— "

"—and cats..."

"And a cat."

"I said cats."

Christ, Beau hated cats.

"Right—gardens and books and cats, what would they do?"

"I suppose they might try making some nice soap and find someone who might be willing to sell it for them."

"Yes—in all the finest shops maybe?"

"Maybe," she said. "But she wouldn't do that, because she wants all sorts of people to have her soap, and she wouldn't want it to be out of reach of the people who would appreciate it most."

"I see," he said. "And maybe she could use some of the proceeds of the soap and give some to a girl's school."

Her eyes went wide then.

"She would," she said. "And maybe she would find a patron, to help defray the costs. And maybe she could even invite some of the women to stay, and work with her. They would get job experience, a small stipend, and their confidence back."

"And what do you think she would call this business?"

"I don't know..I'd have to think about it," she said, and Beau couldn't help but note the excitement in her voice. It made him so incandescently happy to see her this way.

Hearts aside, it was a good idea. A damn good idea. A business venture with a conscience. Small but affordable luxury—he'd known more than a few men to get rich on the idea. Her vision for it was so clear, it made Beau excited not only for her, but for the idea itself. His thoughts instantly went to his grandparent's green book, full of notes and the recipes for soap, tonics, and ointments that she might want to try, using ingredients that could very well only be found on this property. He could talk to Aunt Vee and Jessica about how they might convince their connections to carry the soap in some of the stores. New ideas always sparked a thrill of possibility—novelty always excited him of course, but this was something else.

But he could also imagine himself here with her, helping her choose the recipes, find the customers, and doing all the things he was good at—working with people—while she handled the things she clearly excelled at. He could be her number two. And together, maybe, they'd have something special.

Of course, he couldn't offer for her until his name was cleared. It would hardly be worth tying herself to a wanted man. And unless Dominic Ashe found something—anything—to help him clear his name, it wouldn't be worth offering her.

That is, if she wanted it.

Somehow, the fact that he was wanted for murder seemed like an afterthought—an odd inconvenience. And the idea of going back to take on the helm of Silver Lumber, which had never been a particularly desired future, was more unpalatable than ever. But Neil was there, and his brother-in-law knew more about that company than anyone. Even Jessica showed a keen interest in the business, and if Neil and the directors of the company would get the hell out of her way, she'd do an admirable job with it, too. Hell, she had a better head for numbers than any of them.

They walked up the stone steps, and soon were at the red door. Madeline held up the lantern while Beau opened the latch.

"What if, in your story, there was a fairy godmother—or perhaps a shockingly handsome prince—who would agree to be your main character's patron for this venture?"

Maddy stood speechless at Beau's question. The door had swung open, but she remained rooted to the spot, stunned by his suggestion. Was he joking?

She had to give him a great deal of credit for framing her daydreaming in such a way that it felt safe for her to talk about.

But there was a something else there, lurking just below that joy. It was an old companion, one that had been with her since nearly as long as she could remember—the nagging sense that joy like that was for other people.

"I don't know," she said, standing at the threshold of a house she'd fallen so deeply in love with from the moment she saw it, looking up at the man standing on the other side, waiting for her. "I think she might be afraid to say yes."

"Why is that, do you think?" he asked. "Because it doesn't seem like your heroine is particularly afraid. Indeed, she seems very brave to me."

"But maybe she isn't," Maddy said, swallowing back years of loneliness, of feeling unworthy, that she'd buried underneath a thick plate of anger. "Maybe she just pretends."

"I understand that," he said. "Because I think the hero—if there is indeed a hero and which I hope there is—is also just pretending. He's pretending to be confident and happy and devil-may-care because for so long, he didn't know what it was like to have someone really care about him."

Maddy's eyes widened, fixing on Beau, the lamplight flickering on his perfect face. An evening breeze rose, teasing his hair. The faintest hint of shadow fell across his face, highlighting the lines around his eyes and mouth. He seemed so boyish most of the time, even though they were the same age. But now, she saw the age settling on him. The weariness. The trepidation.

"I also wonder," he continued, his voice low and warm, "if your heroine wasn't stolen by the faeries, and you somehow were mixed up, placed with the wrong family. And that family, those people, didn't know what to do with someone as magical as the heroine. So they did what small people do when they are afraid—they diminish those around them, to feel bigger, stronger, and smarter. And for a while they succeeded."

"Until she escaped."

"Until she escaped," he said. "And found people who were not afraid of her. Who loved her. And let her be the faerie queen she was meant to be."

Maddy pressed her lips together. She felt like she was on a precipice. She loved her fellow spinsters with all her heart, for exactly the reason Beau said. They had taken her in, accepted her when no one else would. Would leaving them be a betrayal? They needed her. How on earth could she do that to them?

"I don't know if I could leave Everwell," she said, voicing her fear out loud to the one person she felt safe doing so.

"Maybe you wouldn't have to," he said. "Not permanently. If you were having people stay, you would be going back and forth all the time, when the roads were good, anyway. Just because you are opening a new chapter of your life doesn't always mean closing off another completely. I believe there is at least one of the ladies in the Society who has a husband."

Maddy nodded, wrestling with her own complicated feelings and regret. She'd been happy, and yet hurt by both Gemma and Elouise's changing status. Not because they'd found love, but because she hadn't and deep down assumed she never would. That the happy bond that had kept her feeling safe and secure would somehow tear, leaving her afraid.

It hadn't happened.

But. *But.*

"It's not chocolate cake," he said. "But I would like to give your heroine a way to live her dream."

Maddy leaned in, because she was certain she misheard him.

"What did you say?" she asked.

"It was your idea, don't you remember?" he said. "Gift it to someone who would treasure it. And I know no one who would treasure it more than you."

Maddy shook her head. "I don't understand," she said. "Why?"

He stepped toward her, cupping her cheek in his hand.

"Because I believe in Happily Ever Afters, Madeline Murray. Especially yours."

Maddy's heart roared so loudly in her chest she could barely hear herself think. Beau stood, just inside the door, the lamplight at his side, bathing him in warmth. His hand was extended in invitation. It hinted at a promise—a promise of something so exquisite she felt herself giving in to its power.

She'd walked in and out of this door countless times in the past few weeks, not giving it much thought.

But tonight, when Beau held out his hand, she somehow knew in her bones she was crossing a threshold. Something was happening, and it felt good. Impossibly good. Every contrary voice—the one telling her to run, or stay and fight, was slipping away from her, drowned out by something tantalizing. A promise for something else. Her own joy.

It was terrifying.

"What is it?"

He stood there, expectant, and somewhere in the haze between fear and longing, it dawned on Maddy that Beau was able to read her expressions. To know her. And not just her body, but something far more vulnerable—her heart.

"Beau," she began as she took a step back, "this evening was lovely. More lovely than I could have imagined. But it's just not possible."

"Why not?" he asked, giving his head the smallest shake, as if he didn't understand her answer. And he wouldn't, she supposed. He just didn't understand what it was like to risk everything the way she had. To lose everything.

"It's a marvellous idea. A sound idea. And it would make you happy."

"I am happy," she replied. "At Everwell. I have everything I need there."

She'd been safe there. The only place she'd felt safe. Accepted. Loved.

He stilled, and she felt strangely compelled to offer an explanation.

"Beau, The Grove would make someone a wonderful home," she said. "And it should go to someone special."

"Don't you think you're someone special?" he said. Frustration edged the normally smooth edges of his voice. He sighed and smiled again. "Perhaps you need some time to consider it. It is a big decision."

"I don't need more time," she replied. "Maybe you need to rethink this. After all, you have a family next door now."

"They have a home they are already in love with," he said. He shoved his hands into his pockets. "Madeline, a few moments ago when you were talking about your dreams you were so happy. Why wouldn't you want that?"

How on earth could she give him the answer to a question she didn't know the answer to herself? Her hands clenched at her sides.

"Why do you care so much if I am happy?" she asked. "I'm nothing to you."

Was it Maddy's imagination, or did he flinch at her question?

"I can't tell if you just insulted me, or yourself," he said, his stare suddenly hard as ice. "But neither of us deserve that censure."

"I was happy at Everwell, Beau." she said. "It was enough. And if you hadn't come and—"

"—taken you away from your books and flowers? Yes. You

said as much. And when they catch the bastard who murdered my stepfather, I will ensure that your inconveniences are added to the charges," he said, naked sarcasm in his voice. "In the meantime, I apologize for any presumptions I had about trying to make you happy."

He turned, about to enter the house, leaving Maddy alone in the moonlight.

"I never asked it of you," she said, calling after him. "I never asked anything of you. And I certainly never needed you to make me happy."

Her words flew through the air, as if she'd thrown a blade that grazed his cheek before it hit the wall behind him. He turned back to her, his jaw tight, and when he spoke next, his voice was brittle, as if he was holding back his own fragile emotions.

"No, you did not. But here is the most remarkable thing of all. I shouldn't care for you, Madeline Murray. I shouldn't care one wit if you are happy or miserable, as you seem so damned intent on being. But I do. I care for you very, very much."

Maddy blinked. Not because of his admission, but because the very idea that he might not want her was somehow more than she could bear. She wanted to push past him and get herself out from under his steel gaze. And she could have done it, if she chose, move him out of the way without so much of a thought. Push past him and every terrifying thing those words stood for. Instead of reaching out with her hands, she used her words.

"What would you have me do?" she whispered, her throat so tight she feared the tears stuck in her throat might erupt in a sob. "Leave all my friends, every bit of safety I have ever known, for some fantasy? You go through the world with your beautiful face, charming smiles, and perfectly cut suits and the world is happy to open whatever door you chose to walk through. It doesn't work that way for me. You cannot be so unfeeling as to disregard why this is so much of a risk. Not everyone gets a happily ever after."

He stood, unmoving and if Maddy didn't know better, she

would have thought for a moment he was waiting for her to continue.

"Unfeeling," he said at last, but it was more of a murmur, as if he was talking to himself than to her. He nodded in agreement with a conversation he was having with himself. "I am unfeeling."

"Beau, that is not—"

"I am not a young upstart that needs to prove himself by marrying a rich man's daughter to make his fortune. I am not so small I need to make someone else small to feel strong." There was something in his voice—a hardness perhaps—she'd heard before, but only once before—directed at Nelson after he'd insulted her. "And I will not turn myself into a rude, obstinate version of myself just because that is what you seem to take comfort in. I grew up with that man, Madeline, but I will not become him. Not even for you."

He turned away and disappeared into the darkness of the house, leaving her alone on the step, the moon at her back. The sound of peepers and crickets were overcome by the pounding of her heart in her chest. And it was breaking.

Chapter Twenty-Three

If Beau had been in Saint John, he would have been tempted to drink himself into oblivion. Between the intoxication and the blinding headache for days afterward, he would have had some kind of reprieve from the hollow pain in his chest. As it was, he spent a restless night, drifting in and out of sleep, wondering how on earth he could have allowed himself, once again, to find himself in need of approval from a person who would never give it to him.

Of course, unlike Frank, Madeline Murray had never demanded anything of him.

At least he hadn't gone and told her he loved her. It was one thing to be a fool, and it was another to be a fool in love. She'd known that heartache once, and never recovered. She'd once been sweet-talked in a way that he now understood had damaged her in a way that still bled into that heart of hers—a heart she kept armoured, lest it be damaged again.

Beau would never wish a man dead, but he could not find it in his heart to be sad about Malcolm Ferguson. He'd treated Madeline so poorly that he'd robbed every man after him of even a chance at her trust and affection. Not that he thought Madeline had anything to do with his death, of course. He had not seen a single indication of the sort of temper that would inspire a person to inflict such grievous injury on another.

He lingered in bed, coward that he was, as he heard her rise. He couldn't face her yet, and he sensed from the cautious way her bedroom door opened this morning that she'd had a similar trepidation. Best not to spoil her morning by inflicting himself on her first thing. He waited until he heard the door below swing open, then rose.

He dressed, then went downstairs and brought the fire back to life to heat water for coffee and a shave. Even yesterday, he'd been considering installing a modern stove. It was 1876 after all, not 1776. Now he had no idea what to do with The Grove. Maybe he would sell it after all. Not to George's College, of course, but there had to be someone who might want the property. He would still come to visit the Chandlers—they were family. But even as he stood in the dining room, gazing out the window, he didn't know if he could bear being here without Madeline. Just out the window was the kitchen garden, which was remarkably tidy given what it was when they arrived. Even he could make out some of the plants now—chives, sitting in thick clumps topped with purple flowers, next to taller plants with blowsy leaves and star shaped tops he recognized as dill.

Christ. Maybe getting back into the boardrooms of Silver Lumber would be for the best. He'd always used the business as a distraction. After last night, he would need it more than ever.

Movement caught his attention, snagging away his self-pity. Teddy Chandler was bounding up path toward the door where only last night, Beau had had his heart properly broken.

"Good morning," Beau said, greeting Teddy with a forced smile. "You're remarkably spry after a late night."

Teddy's eyes narrowed before realization dawned at Beau's joke. His young face broke into the same benign expression that every youth gave every adult who'd thought they were being clever.

"Yes sir," he said, then paused, then looked at Beau with a curious expression. "Can I call you Uncle now?"

"I suppose you can," Beau said. "Can I ask why you're knocking on my door at this ungodly hour of the morning?"

Teddy gave Beau a look of utter confusion. "It's not ungodly. It's nearly ten o'clock. It's not even early."

Not willing to debate the relative merits of birds and their breakfast habits with a grown up that should be extolling such virtues, Beau was about to change the subject when Teddy reached into his pocket and pulled out an envelope.

"This came this morning," he said. "Dad said I should bring it right away."

Beau's heart lurched as he recognized the stamp from the telegraph office and directions to deliver it straight to the Chandler farm. He let out a low breath and accepted the envelope.

"Thank you."

Teddy nodded and was about to leave when Beau called out. "Have you seen Miss Murray?"

"She's in the barn," he replied. "Hitting a big sack really hard."

Beau smiled in spite of himself. Teddy continued on his way, while Beau turned his attention to the envelope, wondering if he should get Madeline before he opened it. While she'd made her feelings toward him quite plain, her future would also be shaped by whatever news Dominic brought. Pushing his discomfort aside, he started toward the barn when he caught sight of Madeline running toward the house.

"I saw Teddy running with a note in his hand." Her skin glowed from her exertions, and she gestured to the note in Beau's hand. "Did you open it?"

She was dressed in a loose-fitting pair of trousers and a simple blouse over her corset. In her hands was the box of knives he'd first discovered packed away with her books.

"Are you playing at pirate today?" he asked, taking in her figure, which, without the draping of skirts and petticoats, was a cruel reminder of the bodily pleasures they'd shared.

"My fighting clothes," she said, giving him a shrug. "A lot was said yesterday. I needed to think."

Despite her attempt at nonchalance, he could tell her armour was back in place. Now, it was protecting both of them.

He tore open the envelope and pulled out the note. As expected, it was from Dominic Ashe.

Good news. Case resolved. Secured confession from new suspect. Bad news. Neil Sweet confessed. Your information was helpful.

There was more—Dominic was asking Beau to meet him in Saint John as soon as possible—but he found himself re-reading that first line over and over. Beau didn't realize his hand was shaking until he felt Madeline's hand steady his.

"May I see?"

Wordlessly he gave it to her, then sat down on the bench before his feet gave out.

"I'm sorry," she said quietly. "Good news and bad news."

She sat down beside him, and he drank in the steadiness of her presence.

"I feel badly for your stepfather," Madeline said. "This must have been a horrible betrayal."

Memories of countless family dinners came into sharp focus, where Frank and Neil had sat deep in conversation, laughing together, while Beau seemed a distant observer. Beau had often joked about Neil being the favourite son.

He rubbed his face with his hands. "I want this to be a mistake."

The job was over.

Beau, consumed by the news he'd hoped for and the news that had clearly rocked him, was lost to his own torrent of thoughts, leaving Maddy to her own.

He probably hadn't needed her at all—the only real threat he'd faced had come from Nelson, and he'd managed that quite well on his own. She'd tell Phillipa that there had been little need for her to be a part of this job, and she might as well stayed in Everwell and looked after her blighted roses.

Funny how there was no sense of victory in that.

The beautiful evening they had spent together, the offer he had made—and her rejection of it—had evaporated into thin air. Maybe she would have regrets later. Blessedly, there was too much else to do.

He would go back to Saint John, be with his sister, and take on the company. And she would go back to Everwell, her library, and her roses.

Maddy should have been satisfied with that. She'd spent the morning lost in the flurry of her training, working through a torrent of emotion she wasn't sure she wanted to feel. Beau had made her the centre of his world, and she, too late, realized she was becoming accustomed to it. Becoming soft.

Every moment she sat beside him, that softness allowed regret to seep under her skin, pulling her down. She had to fight it.

"You go see the Chandlers," she said, getting to her feet. "Let them know they no longer have a wanted murderer as a son and brother. I'll start packing. We can be on the first train home."

Her declaration seemed to startle him. She quelled the impulse to comfort him with a hand on his cheek, and as he rose and walked away, without looking back, she was struck by the sense of longing—and hurt. What had happened to her? The case was solved, and she could only hope that Veronica Turnbull would see her part of the bargain through. It was the only reason she'd come. Everwell would be compensated, she'd have her greenhouse, and Beau would be nothing but a memory.

It should be right. But after years of scraping by on enough, she found herself doing something she once thought impossible—dreaming of a life beyond Everwell. A life of her own.

And maybe, a life with Beau.

The cool water she'd drawn to wash herself helped shake her out of this maelstrom of feelings, if only momentarily. She pulled on her traveling dress and packed up the rest of her clothes. Selfishly, she thought about going back to the keyhole garden and picking out her favourite plant, taking a cutting or two she could take home with her. A souvenir. It wasn't fair that a garden like that would go unloved for so long. Because she would have loved it.

Instead, she retrieved one of her trunks and took it to the parlour. One by one, she started packing her books. As the volumes of poetry, gardens, and most especially, her beloved novels were pulled off the shelves, her mind turned to the green recipe book downstairs. What a wonderful book to add to her library. All of that knowledge, the experiments with plants and that horrible recipe for forcing mustard greens that Rimple would be fascinated by, shouldn't be sitting forgotten on a shelf for another twenty years. It deserved a good home.

She'd been so tempted to take it and tuck it away, as she had so many other books she'd found sitting unloved in dusty libraries owned by rich men who collected them as they collected so many other things—merely for owning them, not for the loving of it. Of course, that wasn't entirely fair, and the memory of Beau's excitement as they'd looked through it that first day he'd found it brought a smile to her lips.

It would stay.

Besides, having a reminder of that moment—the moment she'd nearly made an idiot of herself and kissed him—was not something she'd want in her library. There were fantasies, and then there were *fantasies*, and the latter would be far too painful.

Packing her books was not difficult, especially since she'd carefully arranged her small collection by subject, then by author. And though Beau did help himself to her small collection, he had always managed to put them back exactly how she'd arranged them. As she started packing up her poetry books, she found a volume on roses nested amongst them, as if it had been haphazardly placed there. She frowned as she pulled the book off the shelf and opened the cover. Her fingers grazed over the inscription—*to my dear Madeline, on the occasion* *of her 16th birthday. With love from your grandmother Geraldine Murray.*

It was the one thing she'd taken from home when she ran away. Her grandmother had given it to her—the one person growing up who seemed to understand her. Normally she kept it in her bedroom, somehow the volume being even too precious to keep in the library. Of course she had taken it with her. She went nowhere without it.

She set it in the chest along with all the other books. Before long, the shelves were bare, just the way they'd been when she'd arrived. And yet, Maddy couldn't help but feel they were a little sadder now—like the empty way the front parlour at Everwell felt after they'd taken down the Christmas tree.

Her heart squeezed again. Why had Beau asked her to imagine a life here? Dreams were for other people—the nicer people, the prettier ones, the ones whom people simply seemed to like. Maybe he had meant Maddy to have the cottage, which in the light of day, without the heady rush of moonlight and possibly one too many glasses of Annie's dandelion wine, was a patently ridiculous offer. This was his mother's childhood home. He had once planned to sell it, sight unseen. And now he had family living next door, and a company to run and a sister whose life had been destroyed not once, but twice. He would forget her soon enough.

It had to be a trick of the moonlight.

By the time Beau arrived at the Chandlers, Hollis and Daniel had already hitched up the horses. They must have sensed the news, but even they were surprised at the betrayal of Beau's brother-in-law.

"I'm sorry to be leaving this way," Beau said. "I came here in a storm, and I seem to be leaving in one."

"That can't be helped," his brother said, and Beau's heart

squeezed at the idea that Daniel was his brother. "We can take care of it."

"I'll pay you for your trouble," he said.

"You'll do no such thing," Hollis said, putting his hand on Beau's shoulder and giving it a gentle squeeze. "You're my son. Give me the chance to help you, to make up for all the times I couldn't."

Beau swallowed back his emotions, which were far too close to the bone.

"I'm not sure when, but I'll be back, for a visit at least. Maybe I'll bring Jessica to visit. She could probably use the peace and quiet." Or not, Beau thought. Jessica was her mother's daughter. A socialite.

"Teddy and I will go help Maddy," Annie said. "She must be sad to leave."

"I think she's eager to get back to Everwell," he said, so matter-of-factly it sounded harsh to his ears. "She's packing now."

"And what about you?" Hollis asked, his older eyes narrowing, as if he had a thousand things he wanted to say but had decided to hold his tongue.

Beau paused, choking back an unexpected pang of emotion. Christ, when did he turn into such a blubberer? Frank only valued two emotions—anger and tenacity. Tears were for women and weak men. But here were two men standing in front of him, their bodies hard and lean from working the land, and both of them seemed to have no fear of their own soft hearts.

"I just found a family I didn't know I had." And the glimpse of a future he never could have imagined. "I'm sorry to go."

"I'm always going to be here for you," Hollis said, then pulled Beau in for an embrace. Beau drank in the affection, allowing it to feed him, bringing some lightness and some strength to his heart, which seemed to be torn in a thousand horrible directions. "But right now, you have to take care of your family. So let's go get that done."

Beau unwillingly broke the embrace. There was work to do—a sister to console, a trial to endure, and a company to manage. Beau had always known the company would be his. It had been a fate he'd accepted, even though he didn't want it, which was selfish in the extreme. He was being gifted a massive machinery for making money and he wanted to just walk away from it like a spoiled child with too many beautiful toys. But he was equally certain that if he wanted to turn his attention to something else he could, and those doors would be open for him the moment he chose to do it.

He had risked nothing to have everything. Madeline's words washed up on his skin like a January freezing rain. ... *The world is happy to open whatever door you choose to walk through. It doesn't work that way for me.*

If only he could show her that he would open every door and fight off every obstacle so she didn't have to.

They all piled into the cart and headed back to The Grove. On the way, he thanked Annie again for the absolutely beautiful evening she'd put on for Madeline. An evening worthy of her loveliness. Annie had waved it off, as if it was nothing, even though he knew perfectly well it had not been. Beau was struck once again by this need, so urgent it felt like it was going to burst out of him—to show her how appreciative he was. When he returned, he would talk to Daniel about it and find a way to recognize her in a manner Annie might truly appreciate.

By the time they had arrived, the front door was open, and there were already two travel trunks sitting by the front step. Madeline had wasted no time. There hadn't been much to pack— he'd arrived with so little, and most of it had been hardly the wardrobe of a man who would spend his time mending pergolas and cleaning out attics and scrubbing floors. But he'd liked the work just the same—and as he packed away his best twill pants which now had a few little holes that Madeline had mended, something in his heart flashed and hardened into resolve. Some- how, he would find a way back here. In fact, he emptied out the very small chest of drawers but left his favourite pair of socks as a token.

Madeline moved about with the same efficiency she'd displayed from the moment they'd started this journey. He wanted to make some kind of conversation with her, something to lighten the mood, but she was content in her silence, and he didn't have the heart to impose on it. Both of them seemed to be in a kind of mourning.

There was no time to think about it now. He had to return to Halifax briefly to ensure, as Dominic asked, that Madeline was safely delivered to Everwell, before departing almost immediately for Saint John. There, he would hug his sister and somehow refrain from tearing Neil into pieces. After two hours of scrambling, they were in the cart, trundling down the winding lane, past the canopy of maples, their leaves lazy in the midday sun. The cart bounced them around, and all of them were quiet. He caught Madeline looking up at the house, a subtle swallow in her throat and a flush on her freckled cheeks.

She looked at him, her eyes bright with unshed tears. He wanted to reach out for her, take her hand, comfort her. But even as their gazes locked, she stiffened before turning away. It stung, a reminder of all those times he'd been with Frank, who'd held back his approval like a carrot on a string, always pulling it out of reach.

He pushed the thought away and turned his attention to the road. Frank was dead, and Neil had killed him. The past, and the mess of the present, had to be dealt with before Beau could even begin to dream about his future.

Chapter Twenty-Four

MADDY STOOD on the platform at the Windsor station, a couple of feet from Beau, two tickets to Halifax in her hand as they waited for the late afternoon train. Any relief that had come from the news of Neil Sweet's arrest had been tempered by the riot of emotion of the night before. As part of Beau's family had been torn apart, he'd also found another. Maddy had come to know what it meant to be worshipped by a man so much that he would be tempted, under the intoxication of a full Buck moon, to offer her a dream.

A dream she could not accept.

She'd hurt him. Hurt him in a way she could not ever imagine hurting a man. But he would recover. Maybe she would too, in time. She would go back to Everwell and tend her roses, read her books, and watch over everyone. It would be enough.

It had to be enough. Pursuing a life at The Grove was far too risky, especially with Nelson close by. One word from him and he could ruin not only Maddy, but Everwell by association. She'd given everything to Everwell because they'd given her everything she'd lacked for so long—friendship and respect. She could not repay it by leaving them vulnerable.

The Chandlers stood with them on the platform, their presence a welcome distraction from the strain. Beau was leaving them with promises to return as soon as the trial was over.

Preoccupied with watching the crowd, Maddy caught only half the conversation. The story of Beau's innocence would not make the papers for at least another day, and when she'd gone to buy the tickets from the ticket booth, she'd pulled down one of the public notices about Beau that had been nailed to a nearby pole. Until the news of Mr. Sweet's arrest was widely circulated, Beau da Silva still had an attractive price on his head.

The train whistle rang for boarding, and after the hugs and promises for visits were exchanged, Maddy took a moment to thank Annie for the beautiful birthday supper.

"Will we see you again?" Annie asked, taking Maddy's hand and giving it a gentle squeeze. "You seem very heavy."

"I suppose I am," she said, not wanting to burden Annie with an emotional mess of her own making. "I think I unexpectedly fell in love with The Grove, and I'm sorry to leave it." She'd unexpectedly fallen in love with Beau da Silva, too.

"I hope not for too long," Annie replied. "I think the gardens at The Grove will miss you."

With the luggage stowed, Maddy and Beau boarded the train, going directly to their compartment, which would allow them some privacy. As they settled in, the discomfort in the air made every sound and movement fraught with awkward tension. The jubilance of the evening before was twisted and tempered by sadness.

It was temporary, she reminded herself. Once they returned, Beau, the Chandlers, and The Grove would all be a memory. A story to tell. It wouldn't have a happy ending, but through the lens of time, there might be a memory or two she could smile back on.

She pulled out a book, mostly to hide behind, for there was little hope for her to be able to concentrate on poetry now. For his part, Beau was wrapped up in a copy of the Halifax Chronicle, reading through the business section, the only sound the rattling of newsprint. On the back page, was an advertisement for J Barsalou & Co. Imperial Soap, taunting her with a future she would not have. She found herself staring at it, and at him, waiting for him to say something. To say anything.

His silence shouldn't have caused this dull ache to settle in her chest. She shouldn't have been wishing he might prod her into a smile with a joke at his own expense. And she most definitely shouldn't be trying to formulate a question about the markets just so he might speak with her.

Before she could contemplate any question, her spine began to tingle with awareness. A porter stood at the compartment door, which he'd begun to open. Perhaps it was nothing—a second confirmation of tickets, or a question about their comfort or an unexpected delay, but the train was moving with no sign of slowing down and no whistle indicating a problem that would require anyone to go door to door.

"Can I help you?" she asked getting to her feet.

"Not at all," he said, not bothering to give her a second look. Instead, he looked straight at Beau.

"Would you be Mr. da Silva?" the porter asked.

Beau had already lowered his paper and looked up at the porter with undisguised curiosity. "Who is asking?"

"Just checking the passenger list," the porter replied.

Maddy gripped the book in her hands. She'd bought two second class tickets. She'd given no names.

"Look," Beau said, "I don't know who you're looking for, but if it's a reward you're trying to collect, you're about eight hours too—"

Beau's protest was interrupted when the man grabbed him and pulled him to his feet. The attacker pulled back a fist, ready to plant it into Beau's jaw, no doubt to make it easier to subdue him.

He never got the chance.

Maddy's fist connected with the man's ribs where he'd raised his arm to throw a punch. The force of the blow caused him to contort his body in pain. Maddy lunged at him, preparing to spin him around and incapacitate him when a second person grabbed her from behind. She sensed he was shorter than her, and using her size to her advantage, threw herself backward against the wood-panelled walls of the compartment. She heard the heavy thud of his head against the wall, along with a loud *oomph*, but he still had her, one his hands pressed hard against her throat. Unable to pry his fingers off her neck, she reached for the small stiletto blade sheathed on the inside of her wrist and drove it into the man's arm. He released her amidst a sharp cry of pain and a string of curses.

Pushing herself away from her attacker, she turned around and knocked him out cold with a strong upper cut to his jaw before turning her attention back to the man who'd charged at Beau.

For his part, Beau was struggling with his assailant, but seemed to have the upper hand until the man pulled a knife from his jacket, swinging it close to Beau's face.

Maddy wasted no time. She picked up her book from where she'd dropped it and hurled it at the man's head. He dropped the knife, and Beau grabbed him by the shoulders and pressed him up against the wall.

"Who sent you?" Beau asked.

"No one," came the dazed reply, before he started to blubber. Maddy almost felt sorry for him. There were a dozen reasons why these men thought going after Beau was a good idea, and some of them would have been desperation. But given the angry red mark on Beau's face, and the fact his attacker had tried to use a weapon, Maddy was left with little sympathy for either of them at the moment.

She spotted a thick, folded sheet of paper bulging in the man's coat pocket. She reached inside and pulled out the page. It was one of the public notices about Beau.

"Idiot," Beau said, his voice haggard from the fight. "You're about eight hours too late to make your money." The porter—if he was in fact a porter—was a clean-shaven man in his mid-twenties with a nasty mark on his cheek that was already forming a welt.

The fracas had already brought a handful of onlookers to the door, and one of them must have gone to fetch train staff, for before Maddy could contemplate their next move, the head steward was already present.

"What's going on here?"

Maddy and Beau exchanged a glance before Beau spoke up— the first since they'd left The Grove. While it wasn't unheard of for a woman to get into a public brawl, the potential consequences for Maddy, who had two knives hidden on her body, would have meant some fast talking to keep her out of trouble. Luckily for her, Beau was excellent at fast talking.

"An excellent question," he began, turning from his attacker who slumped to the floor, the fight in him long gone. "Get these two out of here and I'll explain everything."

In a fury of male chin rubbing, hard stares, shared in-jokes about fighting styles or lack thereof, and a more serious threat of legal action, the two men were picked up and pulled away, leaving Beau alone with Maddy once more.

"You were fantastic," Beau said, turning to her, speaking quietly as the hum of the mess being cleared up went on behind them. The warmth in his expression melted away the dull throbbing in her head, twisting the pain back into something tantalizingly like happiness. A happiness she'd rejected last evening.

"Just finally getting to do what you're paying Everwell for," she said, unable to help the smile that came to her mouth when she looked at him.

The smile ran away from his lips then. But she needed to remind him, and herself, that whatever had been between them had to end. He had a life to go back to, and so did she. The contract between The Everwell Society and the Turnbulls had been fulfilled.

Tears pricked at the corners of her eyes. How could she sit

across from him and not show him that her heart was breaking just to look at him?

"You're hurt," she said, gesturing to his cheek. "I should see about getting you some iodine. I'll be right back."

"There's no need," he protested, but Maddy was already at the door.

Beau sat in his seat as the clacking of the train over the rails gently rocked him. Instead of looking out over the countryside, however, he found himself staring at the door, waiting for Madeline's return.

His jaw ached from the punch he'd received only a few moments ago, and no doubt Aunt Vee would be pelting him with anxious questions about it the moment he saw her. Of course, given the situation at hand with his family, a bruised jaw would be the very least of their worries.

His immediate concern now, however, was Madeline. It felt like she'd been gone a very long time. He pulled out his pocket watch, a gift from Frank on his sixteenth birthday, and checked the time. He had no idea how long she'd been gone and did not trust his own accounting for the passage of minutes at the moment. The fracas of the fight had seemed to take forever, though it was probably over in a few terrifying minutes. He'd been afraid for her, but she'd moved with such a cool efficiency that the fight was mostly over before it had begun. The effectiveness at which she'd dispatched those two hooligans both impressed and saddened him. He'd offered her a refuge from all of that. A place where she'd never had to sleep with one eye open, waiting for the next stranger to come banging on the door. He'd hire a damn bodyguard for The Everwell Society if that's what she'd needed. He would move heaven and earth for her.

Beau ran his thumb over the embossed brass watch cover. What a strange month it had been. He'd lost a father and gained another. An unexpected lump formed in his throat at the thought of Frank da Silva and Hollis Chandler. Beau wasn't sure he loved Frank, but he managed to miss him just the same. He would need to channel Frank's sharpness and calculating mind when he walked into the boardroom at Silver Lumber, and when he had to deal with whatever mess Neil had left. For his sister, however, he would find the gentleness of Hollis to soothe her.

The train had pulled into Uniacke Station, nearly halfway between Windsor and Halifax. Still, Madeline had not returned. Perhaps she'd gone to get some air after the fight or to refresh herself. Perhaps she actually had gone in search of iodine or some salve for his face. What he'd wanted to tell her was the medicine he needed was something to cure the gnawing ache in his chest at the thought of losing her.

Unable to sit any longer, he got to his feet. The train started to pull away, and he entertained the momentary panic that she'd disembarked, but he'd set that thought aside seconds after it had entered his mind. She would see the job through.

If he only had an hour or so left to be with her, he wanted every last second of it.

He walked down the narrow corridor of the compartment car, through to the second-class parlour car. It was half full of gentlemen sitting in overstuffed leather chairs, laughing over tumblers of liquor and cigars. Thwarted, he turned around, intent on heading up toward the open coaches further up the line, when two figures appeared up ahead, standing just outside their compartment door. One he recognized immediately. It was Madeline, talking intently to a shorter man. She was still, her eyes hard. He saw her lips moving, but from here it was impossible to see who she was speaking to.

Unease settled on him, and he approached with caution. He'd seen Madeline handle herself with ease, but he would not for a moment take her safety for granted. As he got closer, he could better make out the gentleman she was speaking with. Anger flared in his gut as he recognized Nelson Taylor. Any rational thought Beau might have made about her capacity to defend herself against Taylor evaporated. And it was possible that Madeline had no desire for Beau to intervene on her behalf. Their relationship, she'd suggested, had been based in a contract. A business deal.

As he walked toward Nelson, his hands clenched at his sides, Beau was about to tear that contract to pieces.

Chapter Twenty-Five

MADDY STOOD in the corner of the compartment car, the narrow corridor blocked by Nelson who'd found her as she was returning to her seat with a small bottle of iodine. Her face was hot, betraying any sense of calm she wanted to portray. Damn him, and herself, for allowing him to so easily unnerve her.

"What do you want?" she asked.

"I just wanted to be sure it was you. I had my suspicions of course, but I wasn't certain until I'd spied your name in one of the books in Mr. da Silva's little collection."

Maddy swallowed her disgust at the idea that Nelson had been pawing at her books. He must have been the person who'd shelved her little poetry book in the wrong place.

"I didn't realize you were working for the da Silvas," he continued, his voice oozing that same condescending tone he'd thrown at her when they were younger. "Do they know they have a violent criminal in their midst?"

"I don't need to speak to you," she said, her fingers gripping the bottle so tightly she thought it could break under the pressure. "Now if you will excuse me—"

She moved to get around him, but he stepped into her path.

She cast a glance for a porter, but there were none. And she would not give Nelson the satisfaction of calling for help.

"They called for your head," he said, his mouth twisting into a half-sneer. "You should have seen his parents, distraught after losing their only son."

Maddy knew he was going to drag Malcolm's death into this encounter—they had been best friends after all—but even she was taken aback by how quickly he'd wielded it over her head like a weapon.

"And I wonder how his poor parents would sleep at night knowing that their son was a violent, pathetic drunk grasping for my father's money?" she said.

He blinked, as if he was taken aback.

"You hoyden," he said. "I wonder how you sleep at night."

"Don't waste your time wondering about me," she replied. "I've spent years thinking about that horrible night. I was allowed to defend myself."

"You broke Malcolm's heart," he protested. "He was babbling on about losing you. If you had chosen me, none of this would have happened. I wouldn't have tried to take liberties with you."

Unable to help herself, she laughed at the sheer audacity of his declaration.

"What are you saying, Nelson? That you would have treated your prized sow with more respect?" A rush of memories—pleasant ones, found their way through fog of pain that had enveloped her when she'd thought about the past. Of Phillipa, taking her home to Everwell. Of Rimple and Elouise, both determined in their own way to help Maddy believe in her singular type of beauty. Of Gemma's gentle presence. Jeremy Webber taking the time to box with her, gifting her plants from his hot house. Annie Chandler, who'd made her a beautiful birthday supper and offered her friendship. All these people in her life who'd surrounded her with patience, respect, and even love. And then there was Beau, who'd worshipped her. Who believed in her more than she believed in herself. Who loved her.

Maddy drew herself up, her grip loosening on the bottle of iodine, as she put her hands on her hips and looked down on Nelson.

"I don't think you realize that your opinion doesn't mean a sweet damn to me," she said. "I'm no longer surrounded by people with such small opinions of themselves that they have to tear down someone else to feel important. It took too me far too long to realize that, but that is my fault."

He blinked, sputtering a bit, before he countered with the only weapon he had left.

"You'll care soon enough. Malcolm's mother is dead," he said. "But how eager his father might be to see you swing for that killing."

Before Maddy had a chance to speak, another most welcome voice entered the conversation.

"If you say one more word to her," Beau said, his voice sounding more threatening than she'd ever thought possible, "I am going to shove my boot so far up your backside it's going to lodge in your throat so you can never speak another."

Nelson's eyes widened, and he cleared his throat, then turned to face Beau.

"Mr. da Silva," he said. "Excuse me, but Miss Murray and I were having a private conversation."

"You do not get the privilege of having a private conversation with her," Beau replied. "And if I see you within half a mile of her, I promise you will be very, very sorry indeed."

Maddy saw Nelson's anger bloom under his collar, chasing up the sides of his face. He looked between her and Beau, whose normally joyful expression had turned hard and told Nelson, without saying another word, that he was not to be trifled with. In response, Nelson straightened his hat, nodded to Maddy, then brushed past her and into the parlour car beyond. As the door closed behind him, Maddy heaved a huge sigh of relief.

"That is the last you'll see of him," he said, his expression still serious. "I promise you that."

"Thank you," she said.

"I know you didn't need saving," he said, "but given the events since we arrived on this journey, I at least needed to return the favour."

His mouth quirked up in a smile, a movement that was followed with a wince.

It was dark by the time Maddy arrived home in the cab Beau had hired to take them to Everwell, before he left for his aunt and uncle's residence. Rimple, Phillipa, and Elouise, along with the Everwell matriarchs Lady Em and Tilda, had come to greet her, and Beau excused himself without looking back. It stung, like the first time she'd accidentally tried to pull at a nettle without her gloves.

There were lots of kisses and hugs, and Maddy took in a deep big breath of the familiar scents of home. Elouise had decided to stay at Everwell while Dominic was away, and Maddy was thrilled to see her. It was good to be home again; and yet there was much to say, and so much more she could not. She was weary in both body and soul, and Phillipa eschewed the normal post-job review until Maddy, and the rest of the house, had a good night's sleep. She climbed the stairs and found her room exactly as she'd left it. It was as if everything and nothing had happened, and she could no longer tell what was better.

The next morning, after the breakfast was cleared and Gemma had arrived to get the school day started for the girls, the remainder of the Scandalous Spinsters, along with Lady Em and Tilda, gathered in the parlour. Maddy sat on the settee, Rimple and Elouise on either side of her. Did they sense she needed their support this morning?

"The prodigal daughter returns at last," Lady Em declared, raising her cup of coffee to cheer the ladies. "I am glad to see you. I trust all went well with Mr. da Silva."

Maddy prayed a well-timed sip of coffee would mask the heat

creeping into her cheeks or the threat of tears pricking behind her eyes.

"He didn't return without a scratch, but it was only one," she said, relaying the story of ruckus on the trip home. Even so, her assessment wasn't entirely true. She'd clearly hurt him. But he would recover easily enough, wouldn't he? Maddy sat for a moment, lost in her own thoughts, before the rattle of a nearby teacup drew her out of her woolgathering. She took measure of the ladies around the table who looked at her with unspoken curiosity.

"Your flowers are perfectly fine, by the way," Rimple said, blessedly changing the subject. "We've managed the blight very well. Sylvie has been fussing over them so much we hardly missed you."

Rimple's comment, though it was no doubt kindly meant, startled Maddy. She couldn't remember the last time she'd given even a passing thought to her blighted roses.

Whether it was the fatigue or the heart sickness or something completely different, Maddy was unable to school her features. A flush of heat ran into her face, probably turning it as red as ripening tomato. In response, Rimple put down her cup, and reached her arm across Maddy's back and pulled her close.

"I'm sorry," she said, "I didn't mean we didn't miss you. Of course we did. I just didn't want you to worry."

Maddy turned and planted a light kiss on Rimple's forehead. Her dearest friend could find the sunshine on the darkest day, and if she couldn't find it, she'd go up into her little workshop and create it herself.

"No need to apologize," she said. "I'm tired. Yesterday was a blur, and Beau is distraught from the news."

As soon as she'd uttered his name, she took another swallow of coffee, if only to distract herself from the marked exchange of glances between Elouise and Phillipa, who carefully arched her brow.

Nothing good ever came from Phillipa arching her brow.

"I'm eager for the details," Elouise said. "Dominic only gave us the smallest bits of information, and he won't be home for a least another week."

"I expect we'll see it in the papers." Tilda said. "It will be today's headline."

"Speaking of the papers," Maddy said, eager to learn more of the business that had sent her on this journey, "has there been any retraction yet from Mrs. Turnbull?"

Maddy's heart sank as she looked around the room, the answer to her question apparent without any of them yet to say a word.

"Why?" she pressed, anger creeping up the back of her neck. "We did the job as asked."

Did she have her heart broken for nothing?

Phillipa cast a glance around the room, tension building. Had it been there all along, and she hadn't seen it? Or was she so caught up in her own emotion she hadn't noticed that something was wrong?

"A note came from Veronica Turnbull this morning," Tilda said, setting down her teacup with a calm but deliberate clink that alerted Maddy that all was not well. "She has apparently received troubling news that makes her retraction of the original article not only impossible, but further verifies the NWL claim."

The coffee churned in Maddy's stomach, and for a moment she thought she was going to be sick.

Nelson's words rang in her ears. *You'll care soon enough.* He must have sent that letter the day he'd arrived at The Grove.

Phillipa reached across the table, taking Maddy by the hand, her lips pressed together and her head cocked slightly to the right in that way of hers when she had to say something unpleasant. Phillipa was a master of secrets, but even she wasn't perfect. Everyone had a tell, Maddy had overheard Elouise say once.

"Someone has linked you to what happened all those years ago," Phillipa said at last.

To what happened.

Murderess.

"He was there, Phillipa. Nelson Taylor. We had words." She stood abruptly, rattling the tea table and nearly sending a few of the delicate teacups crashing to the floor. "I will leave before the end of the day. I'm already packed."

She turned to bolt up the stairs, ignoring the pleas of her friends. But there was one voice above the rest she dared not disobey.

"Stop this at once!"

Lady Em's voice cut through the others, silencing them all. Lady Em did not need volume. It was direct and laced with that aristocratic tone she purported to despise but still managed to use to great effect.

"You, Miss Murray, are not going anywhere," said Lady Em in a tone so imperious that it stopped not only Maddy in tracks, but everyone else too—save Tilda, of course. "Except to put on your best visiting gown."

"But staying here puts Everwell in danger," she said, confused by Lady Em's request.

"If they know we will break so easily, Miss Murray, we will open the door to more pressures, not less. So we will not break. Do you understand?"

Maddy had only seen Lady Em this angry once, and it had been directed squarely at Emily Coughlin, their next-door neighbour and generally awful self-important person who had once made quite public disparaging remarks to Tilda in Tilda's own home.

Lady Em rose. "Ladies, wear your best. We are going to visit Veronica Turnbull."

Chapter Twenty-Six

UNCLE ARCHIE and Aunt Vee had greeted Beau with such open arms it almost made up for the fact that his world was pulling apart at the seams. Aunt Vee was aghast at the rather nasty bruise that had formed on his cheek from the incident on the train. Even though it was late when he'd arrived, they'd tried to stuff him with food he had no interest in eating, and even the brandy he'd indulged in had done little to induce him to sleep.

He was up before dawn, writing messages to his sister Jess and his lawyer. He'd considered giving rather specific instructions about firing the board, who seemed a little too eager to support Neil's witch hunt for him, but decided he would allow himself a few days let his emotions settle before he did anything too rash.

Between the dealings with his family and the business, there was Madeline. Christ, he missed her right now. His body missed her lush curves, full lips, and silky skin. He missed her steadiness. Her quiet. His gut twisted with regret as he remembered the way the moonlight shone down on her, illuminating her skin as eyes lit up with excitement, then just as quickly, darkened with fear. He would give anything to take that back now.

Eager for the morning's headlines, he dressed and came down to the parlour with the handful of messages to be sent to the telegraph office. He paced the floors, waiting for the early edition of the Halifax Chronicle to arrive. When it did, he didn't bother to wait for Davis, their butler, to iron the pages.

Case of Lumber King Murder Takes Turn, the headline proclaimed in huge letters, followed by *Son expected to be absolved of crime after true killer confesses* in smaller font. Alongside the column was an image of Frank, looking out at Beau, his eyes as Beau remembered them—grim and a little angry. Perhaps he was angry at losing the love of his life.

Maybe that anger was something else. A way to manage grief.

He scanned the article, written by Benjamin Miller—the same reporter Dominic had contacted to get details, such as they were, and they were grim.

Good news, and bad news. Dominic had warned him, but it was still hard, and somewhat surreal, to read such a sensational story when all the players were people so intimately connected to him. People he loved. People he'd liked, and thought he knew. His attention was so firmly captured by the article he didn't notice his aunt entering the room until she spoke.

"You look like you haven't slept a wink," she said, tsking him in that maternal way she had with him. "Not that I could blame you. Still, I'm glad to see you safe and sound."

There was something in his aunt's voice—a note of concern that stretched her normally relaxed demeanour just a tad too thin. He wondered if she'd known anything about his parentage. Aunt Vee, and even Uncle Archie, were, compared to many of their social standing, rather relaxed in their outlook on propriety compared to most—more devil-may-care than Godfearing—but they were hardly reformists.

"Except for the fact I had no valet, I think I managed remarkably well," he said, attempting a joke that, upon seeing the rather pale complexion in Aunt Vee's normally rosy cheeks, fell rather flat. "If you are worried about my face, it is a little sore, but it will heal in a few days. If it weren't for Miss Murray, I'd have been far worse off."

At the mention of Madeline Murray, Aunt Vee bristled.

"You should have my physician look at that," she said, gesturing to his face.

Beau shook his head. "I expect to be on a train for Saint John by late afternoon. The sooner I can meet with Mr. Ashe about the case, the better."

Her mouth fell into a scowl, then she squared her shoulders and took a seat in her favourite chair. Her back was absolutely rigid.

"While I am pleased that Mr. Ashe was able to help sort through this awful business with your father, my confidence in him and his relationship with the Everwell women has been somewhat shaken."

"Whatever do you mean?" he asked, setting down the paper.

"You are back safe and sound, and for that I am grateful," she said. "But I am afraid I was far too hasty in my agreement to repudiate these rumours about The Everwell Society."

"Why?"

"Because they are true!"

Aunt Vee's answer came out in such a harsh whisper it made Beau blink. She was not a woman given to hysterics. Something had happened.

"Aunt Vee," he said, giving her his full attention, "surely you cannot believe the accusations of gossips. If people believed what was said about me, I would be in a jail cell now, or worse."

She rose and went to a small secretary desk, where she pulled out a slim envelope and handed it to Beau.

"This came yesterday morning by special post," she said. "I'd planned on taking it to the police, but the news about your brother-in-law arrived at nearly the same moment."

Beau scanned the letter, sent by none other than Nelson Taylor, which detailed a stunning accusation against Madeline Murray in relation to the death of Malcolm Ferguson. It was the same story she'd already shared with him, though told from a completely different point of view. But here it was, a tale told about a fine young man, killed in cold blood by a conniving woman who'd wanted his money, and finding he had none, murdered him.

It was an astonishing tale. And completely untrue.

Taylor added that he would withhold any information he had about Beau's association with Madeline Murray if Mrs. Turnbull would convince Beau to sell the property, as intended, to George's College.

Beau swore under his breath, then folded up the letter.

"This letter is preposterous," he said. "And with my case close to resolved, his threats mean nothing to us."

"It is a threat to my reputation and yours. I should never have allowed myself or you to come under the influence of that damned Everwell Society! Sorrowful Spinsters they maybe, but they are also scandalous. And apparently, murderous."

He couldn't recall the last time he'd seen his aunt this angry.

"Aunt Vee," he started, trying to keep his tone conciliatory but she held up her hand.

"There have been rumours about what goes on within those walls for years," she said. "Those women carry on, spitting in the face of good society and all the rules the rest of us are supposed to abide by. And here I am, my trusting nature being taken advantage of, to further their own ends and silence rumours that may in fact be absolutely true."

"Aunt Vee, are you angry with them because they don't follow the rules you are bound to?" Beau asked.

She reddened slightly, then rose. "I am angry at being made a fool of."

"You are not a fool," he said, "and if you want to be angry at anyone, be angry at me. I'm the one who drew this bastard out of the woodwork. And I can tell you that if anyone is trying to play on your fears, it's the man who wrote this letter."

"How can you know that?"

Beau told Aunt Vee everything. About meeting Taylor in Windsor, when he insulted Madeline. The pressure he'd exerted on the Chandlers. Then, lowering his voice, not entirely trusting that the Turnbull's trusted servants weren't on the other side of the door, he told Madeline's story.

"Ferguson paid for his deeds with his life, but Miss Murray did not murder him," he said. "The man who wrote this letter was intimately involved with both Miss Murray and her former fiancé and arrived on the scene of the argument as Madeline left. He is also of a highly questionable character. He tried to blackmail me once he discovered my identity, but I would not be swayed by him. Clearly, he found a different target for his schemes. And unlike you or me, The Everwell Society are far more vulnerable to threats like this. This may be a threat to your reputation, but a minor one. This story, false as it is, could threaten their very existence."

Aunt Vee was silent for a few moments, turning over everything Beau had said.

"Are you certain, Beau?" she said at last. "Are you certain about all of this?"

"Madeline Murray is a woman of incomparable character," he said, his heart filling with a yearning for her that ached in places he didn't know could be touched by such things. "Your trust in Everwell, and in her, was well founded. If she hadn't been on the train yesterday, I might have been bundled in a sack by a couple of ruffians, one of whom was armed. They deserve your support, Aunt. This cretin is preying on your fears for his own ends, and those women, and everyone they help, will pay the price if you do not trust me."

She pursed her lips together, rocking slightly, her mind clearly working through some tangle. It was odd to see Aunt Veronica so much at sixes and sevens.

"I will set Dominic on to this case as well if need be," Beau continued, "and get the truth out in the open. Creatures like Nelson Taylor clearly thrive on people's fears, but scuttle away fast enough when light is shone on the matter. Do not trouble yourself, Aunt Vee. I will handle it."

"I have to trouble myself." She stood and walked to the

window, her hands clenched in front of her. "I wrote to them, informing them I knew the truth about their infamous society. And I promised to speak to Mr. Miller at the Chronicle and confirm the stories."

"You did what?"

He'd spoken so loudly, his response so loud, he surprised both of them.

"It was rash, but I was angry—and terrified, I'm not too proud to say," she said, standing now. "I told him I had a story to break about Everwell. I expect him early afternoon."

Beau rose and crossed the room to meet his aunt. Aunt Veronica was a strong woman, yes, and an independent one. Even now, he could see her mind working, trying figure out how to undo the harms she'd inflicted in a moment of anger and fear.

"Aunt Vee, we have to fix this," Beau said. "Everwell helped us when no one else would."

"Of course we have to fix it," she said. "I don't run away from my problems."

She lifted her chin, a fire in her pale grey eyes he couldn't recall seeing in quite a long time. Instantly, he thought about his mother. Had she run away from her problems with Hollis? Or from a life she knew she couldn't bear? And what about Beau? He'd spent a lifetime running from one problem or another, trying to busy himself with the next thrill.

But Aunt Vee never did. Brushing Beau's hands away, she crossed the floor of the morning parlour in a rustle of silk and pulled the bell for the housekeeper, who, in that magical way of attentive servants, appeared a moment later.

"Mrs. Hayes," she said, "I have a note to send to Everwell. I need it sent immediately. Bring the carriage and wait for their reply."

"Excuse me ma'am," the housekeeper said. "But I do not think that will be necessary."

"Why ever not?"

Movement outside the front window caught Beau's eye.

"Because ma'am," she continued, "they are already here."

There were a million places Maddy would rather be at the moment, and none of them were the Turnbull mansion. She was too furious at the world right now—at Malcolm for humiliating her in public; at Nelson, being free in the world and not allowing her past to rest. She was absolutely vexed with the Turnbulls and the entire upper strata of Halifax society who made arbitrary rules about how the world worked, and then broke them at no cost to themselves.

Of course, there was Beau. She didn't even know what to feel about him anymore, and the fact she was having even that argument with herself was bothersome.

Then again, she thought as she climbed out of the carriage wearing her best green day dress, what if Beau was gone? Maybe he was already on his way back to New Brunswick. Given how intent he'd been since receiving the news, she wouldn't have been surprised.

The sudden grip of panic at the thought he was already gone made her feel even worse.

The Everwell contingent had come out in force. Lady Em lead the charge, along with Phillipa, Rimple, and Maddy. Gemma and Elouise stayed behind with Tilda to mind the children.

She wished Elouise was here—she had a natural charm that seemed to ease a thousand uncomfortable conversations. In some ways, she wasn't unlike Beau—she knew how to use a smile or a witty remark to soothe or distract and direct conversation in a way that served her needs. Instead, it was up to Phillipa and Lady Em to confront Veronica Turnbull about her choice to renege on their agreement and expose Everwell to further damage. Rimple, ever faithful to her friends, came to support Maddy.

Maddy had been on far more dangerous jobs than this. She'd ferried young girls out of the hold of a ship that was going to take them to New England and then on to parts unknown to be used as pleasure things for wealthy men. That hold had been guarded by at least four well-armed men. She'd also confronted more than her fair share of drunken husbands looking for their wives at Everwell.

But this was different. This was an enemy she couldn't fight with a jab in the gut or disarm with a knife. This was the power of words, and the words of people in power. She'd never managed to find a way to defend herself against those.

Phillipa had not even managed to ring the door chime before the massive oak door opened on thick brass hinges. On the other side was an older woman of average height, with greying blonde hair pulled back into a neat knot. She wore a dark brown dress with a chatelaine that marked her as the Turnbull's housekeeper.

"Good morning," she said, nodding her head with a certain degree of respect that Maddy had not expected. She held open the door even wider, her hand extended. "Please come in."

Phillipa looked to Lady Em before casting an eye to Maddy. While they hadn't expected to be tossed immediately to the street, even Phillipa could not hide her shock at this greeting.

They had barely set foot on the beautifully polished parquet floor when a familiar set of footsteps set Maddy's heart into a flutter.

"Madeline," Beau said, appearing from behind a door to her right. Though it was late morning, she could tell by the small lines at the corners of his eyes he'd had a restless night. But he'd washed and freshly shaved, dressed in morning attire befitting the grandeur of the house.

It took all of Maddy's resolve to keep her hands clenched at her sides, instead of throwing her arms around Beau and burying her face in his neck so she could breathe in his warm, soothing scent. His stare washed over her, and, unless she was deceiving herself, she sensed his need to be close to her, too.

But how could she be with a man like him? He belonged in a place like this—grand and beautiful, just like he was. Power such as this only represented a threat to Madeline. In her youth, her parents had used her dowry as a prize and put her in the centre of a heartless game. Now, her entire future—and the future of Everwell—was in jeopardy because of Veronica Turnbull's unwillingness to see past her own impressions of what was true. Maddy didn't have the power to just wipe this all away.

But there was something in Beau's eyes—that fierce determination, like she'd seen yesterday on the train when Nelson cornered her, that made her want to hope she was no longer fighting these battles alone.

She opened her mouth to acknowledge him when Lady Em raised her voice to speak.

"Mr. da Silva, I see you are in one piece." she said, not bothering to hide her indignation. While Lady Em had a fraught relationship with her aristocratic past, she used the power of the privilege she was born to with great effect when it suited her. She frowned, then pulled out her pince-nez and held it to her nose, inspecting him with the same discriminating gaze one might use to ascertain the value of a painting. "Or maybe not."

"Miss Everwell, Mrs. Hartley," he said, turning to Lady Em and Phillipa. "Thanks to Miss Murray, I am very much so." His gaze lingered on Maddy, and her skin prickled with desire. "I know why you are here, and I can assure you this is a grave misunderstanding. Please, come in."

He waited until Lady Em nodded, then escorted the women into a brightly lit morning room. Unlike the foyer to the great house, which was cavernous and meant to impress, the parlour was cozier, with a little less of the affected Tudor style the exterior of the house and the entry exuded. Veronica Turnbull's sharp stare bored into her as she entered the room, and Maddy couldn't help but wonder if the woman had somehow sensed what had happened between Maddy and Beau.

Which had been an utter mistake.

To her surprise, however, Mrs. Turnbull stood and turned directly to Lady Em.

"Miss Everwell," she said, "I cannot allow a moment more to pass before I extend my sincere apologies."

"I should say so," Miss Everwell replied, still incandescently angry. "You sent my entire household into an uproar. Come Mrs. Turnbull, I know you're smarter than that."

Maddy slid a glance to Beau, who stood beside his aunt.

"Well," she replied, "I should have been. But you can appreciate that my entire family has been turned upside down by this dreadful news. My nephew-in-law, who I believed as amiable as the day is long, shot a man in cold blood, and attempted to frame my nephew—" She took a pause, the events of the last few weeks clearly wearing on her. Beau jumped in instead.

"My aunt was in a vulnerable state when she received a note from a reprehensible villain," he said. "He told her a very convincing story—one that has been told and retold so many times and fooled so many others."

"Well," Phillipa said in that no-nonsense way of hers, bringing everyone back to the issue at hand, "it seems we are in agreement at least about the rumours at hand, and I hope, Mrs. Turnbull, about how we deal with them."

"Of course," she said, sitting herself down just as a rather large service of coffee and pastries was brought in by one of the Turnbull's staff with, Maddy had to admit, an impeccable sense of timing. "Let's start over, shall we? If there is one thing I cannot abide, it is being taken advantage of in such a way. Aside from the fact I do not like to be made a fool, I am equally enraged by the fact I have put others in harm's way. For that, I am truly sorry."

Lady Em seemed to accept Mrs. Turnbull's apology, which felt for all the world genuine. Regret had softened her spine for but a moment, before her shoulders squared again as resolution took its place.

"Mr. Miller is expected here within the hour," she said. "Perhaps we can use the opportunity to speak together about the good work of Everwell."

"What if he asks about Miss Murray?" Phillipa said. "You

know as well as I that such stories are hard to refute, especially when so expertly told."

Beau set down his cup of coffee, his voice taking on an air of authority that seemed to come naturally to him, but, it occurred to Maddy, he had never used with her. He looked straight at her when he spoke.

"Leave that to me."

Chapter Twenty-Seven

BEAU'S INTERJECTION brought banter between his Aunt and the Everwell ladies to a halt, but the only reaction he cared for was Madeline's. While he owed both his Aunt and the Everwell Society a huge debt, it was her wellbeing—and her opinion—that mattered most to him.

"What are you suggesting?" Miss Everwell asked between bites of strawberry tart. "You have something concrete to dissuade him from making his accusations public?"

"Not yet," Beau said. "But there must be something out there and I will find it."

"There is something that might help," Madeline offered, drawing the attention of everyone in the room. "I didn't give it much thought at the time. It was something Nelson said, while we were on the train."

"You spoke with him?" Mrs. Hartley asked, her expression turning from surprise to sympathy. "I'm so sorry, Maddy."

"It was somewhat cathartic," she said, pressing her lips together, her gaze turning to Beau. "He said that he'd heard Malcolm speaking—babbling was the word he used. He said it was after I left."

"I thought you were supposed to be the last person who saw Malcolm alive," Mrs. Hartley said.

"That was in the papers," Madeline answered. "But clearly that's a lie. Nelson kept insisting I should have picked him."

Beau sat forward in his seat.

"I'm meeting with Dominic Ashe as soon as I return to Saint John," he said. "While the Ferguson crime is old, it was no doubt sensationalized and people would remember it. There had to be something—or someone—who might know something."

He would be damned if that bastard Taylor would continue to haunt Madeline Murray. The doorbells chimed and soon another visitor was presented to the parlour.

"Mr. Benjamin Miller, of the Halifax Chronicle."

Miller entered, wearing a well-worn brown suit. If the journalist was shocked at seeing the Everwell ladies sitting in Veronica Turnbull's parlour, he gave no indication.

"Please sit, Mr. Miller," Aunt Veronica said, gesturing to a chair next to Mrs. Hartley. "I was just taking some late morning refreshments with members of The Everwell Society. Have you had the pleasure?"

Beau wanted to smile but tried to keep his emotions in check. Aunt Veronica was an effortless hostess, and at moments like this, Beau wondered if his ease with people had come from her.

"I have," he said, nodding politely to the Everwell ladies. "I believe I did a piece on a Christmas pageant at the Manor several years ago."

"And you have not returned," Miss Everwell said, not small amount of judgment in her voice. "You must come back this year. Mrs. Ashe has quite outdone herself of late."

He nodded, giving the matriarch a polite smile. "I will do my best to make amends."

Beau wondered what a man like Ben Miller, who had helped provide Dominic with some contacts in Saint John and who, no doubt, regularly reported on murders, corruption, and other sordid details would find so intriguing about a Christmas pageant at a girl's school, no matter how noble the cause.

"Congratulations on your innocence," he said, shaking Beau's hand. "And thank you and Mr. Ashe for the scoop."

Mr. Miller's piece on his innocence screaming across the front page of the Halifax Chronicle had been as close to a relief as Beau could muster. No doubt the reporter was the second person Dominic had reached out to.

"I'm catching the train in a couple of hours," Beau said, feeling Madeline's moody stare as surely as if she were touching him. "All those messy details you reported on this morning are my life."

The reporter nodded, apparently unbothered by that. "I want an exclusive as soon as you have time to breathe."

"As for me, I am afraid I invited you here with a misunderstanding." Aunt Veronica did her best to appear nonplussed by her misstep in inviting one of the city's most dogged journalists to her door to discuss an old murder case.

"I'm not certain it is an understanding," he said, politely declining a cup of coffee as he pulled out his notebook. "I received a telegram this morning from an informant with quite a shocking revelation about one of the staff at Everwell."

The journalist took a sideways glance at Madeline, and if Beau had no opinions of the man before he walked in, he sure as hell had some now.

"Mrs. Turnbull received a very troublesome letter yesterday, as you know," Mrs. Hartley said. "Almost immediately, she reached out to inform us of this rather slanderous note, which had no other purpose than to blackmail The Everwell Society."

Beau wasn't sure if he managed to keep his eyebrows in place as he took in Phillipa Hartley's smooth—and utterly false—tale of events that had brought the current occupants of Aunt Vee's parlour together. If his aunt was thrown off by it, however, she recovered quickly enough.

Miller was already scratching down something in his note-book. If he sensed there was anything amiss, he gave no sign.

"May I see the letter?" he asked.

"No—" came a chorus of voices that included Beau, Mrs. Hartley and Aunt Vee.

"Yes."

All eyes fell to Madeline, who had been the sole—and most important—contrary voice. Not even Aunt Veronica could contain her surprise.

"Are you certain, Miss Murray?" she said. "After everything you have done for my nephew, I do not wish to have you injured any more than you have already been."

Admiration swelled in Beau's chest at his aunt's gesture.

"Quite," Madeline said, straightening her shoulders, looking Mr. Miller straight in the eye. "I have given Nelson Taylor far too much power over me. My silence does nothing but give his story strength."

Aunt Veronica handed the letter to Miller, who read it care-fully. The collective room held its breath. He read it through once, and then went back and forth over several passages a second time.

"I heard rumours about this murder, years ago," he said. "I never thought I would meet the accused in person. It was rumoured the woman in question had disappeared."

"I went to Boston," Madeline said, and then relayed the story to him, save the most private of details about the nature of the cruel game Ferguson, Taylor, and the others had played to win her hand. "When I left Malcolm, he was most certainly alive. I know, because he was calling me every cruel word in the book as I stormed out. The fabricated story has been told with such assurance that I have been made to doubt my memory, but that is the truth."

Beau wanted to reach across the room and hold Madeline. To tell her how proud he was of her. Her bearing was as it had been when he'd first seen her. Commanding. Proud.

"The blackmailer is obviously close by," Miller said, unmoved by Madeline's confession. "If you've become a threat to him somehow, he is feeling both emboldened to show himself and confident in his threat."

"We encountered him in Windsor," Beau said, relaying the story of his connection with George's College, and the substantial commission he was going to lose. "This was clearly done to threaten me to rethink the sale of a property I had promised to sell him. And now I think he's just out for revenge, which given Miss Murray's story, indicates a certain pattern of behaviour."

Miller's eyes narrowed, and Beau realized he'd revealed something he hadn't intended. The reporter missed nothing.

"It's interesting to me that he is using her circumstance to threaten you," he said. "Clearly The Everwell Society is well intentioned, but hardly in a financial position to pay Mr. Taylor what he demands."

Now Beau was fidgeting in his seat, unwilling to reveal more than he already had. He had his own feelings for Madeline, but she'd made it clear she wasn't able to return them. And no one here knew the depth of what had happened between them. But Miller, damn him, may have guessed.

"So why did you bring me here?" Miller asked. "Keeping a letter like this away from the public eye seems like the thing to do."

"We wanted insurance," Aunt Veronica said, looking carefully at Mrs. Hartley, the two spinning a web between them. "It seemed likely that this Taylor fellow might decide, owing to the rather public nature of both The Everwell Society and my own family, to send a note to the press, or threaten to push the matter. I thought this preemptive measure would give us the opportunity to ask you to help us keep this quiet, at least until we could address it. However, it seems he has taken it upon himself to press the issue."

Miller closed up the note and handed it back to Aunt Veronica.

"An old murder case, a connection to a local charity with a history of rumours—"

"—no thanks to you," Miss Jones said, her dark eyes narrowed and filled with accusation.

"I don't work the society pages, Miss Jones," he said, waving away her ire with a casual tone. "But as I was about to say, a story like this would sell a lot of papers. What is in it for me to keep it quiet?"

"How about your job?" Aunt Vee said. "I know Simon Nickerson well enough to ask him to help us."

"Mr. Nickerson seems to like the way I do my job, Mrs. Turnbull," he said, not budging from her threat. "And we both know he likes it when I sell a lot of papers."

It was maddening, but at the same time, Beau had to admire the man for not being threatened. It was probably the same guts that allowed him to report on the goings on of the society kings in a way that got other reporters working in papers back home fired.

"What if you get a larger story out it?" Beau said.

"What do you mean?"

"This old murder case is old news, like you said," he said. "And do you really want to harm an institution like The Everwell Society, given the good work they do? I don't think that would reflect well on the paper, or on you."

That seemed to get the man's attention. "I'm listening."

"What if I give you something new to report on," Beau said, talking faster now, excited by the possibility. "You debunk the story, the Turnbull family is grateful, George's College is spared another scandal, and Everwell's reputation is intact—saved from a horrible story. You and your paper are heroes."

Miller closed up his book. "I'll give you a week."

Chapter Twenty-Eight

It had been five days since Beau had left for Saint John. Five days of the women of Everwell watching the paper, holding their breath, hoping that Ben Miller would hold off on publishing his story. To her credit, Veronica Turnbull had, through the society papers and her connections at the New Women's League, posted some glowing recommendations about Everwell, including the long-promised repudiation of the rumours that had made it into the same society columns a month before. But Ben Miller's threats to publish the story about Maddy hung over them like Damocles' sword.

"Mr. Miller is a horrid, wretched man," Rimple said as she and Maddy headed out to the garden. Her normally bright expression had clouded over at the mere mention of his name. "I hope he trips and breaks his wrists. How can he be so cavalier about something so serious?"

"He's a journalist," she said. "A journalist who has to help his employer sell papers."

"That's hardly an excuse to ruin someone," Rimple said, her bottom lip positively pouting. "I knew he was an awful person the moment he came to our Christmas pageant."

"I thought you didn't like him because he made fun of your sugarplum jelly", Maddy said.

"The plums were too heavy for the gelatin. I was explaining it was an experiment," she said, "but he laughed at it! Horrible man. And one who clearly does not appreciate the trial and error of the scientific method."

Maddy almost wanted to smile, but her own mood was too heavy. The sun was high overhead, the afternoon air sultry, but with a hint of a breeze moving up from the Northwest Arm. It was a perfect day to be in her garden, away from everything and every care. Except even here, the worries that had haunted her could not be driven away. Nelson Taylor was like the blight on her roses, persisting even with the most diligent treatments.

And truth be told, it wasn't just the awfulness of that man haunting her. It was this ache, as deep and persistent as blight, that weighed down her heart. There hadn't been anything from Beau—not a telegram, not a word.

What had she expected? He had his sister to console, a company to run. Of course he'd promised his aunt and Lady Em that he would deal with Nelson Taylor, but what could he reasonably do?

"Miss Murray!"

Maddy's attention was pulled out of the doldrums by the bright sound of a student's voice. There, standing in the garden, her face as bright as a daisy, was Sylvie LeBlanc. The girl, who'd turned fourteen this year, had arrived at Everwell two years ago, as quiet and inward as a church mouse. It had taken a lot of patience and effort to bring the child out of her shell, formed from years of latent neglect. With her brown wavy hair, fair skin, and lean frame, she was still a girl of few words. To see her waving with an enthusiasm comparable to the more confident students, brought a much-needed smile to Maddy's face.

This was why Everwell mattered. To give girls like Sylvie somewhere to bloom.

"Good afternoon, Sylvie," Maddy said, suddenly feeling a

sharp tinge of guilt. She'd left the roses in Rimple and Sylvie's care, and she'd been home three days before even thinking about looking at them.

"I have exciting news," Sylvie said, casting a glance to Rimple, as if looking for permission to continue, which Rimple granted with a familiar warm smile. "We have managed to isolate the blight. It hasn't spread, and even better, it's nearly gone on this bush."

"It's gone?" Maddy parroted. "Are you certain?"

"Sylvie's been out here every day, checking the plants, applying the tonics. She even did a test with two separate plants to see which one worked better," Rimple said, her facing beaming with pride. "I think Everwell has a budding horticulturist on their hands."

Sylvie's cheeks flushed scarlet, but there was an unmistakable sense of pride in her normally reserved looks.

"I can show you," Sylvie said, turning her body and nodding in the general direction of her handiwork.

"Absolutely," Maddy said, following the girl, who practically bounced with every step. Soon they came to the spot where Maddy had discovered the blight weeks ago. The place where she'd encountered Beau, idly plucking a rose and putting it in his lapel.

She inspected the stems and the leaves. While the blush pink colour of the flowers were now faded, the shiny deep green of the leaves looked remarkably healthy.

"We removed the worst of it, then I came out and treated the spots," Sylvie said, pointing out the two bushes where she'd tested two different compounds. One clearly was healthier than the other. "When it seemed that one was working better than the other, we continued the treatment with the entire plant."

Joy, tinged with bitter sweetness, sat side by side in Maddy's chest, and she was struck by a curious sense of the passing on of something. That this garden, which she'd guarded so jealously since she first came to Everwell, was no longer just hers anymore.

That she didn't need to be here for her flowers to be loved. And that maybe, they weren't just her flowers anymore—if they ever were.

And that was just fine.

"Thank you Sylvie," Maddy said. "This is excellent. I don't think—no, I am quite certain. I couldn't have done better."

If Sylvie had been pink before, she was practically incandescent now.

"I would like to know the recipe that you used," Maddy said, her mind going to another garden, filled with overgrown roses and sage bushes. A garden that could have been hers, if she'd trusted Beau enough to accept it.

"Miss Jones and I kept excellent notes," she said, hands clasped behind her back, looking to Rimple with so much pride it made Maddy smile. "I will show them to you."

What would Rimple make of the big green recipe book at The Grove, Maddy wondered.

"Would you like to work here in the garden with me?" Maddy asked. "On a more regular basis? I could give you a section to look after, and it could be yours. Of course I can help you with it, but it could be yours to be in charge of, to manage as you like."

Sylvie looked to Maddy, her eyes wide. "Really?"

Maddy nodded. "Really. I can't think of anyone better."

Sylvie nodded, her eyes bright, then threw herself at Maddy, wrapping her arms around her and squeezing hard. Maddy, overcome, started blinking back her own tears, patting the girl on her head. After a moment, Sylvie ended her embrace.

"Right," Maddy said, clearing her throat. "Well, how about you take a look through the garden, and make a list of some areas you might like to take on. Tomorrow I'll review and decide."

"Thank you!" Sylvie said, then scurried away, leaving Rimple standing there, hands on her hips.

"What happened to you while you were away?" she asked.

Maddy pasted on a smile, which in itself was probably a mistake.

"Nothing," she said, feigning nonchalance. "Aside from fixing up an old house to make it livable and trying to keep Beau da Silva out of trouble." And out of her heart.

She failed at that one.

"Maddy," Rimple pushed, cocking her head in that way of hers that she did when she was trying to solve one puzzle or another. Unlucky for Maddy, Rimple's propensity for solving problems with only the barest whiff of a clue was quite high.

But Maddy wasn't a riddle, or a piece of broken machinery. Broken, perhaps. But just as illogical as every other person with a brain and a heart that seemed to be forever at odds with each other.

Maddy turned on her heel and started walking back toward the manor house. While she was gone, the school had received a box of books from an anonymous donor, and to her great surprise, the rest of the spinsters had left it more or less undisturbed until she returned. That was something she could bury her nose in while trying to distract herself from Beau.

"You can't ignore me forever you know," Rimple said, persistent as always. "I just witnessed a miracle, and I need an explanation."

"That was not miraculous," she said. "Just rewarding someone for being good enough to manage the garden."

"That is exactly my point," she said. "I didn't think that was anyone. Next you're going to tell me you're going to let Ivy Webber manage the library."

Maddy rolled her eyes. "Ivy Webber is a bright girl, but the only person I'd trust with that collection is her father," she said. "And he's busy."

Before long, the manor house was in sight, and she could see Phillipa on the front step, waving to them. Maddy's heart leapt into her throat. She picked up her skirt and ran toward the house, Rimple a few steps behind.

"What is it?" Maddy asked, bounding up the steps, fear crackling underneath her skin.

Phillipa shook her head. "It's from Dominic. He says he has some encouraging news. He's on his way home."

"Has he contacted Ben Miller?" Rimple asked, clearly not trusting any motives of good will or patience from the journalist.

"He hasn't said," Phillipa said, an unmistakable line down the centre of her forehead betraying her calm demeanour. Maddy had seen little that could ruffle Phillipa's feathers, and as yet, that hadn't changed. "However, at this point I would say no news on that front is good news. Perhaps the Turnbulls have managed to exert some influence on Mr. Miller though Simon Nickerson."

Maddy nodded, stifling her urge to ask about Beau. She hated herself for thinking of him, for wishing he was here. How had he become so necessary to her? She had gone so long without missing anyone—especially a man.

But she missed Beau da Silva.

After Malcolm died, after she'd fled and learned to protect herself. And she'd done it so well it was almost as if she didn't know how to stop doing it anymore. Even with the people who'd tried to be good to her.

Beau had been so hurt. She hadn't thrown so much as a punch, and her knives had all been sheathed, but she'd injured him nonetheless. And he was still trying to help her.

The door swung open again, and Elouise, looking for all the world the beauty she always was, breezed in the front door. Her sunny expression, no doubt warmed by the news that Dominic was coming back, dimmed when she saw Maddy.

"What's wrong?" she asked, coming straight to Maddy, and taking her hand. "Did something happen?"

The warmth of Elouise's touch loosened Maddy's careful control. Maddy caught Elouise's wordless exchange with Rimple, then she pulled Maddy into the parlour as Rimple closed the door behind her, leaving just the two of them.

"Maddy," Elouise said again, and though she was at least six inches shorter and five years younger, somehow seemed matronly —or at least, big sisterly. "Oh Maddy, my sweet friend. Why is

your heart breaking? Did that man hurt you? Because if he did—
"

Maddy shook her head, barely able to see Elouise through tears she'd been determined not to shed.

"I love him," she said, her voice a rough whisper.

"I see," she said. "And do you think he returns the sentiment?"

Maddy squeezing her eyes shut, recalling every moment they'd been together. He'd shown her, over and over, that he cared for her.

"I think so."

"Then what is the problem?"

"We can't be together," she said. "I can't be with a man like him."

"Is he heartless?"

"No—the opposite."

"Then what?"

"Because he's rich, and beautiful, and I—" She faltered. "I am not."

Elouise straightened. "Did he tell you this?"

"No," she said. "The opposite. The reason why we're in this mess is that he nearly took Nelson Taylor's head off in a public square for insulting me."

"Well then, it sounds like he's a man of good character who cares for you."

"He does," she said. "But it's hard, Lou. So hard to believe."

"Maddy," Elouise said, taking Maddy by the hand and leading her to the settee, where the two sat, facing each other. "I know what it's like to have a man's attention. And I know how utterly meaningless it can be. Or at least I did, until I learned to trust the one man who gave me what I truly deserved—his respect and his love."

"Wasn't it scary?"

"Terrifying," she said, her smile radiant. "But the thought of being without him was scarier still."

"But what if being with him means not being here?"

Elouise took Maddy's hands in hers, giving them gentle kiss.

"Maddy, my sweet warrior. You have a life to lead, and if you are letting your happiness slip from your fingers because of some misplaced idea that you must be here at the expense of your own joy, then Everwell isn't your home. It's your prison."

Maddy blinked. She thought of Sylvie, so able to mind her flowers. And The Grove, with the berry patch, and the keyhole garden, which could be enough work for a dozen girls like Sylvie who might want a chance for something better.

Was it too late for that now?

The past week had been one of the most emotionally exhausting efforts in Beau's entire life. His first concern was Jessica, who was one part fury at her husband's betrayal, and the other pure anguish. It had been Jess who'd made the connection between them, after she'd discovered papers tucked away in the back of Neil's drawer.

"He'd always been jealous of you, Beau," she'd said, the two speaking quietly over a glass of their father's best Scotch. "And maybe he accepted that the company would be yours, because you were the son. And then—"

She'd trailed off, apparently unwilling to say aloud the secret that had been untold.

"—and then he found out I wasn't."

"You know?"

"I think I've always known," he said, then relayed how he'd met Hollis and learned the truth.

"Well, Neil didn't like it," she said, wiping a tear from her cheek, her voice rough tears and lost sleep.

"What are you going to do now?"

"Get a divorce," she said. "Yes, it's a scandal, but so is being married to the man who murdered my father and tried to take the company away from us."

"You know the irony is that I probably would have let him run it," Beau said. "He just needed to wait."

"He couldn't run that company," Jessica said, swallowing the remainder of her drink in a single gulp and placing the thick crystal glass down with a heavy thunk on a nearby mahogany table. "The man didn't know how to make a decision. The trick with a man like Neil was to make him think every good idea was his."

"Well Christ, Jessica," Beau said, sitting back. How in the hell did it make any sense that the one person who had the talent to run the company and the desire to do it, wasn't entitled to it? He would fix this—and if the board didn't like it, then they would find themselves out of job.

"What about you?" she'd asked. "You've spent half your time with the police, and half with this Dominic character."

Beau told Jessica about Madeline and the threats she'd received from Nelson Taylor.

"I remember that case," she said. "In Cape Enrage."

"You do?"

"Of course—a woman killing the man who betrayed her like that?" she said. "There isn't a woman in southeastern New Brunswick who hadn't heard of that case. And half of them probably sympathized with her."

"She didn't do it," Beau said. "But it happened so long ago, and it's this Taylor's word against hers."

"I'll talk to Sandra Tisdale. She's Nelson's cousin, and part of my ladies' club," she said. "She's told me some absolutely horrible stories about that man. She might know something."

It turned out that Mrs. Tisdale knew quite a bit about her cousin's character and antics, and thanks to Dominic's incredible detective work and Jessica's connections, they'd uncovered enough evidence to cast a more than reasonable shadow of a doubt on Taylor's story. Enough to send word to Miller that the story Nelson Taylor was telling might end up getting the Chronicle sued for libel. Dominic turned the evidence over to a detective he trusted on the Saint John police force, who was quite keen to learn that the last person to see Malcolm Ferguson alive was the same person accusing Madeline of the crime—Nelson Taylor.

Before he and Dominic boarded the train back to Halifax, he sent a second telegram to Aunt Veronica, and a third to Miss Everwell.

By the time the train had pulled into the station in Halifax the next day, it was mid-morning. Both he and Dominic had had a restless night of travel. Dominic was fuelled not only by solving two mysteries which would only boost his business prospects for even more higher profile cases, but by the desire to be reunited with his wife. It was the longest they'd been parted since he'd moved to Halifax from Boston two years ago, and one might have thought he'd been away for a year, rather than weeks. When they disembarked, she was indeed waiting on the platform, clad in a lovely blue dress and waving her hand to catch his attention. Beau had hoped to see Madeline there with her, which was ridiculous, of course. The disappointment at her absence created a hollow sensation in his gut. The only other person present was a gentleman he'd never met, in a brown tweed sack suit. He doffed his brown derby to Dominic, then went to fetch the luggage.

Dominic walked ahead, and Beau watched as Mrs. Ashe quite literally threw herself into her husband's waiting arms. It was a charming display of affection, and the two didn't seem particularly bothered by the stares of onlookers. Beau was tempted to look away and give the two a moment of privacy, when Dominic looked over his shoulder and waved him over.

"Mrs. Ashe," Beau said, putting his hand to his hat in salutation. "I apologize for monopolizing your husband's time."

"For a good purpose, I hope," she said.

Beau smiled. "I hope."

Mrs. Ashe whispered something in her husband's ear, and after a quick exchange and peck on the cheek, he went off to gather their luggage. Mrs. Ashe led him past the busy crowds to where the carriage was waiting.

"I just want to say, on behalf of all of us at Everwell who love her, that we appreciate what you are trying to do for Maddy." She looked up at him, her manner soft, as if she knew she was treading on tender ground. "Everything."

"I think very highly of her," he said. "She bewitched me the moment I first met her."

She looked him over, as if appraising his worth. He didn't squirm. This was the one test he didn't want to fail.

A sparkling black coach was waiting for them, where two porters had assisted the driver in loading their trunks. The driver nodded respectfully to the gentlemen.

"Good to see you back, Mr. Ashe, sir," he said.

"Good to see you, Harold. I'll have to thank Jeremy for the first-class transportation" he said, shaking the man's hand before turning to Beau. "Beau da Silva, this is Harold Babcock, a friend of Everwell. He'll be taking us there directly."

"Your aunt is already enroute, Mr. da Silva," he said, giving Beau a quick nod. "We shall meet everyone there."

"Let's go then," he said, his fatigue leaving him. He had one last chance. One more idea. One more try at giving Madeline the dream she deserved. Maybe he wouldn't be a part of it, and that would hurt like hell. But he couldn't give up on her. Not yet.

They climbed inside the cab and made for Everwell.

Chapter Twenty-Nine

MADDY STOOD AT THE WINDOW, Gemma and Rimple on either side of her. Lady Em and Tilda were having tea with Veronica Turnbull, who had arrived a few moments earlier. Phillipa had arranged for Dominic's sister-in-law, Claire, who normally worked in his office, to take the students down to the Arm for a picnic and a swim, leaving the spinsters to the business at hand.

A telegram had arrived earlier that morning for Lady Em, and she wasted no time in sharing the good news, confirmed by Veronica Turnbull, that Nelson Taylor's threats were exactly they belonged. In the past.

Rimple crossed her arms as she saw Jeremy's carriage coming up the front park. "I can't wait to take Dominic's evidence and shove it straight up Mr. Miller's—"

"Language, Rimple," Maddy said.

"I wasn't going to say anything vulgar," Rimple protested. "I know all the anatomically correct words."

"They're here," Gemma said. "Come, let's go join them."

Maddy turned away as Dominic, then Elouise, beaming with the return of her husband, got out of the carriage. Something twisted in her chest then. It might have been envy. It might have been anger.

But she understood it was simply grief. Grief for something she might have had.

The love of a good man.

She turned away when more movement caught her eye. At first, she thought it was Jeremy, but he was at Government House today. But another person did get out of the carriage.

She put a hand to her mouth and blinked, unsure if her eyes had deceived her. They had not.

She spun around, shaking. And then she bolted out the door, her hands gripping the iron rail looking down at… him. At Beau.

"You're back," she said.

He turned and looked up at her, and though she was looking down at him, she blinked away tears, as if she was looking straight at the sun. His smile was radiant and, she realized, it was for her.

"I couldn't stay away."

She raced down the stairs and stopped short in front of him. Even though he looked a little rumpled from the travel, and lines of fatigue creased at his mouth and the corners of his eyes, he was still the most beautiful thing she'd ever seen. She wanted to reach out and adjust the lapel of his coat that had turned up as he'd gotten out of the carriage.

"I didn't expect to see you again," she said. "I thought you were too busy. That your company needed you. Your sister. That—"

He reached out and grabbed her hands.

"I spent a week trying to solve this case," he said. "and I definitely wanted the satisfaction of seeing the look on Miller's face when I give him the evidence about Taylor. And I selfish being that I am, I definitely couldn't wait to see you again."

Maddy couldn't help but smile as she turned away, her body trembling. They went upstairs and into the parlour where Beau greeted his aunt with a kiss. It was clear that she was thrilled to see him. She lingered a moment, giving herself time to get her emotions in check before joining them.

Beau relayed the entire story, and though he didn't express it, it was clear to Maddy that instead of worrying about his own future, he'd spent every waking hour leveraging every connection and favour he had to help ensure that Maddy never had to look over her shoulder. So that she had a future, too.

"Oh Maddy," Phillipa said, relief in her voice. "That is a relief."

"Well," Lady Em said, "this calls for something more celebratory than tea, don't you think? Tilda, I think this deserves the good sherry."

Animated discussion broke out in the room, joined by the clinking of glasses and the passing of plates of cookies that Rimple had baked in a fury last night in anticipation of the hints of good news in Beau's telegram. Maddy was subjected to hugs from her fellow spinsters, which she accepted, and all seemed to be well.

But Maddy was not. She rose, and feigning then need for air, went to her library to sit.

This job was coming to an end. And it was happy... for Everwell.

But not for her.

She blew out a shaky breath and cursed herself for wanting the visit to end. For Dominic and Elouise to go home, for Beau to leave with his aunt, and for everything to go back the way it was. Except the way it was meant Maddy having sleepless nights thinking she had blood on her hands. The way it was meant not knowing about the beautiful stone cottage and the magical garden, laughing with Annie Chandler or picking berries with Hollis. It was a life that had not known the love of a man like Beau. Who'd offered her everything she wanted, but she had been afraid to have, because he saw what she could not. Her worth. That her happiness was worthy of fulfillment.

She pushed aside a traitorous tear with the palm of her hand.

A knock at the door jolted her out of her sorrows. Quickly she rose to her feet, dabbing her eyes and preparing to mumble an apology about pollen reddening her eyes when she realized it was Beau standing in the door.

"If I'm disturbing you, I'll go," he said.

"Not at all," she said, gesturing him to come in. "I owe you a debt of gratitude for what you've done for me. You didn't have to do that."

He wore a smile, but it did not meet his eyes.

"But I did," he began. "I am a selfish man, after all. What I want, I want."

Maddy swallowed, nearly afraid to breathe. "And what do you want?"

"I recently had an unexpected meeting with someone who opened my eyes to some novel business possibilities. Exciting ones. However, there were a few obstacles in the way." He rubbed his hands together, then pantomimed what looked like a living advertisement for some kind of beauty cream they advertised in the *Ladies Home Journal*. "What is this charming smile and lightening intellect for if not for removing those obstacles, and opening the doors so they can walk through them?"

There was not a drop of sarcasm in his voice. If anything, there was more than a generous dollop of self-deprecation, which brought a bit of lightness to her chest. She pressed her lips together, trying to suppress an unwanted smile.

"But then, I had an even more remarkable idea that may help in that effort." He came closer then paused, uncharacteristically cautious. "That is, if you would be open to hearing it."

That effort. He was talking about her little dream. She'd shut the door on that dream. Slammed, more like. Or so she'd thought.

She nodded, unable to speak.

"I would like to gift The Grove, and its fifty acres, to Everwell."

Maddy's mouth fell open, but she had no words. She wasn't even certain if she'd heard him correctly.

"I would consider it part of the payment for services

rendered," he continued, his voice warm. "And I would also donate to its upkeep, of course. An annuity."

"Why would you do that?" she asked at last.

Beau approached her, cautiously, as one might approach a wounded animal. He was so close to her now she could smell the familiar scent of his shaving soap. My God, how she'd missed it. She missed him.

"Because then you would never have to leave it. Everwell could be wherever you are."

Maddy put her hands to her mouth, trying to contain the sob at the back of her throat. Beau gently pulled her hand away, kissing the back of her knuckles, his lips grazing her skin. She didn't pull away.

"I want what I want," he continued, looking at her, his amber eyes warm and smiling at last. "And what I want, more than anything, is for you to be happy. I love you."

She had his heart in her hands. It was an odd thing, a powerful thing, to accept. He loved her. He'd even said so, and it had been real.

Maddy looked away, focusing on some random spot on the wall, using every ounce of self-control to keep the tangle of emotions that were threatening to dissolve her into a sopping puddle. She looked at her books, sitting prettily on the shelves. And then she remembered those lovely shelves at The Grove. The study, that had held their trunks. It would make a lovely little library.

"I'm so sorry I didn't appreciate how big a decision this was for you. I was so wrapped up in my own desires, I forgot you were at the centre of them," he said.

She pulled his hands to her lips, pressing a firm kiss to his fingers, then running her thumb over the spot where a small callus had started to form on his hand.

"I'm sorry I didn't have as much faith in my dreams as you did," she said, her bottom lip trembling. She released a ragged breath and dared to look in his eyes. "I love you, too. So very much."

It was so hard to speak above a whisper. She was trembling, as she was letting go of years of heartache, fear… and grief. Beau pulled her into his arms.

"Congratulations, Mr. da Silva."

The unexpected, and slightly bored tones of Lady Em startled both of them. They broke the embrace, but Beau did not let go of her hand.

Lady Em stood in the door, a single eyebrow raised, her mouth tipped up in an amused smile. She looked back and forth between the two of them.

"I see you have managed to discombobulate my dearest Miss Murray," she said, giving him an appraising look before turning to Maddy. "Before this dissolves into something that might actually give the neighbours something to put in Mr. Miller's wretched columns, perhaps you could take a stroll outside, where you can discuss the terms of our new arrangement with a bit more privacy?"

"You know about this?" Maddy asked. She knew Beau had sent word about his own case and the Taylors, but apparently Lady Em, Tilda, and Phillipa hadn't shared everything.

"Indeed. Tilda and I agree it is a splendid idea," she said. "I will leave it to you, Madeline, to work out the particulars of the arrangement."

Lady Em continued on to the festivities in the parlour, and Beau stepped to one side, waiting for Maddy. She took his hand, because somehow her body always seemed to know what to do even when her words failed her. When she was afraid. And she'd feared so much, for so long. Here was the one person, more than any other, who told her she didn't have to be afraid anymore, because he would be there for her.

She led him to the side garden, a lovely border of hollyhocks and calendula, lambs' ears, lavender, and lily of the valley. Every year this garden changed a little, as it was, until this week, the only part of the flower gardens she'd let the students help manage. At the end of the path there was a little bench, beneath a soaring maple tree, its full canopy lush and moving with the summer breeze. It would have been a lovely sound, but she could not hear it over the beating of her own heart.

"Beau," she said, breathless.

"Madeline," he replied, idly running his thumb over her knuckles. God, it felt so good to be touched by him. "Being away from you was absolutely the longest week of my life."

"Before we go any further, I need to tell you something," she said. "Something important. It might make you change your mind."

He pulled her close and put a kiss on her brow that threatened to weaken her at the knees.

"Nothing is going to make me change my mind," he said. "The Grove is yours."

"Beau," she whispered, trying to keep her wits about her, which was desperately hard when his kisses were robbing her of her capacity to think. "This is serious. But I trust you will not tell a soul."

"Or you'll throw me over your shoulder?" he said, cocking an eyebrow in the air.

"It's about the rumours," she blurted out.

His brow crinkled in confusion. "My aunt has dispelled the rumours in the papers about Everwell being some haven for thieves and murderers—"

"Beau—" She stepped back a moment, grabbed his hands, and took a deep breath. "The rumours are not exactly rumours."

It seemed to take a moment for her words to sink in, and she could see a line forming across his brow and his head tilt ever so slightly.

"Not exactly?"

"Not the murders part—that is, as you have helped prove — those are completely and utterly false," she said, the words coming out of her in a rush to quell any fears that his life was in actual danger.

"And the thieving?" He asked, a new note of caution in his tone.

Maddy took a deep breath and hoped the other spinsters would forgive her. She told him everything. About forged insurance policies and missing wills, about Chinese vases and stolen jewels that had to be stolen back so that the owner had something to live on, because having a bank account in her own name was impossible. About the missing girls that were about to be carted off to Boston to work until The Everwell Society of Scandalous Spinsters and Wayward Women managed not only to free them but blackmail the ringleader into never returning. And because she was spilling every secret, she may have mentioned where a few of her books were borrowed from… including the one from Government House. And finally, she told him about the priceless poetry book that she'd gone to MacAskill's to steal back on behalf of the owner, who'd been duped into relinquishing ownership of it.

Maddy wasn't sure she had spoken so much in her entire life. But when she stopped, she forced herself to be patient while Beau took it all in. Allowed herself to trust that he loved her and would somehow understand.

"Well, I suppose I shouldn't be surprised," he said, after what felt like a painful amount of silence. Maddy wanted to laugh at the irony of it. He put a hand to his chin, idly rubbing it as he seemed to be turning over everything she'd just told him. "After all, it was as plain as day the moment I met you."

"What do you mean?" she protested. "I know I'm a horrible thief—a fact I tried to impress upon Phillipa, but— "

He put a finger to her lips.

"You ruthlessly stole my heart right in the middle of a bookstore," he said, his voice low and warm like honey that seemed to flow right through Maddy's body. "And as for the price of the book, it was a fair price to pay for the attention of a faerie queen, don't you think?"

"Entirely fair," she said, her voice barely above a whisper. She wanted to melt right into him.

"Now," he said, clearing his throat, and holding up the deed to The Grove. "Back to the matter at hand. Your happily ever after."

Maddy looked at the folded sheaf of papers in his hand, her heart squeezing one more time. She thought of Elouise and her wise words, too often ignored by those who only saw the exquisite objective beauty of her face. And Sylvie, who flourished when given the chance to look after the garden and would flourish more if she was given the same opportunity that Lady Em and Tilda had given Maddy. Gemma and Rimple, Phillipa. They had their lives. And then she thought of Annie and Daniel, and Hollis and his berry patch, Teddy, and the magical garden hidden and waiting for her. And her happy ending. And maybe it would mean that she wouldn't see Beau that often. He had his life in Saint John, and a company to run.

"I want this," she said. "But I've become greedy."

Beau cocked his head. "What do you mean?"

"I want what I want," she said, trying to mimic his devil-may-care charm. "And I want to share my cottage with Prince Charming."

Beau threw his head back and laughed, then pulled Maddy tight. "You've got him."

"Are you certain?"

"I gave Jess the company," he said. "She's the only one with the head to run it. I might have to go back to Saint John from time to time, but if you like, you can come with me. And it would never be for long. But I didn't want it, and she did. It's her legacy, too. Both her parents are gone. She needs to disentangle herself from Neil. She can do it, and I'll be there for her if she needs me. Just like you would be here for The Everwell Society when they need you to shake down a crooked politician or whatever it is you do."

Maddy held her breath. "I don't know what to do," she said. "I'm scared and nervous and normally when I feel this way I want to go hit something, but I'm too happy."

"How about you stand there looking gorgeous while I kiss you?"

And that's what they did, Maddy leaning into Beau as he took her face in his hands and devoured her in a kiss that she felt down to her toes. Somewhere, in the distance, she heard a chorus of whoops and hollers and… was that clapping? Perhaps clapping.

Clapping not for a happy ending. But for a happy beginning.

THE END

Epilogue

FEBRUARY 23, 1877

The fire crackled the hearth of the royal suite at the Duke of Wellington Hotel, adding a welcome glow to an otherwise gloomy winter day in Halifax. The pristine snow that had fallen yesterday had already begun to darken from the mud and smoke that belched from countless chimneys in the city in the unified effort to stave off the cold damp of a Nova Scotia winter.

Maddy sat at a mahogany desk in one corner of the beautifully appointed room, staring down at the latest version of her plans for the revitalization of The Grove. Beau had taken the rooms in late summer, and they had become her temporary Halifax residence since their marriage last autumn. This past September, they had married under the graceful branches of the maple tree where Beau had proposed and the Turnbulls, Beau's sister Jessica, and the Chandlers had all been present. While many of the summer flowers had faded, the asters, goldenrod, coneflowers, and ironweed had put on a lovely display, and Maddy herself picked some of the late blooming roses that created her wedding bouquet. A vial of oil from the roses was now at her dressing table, made from the petals of that bouquet.

Beau was having a late breakfast with his uncle at the Halifax

Merchant's Club, which allowed her time to pore over the latest sketches of plans for The Grove, which now included lodgings for staff and a second building that would support the creation and packaging of soaps. She was so involved that she didn't hear Beau return until he appeared in the doorway, wearing a smile she would never tire of.

"Mrs. Da Silva, you are going to get a crook in your back if you don't mind your posture," he said playfully as he rested his hands on her shoulders. As he gently massaged her neck, she sat back, allowing herself to melt into the firm but relaxing pressure of his touch.

"If I wanted a lecture on my posture, I would go back to Everwell and let Tilda do it," she replied, sighing with pleasure.

"I promised Mrs. Gilman, Lady Em, and your friends that I would look after you," he said, bending over and planting a gentle but firm kiss on her cheek. "If you thought you were intimidating, you have no idea how it feels to be stared down by six formidable women. If we arrive for supper and you have a crook in your back, my wellbeing might be in jeopardy."

Maddy smiled. She could well imagine what had transpired in that discussion—given that she'd been part of similar discussions with both Dominic Ashe and Jeremy Webber before they were welcomed into the Everwell family.

"Don't worry," she said. "Promise me a back rub every night, and you'll be quite safe."

She sensed his smile as he nestled a kiss on her ear. "As long as I don't have to stop with your back."

Maddy smiled, her body softening under his touch. It was a sensation she was certain she would never tire of—this idea that she was so utterly safe with a man. And that he was happiest when he was making her happy.

"How was your meeting with your uncle?" Maddy asked. Beau's uncle had been quietly intrigued by the business opportunity, and with the urging of his wife, had been persuaded to invest in Maddy's new venture.

"Uncle Archie was in a remarkably good mood," he said, "though I suspect it might have something to do with the fact that his last quarter was better than some of his cronies. They'll be attending the musicale this evening. Aunt Vee loves music."

Maddy stifled a groan. She and Veronica Turnbull had come, if not to entirely like each other, certainly to respect each other. The Turnbulls still had no idea about the Scandalous Spinsters, but their public support of The Everwell Society since the events of last summer had been appreciated. Tonight, Gemma and Jeremy Webber were hosting a musicale in their beautiful home, featuring some of Everwell's students as fundraising effort for the society and expanding their efforts to find excellent employment opportunities for their students as they got older. The Turnbulls' appearance was another important marker of support. Veronica Turnbull might love music, but her talents were, to put it kindly, best left to clapping for the performers.

"As long as she leaves the performing to the girls," Maddy said.

Several hours later, they arrived at the Webber's stately Halifax house. The house glowed with gaslight, welcoming all coming in from the dark, gloomy evening. Jeremy's position as private secretary to the Lieutenant Governor, and his connections to the British military establishment in the city, helped to attract some of the more influential citizens to the event. Lady Em held court, and Jeremy ensured that every officer in a red coat met Tilda, who had once used her skills as a doctoress in support of the British Army. Tilda and Jeremy had met in Persia years ago, when Jeremy had been a young officer, and she saved the life of his soldier valet, Harold Babcock.

As Beau went to fetch a glass of champagne for the two of them, Maddy stood alongside Rimple, Elouise, and Phillipa, marvelling at how naturally Gemma had taken to the role of hostess. She dazzled in a gown of deep plum velvet, which complimented her olive-toned skin and thick dark hair.

"She's a natural at this, isn't she?" Elouise said. "All those years performing under the circus tent have been channeled into something new."

"I'm so proud of her," Phillipa said, beaming at the once painfully shy Gemma. "This is a wonderful evening."

"Who invited him?" Rimple asked, her lip uncharacteristically pulled into an expression bordering disgust. Maddy followed her gaze through the crowd, where she spotted Benjamin Miller speaking with Simon Nickerson.

"Jeremy and Gemma, I suspect," Elouise said.

"He's not a society reporter," she countered.

"No, but where society goes, news follows," Phillipa said. "And many of them are here tonight. And if we don't look away, we are going to end up in his column, so let's just ignore him, shall we? We want the girls to shine tonight."

After all the guests had been greeted and provided with a glass of warming punch, they were invited to be seated while Elouise brought the students on the stage. The evening's event was a mix of music and poetry reading, including some original pieces written by some of the students. Phillipa had gone to assist. Maddy went to take her seat with Beau in the front row, instinctively taking stock of who was already in their chairs.

Rimple was missing.

"What's the matter?" Beau asked, then, as if immediately sensing the problem, looked up and down the row to see who was missing. The entire front row had been claimed by Everwell Society members and allies to give the students the moral support they might need.

"If you're looking for Rimple, she's speaking with Aunt Vee," Beau said.

Maddy breathed a little sigh of relief. Rimple, being of obviously mixed heritage that polite society called "exotic" to her face and far worse behind it, was often subjected to indignities that were spared the rest of the spinsters, save Tilda. Maddy knew Veronica Turnbull would support Rimple if needed and treat her with the respect she was entitled to.

A moment later, she spied them, along with a tall, elegantly dressed, gaunt woman Maddy recognized as Rebecca Beveridge.

Veronica Turnbull was still a member of the NWL, as was Rebecca. As a founding member, and one of its most influential, she'd recovered from what was judged by some as a severe breach in the ranks when she not only put her public support behind The Everwell Society, but the union between Beau and Maddy as well. Still, it was odd to see both those ladies in the same space with Rimple, having what looked to be a quite earnest conversation.

Jeremy rose and went to the little makeshift stage at the end of the room, drawing the attention of the crowd with his commanding presence. Maddy took her seat, and a moment later, Rimple was alongside her.

"What was that about?" Maddy whispered under her breath.

Rimple leaned in and revealed a small envelope she had tucked into her glove.

"It's for Phillipa," she whispered. "I think we have another client."

Thanks for reading!

I hope you enjoyed *A Tantalizing Treasure*, Book Three in my *Scandalous Spinsters* Series. If you haven't yet, try **A Dangerous Diversion**, and introduce yourself to the Everwell Society and meet Elouise Charming and Dominic Ashe, and then continue on with **A Captivating Caper.**

Stay tuned for Rimple's book, coming in 2025.

Reviews are welcome - and super important to indie authors, and helpful to readers as well, so you if can leave a review, I'd be super grateful! Feel free to post one where you purchased the book, or on Goodreads.

My website is www.michellehelliwell.com, and you'll find me on Facebook and Instagram as well. Join my mailing list and get a heads up on new releases, and special giveaways that are only for my subscribers.

very last thing for Gemma wants…except there's something under that button down demeanour she finds utterly captivating.

After the death of his wife, Colonel Jeremy Webber is determined to raise his daughter on his own, but the busy aide-de-camp can't keep an eye on his strong willed child and a busy Lieutenant Governor at the same time. Jeremy's a man of schedules and rules, but his alluring new governess manages to manoeuvre around every one - including his most important rule…never fall in love again.

Normally Gemma is the thief, but Jeremy is stealing *her* heart -- even as he's dangerously close to uncovering secrets that put her and her fellow Scandalous Spinsters in jeopardy. To let him in could risk everything… but shutting him out may break her heart.

Enchanted Tales

All titles are available at Amazon and select online retailers. Ask your local bookstore or library to order your copy!

NOT YOUR AVERAGE BEAUTY

When beauty is a curse, only love can break the spell

Stephen Pembroke, the Marquess of Barronsfield, believes that where his love of beauty goes, death follows. Cursed to a loveless existence, and with his legacy at stake, Stephen makes a desperate proposal of marriage to Rosalind Schofield, his steward's new ward - and the plainest girl he has ever met. Rosalind has spent a lifetime being overlooked for prettier faces. When she is singled out for her lack of beauty by the Marquess, she begins to doubt if she is deserving of the love she inwardly craves.

When unusual things start happening around her, Rosalind can't help but wonder if Lord Barronsfield or his curse are who and what they appear to be. When she openly challenges Stephen about the curse, he begins to doubt everything – and comes to realize that this apparently plain, ordinary woman is not as unremarkable as he believed. Strange things *are* happening in Barronsfield. As they move closer to the truth, Rosalind unwittingly finds herself in the sights of the real beast in Barronsfield, and Stephen must decide if his growing love for Rosalind will be his salvation or her doom.

NO PRINCE CHARMING

Love is the fairest of them all

Dashing off in a daring elopement with a prince handpicked by her mother, Lady Gwyneth Snowdon anticipates a lavish future. But when a mysterious stranger kidnaps her, Gwyneth fears her happy ending is doomed.

Used by his maniacal father, Edmund Pembroke turned his back on society. Seizing the opportunity to say good-bye to his past forever, he makes a deal to separate the pampered countess from a gold-digging imposter. But when Edmund discovers her life is in danger, he is forced to protect the beautiful, well-born Gwyneth Snowdon and to confront his ghosts.

Separated from her plush surroundings, Gwyneth learns she's capable of so much—including love for a man with neither title nor fortune. But she begins to suspects there is more to her rugged, handsome guardian than he's chosen to reveal. After finding herself at the center of a sinister deception, can she dare to trust her heart to a man who's spent years deceiving himself?

NEVER TRUST A ROGUE IN WOLF'S CLOTHING

A heart all the better to love her with...

After three torturous seasons, Lady Eleanore Pembroke is finished with husband hunting and happy ever after. Following the scandal of a broken engagement, eager to bury herself in her work at the local infirmary, she returns home shocked to discover their trusted physician gone, replaced by a dashing scoundrel. Bastien DuMont is a talented doctor, but Eleanore senses his restless heart. She's no longer prepared to risk hers, nor the trust of the people who've come to depend on him.

Caught up in a revolution that dissolved into terror, Bastien learned that devotion is for fools. On the run from a growing list of men who'd love to see him dead, he's forced out of the shadows and into the shoes of a respectable country physician, putting him under the scrutiny of Lady Eleanore, a local do-gooder immune to his roguish charms. When a mysterious figure emerges, threatening his life and the safety of those around him, can Bastien hunt down his opponent before he becomes the prey? Or is exposing his heart the greater danger?

About the Author

Michelle Helliwell started writing her first novel, a time travel fantasy, when she was 15. She moved on to half-hearted attempts at something more literary, then nearly gave up on the writing all together until one fine day in 2005 a co-worker put a romance novel in her hands and told her to "get over yourself".

She did, and the rest, as they say, is history.

Michelle lives with her husband and two sons in Nova Scotia, Canada where moody weather and bagpipes are plentiful, but alas, guys in puffy shirts are too few.

Find all my books at
www.michellehelliwell.com